Louis Saunders, a London-based author, writes stories which revolve around deeply authentic and true-to-life characters. Praised for his clear and refreshingly candid style, Saunders' debut novel, THE RETREAT, takes place in a post-pandemic world. It offers a renewed perspective on the idea of teenagers trying to overthrow a dystopian government. Louis is equally passionate about contemporary fiction that explores the messiness of relationships and current issues in today's society, particularly those affecting younger generations.

Discover more about Louis and his work on his author website: www.louissaunders.co.uk

ISBN: 978-1-3999-6628-3

Cover design by Onur Burc

THE
RETREAT

LOUIS SAUNDERS

PART I

01
Buried Under

01/09/0017

Morning in the Bunker

Jasper hunched over the desk by his bed, his pyjamas covered in sweat. He was speed-reading his way through a biology textbook, guided by the light of a neon-blue lava lamp. It was technically curfew still, and the officials had yet to switch the ceiling lights on.

Despite the fog of fatigue that clouded his mind – which no amount of sleep could ever fully clear – Jasper's eyes ran like lasers along the textbook's pages. Energised by a mouthful of chewing tobacco, whose nicotine danced on his tongue and trickled through his veins, he turned to a passage whose quirky title read: WHAT IS LOVE? A BIOLOGIST'S HOT TAKE.

Jasper jolted in his seat as the ceiling lights flashed on, announcing the start of the Bunker's workday. Scrambling to switch off his lava lamp, Jasper nearly knocked over the little wooden angel that sat on the corner of his desk: the one that Hattie had carved and painted for him as a Christmas present, nearly a decade ago.

Jasper stood up and, grabbing his towel from the radiator, stumbled over to the door. Commander Tommy's painting lay plastered to its surface, watching over the bedroom with colourless eyes. The canvas jostled slightly as Jasper pushed past the door to step into the hallway.

*

Showered and dressed in a jacketless suit, Jasper climbed the Bunker's spiralling stairs. The metal steps clattered and chimed beneath his feet. Above, he could see the outlines of a few dozen silhouettes, shuffling up towards Level 6.

Jasper walked alone. His pace slowed as a group of yobs lumbered ahead. Their shrill voices pierced the air of the stairwell, each competing to be louder than the other. Jasper attempted to sidestep the youths, but their backs formed an impenetrable barrier.

"E-excuse me..."

Once again, Jasper was ignored.

He gritted his teeth, stomach churning with humiliation. Little power plays like this always irked him. Typically, his inhibitions would keep him in check, but this time, his ego intervened. Jasper pushed past one of the boys, a baby-faced brat named Trent. Trent, caught off balance, grasped the stair's safety rail and, recovering, hurled a stream of juvenile insults up at Jasper. Jasper continued his ascent, straightening his back and puffing out his chest, although his stiff, awkward movements betrayed the self-consciousness that the verbal assault had instilled.

At last, Jasper reached the landing to Level 6. Passing through a series of steel doors, he entered Corridor A. A blood-red carpet stretched along the floor of the concrete tunnel, leading to an open entrance from which the sound of chatter and clinking cutlery emanated.

Jasper entered a trance as he queued up for breakfast. The woman behind the serving station had to click her fingers to get his attention. He was already standing at the front of the queue.

"Oh, err - sorry. Boiled egg and toast. Just one slice of fried tomato."

Jasper took his tray and scanned the masses of Bunker residents, some five hundred people, packed along the long tables. Marcus, his best friend, stood out thanks to his fringe of dirty-blonde hair. After greeting him with a nod, Jasper settled onto the bench opposite. The two had grown up in the Bunker, and having graduated from the Schoolrooms, were now assigned full-time roles. Today was their first day in what people sometimes called the 'real world'.

Jasper looked over at Marcus. "Not too stressed, I hope?"

Marcus swallowed. He'd been accepted into the Scouts. Tomorrow was his first expedition to the surface. "Nah, nah. Definitely not. Excited, mainly." Marcus rubbed his hands together.

"Great." Jasper shuffled in his seat. "Yeah. I mean - I'm super nervous for my first class, actually. I find it hard to connect with the younger kids, y'know?"

Marcus picked at his food. Jasper had failed the requirements of the Scouts, and was instead assigned to be a biology teacher. Without prompting, Jasper continued. "I'd much prefer the older classes. Oh well. Just gotta make the most of it, I guess."

Marcus scoffed. Jasper ignored this disrespect, for his attention had shifted elsewhere: Hattie Osborne had arrived at breakfast. Jasper's gaze lingered on his friend and former classmate, now a junior medic. She'd dressed up nicely for her first day in the real world, wearing white chinos and a blue shirt that brought out the colour of her eyes. Holding her tray, she stood alone near the serving station, seeking out friendly faces to sit with. Spotting Jasper and Marcus, Hattie beamed with a smile and headed over.

"Sup," she said as she approached. Hattie looked radiant, though Jasper could see that her smile wasn't lighting up her eyes like it usually did. She sat down next to Marcus and produced a container of green powder labelled ITALIAN SEASONING, before sprinkling it onto their food.

"What's this?" Jasper asked.

"It adds a little kick," said Hattie, giving him a cheeky glance. "Noah gave it to me yesterday. Came for another of his visits." She smirked and averted her gaze. "Bit persistent, that one..."

Jasper's leg jiggled. Noah was the revered Chief of the Scouts and Commander Tommy's only son. Supposedly, he possessed the healthiest genes of all the Bunker's men.

Marcus cleared his throat and, appealing to Hattie, flicked his head towards Jasper. "You reckon he'll miss me?"

Hattie grinned and nudged Marcus on the arm. It was his last breakfast in the common canteen. "Onto bigger, better things, eh?" she laughed, before turning to Jasper.

"Yeah," said Jasper, wringing his wrists, "but no... I'm so - so pleased for him..."

Hattie's smile fell and she tucked a lock of brown hair behind her ear. Marcus shot Jasper a pointed look, scolding him for being so weird. Jasper dropped his gaze to the table. He was aware that he wouldn't be seeing much of Marcus anymore, since the Scouts were kept away from the Bunker's ordinary folk. They had separate living quarters and facilities, and they were bound by 'confidentiality rules' that were strictly enforced by the Commander, the Chief, and the rest of the officials.

"Still though," Jasper added, clearing his throat, "I'm sure we'll find ways to hang out again. Right?"

"Yeah." Hattie peered over at Marcus. "Noah will let you come down and see us, won't he?"

"Maybe," Marcus grumbled, taking a sip of water. "Not sure he likes me all that much, though."

The three moved on to other topics. Marcus struggled with the spices on his food, causing Hattie to giggle and tease him playfully. Jasper, stoic as ever, took the seasoned breakfast in his stride. When Hattie pronounced him as the 'bravest' of the boys, Jasper smiled shyly to himself. But the pleasant moment soon became spoiled as Hattie's attention shifted. Her eyes widened and she yelped as she reached out with her arm, but it was too late to intervene.

Trevor – known to most as 'Tiger' – proceeded to douse Jasper with a jug of cold water. The people in the canteen turned to stare as Tiger clutched Jasper's soggy shoulders, singing, "For he's a jolly good fella, for he's a jolly good fella..." while Walter – whose friends called him 'Ace' – smirked and watched on from behind. Hattie shot him a glare and ordered him to grab some napkins from the serving area. Ace complied, returning with a handful of paper towels which he handed to Jasper. The canteen's gaze remained fixed on the drama.

"Thanks, Walter. I'll be able to dry this all off then," spat Jasper as he scrunched the napkins into a ball, which he tossed at Ace's face. Marcus, catching Tiger's eye, cracked a smile and tried not to laugh, but the dam soon broke and the rest of the Bunker joined in, aiming its collective scorn at the awkward lad Jasper Huxley.

*

Level 2-B

Noah Smith stood in the spotlight of the Scout's Theatre. Marcus, Tiger, and Ace sat behind him, while an audience of forty-nine men occupied the rows of chairs opposite.

Noah had been the Scout Chief for six years now, promoted at the ripe age of twenty. The Commander, his father, believed Noah was the only suitable candidate, after the shocking treason of his predecessor. Noah took pride in his appearance and today was clad in a sleek leather jacket, his blonde hair smothered in sticky gel. Apart from stubble, his tanned face was smooth. He leaned over a laptop on his desk and pressed the spacebar, starting the mission debrief. A slideshow projected itself onto the screen, its title taking up the first slide: SEPTEMBER 0017 – EXPEDITION IX.

Noah spoke into the microphone, more for effect than necessity, his shrill voice piercing the air. "After farm pickup, we're heading to an old warehouse in Surrey, just off the M25. Hans reckons this place has what we need, to get the new lab up and running." Noah cleared his throat. "But erm, we'll discuss that in a bit."

He pressed a key, advancing the slideshow: NEW RECRUITS STARTING THIS YEAR.

"We also have the lads from the class of o'seventeen, here with us today." He gestured to Ace, Tiger, and Marcus, who peered up like nervous rabbits. "Right then, gents, please introduce yourselves."

Marcus felt nauseous. Fortunately, Walter 'Ace' Jones volunteered to go first. He confidently stated his name and expressed his enthusiasm to be part of the team. Despite his unkempt appearance and dull eyes, Ace was surprisingly clever and spoke with a clear and articulate voice.

Meanwhile, Marcus surveyed the rabble of Scouts. The younger ones appeared agitated. With their flushed cheeks and the spiteful glint in their eyes, they carried the air of being sexually repressed or on steroids. The older men, for their part, had faces like veteran gangsters: their jaws were wide and bony, and their skin was chiselled with premature wrinkles.

Ace finished, and Tiger took the stage. As he stepped into the spotlight, Marcus blurted out, "G'warn, Tiger!"

His voice bounced off the walls, and he immediately cringed. The room's collective gaze dug into him.

"Err, anyway... What's your real name, lad?" Noah asked, breaking the silence.

"Umm, Trevor Fervor."

Laughter erupted from the crowd, followed by a nasty "oooOOOooo!" at the lad's weird name. His face turned bright red, but Noah told him to continue. After stammering a few more words, 'Travel Further' slumped back into his chair.

Noah's gaze shifted to Marcus as he handed over the microphone. Standing in the glare of the bright spotlight meant Marcus was squinting out at the crowd.

"Hi, I'm Marcus. I'm eighteen like the others, and I can't wait to get going. Being a Scout is obviously a dream for all of us young lads, so erm, yeah, I'm excited to get going, and all that." Marcus paused. The microphone screeched with feedback. "Oh, and, err, Tiger is his nickname. That's why I called him that." Marcus gave a nervous laugh, and the mic screeched once more.

A sudden voice from the audience hissed, "Sit down, dani-handla!"

The men bellowed with mocking laughter. Marcus, blushing, tried to pass the microphone back to Noah, who stood there with his arms folded. "Think you're forgetting something," Noah said to him.

Marcus's teeth clenched. "Eh?"

"Your surname."

Marcus shrugged. "Don't have one."

"Very funny," Noah said, and then the realisation dawned on him. He snatched the microphone back, gestured for Marcus to sit down, then turned to face the audience. "Oh, wait, that's right!" Noah said. "You're Marcus X. That's the one. Of course. Heh, my bad!"

Tiger slapped Marcus on the shoulder. "First day's always the worst, am I right X-Rated?" he said, and Marcus felt his face blaze.

Ace winked at Marcus and blew him a patronising kiss. Marcus tried to laugh, but in that moment it dawned on him why he'd always preferred Jasper over these two tommy-dazzlas.

*

Noah wrapped up his presentation, and the Scouts headed to their exclusive dining space on Level 2-B. After finishing lunch, Ace opted for a workout in the Scout's gym, while Marcus, Tiger, and some others headed to the shooting range on Level 4.

The metal steps chimed like bells beneath them as they descended the dimly lit stairway in a group. Looking down at his feet, Marcus noticed one of his laces had come loose. He paused on the next landing – Level 3 – and moved over so the others could continue their journey, then knelt to re-tie his shoe.

With his laces firmly tied, Marcus stood, the metallic scent of the iron stairs filling his nostrils. He looked around. Above and below, the dark staircase coiled in a colossal helix structure, the voices of the other recruits becoming quieter as they descended. His eyes returned to this level, his eyes resting on the door to Level 3. Its window was covered in tinfoil, preventing any light from coming through. Marcus moved closer—

"Done yet?" a voice came from behind him.

Startled, Marcus turned to see Tiger grinning at him. He nodded. "Yeah, just taking a look around."

"Come on, freak," Tiger said, pushing past Marcus and leading the way down to Level 4. They spent the afternoon at the shooting range, practising with the others. Life-sized cut-outs of various figures were set up – pictures of shackled convicts, startled deer, scared bunny-rabbits, and a devil-horns photo of the old Prime Minister, along with some caricatures of her Cabinet – that the men mowed down in a stream of raging bullets as they roared with hateful laughter.

Dinner was served at 7 o'clock in the Scouts' dining room. Roast chicken and creamy mashed potatoes. Marcus ate quietly, then retired early for the night. He tossed and turned for five hours straight, restless in the comfort of his luxury suite on Level 2-A.

02
Surface-Level

10:00

The ceiling lights buzzed with an industrial yellow, jolting Marcus out of a slow-burn nightmare. A fist pounded on his bedroom door.

"Let's go! Let's go! We need to be out and ready by 11 o'clock!"

Marcus groaned and responded to Noah's rally-call. He showered and dressed in just under ten minutes.

Breakfast went by in a blur. Sausages and toast with fried tomatoes. And the first cup of coffee he'd ever legally consumed. Its caffeine made him jittery with nervous energy. He kept to himself as the others at his table exchanged banter. Tiger and Ace were already well-liked among the lads.

After breakfast, the fifty-ish Scouts lined up in the corridor, placing their backpacks on the floor beneath their feet. Noah and his second-in-command, Albert, strolled along and inspected the contents of the men's bags, ensuring that they'd each packed the requisite gear: a first-aid kit, a canister of 'antiviral' spray, some emergency snacks, a water bottle, their walkie-talkies, sleeping bags, and, importantly, a fully-loaded Glock pistol each, in case the last 'Retreaters' ever staged another assault.

Next, Noah led the men into the cramped locker room at the end of the hall, where they each put on a set of freshly sterilised gear: orange hazmat suits, sturdy black boots, and gas masks with beady goggles. Dressed in their fluorescent uniform, the Scouts ascended the spiralling stairs like a winding human centipede.

The men reached the top of the staircase. Noah unlocked the door to Level 0 with his master key, allowing them all to swarm inside. The space was shaped like an underground hangar, with its high ceiling and flat tarmac floor. In the dim, buzzing light of the artificial cavern, Marcus made out a row of sleek cars at the far end – ten silver Jeeps and a matte-black Rolls-Royce – whose noses were pointed at the concrete gates.

Marcus took a deep, trembling breath, feeling queasy. He watched as his old biology teacher, Maya MacNair, a middle-aged lady with short black hair, was being dragged by Albert towards the line of cars. The woman was dressed in an orange jumpsuit, and her eyes were bound by a blindfold. She squealed as Albert shoved her into the trunk of a Jeep. The men erupted with vile laughter. Marcus remained silent, plagued by a rush of unease. Albert ordered the screaming woman to "stop her whinging" before slamming the boot shut. Tiger nudged Marcus on the arm and whispered:

"Better her than us, eh lad?"

Marcus let out a nervous laugh. Mrs MacNair had been convicted of abusing her husband's painkillers. As punishment, she'd been sentenced to serve on the Estate. Drug use was strictly prohibited in the Bunker, but most people had their vices nonetheless.

Noah waved the men over, where he gave them a rather generic pep talk. After that, he instructed the three new recruits, Marcus, Tiger, and Ace, to step into the Rolls-Royce with him. The other men leered at the young lads and complained that they were "lucky pricks" before flocking into the Jeeps like a mischief of rats.

Tiger and Ace climbed into the back seats of the Rolls-Royce together. Marcus sat in the front passenger seat. He yanked the door open and set himself down on the soft leather chair. The interior of the car was pristine white and smelled of air freshener. Noah took his place behind the wheel. He began to admire his face in the wing mirror and, without turning, asked the lads:

"We excited for our first time out?"

"Totally," said Tiger. Ace mumbled words of agreement. Meanwhile, Marcus didn't react. Noah glanced over at him. The young lad looked like he'd just seen a ghost. "You okay, pal?"

Marcus jerked his head up and down. In a low, trembling voice, he assured Noah that everything was fine.

"If you say so." Noah revved the engine, which made Marcus jump in his seat. Noah snickered, then grabbed his special remote and, aiming it forward, pressed a small red button. The ground rattled with a tremor, as the Bunker's heavy gates scraped along the tarmac, pulling apart from each other. Marcus recoiled as piercing natural light rushed in through the widening crack. His pupils constricted to the size of pinholes. Noah reached into the glovebox and took out a pair of aviators. Marcus, shielding his face, asked Noah if he had any to spare. Noah shook his head and scolded Marcus for not bringing his own. He released the handbrake and edged his foot on the accelerator. The cars crawled towards the blinding abyss that lay ahead.

*

"So, the most important thing is passion! Dedication! And a passion... for learning!"

Jasper stood at the front of the tiny classroom, giving his inaugural speech to the eight pre-teens of '23. This was the first class he'd ever taught, although thankfully Mr Carr was supervising him, sitting at the back of the room for moral support. Meanwhile, the children stared at their new teacher with a shared discomfort.

"Anyway. Yeah... so today we're going to be looking at... let's see here..." Jasper turned on the projector screen. The first slide read, BIOLOGY – AN INTRODUCTION TO HIGHER LEVEL BIOLOGY.

"Biology!"

"This is pointless!" squealed Patty, a loud-mouthed brat who was sitting at the front. The other kids began to giggle and snicker. Mr Carr cringed and prompted Jasper to respond while the ceiling lights buzzed overhead.

"No, it's not! I understand you've learned the basics, but – but – but – you haven't learned higher-level biology yet, have you now! Yes! By the time next summer comes around, you're going to be on your way to being *proper* students. Not just in biology but all your other subjects, too. And I'm going to help you get there!"

Mr Carr smiled pleasantly at Jasper, but the children looked dreadfully bored. Jasper sighed and pressed a button on his remote. New slide. BIOLOGY IN A NUTSHELL: WHAT KIND OF SCIENCE IS IT AND HOW DOES IT COMPARE TO THE OTHER NATURAL SCIENCES?

He turned once again to the class. No enthusiasm whatsoever. This didn't bode well, thought Jasper. It was only the first lesson of the academic year, and yet his pupils already despised him.

Jasper slogged his way through a long hour of teaching, like trudging through a tunnel that would carry on without an end. The children left the classroom with an unspoken disdain. Mr Huxley, who himself was more or less still a child, had just set them an enormous load of homework. Not like good old Mrs MacNair, who'd always made life easy for the children.

Jasper slumped on his swivel chair and rubbed his forehead. "That was terrible, wasn't it."

Mr Carr stepped forward from the back of the room. "Dinnae worry, Jasper!" declared the English teacher. Kind and worldly-wise, the old Scot was in his early sixties, and – despite his regrettable past – he was widely regarded as a soft and gentle man. "A' though' it went rather well, considerin' it was your first-ever class."

"Oh, come off it. You're just saying that to be polite." Jasper flapped his hand, dismissing Mr Carr's white lies.

"Nonsense." Mr Carr walked up behind Jasper's chair and started to massage the young man's shoulders. Jasper was a little startled – but not surprised. This was just what Donald was like.

"When you're up in front of a class, sir," said Jasper, "it's like the children really listen to you. They take you seriously. They actually laugh at your jokes. Why not with me?"

"Well, a' thenk you're quite the funny one, laddie." Mr Carr ruffled the young man's scruffy hair. "An' a' wouldn' worry too much. You'll grow into it, you'll find your rhythm, an' when you do, they'll star' to really show respect an' listen to what you're sayin'!"

Jasper shook his head. "Never even wanted this job in the first place. It's such a bloody chore, isn't it." He quickly blushed, ashamed of this glaring *faux pas*. Mr Carr stopped rubbing Jasper's shoulders. He made towards the door, but turned around in his tracks.

"Look. A' know this weren't your first choice, Jasp. But a' thenk you're well-suited to the task. An' a've every faith in your teachin' abilities." Mr Carr licked his lips. "Bu' in any case, if you'd like someone to talk to, how abou' you come for a chat with me after dinner tonigh'? You know where ma' room is. 12-B, number 15." He gave Jasper a cheeky wink. "You know a've always got ma' words o' wesdem to share, laddie."

"Yeah – sure." Jasper waved Donald goodbye, and the man eased the door shut.

Jasper slouched in his chair and let out a muffled groan. He wanted nothing more than to be rid of the Schoolrooms forever.

This tired institution – the same one in which, as a child, he'd bounded through like a little lamb – now felt bland and sterile. But for the rest of his working life, he'd be stuck within its bounds, unable to switch to something else without the Commander's permission. Too substandard for the Scouts, so he'd have to make do with teaching. Jasper inhaled through his nose, taking in the musty smell of old textbooks as he tried to compose himself for the next class of the day. The terrors of '27 were due to arrive outside the door at any minute.

*

Marcus stared out the car window in awe, stunned by the Earth's endless space. The morning sun hung high in the sky, flanked by dense fluffy clouds. Gravel lumps cracked beneath the tyres as the Rolls-Royce crawled along a track. Marcus turned to gaze at the Bunker's concrete gates, which were built into a broad, imposing hill. His eyes moved up to the summit, where a small transmission tower basked in the blinding light. Somewhere beyond lay the Bunker's dam, which was currently out of sight.

After several minutes of driving through wild fields, the small convoy followed the track into a sharp V-shaped valley. Hills sloped like alien pyramids on either side. Dry heather grass covered up the terrain, although bits of surface-rock were exposed in gritty patches.

Like children on safari, Marcus, Tiger, and Ace gawped out the Royce's tinted windows. Their gas masks sat on their laps like toys. For the first time in their memory, the three boys could see the world with their own eyes.

After passing through a dense, coniferous forest, the cars reached the main road and continued winding along. The Scouts passed over a bridge, with a vast lake to their right, flanked by a chain of pylon towers.

Marcus glanced over at Noah, whose attention was fixed firmly on the road ahead. His grey-blue eyes were visible behind his sunglasses. Like the others, he was clad in a hazmat suit, which resembled an orange onesie. Marcus couldn't help but let out a little snicker. Noah furrowed his brow and glared at him.

"What d'you want?"

"Nothing." Marcus averted his gaze.

"I think he *likes* you!" blurted Ace, covering his mouth with his hand. Tiger began to giggle uncontrollably, high on the Earth's natural light.

Noah turned to the boys. "Gone off Osborne then, has he?"

The two chaps in the back burst into laughter. Tiger ruffled the back of Marcus' hair. "Yep! This one still loves his bit of posh! Not so subtle, are you mate!"

Marcus turned and slapped Tiger's arm, telling him to "cut it out". Noah slammed his foot on the accelerator and sped down the deserted A-road, cutting through a gently sloping valley. The Scout Jeeps struggled to keep up.

"To be fair," said Noah, glancing at a lone cottage by the roadside, "she is quite sweet, that one."

Tiger shared an opinion he'd voiced many times before: "I mean, I'm more partial to Melissa for a short-term thing, but I wouldn't want someone like her to be the mother of my kids. Hattie, however, most definitely! But I reckon Marcus here might still have a better chance than me!"

"Which one's Melissa again?" Noah reflected for a moment. "Oh, yeah. The ginger one. How could I forget." He licked his lips and smiled to himself.

Tiger chuckled. "Last I heard, she was getting cosy with Bobby!" He turned to Ace and smacked him on the knee. "Always had a thing for the older ones, eh?"

In the rear-view mirror, Noah exchanged knowing glances with the two chaps. They nodded and let out a shared "aaaaaaaahhhhh" sound in a show of understanding. Marcus remained silent, unimpressed by the Chief's conquests. Noah nudged him on the arm and asked if it were true that he and Hattie were on "really good terms" nowadays.

Marcus nodded. "Yeah..."

"Interesting." Noah made a tsk sound with his teeth.

As they passed a rusty wreck on the roadside — the shell of a hatchback, stripped of all its wheels and doors — Noah cast a pointed glance at Marcus. "Anyway, all I'll say is, I've had my eye on that one for a while now."

Marcus' insides boiled with resentment. He knew that Noah was sniffing around for some younger meat, having dumped his ex, Gina, after she became pregnant. "I know her type, Noah. She's not into guys like you. No offence."

Noah scoffed, raising his brow. There was a moment of awkward silence as Tiger and Ace gaped at Marcus' audacity. The Rolls-Royce continued down the lonely road, due to arrive at the Estate in ten minutes. Tiger, trying to ease the tension, finally spoke up.

"Marcus mate, what about Liv?" He ruffled Marcus' hair. "Yeah, reckon you should go for her!"

Ace concurred. He'd been the one to see Marcus tonguing Liv in a darkened room two summers back, and had leaked the news to Hattie, Marcus' girlfriend at the time.

"What do you say to that, X-Rated?" persisted Tiger.

Marcus remained silent, clenching his fists together. Tiger grabbed the sides of Marcus' seat and shook it hard. "Yeah! You two go well together! I'd go for another romp in the sack and see what happens from—"

"FUCK OFF!"

Trevor backed down.

The car continued to bump along the road, wheels scraping on cracks and patches of vegetation. After a prolonged pause, Noah let out a low, sinister chuckle. "Always been a bit stubborn, haven't we Marcus."

Marcus, caught off guard, sat with his mouth gaping open. He began to formulate a response, but Noah stopped him in his tracks by telling him to "shush". Marcus crossed his arms and kept to himself for the rest of the journey.

Dry heather plains flanked the lonely road. Rolling hills curtained off the horizon. Despite having never been here before, all was familiar in the young lad's head. An inexplicable malaise surged through him as the cars passed an old fuel station, its forecourt empty, and the seashell logo faded from the entrance sign.

Eventually, the convoy reached a roundabout and crossed straight over. A road sign read that Barnsley was eleven miles away.

*

After knocking, Jasper opened the door to Donald's room. The old teacher was waiting inside, perched on the edge of his cradle-like bed. He wore a rouge dressing gown that exposed the flabs of his hairy chest.

Jasper lingered by the entrance. The dark room's walls glowed with a sinister red; sickly-rose candles had been lit around the desk.

"Dinnae be scaird, young lad, come on en!" beckoned Donald with a wavering hand.

Jasper complied. The Commander's painted visage watched from the door, identical to the one in Jasper's room.

"My boy... si' down... si' down..." Donald belched out a disgusting burp, then patted his duvet, inviting Jasper to sit. His pupils were dilated, resembling pools of oil. That typically crisp and articulate voice had turned into a slur.

"Mr Carr – have you been drinking again?" Jasper could smell the booze on his ex-teacher's breath.

Donald pulled a cheeky face and flapped his swollen hand. "Dinnae... worry 'bout me." He hiccupped. "Sometimes... we jus' hav' to admet... that ferbedden fruits taste the sweetest. A' love rum, rum and coke, et's good fer ye." He snorted and, lying down, propped himself up on his elbows. "Good denner tonigh' then, Jas?"

Jasper squirmed, sitting upright on the bed. "Yes, thank you... Hattie and I had a... great chat – is everything okay, Mr Carr?"

"Blegh!" erupted the old man, who rolled on his bed like a playful pig in mud. "Don't call me *Mester*, et's Donald to ye, whe're chums, Jassie, we've always been goo' chums... c'mon now." He hiccuped. "Hattie? Ah, yese two, yese go well togethur... like peas en a basket... pod... She's a nice lass, a' thenk ye shed make a move on hur..."

As Donald rambled on with some generic advice on how to impress 'Wee Lasses', Jasper's eyes darted around the room. Something on Mr Carr's bedside table caught his attention.

"... an' so, back en naintee-eigh', I met ma' furst troo love an' et's just... ye have ta be confi—"

"Sir?"

"Aye?"

"Why do you have that book?"

Donald paused for a second, turned towards where Jasper was looking, and abruptly lunged to the bedside. He shoved his copy of *1984* into a drawer. "Wha' book?"

Jasper rolled his eyes. "I know what it's about, sir. George Orwell? You taught us all about him..." He hesitated for a second. "And then something happened, and you said you weren't allowed to teach the book anymore. Wasn't 'on the curriculum', so you told us. And I couldn't find it in the library either." Jasper bit his lip. He knew he was breaching the Bunker's unwritten code by bringing up such a topic, even in a private domicile. He peered over at the door. Tommy's portrait looked on with its beady grey eyes. Jasper wrung his hands together and turned away. It was time for the truth to come out.

"Please tell me why you have it here, sir."

Donald let out a defeated sigh and sank back down into the bed, lying down with his head on a pillow.

"Ye know, a' always thought ye were special, Jaspur." He played with the ring on his finger. "Someone who nevur agg-cepted the situasion fer how et seem'd. Someone who coul' scratch undur the surfass o' thengs. A' saw et en yer eyes durin' ma' classes bou' Orwell an' Rousseau. An' a' rimembur the look on yer face when a' told ye that *1984* were off-lemets. They nearle' put me on Level 3 fer tha', ye know!" Donald's voice rose. "Aye! I coul' tell ye wurr the onle' one who understood why a' weren't allowed ta teach et! But the othurs were clueless! Frankle', they couldn'a gi'en a hoot abou' any o' et..."

Jasper began to hyperventilate. Donald patted him on the arm.

"Et's alrigh', laddie... dinnae be scaird. You an' Aie: whe're some o' the few with the brain powur ta thenk fer oursel'es, an' the courage ta not agg-ccept the deceit an' lies that's been forc'd down our throats all our lives..."

Jasper shook his head defensively. "I don't know what you mean..."

Donald clapped his hands at Jasper, head jerking with fervour. "'Course ye do! The Commandur, the Scou's, everythin'. S'all twaddle. S'all a pack o' lies. They're keepin' us down here, 'gainst our own Frie Well!"

Jasper breathed in and out through his nostrils, looking into Mr Carr's impassioned eyes.

"Ye know et," the old teacher continued, "jus' as much as a' know et. There's no pleague ou' thur, lad. No' anymore. An' that's the semple fact o' the mattur!"

Jasper folded his arms. "But how – you don't know that, sir..."

Donald scoffed. "So ye realle' thenk that so-call'd Doctur es trustworthe', or wha'?"

Jasper's eyes began to well up. He'd long suspected that the annual viral reports were fabricated. Dr Hans Novak, a retired biochemist, and the Bunker's chief scientist, analysed air samples every year, and presented his findings to the public. And every year, it was always the same. Disease X, always present in the Earth's atmosphere. And Hans' words, always treated like gospel. But Jasper couldn't help but think that something was up. The way the doctor spoke in his presentations. His petrified eyes, his robotic voice, and the outlandish claims he made in those papers – none of it added up. No disease in human history had survived in the air for more than a few days, and yet, according to the so-called 'Science', X was somehow an exception to the rule.

Jasper let out a tired chuckle. A lone tear rolled down his cheek. Donald wrapped his arm around him. "Et's alrigh', lad. Et's alrigh'."

Jasper groaned and pulled away. Donald let out a heavy sigh.

"Look, whe're no' alone, Jaspur. There're othurs like us, othurs who understan' the Trooth. A'll invite ye to our next meetin' if ye like: whe're holden' a wee soirée at mine tomorro' ev'nin'."

The room fell silent, until Jasper broke out with an abrupt quote: "L'homme est né libre, mais toujours, il est dans les chaînes."

Mr Carr smiled and patted Jasper on the shoulder, as if to say 'clever laddie', before falling into a drunken slumber. Jasper stood, wiped his tired eyes, and left the room.

Commander Tommy's face remained on Donald's door, watching over the man as he slept. His massive stomach heaved up and down, the folds of his belly-button pulsing back and forth like the slow blinks of a third eye.

03

The Estate

SPARROWMAN ESTATE, read a rusty sign by the road.

The Scouts followed its pointed arrow, pulling onto a gritty off-road track which passed through swathes of fields. The cars kicked up large clouds of dust in their wake.

At one point, a group of three teens was seen loitering ahead. They dutifully scurried out of the way to let the Scouts pass through.

"Ignore them," said Noah. He put on his protective mask and told the others to do the same.

As he fiddled with his mask, Marcus watched the three youths through the Royce's windows. Two of them were smoking cigarettes. One clutched a half-empty vodka bottle. All of them wore loose-fitting tracksuits instead of hazmat suits. The oldest, a tall, chubby lad who looked about sixteen, glared at Marcus with envy in his eyes as the Rolls-Royce passed them by.

Eventually, the convoy reached a checkpoint. One of the Bunker's hazmat-clad Scouts, currently stationed on the Estate, emerged from the little outhouse. He untied the chain-link gate and waved the lads through.

Led by the Royce, the cars crossed the threshold of the barbed-wire fence, which surrounded the farm's acres as though it were a prison camp. They entered the Estate's car park and found it empty, aside from two Land Rovers, a BMW, and a decommissioned tank. Noah yanked the handbrake and stepped out of the Royce. Tiger and Ace climbed out from the back seats. Marcus took a deep breath, then set his feet down onto the martian terrain. He slammed the door shut and breathed in the cool air of the Earth through his filters. It was nearly twelve o'clock. By now, the sky was layered in a curtain of grey, the white sun cloaked beneath the clouds.

The crowd of fifty Scouts loitered about, resembling a team of alien exterminators, with their bright orange suits and insect-like gas masks. Through his smudged goggles, Marcus peered up at the Estate's stately mansion, which towered at the edge of the car park. Two Grecian columns lined its entrance, and its grey cobblestone façade was adorned with a row of sash windows. To the side of the house, a lone turbine turned in a fenced-off yard. Behind spread the vast swathes of Sparrowman fields: abundant crops and animal pastures, separated by a network of cobbled walls. Five industrial warehouses lay tucked beneath a slope on the near horizon.

Noah tapped Marcus on the shoulder to interrupt his daydream. "Listen carefully and you'll hear the sheep's baas and the cow's moos. Adorable, eh?"

Marcus scowled at Noah. Noah smirked to himself and strolled away. Meanwhile, Tiger bared his teeth like a Cheshire cat. "Why've we been living in a friggin' hole in the ground all this time, then?"

Everyone chuckled at Trevor's light-hearted remark, apart from Marcus, who felt compelled to make an observation. "Those kids back there." He pointed back towards the dirt track, where the trio of Sparrowman yobs lingered outside the bounds of the Estate. They puffed away on their cigarettes, watching the group of strangely dressed men who had penetrated their lands. "Why aren't they wearing any gear?"

Noah shook his head. "Those three are a bunch of idiots, Marcus. They're putting themselves and the rest of the Estate at risk – selfish little shits."

Marcus gritted his teeth. "Right..."

"Believe me," Noah continued, "being up here, it's no way to live. And I don't just mean the field-slaves – I'm talking about the Sparrowmans, too. Nothing but a bunch of alcoholics. There's fuck all to do up here anymore."

Marcus frowned. He peered up at the manor's front, trying to see what lay behind the windows. Meanwhile, a white delivery van drove towards the Scouts from the warehouses. It crunched its way along a makeshift track through a field of oilseed rape, before its tyres rolled onto the grit of the car park.

The driver climbed out and slammed the door. This man was an 'official' from the Bunker, stationed on the Estate to oversee operations. Like the Scouts, he was clad in one of the Bunker's standard hazmat suits, and held a clipboard in his gloved hands. ""'Ight Noah. 'Ight lads."

Noah slapped the man on the arm. "Alright, Pete?"

Pete nodded. Behind the mask, Marcus could see a pair of world-weary eyes. "Brought Maya with you, yeah?"

"Mhm." Noah gestured towards one of the Jeeps and instructed Albert to fetch the woman. Albert opened the boot and pulled her onto the ground, then removed her blindfold. Her body appeared to shake in the cold breeze, and her sharp brown eyes were tinged with fear. Pete gave a satisfied grunt. He instructed Albert to take the woman into the mansion. Her tattered shoes scraped against the dirt as Albert dragged her along. The manor's entrance doors were opened by an unfamiliar old man, who allowed them both to step inside.

Meanwhile, the rest of the men remained outdoors. Noah took the clipboard from Pete and scrutinised it. After a while, he looked up and groaned:

"We're short on flour, Pete."

Pete muttered something about production issues. Noah flung the clipboard onto the ground in an apparent fit of rage. "Oh, for Christ's sake, man! What has happened?" He clapped his hands together, making a point of his frustration.

Pete peered down at his feet. "Last week, one of the field-slaves got... he got..."

Noah drew in a sharp breath. "Someone got *sick*, did they?!"

"Yes." Pete closed his eyes and tilted his head towards the sky. "Derek Platt. Contracted X while toiling in the fields..."

The Scouts observed the two as they played out their discussion. Marcus was bewildered by the peculiar exchange, which felt like amateur theatre.

"...but this was an isolated incident, yes?" Noah crossed his arms. "No one else developed the Cough or tested positive?"

"No. Don't worry. It's all under control," Pete assured him. "We've *disposed* of the infected person."

"Well, alright, then." Noah raised an eyebrow. "In any case, what can the Sparrowmans offer to compensate for the flour?"

"They'd like to discuss options with you, face-to-face."

"Well, let's go and have a word with them, then." Pete and Noah made their way towards the mansion's doors. Noah rapped on the golden handle. The strange old man opened up and let the two men inside. Like a tortoise, the wrinkled fellow poked his head out and gave the rest of the Scouts a curious stare before retreating into the comfort of his home.

*

While waiting for Noah, the fifty-ish Scouts split off into small groups. Half of them formed a circle around the disused tank to inspect it. The other half went to loiter by the slave-yard, which was surrounded by a chain-link fence. Twenty shipping containers had been placed within its bounds. In the middle of the yard, a wind turbine soared above, powering the Estate with its whirring blades.

Marcus grabbed a handful of gravel and tossed it over the fence. It scattered on the roof of one of the containers, causing the metal to chime. "Are Noah and Pete on drugs or something?"

Bobby, a nineteen-year-old chap, who had been a year ahead of him in school, hushed Marcus and told him to "keep shtum".

Marcus swivelled around. Bobby was fiddling with his gas mask in his lap and staring off into the distance, sitting on the gritty surface with his legs crossed.

Marcus raised his brow. "You really ought to put that back on." Bobby scoffed at him. All the other Scouts had taken their masks off. The three new recruits were the only exceptions.

"Don't worry yourself, mate," said Dennis. This man was around forty-two, and resembled an Italian mobster, though he spoke with an Essex accent. "The sky ain't gonna fall if you take it off for a little breather."

Marcus looked to Dennis before lifting the edges of his mask and peeling it off. He took a sharp inhale of the crisp country air, while his face tingled with frost. A sharp breeze stung his teary eyes. "I don't know, guys," he said, breathing in through chattering teeth, "it just felt like Noah and Pete were putting on an act back there. Like, I don't know about you lot, but that's how it seemed to me."

Bobby gave him a stern look and told him to "pipe down".

"I'd drop it if I were you," Dennis warned.

Ace nodded slowly like a zombie. "Confidentiality," came the muffled voice through the mask.

Dennis jerked his thumb at Ace. "Exactly."

Tiger repeated the word "confidentiality" in an ironic tone before lifting his mask and gulping like a fish.

"Don't see why we need those rules, to be honest," said Marcus. "What's wrong with telling the truth?"

Dennis chuckled. "You sweet summer child." Marcus stared at the man with a blank expression, failing to grasp what he'd meant.

"Yeah, shut the hell up, Marcus." Bobby folded his arms. "Didn't you listen to anything Jackson taught us?"

Marcus began to pout. Mr Jackson was the Bunker's 'Scout Recruiter'. He was the teacher responsible for indoctrinating young schoolboys into the ways of the Scouts. One of the core principles ingrained in the children was the all-encompassing concept of 'confidentiality'. In essence, Scouts were prohibited from discussing their missions with ordinary citizens. Additionally, they were forbidden from openly questioning their leadership. The so-called 'confidentiality rules' were essentially a means for the Commander to enforce silence and suppress dissent under the guise of 'maintaining order and civility' through the 'enforced withholding of certain pieces of critical information by relevant persons to the general public' and 'specific and limited qualifications to the otherwise absolute principle of free speech'.

"I mean," Marcus began, "we all know Jacky-Boy's got Tommy's fist up his arse. Like a little sock-puppet. Am I right, men?"

Marcus chuckled to himself. A faraway sheep began to bleat. The others fell silent, their eyes wide with collective apprehension. Bobby stared at Marcus with a fiery expression. Marcus returned his gaze, determined not to look away. Bobby had always taken pride in making the younger lads submit to his whims, but this time, Marcus wouldn't yield to this bully. After a moment, he managed to win the impromptu staring contest. A chicken clucked from somewhere in the distance as Bobby dropped his gaze. Marcus laughed and patted Tiger on the shoulder, before blurting out the following jest:

"Blobby's not so tough now, is he!"

'Blobby' scowled and jumped up from where he had been sitting. He grabbed Marcus by the scruff of his neck and stared into his eyes. In their orange suits, the two boys resembled a pair of angry carrots. Tiger snorted with absurd laughter, while Ace watched on, alarmed. Dennis advised the two quarrelling lads to "take it easy".

"What did you say about me, you little shit?!" shrieked Bobby, spewing flecks of saliva into Marcus' face.

"Step away, weird fucker."

"Who the fuck do you think you are?!"

Marcus clicked his tongue, smiled, then proceeded to spit gob directly into Bobby's left eye. Bobby yelped, dramatically clutched his face, turned around and, with a single punch, knocked Marcus to the ground. He began to kick Marcus's limp body until a group of older men restrained him by the arms and pulled him away.

*

Marcus awoke in the front seat of a moving vehicle. Eyes widening with fear, he yanked on the door handle in an attempt to escape.

"Relax, relax, relax," Noah urged, patting him on the shoulder. "Snap out of it, lad."

Taking deep breaths, Marcus's panic subsided, as he started to recall his surroundings. The pristine waters of a blue lake stretched to the Royce's left.

Trailing them was the white delivery van, now driven by Albert. It held the Bunker's monthly food supply, alongside a stash of tobacco and cannabis. Ten silver Jeeps followed close behind, helping to escort the valuable cargo.

"You alright, mate?" enquired Tiger, from the back of the Rolls-Royce, where he was seated next to Walt. The lads had removed their gas masks and wore their hazmat suits like orange robes.

Marcus rubbed his throbbing forehead, his ears plagued by tinnitus.

"Your friend asked you a question, pal." Noah shot a glance at Marcus and clicked his fingers to rouse the young lad from his daze. "Can you hear me?"

"Yeah, yeah," said Marcus, sinking back into the plush leather seat. "I'm fine, I'm fine." The natural light from outside made his eyes sting. He considered asking Noah if he could borrow his shades, but knew in advance what the answer would be.

"I heard what happened," said Noah. "Seems like Bobby did a number on you..."

The convoy crossed an arched bridge spanning the lake. A red, triangular sign warned of 'black sheep' for the next three miles.

"We'll get you checked up," Noah added.

"Alright." Marcus winced as pain pulsed in his temples. "What about Bobby?"

Noah shrugged. "Still figuring that one out."

"You're gonna send him down to Level 3, aren't you?"

"Don't think so, pal."

Marcus frowned. "Why not?"

Noah remained silent. The Rolls-Royce pulled off the road, its wheels crunching against gravel as it traversed through dense woodlands and wound its way up a low-level mountain pass. At last, Noah offered a cryptic response, mentioning something about there being "aggravating circumstances" to consider with regard to Bobby's conduct.

Eventually, the cars returned to Level 0. The Bunker's imposing concrete gates were gaping open, allowing the outside light to flood the ground floor. Emerging from the vehicles, the orange men began unloading boxes and crates from the delivery van. Once this task was finished, Noah gathered the Scouts into a circle and informed them that they needed to wait for about an hour while Marcus received a brief check-up. He also announced that Bobby would be disqualified from taking part in the rest of the mission. Albert escorted a downtrodden Bobby out from a Jeep and called Marcus over as well. The two young men followed him to a far corner of the cave which housed transparent, human-shaped vats. Albert directed them to take chemical showers. After being enveloped in a cloud of disinfectant gas, the boys removed their hazmat gear and dropped it in a black bin. Albert performed a skin-prick test on each of their thumbs. Following the standard thirty-minute waiting period, both were confirmed as X-negative. Albert then instructed the two to return to their rooms and await further instructions.

04

True Colours

Marcus, now dressed in a funky psychedelic t-shirt and a pair of grey shorts, sat perched at the edge of his double bed. His new room on Level 2-A was spacious and regal. The walls were painted with a soft Mediterranean yellow, and the floor had been laid with wooden planks.

Engrossed in his plasma TV, Marcus was currently watching the *Landview* channel, which displayed a vivid scene of a beach. The sands were white and pristine, the gentle waters turquoise, and the sky a deep blue. Marcus sighed, longing for a life that would never be his.

The bedroom door rattled with a knock. The Commander's paper portrait shuffled in its place. Marcus stood up and peeped through the spy hole. Dr Jones and Hattie were standing in the hallway outside.

Marcus opened the door, shook Dr Jones' hand, then greeted Hattie with an embrace. She was dressed in a white lab coat, having been assigned by the Commander to the medical staff. Strictly speaking, Hattie didn't need to be up here, as Dr Jones could perform the check-up alone. Nonetheless, she had opted to seize this rare opportunity to visit her friend.

Dr Jones had Marcus sit down on his bed with his top off. He assessed the young lad's vitals with a stethoscope. Hattie watched from the corner, fiddling with her silver necklace. "So, Marcus," she said, breaking the silence, "what's it like up there?"

Marcus chuckled. "It's alright." He jumped in his seat and let out an exaggerated "brrrr" as the stethoscope pressed on his back. Hattie giggled, hiding her mouth with her hand.

"All sounds pretty *ace* to me." Dr Jones stood up from the bed. "You can put your shirt back on."

Marcus pulled his technicolour top over his torso. Hattie peered down at her feet. Dr Jones instructed Marcus first to close his eyes and touch his nose, then to stand up and walk in a straight line.

"Yep, all ace," deemed the doctor. He scribbled on his notepad. "Any dizziness or discomfort?"

"Yeah. My head hurts," said Marcus. "And the lights are really strong." He peered up towards the yellow ceiling light and shielded his eyes. "Like, more intense than usual."

"I see... but other than that, you feel... fine?"

"Mhm." Marcus scratched his neck. "Mostly ace, Dr Jones."

"Okay," replied the doctor. "I think you're fit to carry on with your mission. I'm just going to prescribe you some stuff for your headache." Assembling his green briefcase, Dr Jones stood up and said "Alrighttttt?" in his kindly, somewhat patronising manner, then made his way to the door. Hattie ran her fingers through her hair and asked if she could wait up here while Dr Jones fetched the prescription.

"No problem." Dr Jones winked at her and left, off to retrieve some long-expired paracetamol.

Hattie let out a sigh, then gave Marcus a tired but radiant smile. She grabbed the remote and turned the TV on, revealing a paradise beach.

The two friends settled at the end of the bed, watching as clear waves lapped against white shores. The scent of musk pervaded the room's air. Hattie closed her eyes with bliss and stretched down on the duvet, her hair fanning out in auburn curls. "You're really rather lucky, y'know. Having all this space."

Marcus turned to look at her. Hattie returned his gaze. Her blue eyes were soft and lazy with comfort. He shuffled back and lay alongside her. The two stared at the bright ceiling, which hovered low above their heads.

"This space is so 'ace'," said Marcus.

"So 'ace'," she echoed.

They looked at each other for a while.

"Jasper sends his regards," Hattie added.

Marcus snickered. "His 'regards'?"

"Yep." She suppressed a snort. "That's what he told me to tell you."

"Jesus," he laughed, "I swear he thinks he's an old professor or something, the way he speaks sometimes."

"Hey, don't be mean." Hattie turned her attention to the TV. "He really does miss having you around."

"Yeah?"

"We both do. Nothing feels the same without you here." Hattie bit her lip. "He seemed a little bit off at breakfast today, actually. Unstable, like."

Marcus pouted. "Eh... he'll be alright. He's not my pet or something. Anyway, you've got your eye on him now, haven't you," he said, letting out a little scoff.

Hattie's smile returned. "I'll make sure he stays out of trouble."

"Yeah, good luck with that," jibed Marcus. "Completely off the rails, that one."

Hattie playfully bumped Marcus on the arm, scolding him for his sarcasm.

But their intimate moment was spoiled by a knock.

"Marcus?" called Noah from outside. Another forceful knocking of the door. "We ready?"

Marcus groaned and stretched himself up. "I'm just waiting for a prescription from Dr Jones!" he yelled.

"Don't worry about it – I went and fetched it for you," said Noah. "Can I come in?"

Before Marcus could respond, Noah used his master key to unlock the door. He was dressed in a white shirt and a pair of tight trousers. His eyes fixated on Hattie, and a predatory smile broke across his lips. "Alright, Hat?" he said in a sickly-sweet tone. Marcus crossed his arms as he went over to give her a tight squeeze. Hattie patted him on the back as if to say 'easy, tiger'.

Noah broke away from the hug but kept his hands on her waist. Hattie's face turned red as her startled eyes met his gaze.

"How'd you like the seasoning I got for you?" he asked.

Hattie let out a nervous laugh. "It was great." She swivelled around to Marcus. "We both loved it, didn't we?"

Marcus nodded, shooting a pointed glance at Noah that told him to back off.

"Glad to hear, glad to hear," said Noah, "wasn't too spicy for you, yeah?"

Marcus shook his head. "Not really, no."

Noah pointed his thumb at the lad and joked that "this one" was a "god-damn trooper". Hattie, somewhat unnerved by Noah's passive-aggressive banter, played along with the routine nonetheless, and granted him a few stilted chuckles.

"First the spices. Then Bobby's fist in your face." Noah roared with laughter. "You've been in the wars lately, haven't you, mate?"

"Haha, yeah."

An awkward silence.

"Right then," said Noah, casting a glance at Hattie, "better leave you to it. Marcus and I have a warehouse to raid. Isn't that right?" He thumped Marcus on the chest. "Looking forward to our Surrey excursion, yeah pal?"

No answer.

Noah chuckled and led Marcus out of the room. Hattie lingered in the doorway and watched as the two men left down the hall. Marcus turned back and caught her eye. The two shared a quiet regard of unspoken longing. Spotting this, Noah laughed and slapped the boy on the back as they passed through the exit of Level 2-A.

*

"Ma' friends, a' invite ye now to welcome our most special guest – nay, not only a guest, a new Brothur – to the Circle of Frie Thenkers."

"H – hi."

Jasper waved awkwardly at the two men on Donald's bed. These were the other Free Thinkers. Once again, it was curfew and the lights were all switched off, although Mr Carr's room glowed under the spell of red candles.

"Come on, si' down, si' down." The old teacher ushered Jasper to the swivel chair, which he'd oriented to face the bed. Jasper took his seat while Donald sat down on the mattress, to Otto Walker's left. Otto was the *de facto* leader of the Free Thinkers. The man was bald, with coarse black skin, and wore a set of spectacles. Formerly the UK's Health Secretary, he was fortunate not to have been expelled from the Bunker along with the rest of the Cabinet. To Otto's right was Brandon Creak, a rather dishevelled-looking man in his late forties. His hair consisted of long greasy strings, and his eyes, albeit murky and remote, seemed always to contain an undercurrent of despair.

At last, Otto began to speak. His unfaltering, self-confident voice carried the air of a wealthy upbringing. "Did anyone see you on the stairs?"

Jasper shook his head. Otto sighed with relief. "In future, make sure you've got a cover story at hand. You never know when someone might be watching."

"Understood," said Jasper.

"But anyway," Otto continued, rubbing his knees with his palms, "I expect you remember me, don't you?"

Jasper nodded. He knew very well who Otto was. Mr Walker was Tiger's step-dad, and the Bunker's 'Head of Cleaning'. Nonetheless, it was rather strange to see him under these circumstances.

"And that there is..." Otto threw a brief look in Brandon's direction. He swiftly turned back to Jasper. "That there's Brandon. You've probably... erm..." Otto cleared his throat, "heard some things about him."

Jasper turned to Brandon. This man had once been a Scout, until a horrible incident on the road back in o'eight. Otto carried on:

"So anyway—"

"He thinks I'm... he thinks I'm mad, doesn't he..."

Everyone looked at Brandon as a wave of anguish flushed over his face. The room froze with discomfort.

"No one thenks tha' at all," said Donald, reaching to pat Brandon on the knee. "We all thenk you're a friggin' *soldiur*. M'kay, mate?"

A few seconds passed. Brandon creaked his mouth open. "That's what people – just what people – you people have to say to a man like me... a man who's had to see what I've had to see..."

Otto sighed with frustration. "Just wish you'd love yourself the way we all love you, my friend."

Another silence.

"So, what's the topic of discussion today?" Jasper enquired.

"Well," said Otto, "first of all, I just wanted to ask, Don, how exactly did you find out for sure that he's a deviant?"

"A *deviant*?!" Jasper crossed his arms.

"No, no' like tha'," laughed Donald, "he means someone who can be trusted." He turned to Otto. "I managed to force it ou' of him."

Otto reflected for a moment, then gave Donald a cheeky *coup d'œil.* "You finally worked that bloody *1984* thing on him, didn't you?"

Donald laughed and slapped Otto on the arm.

"You cheeky rascal," said Otto. "Unbelievable." He let out a dry chuckle.

"Huh?" said Jasper. "What are you talking about?"

"Ma' boy," began Donald, clasping his hands together, "I left ma' copy of *1984* ou' on purpose when you came to see me. A' wanted you to see it, so you'd let your guard down." He smiled. "An' you know, a' was rather surprised tha' ma' lettle treck worked out so bloode' well." Donald chortled, then pointed his thumb at Jasper. "A' can confirm, this one's as *devient* as *devient* gets!"

Otto made to speak, but was interrupted by Brandon's sharp hissing of the word "official!" which forced the men to fall silent.

One of the Bunker's 'security officials' strolled along the hall. The footsteps came, then returned, plodded past the room once more, and finally vanished.

"How much of my whiskey have you got left?" said Otto.

"Oh, there's plente' for the four of us, stell."

"Good." Otto turned to Jasper, and began to explain. "Tommy – oh, excuse me, the 'Commander' – gave me a whole casket of the stuff for my birthday. Thinks I'm his 'mate', the utter clown." He glared at the standard Big Brother image that watched proceedings from the door.

Donald grabbed a sloshy bottle from his bedside drawer, twisted the lid, and gulped, gulped, and gulped, causing his belly to swell. At last, he let out a violent belch and passed the booze to Otto, who took a gentle swig before asking Brandon if he'd like a sip.

"I'll have some," said Jasper, before Brandon could respond.

"Oh, err, mate. I asked Brandon first." Otto glared at Jasper over the rims of his glasses, in the manner of a stern librarian.

"Yeah – whatever. Give it here." Brandon snatched the bottle, struggled to take the cap off, and then, placing it to his lips, guzzled its contents down his throat.

"That's enough, that's enough." Otto took the rum from Brandon's shaky hands and passed it to Jasper. The young lad took a whiff of the stuff and made a "yeugh" sound.

"Dinnae be such a wuss," laughed Donald. "We're all qui'e aware of wha' you an' the othur kids used to ge' up to aftur school."

Jasper, eager to impress his new friends, took a massive gulp of the Scotch whiskey. His face twisted itself into a grimace.

"Sue Parker," said Otto, staring at his feet. "Was just thinking about her." He turned to Jasper. "Your booze dealer back in the day, correct?"

Jasper nodded. Sue used to trade alcohol and drugs to people in exchange for their food, including the Bunker's teenagers. At the time, she'd been seeing a Scout named Mo Singh, who'd supplied her with the contraband, and had been the main instigator.

Otto folded his arms, staring at the ceiling with an air of nonchalance. Ms Parker and Mr Singh had been sentenced to 'indefinite servitude' on the Estate for their crime. But Otto seemed rather indifferent to this glaring injustice. He opened his mouth to state his verdict on the woman.

"Stupid bloody... cow."

"Tell us how ye realle' feel," said Donald, who nudged Otto on the shoulder. The man's face was marred by resentment.

"I'm right, though, aren't I," he groaned. "It was always gonna end in tears for her. Not saying she deserved what happened – I'm just saying, if you play stupid games, you win stupid prizes..."

"You have to respect hur hustle, though." Donald scratched his chin. "Aye... she an' hur man, dishin' pills an' booze ou' to schoolchildren, all fer some extra scraps o' food. Takes propur guts, tha'."

"Yeah, really brings a tear to the eye." Otto chuckled with disdain. "But I'll tell you what *real* courage looks like, yeah?" He licked his lips and began staring at Jasper with a set of glazy, drunken eyes. "Mickey Ratford. Yeah?"

"Hear, hear," said Donald.

Jasper furrowed his brow. "Mickey Ratford?"

"Aye lad," said Donald.

"But the man was a bloody terrorist..."

Otto scoffed. "You believe that, do you?"

Jasper reflected for a moment. Mickey had been part of Commander Tommy's inner circle and was once the Chief of Scouts. In 0010, he'd been accused of trying to sneak a batch of X into the Bunker and release it. As a result of this 'treasonous plot', Tommy had confined him on Level 3, until he'd 'offed himself' in 0013.

"Yeah, I don't know," Jasper said with a sigh, "I'm just sick of all the lies."

Brandon mumbled in agreement.

"And yet," said Otto, "no one seems to question any of this crap. Not just the lies, but the hypocrisy, too. The degeneracy. The drugs, the binges, the orgies – I've seen it with my own eyes, Jasper. And it all happens under Tommy's watch. But if common folk like you and me get caught with a few pills or whatever it may be, we'll be locked up on Level 3, sent out to the Estate and all..."

"Maya MacNair," said Brandon, "that poor woman – it was... it was horrible... and you know she did nothing wrong, don't you..."

"I mean, yeah." Jasper bit his lip. Mrs MacNair's humiliating trial was still fresh in his memory, having played out a month ago. "But what exactly can we do about it?"

Otto glanced to the side and wrung his hands together. "Bugger all, really."

Jasper felt a pang of disappointment. He leaned forward in his chair to size the men up one-by-one. "So what's the point of all these meetings, then? Do you guys just sit here and rant about stuff?"

"Aye, mostle'. It's a discussion forum, laddie," said Donald. "A safe place fer us to show our Troo Colours."

"That's right." Otto lay down on the bed, propping himself up on his elbows. "Why, have you got any game-changing plans you'd like to share with us, kid?" He leered at Jasper with a mocking smirk on his lips.

"Look there, a' cannae even ge' Tommy's bloode' noggin ou' ma' room," laughed Donald, gesturing towards the Commander's ugly portrait. On drunken impulse, Jasper stood up and resolved to tear that oppressor from the face of Donald's door.

"Easy, tiger!" bellowed Otto.

"Aye, leave it be," said Donald. "It's pointless. They'll notice if someone's tried to take it down from its propur place."

Jasper let out a defeated sigh, returning to his chair. Donald reached into his bedside drawer and offered the sad lad a plastic vape, which he happily accepted. The device snapped and crackled as he sucked on its mouthpiece and breathed in a strawberry cloud.

"Feelin' a wee bit bettur?"

Jasper nodded. He took another drag from the vape pen. His veins pulsed with nicotine. The powerful rush made him feel a little queasy, and in a moment of scattered derealisation, the young lad reflected on his long-standing misery. There had to be more to life than just this Bunker, and yet, the so-called 'Free Thinkers' had done nothing but mope about and complain, treating their predicament as just another unfortunate fact. A tough situation to be coped with through laughter and 'togetherness', rather than taking concrete steps to try and actually resolve it. Meanwhile, Commander Tommy was still busy with his efforts to strip their lives of joy. The Bunker was his trap, and its citizens were the little critters he'd lured inside of it. But the question remained: what did Tommy stand to get from this arrangement? Was it really just about power, or was there something more to it?

At last, a brilliant idea came to Jasper's mind. He took one last puff of the e-cig before returning it to Donald.

"What if we could get our hands on guns?"

The others stared at him in silence.

"Eh?"

"If we had guns, then we could launch some kind of uprising. The officials would lose their monopoly on force. That's the main pillar of the State – according to Weber's notions, at least..."

Otto rolled his eyes. "Max Weber ain't gonna help us here, mate. Besides – all the guns are kept under lock and key."

"But Otto – what about... what about that rascal Little Ted?" said Brandon, peering down at his feet. "You – you said he keeps a... a gun in his bedside drawer..."

"Yeah. He's a wee bit paranoid, that one." Otto playfully slapped Brandon on the knee. "Yeah." He turned to Jasper. "I see it in there whenever I do his room. Probably scared of shadow-people coming in during the night, or something." Otto proceeded to laugh at his own joke.

"Well then," said Jasper, "have you thought about stealing it?"

"I have... but then what would I do with it?"

"I dunno." Jasper scratched his neck. "We could, like, shoot Tommy dead, or hold someone hostage..."

"Nah. Wouldn't achieve anything. Our problems don't start and end with him. Someone else would take his place. And they're all just as bad as the other, really."

Jasper shuddered at the thought of Noah Smith being made Commander. Nonetheless, his thoughts continued to linger on Teddy's loose gun.

"Maybe," he began, "you could grab it and shoot whoever's on checkpoint. Then we all make our way up the stairs – past the forbidden floors – and boom, there we are, up on Level 0, then we run out the gates, and at last, we're finally free of all this misery..."

"See, a' told you he's clevur!" said Donald, breaking out with a pleasant smile.

"*Clever*?!" Otto snorted with disdain. "Jasper, I – really? That's your idea, is it?"

Jasper shrugged. "Yeah. I don't know—"

"What about my wife and son?" Otto raised his arms with righteous anger. "How could I ever convince them to come with me? We'd be leaving our whole lives behind, you cretin!"

"Look," said Donald, speaking on Jasper's behalf, "it's no' a half-bad plan. If we wen' up to the surface, we coul' even try to find Dalton an' the othurs – assumin' they're stell kickin' abou'..."

"Even if they were," said Otto, "there wouldn't be enough of us to do any real damage."

Jasper frowned. He understood that most of the remaining 'Retreaters' had been taken out in an attack five years ago. Only Dani Dalton and Ashley Mirza had managed to escape the wrath of the Scouts.

Donald polished off the last of the rum. He wiped his mouth and stood up. "A' cannae help bu' find ma'self agreein' with Jaspur, y'know. We can't jus' sit here an' moan all our lives. We've got to, y'know, get ou' thur an' do somethin'..."

"I know." Otto sighed to himself. "I know. But I'm sorry, fellas. It just ain't gonna work."

Jasper rubbed his face. His eyes welled up with disillusioned tears. At last, he swivelled up from the chair and left the dark room in a sulk, slamming the door on the other Free Thinkers. 'Utterly pointless,' he thought to himself, as he scurried his way through the pitch-black hall and trudged down the silent staircase, returning to his bedroom on Level 13-B.

Another solitary night without having made any progress, Jasper lay awake for an hour, restless from the nicotine, until he finally drifted off into a groggy half-sleep.

05
The Retreat

The same night, Marcus and the others found themselves in the courtyard of an industrial complex, near a motorway. The fifty-odd Scouts surrounded a barrel fire, akin to a congregation of the homeless. Noah had allowed his men to remove their hazmat suits, exposing their undershirts and various undergarments. The air was nippy, so most of the lads were cocooned in sleeping bags. They had stashed chemicals and equipment in the delivery truck, parked outside the courtyard. A few items on Dr Hans' list were yet to be retrieved from the warehouse.

Marcus was sitting on a roll-up mattress. He took a hearty swig from his bottle of SPARROWMAN BREW. Tiger finished the last of his roll-up cigarette, before he grabbed Marcus and Ace by the shoulders and clasped them both together. "What a life, eh chaps?"

Marcus nodded vacantly. "Yup." Tiger released his grip and stood up, heading off to find another group of 'lads' to 'chill' with. Meanwhile, Marcus continued to stare into the fire's spitting embers. The warehouse they'd ransacked earlier stood in the near distance, its garage door rolled up for all the men to see.

Marcus glanced at Ace, who was staring into the dark forest that lay beyond the yard's bounds.

"Bit creepy, innit," said Ace.

"How's that?"

Ace pointed at the shadowy woods, whose canopies rustled in the breeze. "It's like... I dunno what's in there..."

Marcus took another sip of his beer and told Ace to stop worrying. "There's fifty of us here, Walter."

Ace ground his teeth together. "Yeah, I know." He continued to stare with paranoid eyes. "But still..."

Noah strolled over and crouched down to say hello.

"Alright, kiddos?"

Marcus refused to look at him.

"Yeah," responded Ace. "Just chilling."

"Cool!" said Noah, a grin spreading across his face. Patting Marcus on the shoulder, he said, "Make that your last beer, yeah mate?"

Once again, Marcus refused to acknowledge him.

"Don't want anything to happen to you, do we mate? What, with those pills you've been taking..."

Marcus shrugged, then took a big gulp from the beer. His head throbbed with a migraine. "I'm sure I'll be fine, 'mate'. Those pills barely do nothing anyways."

Noah pulled a funny face. "Shouldn't be drinking at all on paracetamol. That's what the doctor says."

"Yeah, well," scoffed Marcus, "I don't seem to remember asking."

Noah's face flushed with drunken anger. "You got an issue with me or something?"

"Err," said Marcus, a smile of disbelief on his face, "no?"

Noah kissed the insides of his teeth. "I have to say, pal, it really does seem like you do..."

He turned to the rest of the group, his voice filled with mock concern as he exclaimed:

"Hey everyone... I think Marcus here's a bit upset!"

The men fell silent.

"Why's that then!" yelled Albert, playing along with Noah's routine.

"I dunno," said Noah, staring deep into Marcus' eyes. "Keeps giving me attitude..."

Marcus remained seated, while Noah sized him up with his piercing grey eyes. After a tense silence, he poked Marcus' belly and made a "boop" sound. The men burst into laughter. Noah stood up and headed back to his group, whistling as he crossed the yard. Marcus muttered the word "wanker" within Noah's earshot. The men went "ooooooo". Noah gestured for them to be quiet before he spat out a crude joke about Marcus' parents, who'd been "dispatched of" by the Commander during the outbreak's early days. The men groaned and exchanged begrudging laughter. Like Marcus, they'd all lost their loved ones in some way or another. Marcus seized on this fact and yelled that Noah was a "soulless twat", no different to his "scummy father".

A hush fell over the Scouts. Noah, stunned, opened his mouth to speak, then closed it again, struggling to find a comeback. At last, he scoffed and walked away, grabbing his things and heading over to the ransacked warehouse.

"You lot can come in with me, or stay out in the cold. Your choice." Noah passed through the entrance and disappeared into the depths of the warehouse, his sleeping bag trailing by his feet.

One by one, the men gathered themselves and followed the Chief inside. Marcus remained on the ground. Ace stood up, threw a scornful glance at Marcus, and headed off to join the others. Meanwhile, Tiger returned to speak with his ostracised friend. He leaned into his ear and whispered:

"What the hell were you thinking?"

"I was thinking," said Marcus, his voice a woozy slur, "that someone had to tell him, tell him for what he really is..."

Tiger bit his lip. Turning around, he decided to join the streaming men, and crossed the threshold of the warehouse.

Marcus remained outside for a while, until he resolved to head over and clear things up with the Chief. But as he neared the entrance, Albert, who was stood nearby, turned to the others and cried:

"Look! *X-Rated* is trying to come in with us!"

The steel walls of the warehouse howled with laughter.

"Keep out and stay out!" boomed Noah, sitting behind a shelving unit. His taunt was met with cheers of approval.

Marcus frowned and strolled back to the campfire. Albert rolled the door down, cutting him off from the others for good.

He lay down on his roll-up mattress, curling himself into a foetal ball. Even after pulling the sleeping bag over his body, Marcus couldn't stop shivering. The barrel fire kept on flickering and spitting, but its flame was on the brink of dying out.

*

Over the course of the night, Marcus managed to drift off on several occasions. Nonetheless, his light sleep was interrupted three times: first by his bladder, then by nothing in particular, and lastly by the distant whirs of a creature in the sky.

Propping himself up, Marcus strained to listen more intently, unsure if his concussion was making him imagine things.

But there it was again. Marcus saw a shadow flit beneath the stars, like a hummingbird switching positions.

'Odd.' Marcus raised his eyebrows and, exhausted, lay down once more, resting his head against the mattress. And yet, his eyes remained open. After a long minute, he dragged himself up and ambled over to the warehouse in bare feet. He paused, however, before he could knock on the door, as he glanced up at the sky and saw that the flying object had vanished. It had likely been just a bird or a bat.

Marcus chuckled and stumbled away from the warehouse. Dressed only in his psychedelic-patterned shirt and plain-white underwear, a surge of adrenaline propelled him out of the courtyard. With his vacant stare and aimless movements, Marcus resembled a man in a fugue state.

On the slip road outside, the Scout vehicles were parked in a neat row, including the Jeeps, the van, and, of course, the Rolls-Royce. He crossed and entered the fringe of the woods, the same ones that had so worried Walter. Marcus relished this opportunity to explore by himself, before dawn could finally break, before Noah and the others could subject him to more torment.

The damp air of the woods was heavy with the stench of rotting matter. Grass brushed against his ankles as he squelched through the undergrowth. Up ahead lay a large clearing, where an immense trench had been dug. He walked to its edge and, stood between trees, peered down towards the asphalt river.

The M25 had been abandoned for nearly two decades. Aside from the odd crack and pothole in the surface, with tufts of vegetation poking out, the road remained in a somewhat decent condition. In fact, it looked a little sad, as if waiting to be made useful again, not privy to the fact that its masters were deceased. Marcus felt a sudden pang of unease.

On that empty stretch of road, only an old Range Rover remained. Marcus creased his brow. Something seemed off, the way it was parked there. His eyes welled up with inexplicable tears. An abrupt instinct took control of his legs, driving him back into the woods. He scuttled through as fast as he could, stomach churning with adrenaline.

A branch snapped some thirty feet away. His heart raced with painful throbs. He started to pace towards the end of the woods, back to the warehouse, but a strange voice barked for him to stop.

Out of the corner of his eye, Marcus could see a silhouette. Instinctively, he stopped running and raised his hands, sensing that this person was armed.

The shadow-person approached him from behind and ordered him to kneel. Marcus complied, knees squelching into the wet soil. The shadow-man lingered for a moment, then grabbed Marcus by the arms and turned him around.

Behind the balaclava, a pair of brown eyes stared at Marcus. The masked man had an eerie, dreamlike aura. Marcus felt as if he were dreaming, or that they had known each other in a past life.

The man spun Marcus around and pressed a gun into his back. "Move." Compliant, Marcus began to stride ahead, descending the gentle slope and onto the rocky surface of the M25. The two walked along the road for a few gut-wrenching minutes, until the man shoved Marcus into the front seat of the Range Rover, whose doors had been left unlocked. In the back sat a little old lady with a small drone on her lap.

*

The shadow-man switched the electric engine on, and started to roll off his balaclava. Marcus shook with a full-body tremor. Ashley Mirza had just revealed himself, and was sitting at the wheel. Just as Marcus had seen in the photos, Mirza had light-brown skin, a black goatee, and the same old tireless eyes. He must have been about fifty now, and had turned completely bald. The man tapped his foot on the accelerator, and the Rover crawled across the road. The electric motor chimed with the songs of ghostly angels.

Meanwhile, the strange woman in the back seemed to be Dani Dalton herself. Marcus looked at her face in the rear-view mirror, careful not to make eye contact. Once Prime Minister of the United Kingdom, Ms Dalton was now ringleader of the 'Retreaters', and had been committing atrocities against the Bunker ever since o'zero, after the Commander had sent her and her allies into exile. These days, Dani looked haggard, like a criminal on the run. A white drone lay on her lap, lifeless, like a homeless person's little dog. The jawline of her pasty face was sharp and prominent, and her sullen green eyes carried bags of exhaustion. The buckle of her seatbelt, unfastened, shook about on its strap as the Range Rover picked up speed.

Marcus was stiff in his seat, his heartbeat thumping in his ears and throbbing behind his eyes. His mind raced with terrible visions of the aftermath of Retreater attacks: PowerPoint slides of horrific car wrecks, with mutilated corpses strung out on the road: young men slaughtered for no real reason. Dani Dalton stared out the window, her face devoid of expression. Ashley Mirza barely moved, except to edge the steering wheel, holding it between his fingers like a paintbrush.

Marcus gulped, and tried to muster up the ability to speak. "Wh... wh... wh..."

"Sssh," hissed Mirza. He glanced over at the terrified young lad. "Name?"

"M-Marcus..."

"Marcus." Mirza chuckled. "Surname X, isn't it?"

Marcus's voice jittered. "Y-yeah – how did—"

"Thought I recognised them eyes." The Range Rover pulled off the M25 and drifted onto a slip road. "Christ, you've grown, haven't ya? Knew you when you were *this* high." He gestured with his hand, creating an infant-sized space between it and his lap.

The car reached a roundabout, and took the first exit. They passed onto a straight road that cut through an old suburb. Grand Surrey homes stood on either side. The driveways were packed with cars. Marcus felt sick. All the houses lay intact, but they would doubtless be riddled with the dead. The plague had swept across the world within a month and, despite the horrors around them, most people went gently into that good night, spending their last days on Earth with their loved ones.

The journey was guided by full beams, which gleamed in the windows of the desolate buildings. Eventually, the Range Rover approached a small roundabout. At its centre stood a World War I memorial. Thick weeds sprawled in the soil at its base, taking the place of the remembrance-day poppies. Mirza wound past the ancient monument and drove them through the rest of the town. The narrow road was flanked by red-bricked buildings, where 'shops' and 'pubs' had once teemed with life. At last, the car left the 'high street', and a black-striped 'speed limit' sign marked the start of a dense forest.

Ashley Mirza. Dani Dalton's lieutenant. Marcus felt odd, as if he were talking to some mythical creature that had sprung into life. Meanwhile, the dishevelled old lady in the back remained a phantom. Marcus cleared his throat.

"W-what do you, erm, what do you want from me..."

Mirza glanced over at the petrified lad. "I wouldn't worry, mate." He glided the car down the road at a reckless speed, wheels bouncing up and down and slamming into potholes.

"I've still got plans," breathed Dani Dalton, her voice like a fleeting wind.

The Rover screeched to a halt, then veered onto an off-road track. A wooden gate had been opened at its entrance. Mirza passed through, then stepped out of the car to go and click it shut. As he climbed back into the driver's seat, Marcus saw that the man had a Glock tucked in his belt. He shot Marcus a menacing look before he switched the ignition back on and sped the car up a slope. Dirt cracked and crumbled beneath the skidding tyres.

The morning sky was filled with a dark crystalline blue. Dawn was about to break. The Rover reached a flat stretch on the track. Mirza parked the car in an open clearing in the forest. He stepped out and, pulling the charging flap open, connected the car to a black cable that emanated from the soil. He then led Marcus up a rocky footpath through the woods, with Dani stumbling behind, until they reached the summit of a hill. On top of it lay the sprawling remains of an abbey. Among the bricks and rubble, a camouflaged hatch had been fitted in the grass. While Mirza crouched to punch numbers on its hidden keypad, Marcus stared off into the flat world beyond the slope, swarmed by endless forests and the occasional hill. An old spire from a church stood tall in a country village. On the far horizon, Marcus could see the outlines of towers, marking the core of a distant city.

At last, Mirza pulled the trapdoor open, revealing a vertical tunnel.

"Welcome to the *Project*."

He gestured the hostage inside, pistol still tucked in his belt. Marcus took one last gulp of the world's air. He stepped over a crumbled abbey wall and peered down into the vault's depths. Mirza slapped him on the back as if to say 'attaboy'. A rusty ladder railed down towards the darkness of the Earth.

06
Reds Versus Blues

Three days after Marcus' disappearance

Leaving Level 6, Jasper made his way down the metal steps. The Bunker's massive staircase was completely empty, save for an official stationed at the checkpoint outside 5. Jasper peered up. Big Davey's silhouette could be made out through small grilles in the landing.

Holding a crinkly bag filled with his packed lunch, Jasper entered the small lobby space of Level 7 and navigated through Corridor B. At last, he unsealed a vault door, passed through a narrow passageway, and opened another door that led him to the Garden Space, the only part of his world that didn't feel claustrophobic.

The gargantuan chamber contained a lush park and had a row of greenhouses at its far end. The air of the Gardens was humid and light, and the temperature was cool. Its plants oozed with oxygen, and a hydroponic farm had once been operated in the space.

Jasper stepped onto a gravel path that cut through a lawn. Above his head stood drooping willow trees, which had recently reached maturity. Their tops grazed the hexagonal panels, which beamed light from the ceiling. As he walked, the occasional bee buzzed by his ankles, courtesy of the colony that the Scouts had introduced.

The Garden Space teemed with fifty-odd kids who'd already eaten their lunch in the canteen. Incessant shrieks filled the air, drowning out the ambient birdsong and breeze that played on the room's loudspeakers. As he plodded along the path, Jasper was struck in the knee by a rubber cricket ball, which he chucked back at a circle of pre-teens.

"Cheers Jassy-Hux," squeaked Terence, a troublesome twelve-year-old whom he'd taught in the morning. The other kids laughed in unison at their fresh-faced teacher. Jasper groaned, reached into his pocket, stuck a tangled pair of headphones in his ears, and began to listen to some jazz music.

After a minute or so of walking, he reached the heart of the park, where an ornate fountain splurged water on itself. Surrounding the fountain's rim was a large gravel circle, where eight wooden benches had been set up. Jasper looked around. Going clockwise, each of them was occupied by:

Alastair Cash, Josh Brooks and Scarlett Chase – sitting on the furthest bench. Two teenage lads and a lass, whispering about some low-level gossip that made Bunker life a little less boring.

Jonah Reeves and Colin Carrington. Two male 'friends', staring at the fountain and eating a box of jam sandwiches together.

Ursula Wolf. A swotty young lass whose father was German. The girl was seventeen, and would be graduating from the Schoolrooms next year. She'd always been obsessed with science fiction novels, as well as with 'Jassy-Hux', who quickly turned away to avoid her gaze.

Otto Walker and his pretty wife Prim, who was twenty years his junior. Her rosy-red cheeks matched the colour of her dyed hair. They were nattering away about something unimportant. Jasper tried to catch Otto's eye, but the man ignored his presence.

Barry Townsend. A depressed and wrinkled old chap, who'd once been a civil engineer. He had a patchy, unshaved beard and had never moved on from the loss of his pre-pandemic life.

Percy and Steve, clutching their phones. Two scrawny geek-children, immersed in Bluetooth games. They never seemed interested in anything other than themselves, always stuck in their own little bubble.

One bench remained unoccupied.

And on the last, Hattie Osborne was sitting all alone, facing sideways. Her eyes were filled with a quiet despair, still processing the terrible news from this morning.

Jasper took his headphones out and began to approach his friend. His heart was thumping in his ears. A strange tension had grown between the two, ever since Marcus left for the Scouts. And now that he'd gone missing, Jasper felt a duty to break the ice, and make sure that Hattie was doing okay.

"Hi there," said Jasper.

Hattie started in her seat and took her earbuds out. "Sorry, Jas. I didn't see you coming."

"May I join you?"

Hattie furrowed her brow. "Of course..."

A beaming smile spread across her face, and she patted the bench, inviting Jasper to take a seat. And so he did, awkwardly placing his bag on his crotch. He reached into his bag and ruffled out a mutton sandwich. Peeling the clingfilm off, he listened to Hattie as she rambled on about a "hilarious" film she'd seen last night. Jasper took a bite from his sandwich and nodded mechanically as she spoke.

"... but erm, yeah, no, it was great." Hattie cleared her throat and looked to the side. She'd run out of things to say. Jasper broke the silence by asking her if she'd already had lunch.

Hattie shook her head. "I erm," she said, wiping her forehead, "I didn't really feel like it today."

Jasper frowned. "Have the rest if you want," he said, pointing down at the other half of his sandwich.

"Aww." Hattie smiled sweetly. "Thanks, Jas. But I think I'll be okay."

Jasper offered his apple. Hattie shook her head. "No, really, I'm fine."

"Alright." Jasper stared into the waters of the ornate fountain. "Tommy sure does like a good Victorian design."

"Yup." Hattie looked down at the gravel under her feet and started to fiddle with her necklace.

"Marcus," she said, in a low, murmuring voice. Jasper glanced over at her. "He'll be okay, won't he."

"Yeah." Jasper cleared his throat. "Yeah, they'll find him, for sure." He crunched into his apple, eyes glazing over like a horse's. Two screaming boys began to run laps around their bench. Hattie beamed with delight, while Jasper just looked livid.

"Boys, boys, leave that nice young couple alone!" called a distant voice, which belonged to Mrs Sprigg. The old dear was on lunch duty, watching over the children's playtime. "Oh, do take your squabble elsewhere!"

The boys appeared to register this command. As they darted off, Hattie let out a deep sigh. Her gaze trailed the children as they bounded through the grass and vanished behind the leafy curtains of a willow tree.

Jasper took another bite of his apple. "I hate kids."

Hattie burst into laughter and nudged Jasper on the arm. He smiled in return but felt his limbs freeze up, chest burning with an uncomfortable warmth.

"You're such a grinch." She let out another chuckle and leaned in a little closer. The two sat in silence for a while. Hattie, gazing at his unbuttoned collar, was trying to come up with a thing to say.

"Nice suit."

"Thanks." Jasper glanced at her blue jumper and averted his gaze, embarrassed at having seen the outlines of her breasts. "Y-yours look nice today as well... erm, yeah."

Hattie bit her lip.

"Thanks."

She shuffled away a little. Jasper cringed at himself. His body resurged with fear, overcome by a wave of self-hatred. How did he always manage to spoil precious moments like these? Sensing that Hattie was about to leave, he opened his mouth to try and keep her interested.

"You know – I reckon Marcus will be just fine..." he murmured, trying to project an air of mystery.

Hattie nodded. "Yeah..."

"No, I mean – I really do think he'll be okay. Like, objectively speaking."

Hattie's eyes became filled with confusion. Jasper cleared his throat, and tried to explain.

"The disease... you know, it's erm" – he checked over both of his shoulders, making sure no one was listening – "it's not even around anymore." He rubbed his hands and took a deep breath, worried to have broken confidentiality. Hattie stared at him with a perplexed expression, like he'd told her the Earth was flat.

"Right..."

Jasper peered over at the bench where Otto was sitting, on the opposite side of the fountain. The two exchanged a brief look. Otto stood and led his wife Prim out of the Gardens, glancing back at Jasper with a flicker of suspicion. Jasper turned back to Hattie.

"There's a bunch of us," he continued, "who don't buy all this nonsense from Dr Hans. Anyone who knows anything about science will tell you..."

"Jasper," said Hattie, "I really don't want to talk about this. I'm not interested." She stood up and wiped at her sleeves, as if to rid them of imaginary dirt. "You shouldn't say things like that out loud."

Jasper apologised. Hattie stood over him with her hands on her hips, like a mother scolding a child. "What is this, anyway? Some sort of group?"

Jasper, hunching over on the bench, began to shake his head. "Don't worry."

Hattie looked towards the garden's distant exit. Folding her arms, she turned back to Jasper.

"Just promise you won't do anything silly, okay?"

"Of course." Jasper faked a smile. "And besides – I'm only kidding, Hats. There ain't no group!" He scratched the back of his neck and added, "I got you fooled, good and proper," before letting out an awkward chuckle.

Hattie turned and left without saying a word. Jasper watched as she walked down the path in her graceful stride, her silky brown hair bobbing up and down while her upper thighs rippled and waved. The fearful flutters in his chest subsided, turning instead into pangs of desire.

*

That afternoon, Jasper finished marking the prep he had set for the tykes of '25, then headed to the Sports Hall on 6-B. Today was another 'Sports Day'. No classes were scheduled for the afternoon.

That week, all the young boys from the 'Red' and 'Blue' houses were participating in the monthly football tournament. Events like these always had high attendance. In fact, they were considered compulsory, though the officials never bothered taking registers. Most people invariably showed up. Jasper too had decided to come along, obliged to support his young pupils.

As expected, the 'Reds' won the U-8 and U-10 matches with ease, and would undoubtedly win the U-12, U-14, U-16, and U-18 games as well. It was no secret that the Commander assigned the children he deemed 'stronger' to the larger 'Red' house, while the weaker minority formed the little 'Blue' house. Unsurprisingly, Jasper had been made a 'Blue' at the age of five, when the colour system was established back in the calendar year 0006, yet another of Tommy's cruel designs.

Five minutes into the U-12 game, the 'Reds' were already leading 4-1. Jasper winced with second-hand embarrassment for the 'Blues'. Football always conjured up excruciating memories for him, of playing as a goalkeeper, helplessly conceding to boys who were more athletically gifted.

Finally, Jasper shook his head and, for the first time in his life, refused to endure this torture any longer. He made his way through a crowd of excited young girls, then through a large group of adults, including a few Scout lads, who had been allowed to come down and watch the match. Each of them held a cup of vodka and lemonade. Noah was nowhere to be seen, still leading the search in Surrey. Jasper brushed past a kindly older Scout named Dennis, who stopped him by seizing his wrist.

"Jasper Huxley?"

Dennis released his grip. Jasper waited for the crowd to cease clapping, after the 'Red' attacker, Lance Harding, scored his third goal of the game. As the noise died down, Jasper confirmed that this was he.

Dennis, staring at his feet, reluctantly began to explain:

"Look, kid – as far as I know, the guys haven't found him yet. But we're doing everything we can." Jasper's gaze intensified, urging Dennis to continue. "But listen, erm – we can't make any promises, y'know, what with... with the disease, and—"

Dennis stopped abruptly. A guilty look passed over his face. Jasper nodded with a silent understanding. "No worries, Dennis." Jasper smiled politely, then moved towards the exit, the soles of his shoes clopping along the polished floor. Jasper creaked the exit door open. He cast a final glance at the match, but his view was obstructed by the teeming spectators. In that moment, he felt like a repulsive freak, forced to watch the Bunker from afar. Some of the men had their arms wrapped around wives or girlfriends. The young lasses screamed and cheered for the 'Reds', while the sparse 'Blue' supporters kept to themselves. Even the Bunker's elderly residents had turned up, huddled in a corner. They cheered gayly at the beautiful game before their eyes. Full of shame, Jasper turned and left the hall, making his way through concrete passages until he reached the gloom of the staircase.

Jasper stepped on the landing of Level 6 and swiftly descended the steps, trying to avoid Big Davey's gaze. This man, an official, was currently on duty at the landing to Level 5. He was seated on the small metal landing in a deckchair, earphones plugged in. Extremely tall and very grotesque, Big Davey resembled an orc. His bald head glistened in the dim light of the stairs as he listened to tinny music.

Believing himself to be in the clear, Jasper puffed a sigh of relief. Whistling inconspicuously, he proceeded down the spiralling steps.

*

Level 12's lobby was aglow with industrial light. Nothing lay inside the cramped space aside from the Bunker's standard red carpet and a pair of doors. Jasper entered the one marked 'B', revealing a sterile concrete hallway. Each of the bedrooms there was marked by a number. Most remained vacant, but were waiting to be filled by the ever-booming mass of 'Bunker Babies'.

At last, Jasper reached the room marked '15'. On the other side of the door, he could hear Mr Carr, engrossed in an erotic film on his laptop. Jasper turned to leave as low growls became piggish squeals.

Disappointment washed over the young lad. He'd been hoping to talk to Donald, to try and persuade him to have another word with Otto about the scheme they'd discussed the other night.

But Hattie!

Jasper paused for a moment.

Like Donald, he hadn't seen her face amongst the crowd. Perhaps she, too, had decided to hide away in her room, another lonely free-thinker like himself. Jasper continued to walk through the concrete passageway. At one point, he thought he saw a shadow flicker in the corner of his eye, but chose to ignore this paranoid intuition.

Finally, he reached the exit, crossed the lobby, and entered corridor 'A'.

Hattie's bedroom was located at its far end. Jasper could already hear her sobs as he walked down the empty hallway. When he reached her room, he cupped his hand against the door and whispered:

"Hattie! Hattie! It's me!"

The girl's muffled tears came to a stop. There was a long silence until she edged to the door. Creaking it open, Hattie peered through the crack as if answering a stranger in the night. Jasper stared at her with longing in his eyes and a shameful curse in his heart.

"What's up?" Hattie said, injecting cheer into her voice. The whites of her eyes were still red from crying.

"Can I come in?" he asked, well-mannered as ever.

She stepped aside and allowed him to enter. Jasper felt deeply unwelcome, like a pesky fly she'd been too polite to shoo away.

Hattie's room was the same size as Jasper's, akin to a prison cell. Her single bed dominated the space, though a desk and a cupboard had been crammed in there too. Hattie had resided here since she was six, and had decorated the place nicely over the years. Jasper began to examine the walls with childlike wonder. Moving clockwise, the wall opposite him was covered in a pastoral scene, one that Hattie herself had painted. It depicted an idyllic English countryside: plains lush with oak trees and wildflowers. On the wall to his right, she had designed a bleak cityscape, crammed with billboards and Soviet-esque high-rises. On the wall behind Jasper, where the door stood – Commander Tommy's portrait hanging there with a look of disinterest – lay a vast expanse of desert. Pyramids stood on its lone and level sands. Jasper smiled, imagining this to be a cryptic statement about the Commander's 'pharaonic' regime. Before he could inspect the final wall of the room, Hattie interjected by asking if he fancied some 'baccy-chew'.

Jasper nodded with keen enthusiasm. "Oh, yes please – thank you very much." He winced, worried that his voice had sounded like a robot's. Hattie took out a metal tin from her bedside drawer. She opened the lid and revealed its earthy contents. Jasper stuffed a handful of leaves into his mouth.

"You no' havin' any?" he grumbled, releasing a fleck of tobacco-tainted spit that landed and left a mark on her red carpet.

"No," she replied. Hattie wasn't fond of the taste of tobacco. She only chewed at social gatherings, merely because it was something to do. She returned the tin to her drawer and pushed it shut.

As Jasper crunched the dry leaves into mush, the sharp taste of nicotine tingling on his tongue, he began to examine Hattie's final wall, unpainted, which she had adorned with a collection of printed photos.

His heart sank. These pictures were snapshots of their shared childhood. He'd been to her room a couple of times in the past, but both occasions had been drunken and short, and he'd never examined the details in full. The industrial ceiling light buzzed overhead, filling the weighty silence.

Jasper leaned in and squinted. One row of the collage depicted the plays that Hattie had participated in; snapshots of her with the rest of the cast, and a few of her on stage, including that biblical epic scripted by the Commander himself, GOOD AND EVIL. Hattie, who'd been ten at the time, was cast as an angel. In the photo, she was shown gazing up at 'The Devil' with her bright blue eyes, trying to sway him towards the light.

Jasper stopped chewing his mush, as his mind recounted to him that painful tale of how, aged eleven, he'd auditioned for the role of 'Jesus', but instead had been made to play a tree.

A bitter taste seared in his mouth, like the ashes of a dying fire. He stooped down and spat tobacco mush into Hattie's bin. The girl now stood beside him, and, in spite of himself, Jasper felt compelled to continue this journey into their shared past.

All the pictures were aglitter with 'Hattie and Co', but never showed Jasper in the limelight. Sure, there were a few moments of him, her, and Marcus all together – but Jasper was only ever there as a sideman. One such image captured the aftermath of a paintball game on Level 4. Jasper was giving an awkward thumbs-up to the camera, his helmet splattered with yellow paint. Meanwhile, Hattie and Marcus stood with their helmets taken off, smiling and laughing like an old married couple.

In fact, the only picture of just Hattie and Jasper was taken when they were both ten. It depicted them sitting in a library, broadly smiling at the camera with a shared comic book in their hands.

Jasper's heart ached. He and Hattie had once been genuinely close, but ever since puberty, Jasper had been reduced to the level of a satellite, watching his friends as they breezed through their adolescence. He'd always taken a detached interest in it all, thinking, in his anxious disconnect from the others, that he was somehow better off compared to them – but, all in all, he had little to show for his time on this Earth, apart from just sort of being 'there'.

As his eyes fell on the last photo – baby Hattie cradled in the arms of her late mother – Jasper could feel something fire up in his stomach, like the rusty cogs of a long-dead machine. The grinding resentment of a wasted life made his face twitch with hatred. Hattie saw this, and asked if he was alright, to which the young lad gave no response, until at last, he looked her in the eyes and asked if he could pose her a question.

"Sure!" she yapped, forcing a smile.

He closed his eyes, inhaled, then exhaled, contemplating whether he should reach for her hand. He decided against it, and opening his eyes, he released the haunting question that had plagued him ever since the age of nine:

"Am I going to be stuck like this forever?"

*

Hattie's face became a blank canvas. Each movement there was carefully scripted. At last, she parted her lips and delivered a cautious response:

"I don't know what you mean."

Jasper rolled his eyes. "Yeah, you do. I mean, am I going to be a fucking loser 'til the day I die, or will this ever get better? Will I ever get better?!"

"Oh, Jasper!" she cried, holding him by the shoulders as he sat down on the bed. He stood up and began pacing like a restless meth-head, as Hattie tried to calm him, her gaze fixed on the haunted despair that passed through his eyes. "You're not a loser, it's – it isn't true..."

Jasper collapsed onto bed again, this time clasping his face in his hands. "That's just what you have to say – you never mean it!" he cried with a shaky voice. "I'm a waste of oxygen, aren't I? Aren't I?! Go on, tell me!" he yelled, his voice filled with despair, until he found solace in the warmth of Hattie's validation, as she enveloped him with a hug. Face pressed against her shoulder, Jasper buried himself there a little harder while he wailed.

"It's okay..." she said, stroking his back with her delicate fingertips. Jasper's tears began to subside. "You're okay..."

In a flash of awareness, Jasper jerked his head up and stared into Hattie's gentle eyes, as if the two were about to kiss. He held her by the hand, and she looked away, cheeks tinged with an uneasy blush.

"I think we should go look for him, you know," he murmured in a low, brooding voice.

Hattie sniffled, overwhelmed by Jasper's sudden outburst, and the all-but-certain loss of her dearest friend. Slowly, she untangled her hand from his fingers and placed her arm over Jasper's shoulder. He nestled his head against hers, and the two sat in comfortable silence together, staring at the grim concrete jungle on her wall.

"I really don't think he's coming back," she said, eyes closed with a sad finality.

Jasper sighed deeply. He'd never felt so warm and fuzzy in his life. "Maybe not."

Tears welled in Hattie's eyes, and she let out a muffled cry. This time, Jasper took the comforting role, stroking her hair and kissing her on the forehead. "Can't say for sure, though," he said. "Maybe he's still out there. Just maybe..."

Hattie wiped her eyes. "I'm not sure..."

"I know they're lying to us," said Jasper, gazing into Hattie's bleak cityscape. A surge of determination pulsed through him. "Dr Hans – he's a liar. You know they make him present false findings, don't you?"

Hattie pulled away, creating distance between the two. Jasper continued:

"We're – we're called the Free Thinkers. We meet every other night. And erm, Mr Carr's a part of it too, you know!"

The blood vanished from Hattie's cheeks. She urged Jasper to lower his voice lest someone 'official' might hear.

"What the hell are you on about?"

Jasper jumped up and started pacing the room, prancing about like a golden retriever. "That group I was talking about – it's real! All too real!"

Hattie shook her head. "But what's that got to do with—"

"Because," interrupted Jasper, his eyes darting across her walls, "we could go and look for him, you know, find a way to sneak out of this concrete shitheap, go and see the real world!" His eyes sparkled with idyllic visions as he stared into her green pasture. "Oh, Hattie, wouldn't it be nice?!"

"I guess, but – but–"

"But what?!" he exclaimed, clapping his hands before her face. His legs trembled with exhilaration. "Nothing's stopping us! We could be out of here by tomorrow if we really wanted!"

With the grace of a clumsy ballerina, Jasper swivelled and dropped himself down on bed, leaning into Hattie as he spoke excitedly. "Otto's a cleaner, so he can take the gun from Ted, then we use it to kill Davey, grab his master key, and then we make our way to the gates and–"

"Jasper!" cried Hattie, slapping him across the face. She rose from the bed. "What the fuck's wrong with you?!"

Horrified, Hattie stared at Jasper, who remained on the bed, recoiling from the pain she'd inflicted. The girl thought she heard a shuffle outside, but her paranoid musings were interrupted by the maniac.

"Are you fucking crazy?!" he snarled, riding the tides of self-righteous passion. "What'd you do that for, huh?!"

He stood and flung his arms like an angry Italian. "Got an issue with me, do ya?!"

Hattie backed towards the door. The two stared at each other, his brown eyes livid, her blue eyes trembling with fear. Hattie pressed herself against the door as she withdrew from her frenzied friend, her back smothering Tommy's portrait. Jasper hesitated, unsure of what to do or say next.

"Are you finished?!" spat Hattie, panting with heavy breaths. Jasper's eyes flickered, and the mania train came to a grinding halt.

"I – I'm sorry, Hats, I – I didn't mean to–"

Hattie pressed a finger to her lips. Jasper fell silent as her eyes widened in alarm. Her mouth dropped open as she held her ear to the door. Jasper crept over and listened in as well.

There it was. A breath. Moving in and out. The carpet seemed to creep beneath their feet.

A fist pounded on the door – Hattie and Jasper jumped in shock.

They exchanged a glance of terror, before Hattie pulled the door open, revealing Big Davey on the other side.

Davey strode into the room, holding his smartphone out like a platter. He tapped a red button, causing a long recording to stop.

He looked Hattie up and down, surly eyes bulging with desire, then turned to Jasper with a vile sneer.

"Thought you could fool me, did ya?!"

Jasper's knees wobbled, as if about to give way. Davey grabbed him and Hattie by the ear and led them out into the concrete corridor. The red carpet rasped beneath their feet as the brute dragged them over to the exit.

07
Good and Evil

Jasper sat curled in a pitch-black cell. His stomach was churning with dread, although by now, a tired euphoria had made itself known behind his eyes, adrenal glands having worn themselves out.

Jasper shuffled on the rock-hard floor. Four hours had passed since Big Davey locked him inside. He sighed and adjusted his position once more, this time stretching out to lie, although this too could give no comfort.

As he stared up into the darkness, Jasper's windpipes hacked out a laugh that sounded like a cough. His scattered mind ventured into the past, as long-suppressed memories came to the fore.

*

His slow descent had been set off long ago. It was on the fourth of April, back in double'o'ten.

Jasper had been a gangly pre-teen at the time. For the Bunker's spring play that year, the young lad had been cast as a tree in the Commander's morality tale, Good and Evil, which took place in the Sports Hall.

There he was, up on the stage, all self-conscious and embarrassed in a tree costume. 'Adam', played by an older boy named Reece, and 'Eve', played by Jasper's classmate Liv, both flanked him at his sides. 'Eve' tore an apple from his foliage.

"What's that?" cried 'Adam' in a melodramatic tone.

"This," 'Eve' began, "is an apple from the Tree of Knowledge of Good and Evil!"

Even at the time, Jasper could sense how odd and disjointed this line sounded. The Commander had done a bad job with the script.

"Eat my fruit at your peril," mumbled 'Tree', voice barely audible to the audience. The line was intended as an exclamation, but Jasper refused to put any effort into the execution.

After this brief cameo, Jasper strolled off the stage and ventured into an empty classroom, ridding himself of that cringeworthy tree costume.

He recalled how Hattie had been the only one to come and visit him. Dressed as a bright angel, young Hattie gave him a hug and a crumb of forced praise, which Jasper cherished dearly, but nonetheless sensed the emptiness of her words.

"Aren't you due up soon," he grumbled, staring down at his feet.

Hattie nodded. She glanced at her little pink watch. Five minutes to go.

"D'you mind looking after this for me?"

Jasper said "Fine" and seized the watch from her wrist, careful to avoid her gaze. Nonetheless, Hattie saw the tears that were building in his eyes, and she gave him another hug, which caused young Huxley to burst into a whine.

"It's okay," she assured, immediately grasping why Jasper was upset. The boy had auditioned to play the part of a young Jesus Christ, but had lost out to Bobby Stephens. "You'll get something brilliant next time, I promise..."

"No I won't," sniffled Jasper, "I'm rubbish at this..."

Hattie broke away from the embrace, realising that she was going to be late. "I've got to go now – sorry. Come and see me once the show's over, alright?"

The girl beamed a smile at her miserable friend and left the room, bounding through the corridor. Jasper wiped his tears and, after a minute or so, decided to return to the Sports Hall. Standing at the back of the crowd, Jasper observed his friend's performance from afar.

The Devil, played by a fierce sixteen-year-old named Derek Platt – later sentenced to the Estate, for something unspeakable – was staring down at sweet little Hattie, who gazed up at him with petrified eyes.

"...and why should I listen to YOU!" he boomed, voice blaring through the loudspeakers.

'Angel-Girl' gulped. "Because – well, because—"

"Because WHAT?!" interrupted 'Devil'. "What, because you've got those big fluffy wings and that sanctimonious golden halo?!"

The audience guffawed at this bizarre line, expertly delivered by the talented Derek. Even Jasper couldn't help but crack a smile.

"Leave her ALONE!" cried a voice from the front rows. The crowd gasped. Bobby Stephens stood up from his chair, dressed in rags and a long Jesus wig.

"Oh yeah? Or else you'll do WHAT?!" bellowed 'Devil'.

"Or else WE'LL do THIS!" cried 'Jesus'. Ten boys dressed as angels stood up at his command.

"Angel-Team Assemble!"

Jesus and the Angels stormed the stage, swarming around the Devil and kicking at his shins. The script abruptly instructed them to scurry out of view. The room's lights turned a malevolent red, and Hattie remained trapped there, alone in this personal Hell. The young girl screamed for help while Derek let out a villainous "Muahahahahaha".

A sudden white flash, and Noah appeared on the stage, dressed in Zeus apparel. He was eighteen at the time, and the Commander had cast him to play the role of God. He pointed his wooden staff at Derek and exclaimed, "Prepare to die, my woe-betided fiend!" before the two engaged in dramatic combat, culminating in Noah tossing 'Devil' into a fake pit of fire. 'God' brushed his hands together, and the Angels returned to the stage, along with his Son.

"Nice job, Dad!" said 'Jesus'.

"Yeah, thanks for saving me!" exclaimed 'Angel-Girl', reaching up to give Noah a fist-bump.

'God' waved his hand in humble dismissal. "I'm just doing my job, after all!"

The main characters read some 'thoughtful monologues' to conclude the play, then the lights went out. The audience leapt to its feet and cheered as the cast returned for the curtain call. Jasper wasn't a part of this parade, for the Commander felt that 'lifeless props' like him didn't deserve the spotlight. The young boy tried to catch Hattie's eye while she was on stage, but her attention was fixed on someone else in the audience.

Then, out of nowhere, the Commander started doing laps around the stage, hyping the crowd by waving his hands. The Bunker erupted with collective adulation, as if their dear leader were a rockstar. Some cried genuine tears. Finally, the Commander took a *bow and stood next to his son, Noah. And Jasper seemed to recall how, while waving at the crowd, the Commander caught his gaze and, although the teeth wore a smile, his sullen eyes were livid, and clearly spoke to say:*

'Do better next time, useless little shit.'

*

The lock rattled on Jasper's cell. Adrenaline surged through his body once more, as 'Little Ted' swung the door open.

Jasper was dragged through the bleak tunnel of 3-B, which felt like an underground prison. The rows of cells were currently unoccupied.

At the far end of the hall, a door had been left open. Lurid yellow light glowed from within.

Jasper was thrown into the room, and had to steady himself on the central table. Little Ted slammed the door and took his place in a corner chair.

Commander Tommy, waiting at the interrogation table, gestured for Jasper to take a seat. Jasper complied, his back scraping against the metal as he lowered himself down.

Slouching in his chair, the Commander ran his fingers through his beard, whose wiry strands were tainted with grey on the ends. Jasper avoided the man's piercing gaze. Meanwhile, Little Ted sat watching Jasper with jaundiced eyes.

The Commander placed an iPhone onto the table and slid it towards Jasper, instructing him to press 'play' on the touchscreen. Jasper did as he was told, playing Davey's tinny recording of the 'Osborne Conversation'. Jasper closed his eyes in shame, as the long audio played itself out, filled with long pauses at the start, until it gradually gained volume, culminating in his manic screeches.

The Commander snatched the phone back, tucking it into his pocket.

"You know, I always thought you were a bit broken, Jasper. Like someone dropped you on the head as a child." He clasped his hands together. "Now. Tell me more about the 'Free Thinkers'."

Jasper gulped. "I-I don't... I don't—"

The Commander slammed his fist on the table, causing Jasper to jolt with a yelp. Little Ted cackled from the corner with a crow-like laugh.

The Commander mimicked the boy's petrified voice – "I don't, I don't, I don't..." – and let out a dry chuckle, watching Jasper's face with interest. Jasper squirmed in his seat. The Commander continued to stare at him in silence. Eventually, the dry lips cracked open, and a low growl slithered through:

"Shall we try that again?"

Jasper took a deep breath, glancing at Little Ted in the corner, who sat there, slumping, like a ragdoll in tatters. Fighting through his nerves, Jasper tried to formulate a response.

"We – we're a group, it's a group that met every other evening, the guys, they talked about stuff, and—"

"What 'stuff'?" interjected the Commander, folding his arms with disdain.

Jasper gulped. "The Free Thinkers, they were basically saying – erm – that the disease might not be around anymore, and so, erm, they wanted to—"

The Commander let out an odd, delayed chortle, as if he'd only just registered the stupidity of these words. Little Ted joined in with the laughter and stared intensely at Jasper. Jasper stared right back. Little Ted was now forty-five years old. Tufts of greasy blonde hair obscured his sullen eyes, the right one black and blue with a bruise.

"So let me get this straight," said the Commander, "you wanted to kill my guy and then run out of the gates. Is that right?"

Jasper paused. He closed his eyes and gave a grave nod. The Commander scoffed in response, then swivelled around to his minion. "What do you make of that, Ted?"

"Shocking, sir! Disgraceful!"

"Yeah. It is, isn't it." The Commander turned back to Jasper. "What else were you planning on doing?"

"I – I don't know." Jasper gulped. "I only ever went to one meeting, sir – I promise."

"Really?" The Commander leaned back in his seat, crossing his arms. "And who else was in attendance?"

Jasper cleared his throat. "Well, erm – like I said on the... thing, erm, it was Mr Carr, and Otto. And, erm – Brandon. Brandon Creak. He was there as well."

The Commander reflected for a moment. "And what about Osborne?"

Jasper's eyes bulged with horror. "No, sir – she had nothing to do with any of it!"

The Commander nodded repeatedly, as if listening to an internal rhythm. "So why did you discuss those plans with her?"

Jasper violently shook his head and opened his mouth, but the Commander interrupted before he could speak:

"Seems to me like she was a kind of... *confidante*, to you. Was she not?"

Jasper breathed a heavy sigh, and his eyes began to well up. "Please, sir, don't hurt her, please, I'm begging you—"

At last, he burst into pathetic tears. The Commander leaned across the table, and, in the precise manner of an experienced abuser, smacked the young lad in the cheek and left a lingering rash.

"Now," he began, "you're going to tell me everything you know about this group. If not, I can make this a whole lot nastier for the *both* of you." In the corner, Little Ted had started to play with a butane lighter. The Commander turned towards him.

"You've been desperate for a romp in the sack, haven't you lad?"

Little Ted's eyes were fixed on the hissing flame. "Indeed sir, indeed!"

"Is pretty little Hatt up to scratch?"

Little Ted licked his lips. "Ooh, yes. I'd be a very lucky man!"

The Commander chuckled, then returned his gaze to Jasper. "Tell me about Otto Walker."

Jasper took a breath to compose himself. "Well," he began, "Otto, erm, Mr Carr said Otto was the ringleader, he was the one who initiated the first meeting, and erm – then they managed to get Brandon to start coming along, and then Mr Carr managed to web me into it..."

The Commander scoffed. "Donnie 'webbed' you into it, did he?"

"Yes," said Jasper. "He... I guess he *used* me, is the word..."

"*Used* you?" The Commander laughed incredulously. "Alright, fine. Carry on."

"Otto... yeah, erm – apparently, he erm, he really despises you... Mr Carr said it was to do with what happened in o'zero..."

"Really?" The Commander tilted his head, gazing up at the buzzing yellow light. "Wow. Never got over that whole thing then, did he."

Jasper gave Tommy an odd look, taken aback by his naivety. Mr Walker had been a Cabinet minister, so naturally, he'd been a little disgruntled after Tommy ousted all his old colleagues from the Bunker.

"Thought Otto and I were good friends, y'know. That's sad." Tommy drummed the table with his hands. "Anything else you'd like to share with me, Jasp? Anything juicy?"

Jasper took a breath and began to rack his brains. "Well, erm – apparently, they literally met every single week, and—"

"You already told me that!" hissed the Commander, "give me something else!"

Jasper cleared his throat. "It was a kind of discussion forum, y'know. Like, they basically went on long rants about stuff, and things like that."

The Commander yawned and rolled his eyes. "So tell me," he began, "who was it that came up with the plan?"

Jasper's eyes widened. The Commander leaned in, his face contorted with a cruel sneer.

"It wasn't *you*, was it?"

Jasper gritted his teeth. "I, erm – they all sort of worked it out together, I suppose..."

"They?" said the Commander. "So you had no part to play whatsoever?"

Little Ted glared at Jasper, flicking the flame of his lighter. Jasper kept his mouth shut, unsure of what to say.

"Remember what's at stake," the Commander warned. Jasper's stomach churned with horror. A tortured vision of Little Ted polluting Hattie flashed before his eyes, her muffled shrieks piercing his ears. A sore lump formed in his throat, and he pressed his eyelids shut.

"I came up with it." Jasper's shoulders seemed to ease. "That's right. I put it all together." He looked over at the Commander, expecting a surprised reaction, but the expression there remained blank – tired, even.

"Uh-huh." The Commander scratched his beard. "Thought so." He peered over his shoulder. "Go and fetch Davey for me now, would you?"

"Yes sir." Little Ted stood up and scurried out of the room. Meanwhile, the Commander began scribbling in his notebook, his tongue sticking out like a child lost in thought.

Five minutes later, Little Ted returned with Big Davey. The two resembled a depressing comedy act. Ted sat down in his corner chair while Davey loitered about with his hands in his pockets. The Commander penned the last lines of Jasper's script.

"All done." The Commander blew on the ink, then presented the book to Jasper. "Have a little read, and let me know when you've finished."

Jasper's eyes skimmed the pages. His scattered brain struggled to comprehend the messy writing.

After a few minutes, he looked up and nodded at the Commander. "I'm, erm – I'm finished."

"Alright." The Commander took Davey's phone out, which he used to record the confession. Its camera flashed on like a spotlight, and Jasper cleared his throat to speak.

"My name is Jasper Huxley. I – I would like to confess to a very grave crime that I planned to commit."

Jasper read through the rest of the piece, stumbling on every other word. After he finished reading, the Commander smacked him and told him to "try again, but with a bit more fucking oomph".

The next time around, Jasper managed to read his lines somewhat convincingly. The Commander stopped the recording, then handed the smartphone back to Big Davey.

"What do you make of all this drama then?"

Davey tutted, shaking his head at Jasper. "I could tell this one were up to no good. Had a weird way abou' him!"

"Interesting." The Commander chuckled. "Didn't take his rejection so well, did he."

Big Davey bellowed out with laughter. The Commander smirked and patted him on the arm. "Good work today, mate."

"Cheers, boss." Davey was seen out the door by the Commander, who then returned to his seat.

"Right then," he said, rubbing his hands, "I think you'd best be scooting off as well." He gestured for Ted to escort Jasper back to his cell. In the doorway, Jasper turned his head and begged that Hattie be freed.

"Yeah, yeah," said the Commander, who idly twirled his pen around the tabletop.

Little Ted led Jasper away, then tossed him into a darkened room, the door of which had no number.

*

Hattie's door began to rattle. Its metal hinges creaked, as Noah opened the cell.

"Dad says you're free to leave."

Hattie wiped her tired eyes, then rose to her feet. She'd been locked in that cell for nearly five hours. During that time, Noah and his search team had returned from Surrey, on the orders of Commander Tommy, who had spoken of a "possible coup d'état" via radio.

"We'll carry on looking as soon as we can," he said, accompanying her through the dim corridor of 3-B. "I promise."

"Thanks," she said, not even bothering to turn around. Noah grabbed her by the wrist, stopping the girl in her tracks.

"No one *did* anything to you, did they?"

Hattie shook her head. "No."

Noah seemed relieved. "Okay, good. And erm" – he paused for a second – "I'm really sorry about Jasper."

Hattie bit her lip. She peered over her shoulder, in case anyone could hear. "Noah," she began, "please don't let them hurt him. He's not a bad person, he's just – he's just a bit lost at the moment..."

"I understand. Yeah." Noah rubbed his chin. "Thought it was harsh, turning him down the way he did. If it were just up to me, I'd have let him join. His test results weren't *that* bad."

Hattie peered up him. "So you'll have a word with Tommy?"

He ground his teeth together. "I'll see what I can do."

The two continued towards the exit of Level 3, walking side by side. When they reached the stairs, Noah lingered in the doorway, watching Hattie make her way down towards the lower levels, stepping past Big Davey as she made her slow descent.

08
Really Sorry

18/09/0017

At present, the Bunker's populace was seated in the shadows of the Sports Hall, peering up at the lurid, empty stage.

Hattie, dressed in all-black clothes, was sitting in the back row, with only Dr Jones to keep her company. Her stomach was tied in knots, and her chest ached with a lingering pain. Although Noah had ensured she wouldn't have to testify against Jasper, he'd been unable to disclose what Tommy had in mind for her unfortunate friend.

Her head turned sharply as she heard footsteps outside. The door of the Hall was pushed open, revealing a procession of officials, spearheaded by Big Davey, Little Ted, and Eddie Lee. All of the Bunker's security checkpoints were now unmanned, except for on the hilltop, where 'Freddy Krueger' was stationed with a sniper.

Eddie, a rugged man who'd grown up in Singapore, was followed by Noah, and then Commander Tommy himself, who led the shackled Free Thinkers with a massive chain leash. Hattie's heart wrenched, as she looked at the men one-by-one.

Mr Carr trudged along at the front with his hands bound together. He had two black eyes, and his massive face was swollen. The man resembled a dying panda.

Otto Walker lagged behind. His signature glasses were missing, his saggy eyes exposed to the open air.

Next, Brandon Creak, who had a long scratch over his swollen left eye, etched there by a sharp knife.

And last of all, Jasper Huxley. His attention was fixed squarely ahead. Although his hair was greasy and his face sullen, Hattie felt a measure of relief, as, unlike the others, he appeared to have avoided physical torture.

The officials stepped onto the stage. Each of them took their places. Davey, Ted, Eddie and Noah sat in their seats at the back. Meanwhile, Commander Tommy stood before the podium. Directly ahead of him, Donald, Otto, Brandon and Jasper were made to kneel in a line of shame. Their cuffed hands dangled over the edge of the stage.

"My friends," said the Commander, his harsh voice booming through the air of the hall, "once again, we find ourselves under attack. But this time, our enemy has been working from within." He glared at the four suspects. Each of them looked terrified, except for Otto, whose eyes burned with defiant rage. Commander Tommy pressed his lips against the microphone, and the whispering crowd fell silent.

"Each of these men has been scheming against us. Clandestine meetings in the night, where they indulged in wild conspiracies, and threatened violence against our people!"

The Commander left a deliberate pause, allowing the room to seethe with anger. In the front rows, the Scout-men glared at the four with collective scorn, directing most of their hatred at Jasper Huxley, the Blue-Boy whom they'd rejected that year. Jasper did his best to avoid Tiger and Ace's unsettling gaze. Meanwhile, the Bunker's young children, scattered throughout the audience, scowled furiously and growled like lion cubs. Commander Tommy opened his mouth to continue his speech, but stopped himself in his tracks. He looked to Big Davey, then gestured for him to take the stand.

Davey adjusted the mic, then gripped the sides of the podium with his enormous hands. "Last Saturday, I watched Mr Huxley" – he jabbed his trembling finger at the hunched lad on the stage – "I watched this one as he were leaving the match, even though it were still going on. He come out the door of Level 6, then I saw him lookin' at me to see what I were up to." He turned to the Commander with a confused and nervous expression, like a labrador pleading with its owner. The Commander told him to keep going.

"Yeah," said Davey, turning back to the crowd, "then he went down the stairs, and I watched him, thinking, well, he's actin' a bit odd. Whistling in the way what a wrong'un would do. So I decide to follow him. And then he walked through Le'el 12 for a bit, and decided to visit a lady friend. Went into her room, and started rambling about being upset, or something. Then he starts talking about shooting me!" Davey's eyes wettened with a sad puppy look.

"I don't know what I done wrong! But anyway, he said he wanted to kill me, then, erm..." – here, he looked to the Commander again, who gestured for him to continue – "then, erm, what happened was, well..." He tapped his lips. "Well, he said he were gonna nab me gun, then – ah, bollocks, what was it again..."

The Commander intervened. "Otto was going to steal a gun from someone's room, then Jasper was going to shoot you. Isn't that what you said?"

"Oh yeah." Davey turned back to the audience. "Tha'ss right. Otto were gonna nick it from Ted's drawer!"

'Little Ted' squirmed in his seat. His bruised eye bore the mark of Commander Tommy's beating.

"And then," Davey continued, "Jasper were gonna use it to kill me while I were on duty. Then they were going to swipe *my* gun, too, and storm all the le'els, takin' out ordin'ry people one-by-one! I reckon they was somehow in cahoots with Dani Dalton and such, what with Otto being part of the old Cabinet n' that..."

Big Davey, like a shy child, began to twiddle with his fingers. "But yeah. Tha'ss all I've got to say, I s'pose."

"Thank you, David." The Commander patted him on the arm and gestured for the man to sit down. "Now," he said, his hoarse voice booming through the speakers, "I think it's time we heard from the man of the hour."

At this moment, Davey rustled in his trouser pocket and took out his smartphone. Little Ted swiped it from his palm and plugged it into the projector. After a minute or so of setting it up, a white screen was lowered over the stage, with Huxley's meek face projected onto it.

*

Hattie watched in horror as the recording began.

My name is Jasper Huxley. I would like to confess to a very grave crime that I planned to commit.

The audio picked up a quiet gulp.

This summer, I was rejected from the Scouts. My aim and stamina was proven to be poor, and I failed to impress either the Commander or the Chief in my interviews. Unable to take responsibility for my own failings, I blamed others and turned to the commission of treason.

My old schoolteacher, Donald Carr, introduced me to the group one day. When I arrived, I saw that Brandon Creak and Otto Walker were also in attendance, and as I understand it, these men were the only others involved in the group. It was made very clear to me that this was not only a discussion forum for vile conspiracy theories, they were also planning an attack on the Bunker.

These men coerced me and persuaded me into being part of a vile plot. This had been in the works for a very long time. Mr Walker, the ringleader, intended for me to play a crucial part in it. He was going to steal a gun from an unnamed official's room – which, of course, should NOT have been there – and then he was going to make me shoot whoever was on duty with it, as a kind of test for my loyalty, or something. Then Mr Walker and the others were going to come and join me, and steal the gun from whichever official we just murdered, as well as the gun we had already, to go and slaughter innocents, as well as Scouts and officials maybe, until we ourselves were finally put out of our misery.

Now, what was our motive?

Jasper turned to a new page, and continued reading from the notebook.

Well, I suppose we all hate the Commander, and everyone in the Bunker, deep down. All four of us have our petty grievances.

Donald has already proven himself violent – I think he got a kind of bloodlust from when he made that poor little girl tumble down the stairs.

Brandon, for his part, was no doubt still bitter about being made redundant after what happened in o'eight. But it's not the Commander's or the Scouts' fault what went wrong in his brain.

Next, Otto Walker. Apparently he was still resentful about what happened to Dalton and the other old ministers, but he fails to remember that the Commander could only do what was best, and we even gave them protective gear to ensure that they might survive in the contaminated air. Not that they needed it, filthy rats. But of course, just like the 'Retreaters', nasty Otto Walker is deeply ungrateful for everything that our faithful stewards have done for us, and would perpetrate senseless violence to satisfy his insatiable ego.

As for I, Jasper Huxley: in truth, I am but a veritable loser at heart. My friend and apparent love interest, Hattie Osborne, I always fell short of her expectations, which made me extremely resentful, and then I seemed to snap after my rejection from the Scouts.

I deeply regret my actions now, and I understand that neither senseless violence, nor slandering of officials, can ever be sensible things.

The video came to a stop. Jasper's face remained frozen on the screen, like a deer forever stuck in the headlights.

*

The projector screen was rolled up.

The Commander called Primrose Walker to the stand. She had managed to avoid being detained like the others. Otto had covered for her during his interrogation. Nonetheless, the officials suspected her involvement. From the front row of the audience, supported by his best mate Ace, Tiger watched on, horrified, as his mother was subjected to questioning. These last few weeks had seen his world turned upside down.

The Commander paced behind the four kneeling convicts. His hands were placed behind his back. Prim stood at the podium, her knees shaking uncontrollably.

"Now remind me," said the Commander, his voice booming throughout the Sports Hall, "how long were you and Mr Walker married?"

Primrose gulped. "Eleven years." The microphone screeched with feedback.

"Congratulations." The Commander cracked his knuckles. "What do you like about your husband?"

"Well, erm," said Prim, "lots of things, I suppose. His charm. His dry wit. And he really stepped in to help out with my Trev, after his dad passed away."

"Right, right, right," said the Commander, "so you were in love with him, then?"

Prim furrowed her brow. "Of course." She peered down towards her kneeling husband, whose stern gaze was fixed directly ahead.

"Did a lot of things together, didn't you?"

Primrose nodded. "Yes..."

"What kinds of activities did you two enjoy?"

Primrose cleared her throat. "Well, erm – we loved going for walks, and we, erm – we went to the gym together, spent afternoons in the library... just normal things, things of that kind."

The Commander's eyes flickered with a cruel glint. "What about during the night?"

Primrose remained silent.

"Is it true that he saw other women, right under your nose?"

Primrose shook her head. The Commander scoffed and raised his eyebrows. "Well, that's what he told me."

Prim's eyes appeared to widen. She peered down at Otto, who had solemnly bowed his head. Suspense heavy in the room's stale air, the crowd's eyes fixed on her face.

"Well, erm," Primrose began, "I – I suppose he did, actually. Sometimes." She cleared her throat. "But only sometimes."

"Only sometimes?" The Commander let out a dry chuckle. "Is that why he was sneaking about in the stairs every other evening? Off for a shag – but only sometimes, yeah?"

Primrose bit her lip, then gravely nodded.

The Commander raised his eyebrows. "M'kay." He stepped to the edge and peered down at the sea of faces. "Anyone here who's slept with Mr Walker, please raise your hand."

The air remained still. The silence was broken by an old man's cough.

The Commander smiled, then turned back to Prim. "Yeah. See, I thought that was a lie."

Otto squirmed in his place, his cuffs rattling. The Commander positioned himself right behind the man and turned back to Prim, who watched on with horror. He rubbed his hands together, and explained:

"It didn't go unnoticed, you know. Your husband moving between floors every other evening. We asked him about it once, and he mumbled something about you two being in an 'open relationship'." The Commander shook his head, his eyes filled with regret. "I should've fucking known…"

Primrose gulped. The Commander noticed this and began to smirk.

"Were *you* seeing anyone?"

Prim's eyes began to well. "Wh – wh—"

"W-W-What?!" bellowed the Commander, mimicking her shrill voice. "Go on then, tell me!"

Prim burst into tears. The Commander rolled his eyes and muttered a curse beneath his breath. He began to prowl towards the witness, a predatory smile on his lips. Otto turned his head to watch him with a side-long stare.

Meanwhile, Prim continued to weep, her distraught voice warping. "I don't, I don't, just, just ask him, okay, he'll tell you everything, just ask him," she sniffled.

The Commander stood directly opposite her. He smiled with a feigned understanding, and his empty eyes gleamed with a phoney compassion – until his face turned to snarl and his fist slammed the stand.

"ANSWER ME NOW, WOMAN!"

Prim recoiled and let out a yelp. The audience jumped in their seats. Otto stood to his feet and began to yell obscenities at the Commander. Big Davey stood up and tackled the man to the ground, before dragging him back into his place on the stage. A dozen young women had to leave the room, as their children had started to cry.

*

Primrose eventually confessed to knowing all about the Free Thinkers. The Commander had discerned that Otto's 'open relationship' story was a fabrication. Now, he had obtained the last piece of the puzzle – one that Mr Walker himself had stubbornly withheld – the fact that Prim had been an accomplice to the treason.

Following the Commander's orders, Little Ted placed a set of handcuffs on Prim's trembling wrists and made her kneel at the edge of the stage, next to Jasper Huxley. The distraught woman stared down at her son, Trevor, with horror in her eyes. Her little tiger cub stared right back, his face contorted with anguish, as if to say, 'What the hell's going on, Mum?!', to which she could give no answer.

The Commander called his officials into a circle, where they each gave their final verdicts on the convicts. They stood at the back of the stage, engaging in hushed deliberations that the audience couldn't hear. However, Jasper could make out what was being said.

"As I says earlier, I reckon we send 'em to the Estate," hissed Davey, "but we keep Huxley locked on Le'el 3. Gives me the heebie-jeebies, he does."

Meanwhile, Little Ted suggested that all the men be sent to the Estate, but that Primrose be kept on Level 3 as an "outlet for the lads".

Eddie was insistent that all five of the convicts should be sent to the farm. He argued that food production needed to be significantly increased over the next few years, based on the Bunker's projected population growth.

Noah strongly advocated for Jasper to receive a shorter sentence than the others, given his full cooperation during the interrogation, and his sharing of details about the other suspects. Additionally, he conveyed Pete's verdict *in absentia*, who was happy with whatever decision was made, and had no strong opinions either way, as well as Freddy's, who wished to see that "nonce" Mr Carr locked up for life and that "slimy" Otto Walker given the "Mickey Ratford treatment".

The Commander, standing with his arms folded, thanked his officials for their input and told them to return to their seats. He strode over to the podium, peering into the faces of the audience, and started to speak.

"Brandon Creak." The Commander turned to the man, whose body seemed to teeter on the edge of the stage. He proceeded to read from his judgment. "As you should be aware, the principle of free speech, albeit sacrosanct and absolute, is governed by a common-sense list of specific and limited qualifications. You engaged in a forum dedicated to the spread and discussion of extremist conspiracy theories, and were actively involved in plotting a violent attack against our citizens. Consequently, you are sentenced to indefinite servitude on the Estate, from which there can be no appeal."

"Donald Carr." The Commander turned to the heavyset man, whose head was bowed in shame. "You too have been found guilty of engaging in non-legitimate speech. Indeed, you played a central role in the Free Thinkers, and recruited Mr Huxley into the group. You are therefore sentenced to indefinite servitude on the Estate, from which there can be no appeal."

"Jasper Huxley." The Commander didn't even look at the young man. "You are guilty of the self-same charges. However, considering your age and cooperation during the interrogation, you are sentenced to serve on the Estate for a maximum of five years. Should you survive without contracting the disease, you may return to the Bunker, subject to a reintegration process."

Jasper was surprised by the leniency of his punishment. No one had ever been offered a temporary spell on the Estate before. Behind him, Noah shuffled in his chair, trying to catch the attention of a distant audience member.

"Primrose Walker." The Commander's voice boomed through the air. Primrose appeared to shrink on her knees, and a frightful expression crossed her face. "You possessed full awareness of Otto's activities, and yet you turned a blind eye to them. Furthermore, you attempted to deceive me. Therefore, you are sentenced to indefinite detention on Level 3. Your fate beyond that depends on your conduct. We may decide to let you go, if you're able to provide us with some restitution."

"Finally, Otto Walker." Commander Tommy's grin was sinister. He addressed the crowd directly. "It's so interesting – you think you know someone, they smile as you shake their hand, but they've got a plan to ruin you; to take your life's work away. So yes. I'm going to send him to Level 3, where he can fester in all of his thoughts and regrets."

The Bunker fell silent. The Commander had just uncovered an awful truth, one that had been concealed for nearly two decades: that Otto Walker, once a beloved and charismatic figure, was revealed as a traitor, like Mickey Ratford, like Dani Dalton, like the rest of those vile individuals who'd tried to tear their lives apart over the course of the years.

The Commander began to prowl behind the convicts. Approaching Walker, he slapped the man hard on the shoulder, nearly knocking him over, before turning his attention to Jasper and whispering something into the young man's ear.

"S-sorry?" asked Jasper, voice trembling.

"You heard me." The Commander's expression transformed into a smile. Turning to the audience, he announced:

"Mr Huxley has something to say, everyone!"

Reluctantly, Jasper spoke.

"I'm, erm – I'm really sorry."

"Louder," the Commander ordered.

Jasper gritted his teeth. "I'm *really* sorry..."

"Louder!"

"I'M REALLY SORRY!" he snapped, voice sweeping across the room.

The Commander smirked and ruffled Jasper's hair. "See? That wasn't so hard, now, was it?"

He instructed Big Davey to tie the prisoners together, forming a shackled line. The Commander then led them out of the hall, whistling as he went, holding their chain as if taking a dog for a stroll. The officials tailed behind. Noah cast a regretful glance at Hattie, and mouthed words of apology, before leaving through the door with his father. Meanwhile, Jasper avoided her gaze as he clinked down the aisle, his tired eyes budding with a lifetime of resentment.

PART II

09
Closed Doors

Late September

In a dark corner of the Bunker's ground floor, near the rows of chemical showers, Dr Hans Novak's new lab had been established. The space was dimly lit and packed with mismatched equipment: colossal steel vats, stacks of barrel drums, and a long row of industrial tables, cluttered with papers and assorted glassware.

At present, Dr Hans sat at his desk with a steaming cup of coffee. He admired the afternoon's work that dangled from a line above his head. Eight wet sheets, stuck there with clothespins. Each of them was dotted with a sea of tiny tablets. The air reeked with the stench of chemical fumes.

The door to Level 0 creaked open. A set of footsteps echoed through the vast cavern, plodding along the flat tarmac surface. Acting on instinct, Dr Hans put his mask back on, stood to attention, and extended his arm to shake Commander Tommy's hand.

"I see you've been busy," Tommy remarked, admiring the lab that he'd helped set up.

Dr Hans nodded. He glanced back towards the papers above his desk, drying like pieces of laundry. "I have made enough to last a long time," he said in his faintly German accent.

Commander Tommy strolled to the doctor's workstation to take a closer look, with Hans trailing behind, wringing his hands.

"Very good," said Tommy, inspecting the rows of LSD tablets. Behind the goggles of his protective mask, his eyes lit up with an almost boyish delight. "The lads will love this, I'm sure..."

"I hope so," said Dr Hans, with a hint of false modesty in his voice. He was confident of the batch's excellent quality, having been a top chemist in an 'industrial lab' back in the day. His firm had specialised in the synthesis of 'research chemicals'. "You're welcome to try one, sir."

Tommy raised an eyebrow. "I'm alright, thanks."

Dr Hans bowed his head as if to say 'very well'. Tommy turned to survey the rest of the lab's equipment. "Painkillers up next, then?"

"Yes, sir," said Dr Hans, "I'll get to work on some paracetamol."

"Good, good," muttered Tommy, "it'll be nice to have some stuff that actually works. Something with a real *kick* to it."

"Indeed. But there is one issue" – here, Dr Hans scratched his neck – "I wanted to let you know that, unfortunately, it's not possible for me to produce codeine... however, I could prepare a similar substitute if you wish. It will be possible to create something synthetic. Tramadol, this should not be a problem. But fentanyl, I'll need a chemical called NPP. It's still missing from my list. It's quite hard to find."

Tommy's eyes glazed over for a second, plagued by a distant memory. Abruptly, he snapped himself out of it. "Alright then. I'll let Noah know."

Dr Hans gave an appreciative nod. "But erm... it's possible I could get to work on other things, sir, with the inventory we currently possess..."

Tommy winced. His gaze became fixed on a barrel labelled 'methylamine', which was stacked against the wall.

"Not too much," he warned. "Just enough to keep the lads happy."

"Naturally," said the chemist.

Tommy's eyes shone with respect as he patted Dr Hans on the shoulder. "You can have Primrose this week if you want. You've done an excellent job here, my friend."

Dr Hans smiled. "Thank you, sir. But I feel I must decline. My Eva would certainly be a bit upset." He chuckled before gesturing towards the lab's shiny equipment, like a boy showing off his toys. "This, I consider my just reward!"

Tommy narrowed his eyelids, watching the childish man as he started to inspect a round-bottom flask, holding it up as though it were a rubber chicken.

"Remember, Hans – the annual report's coming up soon." Dr Hans set the glassware down and submissively nodded. Commander Tommy sauntered out of Level 0, leaving the chemist to his own devices.

Settling into his swivel chair, Hans peeled his mask off and inhaled the lab's dizzying fumes. He peered towards the far end of the space, where the Bunker's concrete doors remained sealed. He shook his head, as if dispelling an unwelcome thought, and continued to skim through his papers.

10
Woodhead

Early October

An electric impulse jolted Marcus awake, his head concealed beneath a tight hood.

He pulled the thing off with his left hand, and sat himself up. His cubicle was surrounded by a surgical curtain, granting him some privacy, though his right hand remained cuffed to the bedframe.

Marcus' time in this place had left him numb and exhausted. Throughout his entire body, he felt a slight unease, as if nursing a lingering hangover.

Behind him stood the massive *MaxSimi* CPU, its electric fans whirring. Its matte-black casing was dotted with air vents, out of which glowed a gentle blue light.

Boots plodded in the hallway outside, until a brown hand grabbed the curtain and pulled it back.

"We ready?" Ashley Mirza asked, poking his head through a gap.

Marcus groaned in affirmation, rubbing his sore forehead. Mr Mirza stepped into the room, removed Marcus from the handcuff, and led him down the sleek corridor of Ms Dalton's lair. They called it the 'Project': a vast, open-plan facility, built into the depths of Surrey well before the pandemic.

Mr Mirza and Marcus walked silently through the wards, passing endless rows of identical beds, each fitted with their own dormant machines.

At the far end of the hall, a rusty ladder leaned against the white wall, railing up into a burrow-like tunnel. Mr Mirza began to clamber up towards the surface. A reluctant Marcus followed behind, his malnourished muscles shaking on each exertion.

Finally, Mr Mirza pushed the exit hatch open. Twilight flooded through the tunnel, accompanied by a howling wind. After a laborious climb, Marcus reached the top. Exhausted, he sprawled onto the grassy hill, panting as he lay on his back. A small drone buzzed in the pre-morning sky.

Ms Dalton sat amidst the abbey's ruins, crossing her legs like a Buddha imitation. Her tear-shaped earrings swung as she raised her chin, clutching a pronged remote control. Her silvery hair was dishevelled as ever.

"You're up early!" said Mr Mirza. Ms Dalton, however, remained captivated by her airborne toy.

"Don't see why we need the *boy* with us."

"Well," replied Mr Mirza, "I think it's easier if he tags along." He turned to the hostage. Though his hands were unshackled, neither Mr Mirza nor Ms Dalton could fully trust him yet. "You'll behave for us now, won't you Marcus?"

Marcus stared down at his feet. Mr Mirza patted him on the arm.

"Look," he said in an avuncular tone, "it'll be over soon. We strike, we swoop in, and we leave with some fresh fuckin' food. Alright?"

Marcus remained silent. Mr Mirza ground his teeth. "There'll be no violence," he added. "We only want the van – that's all."

Marcus turned to watch Ms Dalton as she fiddled with the remote. The old woman's eyes twinkled with a girlish delight, though her face had been worn out by the passage of time. Marcus gulped, leaning in to whisper to Mr Mirza.

"Is she fucked in the head or something?"

"Don't," he warned.

"Alright..." Marcus crossed his arms. "It's just – I know this is gonna end in violence. I'm not an idiot."

Mr Mirza glanced over his shoulder, then turned back to Marcus. "Look – I'll do whatever I need to make 'em abandon the truck. But I'm no killer, me."

"Yeah, right." Marcus scoffed. "I'll tell that to the *fifty-six* then, shall I?"

Mr Mirza's face reddened. "You don't know anything, kid. You're too young to understand."

"No, no, I get it alright," Marcus retorted, raising his voice, "it's just – you had no fucking right to butcher all those men!"

Mr Mirza thwacked Marcus in the face, sending him sprawling across the grass. He drew his pistol and aimed it at the young lad's head. Ms Dalton turned, groaned, and dragged herself towards the commotion, her drone lingering overhead.

"Calm yourself, Ashley," said Ms Dalton. "He'll come to understand; all in good time."

Marcus, his hands raised and shaking, tried to appeal to the old politician. "Listen, ma'am, I do have sympathy for what happened to you lot, it's just – I don't think this is the right way—"

"Enough," Mr Mirza snapped, although by now he'd lowered his weapon.

Ms Dalton gave Mirza a reassuring pat on the shoulder, then settled her gaze on Marcus. "You reckon there's a better way, do you?"

Marcus clenched his jaw. Her tone called for an answer. "Well, erm, the Estate – it's got warehouses, where they store the goods before delivery. Maybe we could break in there. Could maybe get more, than if we just went for the van."

"Thought of that," said Mirza. "Took the drone there last year for a recon. It's well-secured now. Whole farm's got fencing around it."

"I dunno," said Marcus, "there must be, like, a weak spot somewhere. Seven-hundred acres? It's gonna be difficult to secure every inch properly..."

"Too many guards," Ms Dalton replied in her usual laconic tone. She turned her attention to the horizon. The sun was due to rise at any minute.

"Exactly," said Mr Mirza. "Normally six at any one time. One of Tommy's lot, then four or five of his 'Scouts'. All of them armed."

"So use a sniper," blurted Marcus. He creased his brow, a little surprised by his own vile suggestion.

Mr Mirza smirked and patted Marcus on the arm. "Didn't think you had that sort of thing in you!" he laughed, but stopped to shake his head. "In any case, the terrain's too flat around the Estate. No good vantage points for a shot."

The atmosphere flared red as dawn began to break. On the skyline, London's glass towers gleamed in the fiery light.

"Best get moving." Mr Mirza motioned for Marcus and Ms Dalton to follow him down the path through the woods, leaving the remnants of the abbey behind.

As they drove down the dirt road, Marcus's thoughts drifted back to a violent dream he'd concocted for himself, in which he'd pummelled Noah Smith to death in a boxing match.

* *

The Range Rover glided over the vacant M25. By the time they reached the M1, the sky was fully lit, although the sun had been obscured beneath grey clouds.

Their journey was like an early-morning trip to the airport. The world had turned into a liminal space. On their way, they saw no major built-up areas, apart from faded signs that listed where places once stood. At that moment, the car had just passed a town called Watford, and a road sign read that Luton was somewhere nearby.

Above their heads, concrete bridges led to nowhere. The odd service station sat by the roadside, their courtyards empty, save for a handful of long-abandoned cars.

Marcus, sitting in the passenger seat, began to chow down on his breakfast: an expired protein bar that tasted like animal fat. Nonetheless, he wolfed his portion down with hungry enthusiasm. Mr Mirza's eyes remained fixed on the road ahead, while Ms Dalton, sitting in the back, stared out of the window with her head propped in her hand.

A couple of hours later, the Range Rover arrived in the Peak District. They parked on a narrow lane at the base of a colossal green hill. Ms Dalton stepped out into the fresh air to get her drone up and running, while Mr Mirza went to retrieve his sniper from the boot.

Marcus looked in the rear-view mirror, watching Ashley Mirza as he rummaged in the back of the car. Outside, the air was breezy. The sky hummed with the faint noise of a small drone, which Ms Dalton controlled with her wireless remote. On her lap, she had a tablet, similar to an iPad, which she used to view the drone's camera feed in real-time.

"You sure today's the right day for this?" said Marcus. "Bit choppy, no?"

"It's only a breeze." Ashley peered inside a black duffel bag, sitting on the boot with his legs dangling out. "I've seen worse."

"Drone's got eyes on them," said Ms Dalton, raising her hoarse voice. "They're headed up the A628 as we speak."

Ashley Mirza rubbed his hands. He nodded at Marcus. "D'you wanna take a look?"

Begrudgingly, Marcus stepped out of the car and went to sit with Ashley and Ms Dalton, all of them forming a circle around the tablet screen. It depicted a long line of vehicles – Noah's Rolls-Royce and ten silver Jeeps – all winding through a vast, barren landscape. The drone tailed far behind, undetected, zooming in on the convoy as it approached the Estate.

"Mr Mirza," implored Marcus, "please, don't aim for the younger guys. Some of them... they're my—"

"Yeah, yeah," said Ashley, "I'll try not to hit your mates. But it's gonna be difficult if they're wearing their masks." He licked his lips. "You know what? I'll try and aim for their lower halves. Go for their ankles. How does that sound?"

Marcus felt somewhat reassured, although the prospect of Tiger or Ace being harmed still made him queasy. Ashley patted him on the arm and, grabbing the duffel bag, started to trudge up the hill.

Marcus and Ms Dalton continued to watch the Scouts' movements. After a while, the long convoy crossed onto the Estate's dirt road, gliding past three Sparrowman yobs as it sped towards the checkpoint. A small figure in orange emerged from a hut and opened the chain-link gate, waving the cars into the car park. The Scouts pulled up in front of the mansion's façade. The turbine creaked in the slave-yard.

After a minute, the white delivery van headed over from a distant warehouse, and entered the car park. Out stepped Pete, holding a clipboard. Noah, clad in his hazmat suit, snatched it from Pete's hands and read it over. Albert went over to the Scout vehicles, and, from the boots of three of the Jeeps, dragged out a series of blindfolded men.

Marcus gasped. His eyes grew wide.

Ms Dalton looked down at her tablet and tapped a button, zooming the camera in on the three shackled men.

"What the fuck," said Marcus. "What the fuck," he repeated, as though these were the only words he could muster.

"Let's see who we have..." Ms Dalton leaned into the screen, eyes squinting at the pixelated faces. "Interesting..."

Marcus remained silent. Ms Dalton's finger pointed towards a young lad's blindfolded face. "Never seen him before..."

"All set," said Ashley, speaking on Ms Dalton's walkie-talkie. "What's happening down at the farm?"

Dalton pressed the radio button. "They've brought prisoners."

"Oh," replied Ashley. "Can you see who it is?"

"Donald Carr, Brandon Creak, and erm..." Ms Dalton turned to Marcus. "Which one's that?"

"Jasper Huxley..."

Ms Dalton raised an eyebrow. "Blimey." She pressed the walkie-talkie button again. "It's Jasper, apparently."

"Bloody hell," came Ashley's tinny voice. There was a moment of silence. "Marcus – are you alright?"

Marcus didn't respond. His face had gone pale, watching as these familiar prisoners were led across the car park and into the recesses of the mansion. The slave-yard, full of shipping containers, could be seen to the side, where they'd likely be housed for the rest of their lives.

"I don't get it..." said Marcus, although his words fell on deaf ears. Meanwhile, the fifty bug-men began to fill up the cars and leave the massive compound. Ms Dalton's drone followed them. As the convoy reached the end of the off-road track, the Rolls-Royce turned right towards the roundabout, followed by the delivery van, and the ten Scout Jeeps, trailing behind for protection.

"That's rather a nice set of wheels," said Ms Dalton, pointing towards Noah's car. "One has to admit..."

Marcus, filled with resentment, snatched the walkie-talkie from the old Prime Minister. In response, she instinctively reached for her pistol and levelled it at Marcus with a shaky hand, before lowering it, realising that the boy had meant no harm.

"The fuck d'you think you're doing?"

Ignoring the old woman's question, Marcus spoke into the radio. "They're on their way to the bridge."

"Thanks, Marcus." Ashley paused for a moment. "Listen – I'm really sorry about your friend. I don't know what to—"

"I think there's a better way to do this," he interrupted, voice bristling with rage. "Take Noah out first – make the van crash into his rear."

The convoy of Scouts made their way towards Woodhead Pass, snaking along the bendy road. They began the approach to a quaint little bridge that spanned the lake, where Ashley had been planning to shoot the van's tyres out.

* *

The Rolls-Royce crossed the threshold of the bridge, followed by the rest of the convoy. Unbeknownst to them, a mechanical eye in the sky watched on with silent indifference.

A loud bang sounded from the hilltop. Marcus stared at the screen, his stomach alight with butterflies.

On the bridge, Noah's car skidded to a halt. The white van tried to swerve to avoid a collision, but was too late, and smashed sideways into the back of the Rolls-Royce. The ten silver Jeeps slammed on the brakes. After a pause, orange-clad men poured out of the doors, brandishing their rifles like an agitated tribe.

Another shot pierced through the atmosphere. Half a second later, Marcus saw a masked head erupt with blood. The body collapsed to the side and, pivoting over the low safety rail, tumbled down into the clear waters below.

The Scouts began to fire aimlessly, bullets scattering in the air. Ashley fired another shot, this time hitting a Scout in the thigh. The man fell to the ground. As someone tried to drag him into one of the Jeeps, Ashley shot him again, this time with a lethal blow. He collapsed to the floor and bled out from his chest.

In a panic, the rest scrambled back into their vehicles, firing a few more useless rounds. Four men ran towards the Royce and dragged Noah's limp body from the driver's seat. Ashley fired another shot, and four became three, but the others managed to heave Noah into one of the Jeeps before speeding off, leaving behind the wrecked Rolls-Royce, the delivery van, and two lifeless bodies splayed on the tarmac.

Ashley hurled his duffel bag down the hill and, as though giving it chase, bounded behind it.

Ms Dalton and Marcus climbed into the Range Rover. Moments later, Ashley reached the bottom of the hill, grabbed his bag, and shoved it into the car's boot. He slid behind the wheel, panting heavily, and switched on the electric engine. The Rover sped across a series of narrow country lanes, past rolling hills and dense forests, until at last, they reached the scene of the ambush. Massive pylon towers loomed nearby, their cables clattering in the wind.

Ashley parked behind the white van. He and Marcus leapt out, while Ms Dalton stayed in the car, still tracking the Scouts with her drone. Marcus moved to open the van's back doors, but Ashley stopped him, judging that the van might still be drivable.

"Listen," he said, "have Dani take the Range Rover back. I'll be driving the van."

"But—"

"Just do as I ask!"

Marcus nodded, chest pounding. He noticed a trickle of blood on the road. Drawn to it, he followed it to its source. He bent down and lifted the mask from the limp, lifeless body, revealing the face of his childhood friend 'Ace'.

"Hurry up!" shouted Ashley.

With hardly a moment's notice, Marcus found himself sitting in the front seat of the Range Rover. His body felt numb and tingly, as if overcome by chilblains. "Ashley wants you to drive; he's taking the van." Marcus' thoughts seemed to speak with no sound.

"Alright," replied Dani. She took the wheel and started to drive, allowing Ashley to overtake and lead the way with the van.

Marcus picked up the drone's remote. Following Dani's instructions, he guided the drone away from the Bunker's gates, where the convoy had returned. After directing it over some barren hills, Marcus caught up with the van and the Rover as they travelled in unison. Marcus flew the drone alongside his window and, using the touch-screen tablet, began to zoom in on his own face, observing himself with a little third eye.

11

Knocked Out

Level 7-A

Hattie, sitting in her solitary office in the medical wing, was reading a manual on psychiatric conditions. Turning the page, she began skimming through section 8.2, which was titled CLUSTER B.

> *Emotional instability is a common experience for people with these conditions. They often encounter intense emotions, feelings of emptiness, and a pervasive sense of dissatisfaction.*

Her eyes started to drift, overcome by weariness. She had been sitting with her book all afternoon, attempting to fill the void. Work had been slow, and her life was uneventful. Her remaining social network consisted mostly of acquaintances and surface-level friendships. Not to mention, Melissa and Liv were still giving her the cold shoulder. At breakfast, they had made a concerted effort to exclude Hattie from the conversation, steering the chatter towards Bobby Stephens and some other 'blokes' from the 'forbidden floors'. They both knew perfectly well that Hattie detested this lot, owing to a nasty incident that had occurred in 0015.

Hattie shook her head and continued reading.

> *Impulsivity is also a defining characteristic for those on the Cluster B spectrum, particularly borderline personality disorder. The patient may engage in risky activities such as drug abuse, hypersexuality, gambling, overspending, or other compulsive behaviours. Although such tendencies are clearly self-destructive, the patient may use them as self-soothing strategies to cope with emotional problems. Diligent practitioners will work with patients to explore alternative coping skills. Attempts to address the underlying traumas*

involved should only be carried out as and when the patient feels comfortable.

Hattie knew all too well why she felt so compelled to read this manual. Laying the book face-down on her desk, she closed her eyes and ran her fingers through her hair, trying to release those buried emotions. A sharp pain in her chest made her wince. Sensing a lump as it swelled in her throat, Hattie reached for her phone and began to solve a mindless puzzle, killing the feeling in its tracks.

But before she could finish *Round #2618*, someone hammered on the door to her office.

"Hattie!"

She leapt up and hurried to the door. Dr Jones and the other three medical staff were sprinting down the corridor. Each wore a mask and a pair of blue gloves.

"What's happening?" she called.

Dr Jones halted and took a deep breath. "There's been an attack on the road."

He handed Hattie some gloves and a mask before turning around and resuming his dash.

The medics hurried up the stairs towards Level 0 where, in the middle of the colossal cavern, surrounded by a throng of orange-clad men, the wounded Chief lay sprawled on the floor, his hazmat suit torn and bloodied. His sheet-white face was contorted with a grimace.

Calmly, Dr Jones strode up to the wounded boy. "Tested negative?" he asked in a hurried tone.

"Negative," Albert confirmed.

Dr Jones turned to the rest of his staff and called Mr Dacosta over. The two men lifted Noah onto a stretcher. After strapping him in, they hoisted him up and headed back to the staircase. The other three medical staff followed behind. Hattie's heart was racing. Her gaze became fixed on a curtained-off corner of the cave, from which a foul chemical stench emanated.

"HURRY UP!" shouted Dr Jones. Hattie snapped out of her brief reverie and quickened her pace. The medical staff began clambering down the stairs. Upon reaching Level 5, Big Davey moved his chair out of the way and allowed them to pass through.

Within a minute, they had all reached the emergency room on 7-B. Dr Jones and Mr Dacosta placed Noah on the bed. The five-strong team swarmed around him, donning surgery gowns and clinical masks.

"It's okay, Noah," said Dr Andersen, a former vet in her early sixties. "We're going to fix you up."

But Noah remained catatonic. The eyes were open, but his face was frozen over, save for the occasional wince or twitch of the mouth.

"Christ alive," she said under her breath, as she prepared a vial of anaesthetic.

Meanwhile, Hattie prepared an IV drip as Mrs Novak checked his vitals, none of which were stable. The urgent sound of a monitor's beeps filled the air of the room.

Hattie grasped the IV needle and seized Noah's limp wrist. She inserted the needle into a vein, causing his whole arm to jerk. An uncanny sickness passed over her, as though she were interacting with a semi-animate corpse. Dr Andersen injected Noah with a clear liquid. Mrs Novak strapped a mask over his face, supplying the patient with a stream of oxygen. Eventually, the dull eyes rolled lifeless.

Removing the crusty, blood-soaked bandage that someone had applied to Noah's right shoulder, Dr Andersen began to inspect the grisly wound with a penlight. "There's a bullet lodged inside. Two centimetres in diameter, level with the second rib."

Meanwhile, Dr Jones failed to suppress a worried sigh as he inspected the young man's airways. "His right lung's collapsed." On this cue, Mr Dacosta fetched a large needle-pump. Dr Jones took it and inserted its shaft between the patient's broken ribs and, as if deflating a football, began to draw the air from inside, relieving the pressure that had built in his chest, allowing the lung to re-expand. The beeps of the monitor seemed to ease.

While Dr Jones was performing a needle thoracostomy on Noah – inserting a plastic tube into his chest and draining all the fluids that had accumulated inside – Dr Andersen got to work on the patient's shoulder.

"Scalpel."

Ms Osborne passed her the scalpel. Dr Andersen made an incision in Noah's skin.

"Retractors."

Hattie fetched some retractors. Dr Andersen pulled the wound open.

"Haemostats."

Hattie grabbed a pair of narrow clamps. She held up the penlight while Dr Andersen probed Noah's shoulder, clamping his blood vessels, before Hattie took a pair of forceps and, after a minute, extracted a tiny golden pellet. She placed it into a glass tray and rinsed it in the sink, while Dr Andersen worked on disinfecting the wound.

Eventually, with Mr Dacosta's assistance, Dr Jones completed the thoracostomy, which was followed by Dr Andersen stitching Noah's shoulder shut. Mrs Novak confirmed that Noah's vitals had stabilised. The young man lay still in the surgery bed, consumed by a narcotised dream.

After disposing of their soiled PPE, the medical team stepped out of the surgery room for a moment, except for Mrs Novak, who continued to watch the patient from a corner chair. Hattie stared at her through the door's small porthole, but quickly averted her gaze after the woman peered up.

"What next?" asked Mr Dacosta. This man, an inexperienced junior nurse, was stocky and in his early twenties, and had been turned down from the Scouts two years ago.

"Well," began Dr Jones, "I expect he'll wake up at any moment. We'll have to check for concussion or a TBI, then perform a CT."

"He'll be okay, right?" asked Hattie earnestly. This was the first real surgery she'd ever participated in, and she had no idea what to expect.

Dr Jones shrugged his shoulders. "I don't know, Hattie. We'll need to keep an eye out for sepsis. Hans still hasn't gotten around to making antibiotics, so we'll have to rely on the expired stuff."

Hattie clenched her teeth, eyes plagued by a distant memory. Dr Jones saw this and gently reached for her arm.

"But, in any case, I'm sure we can get some fresh stock prepared by tomorrow. I'll have a word with the officials." He looked into

Hattie's eyes and gave the young woman a reassuring, albeit patronising, "Alriggghhht?", in his usual manner.

Dr Andersen peered through the window and noticed that Noah was beginning to stir. She alerted the others with a wave, and the four of them returned to the operation theatre.

* *

That evening, Marcus, Ashley Mirza, and Dani Dalton sat at the counter in the Retreat's little kitchen. Marcus stared vacantly at the wall, taking reluctant sips of the nasty tomato soup that Ashley had prepared for them all. Their mission had been a failure. No fresh food was found in the van; instead, it had been packed with plastic barrels of biodiesel produced from the farm's rapeseed fields.

"Still a win," Ashley insisted, breaking the uncomfortable silence, "since we've now got backup fuel for our generator, in case anything happens to the solar panels."

"Oh sick, that makes it worth it, then," Marcus quipped sarcastically, though his voice was low and grave.

Ashley winced and set his cutlery down. "Look, kid..." He cleared his throat. "I'm sorry. But I couldn't see any of their faces. How on Earth was I to tell them apart?"

Marcus gave a dismissive shake of the head and carried on eating. The rest of their meal passed in awkward silence. Ashley stared down at his food, while Dani cast occasional glances in Marcus' direction. Marcus returned the favour, his gaze falling on her face, her wrinkly chops smothered with the blood-red soup. After a pause, Ashley tried to engage Marcus in conversation to lighten the mood.

"You know, I was thinking about what you said about the farm."

Marcus wasn't interested. Ashley kept going anyway:

"If we did it right, we could certainly break in there. Not for food, I mean – to get all those captives out. Wouldn't that be something?"

Marcus stared down into his bowl, not bothering to respond. Meanwhile, Dani continued to glare at Marcus, taking his silence as a sign of disrespect. At last, in her whispery voice, she spoke to say:

"You should be more grateful to Ashley."

Marcus raised his brow, idly picking at his soup. "Why's that?"

Dani let out a cackle and stared into Marcus's face with her lizard-like eyes. "He's soft," she continued, "still thinks you're worth keeping around..."

Marcus glanced at Ashley. "Eat your food," Ashley muttered, avoiding the young man's gaze. Marcus looked down and swallowed a reluctant spoonful of the soup before finishing it off. He declined dessert, so Ashley led him back to his makeshift cell and chained his right hand to the bed's metal frame.

Ashley gave him an apologetic look before pulling the curtain shut.

Marcus sighed and rubbed his eyes with his left hand. He pulled the *MaxSimi* hood up from the pillow and slid it over his head. It sealed tight around his neck, like a coiling snake. Shifting on the rough mattress to lie down, he uttered the words:

"*MaxSimi*, Go."

"*MaxSimi*, I'm Sure."

In an instant, Marcus was rendered unconscious, his mind taken to a plane that didn't exist. His free arm dangled down from the side of the bed, while the cuffed one was stretched above his head, pulling him into a contorted pose.

* *

Marcus found himself immersed in a familiar dream, one that had recurred several times in his youth – one which, at last, he could finally bring to life.

There he was, at a techno rave on some faraway beach. He'd seen it in a film when he was younger, and his brain had evidently latched onto it. All its details had been captured to perfection: the bustling crowds, the blaring techno sounds, and the flashing disco lights, which made the starless night sky pulse with technicolour. The throbbing bass vibrated in his eardrums, and like a compressed particle, Marcus was bounced and jostled about by the teeming, agitated crowd.

The young lad tried to join in with the dance, jumping mechanically in the air and screaming mindlessly, attempting to drown it all out, but the emptiness inside of him was still ever-present.

"*MaxSimi*, Give Me A Molly."

Certainly, replied the female voice in his head.

"YEEEEAAAHHH!!!" he cried, as he began to feel a little less numb, and the warm bodies around him a little more human. The chemical rush made him feel an inexplicable love for his neighbours, and, driven by oxytocin, he decided to go in for a random embrace. Pulling away, he looked into the dream-boy's face and saw that it was Jasper.

"JASSSPEEEEYYY!!!!"

Jasper responded to Marcus' screams with a terrified smile, while he continued to execute a set of stilted dance moves.

"HUXXXLEEEEYYY!!!" Marcus affectionately draped his arm over Jasper's shoulder. "HOW WE FEELING TONIGHT?!?!"

'Good, man!' Jasper replied, awkwardly raising his voice, 'really good!'

"NICE ONE!!!!"

The eclectic rave music mellowed out into ambient sounds. The crowd dispersed across the beach, settling down at separate fires on the sands. Marcus found himself leading Jasper to one where Hattie and Trevor were seated.

"Look who I've found!" he exclaimed. He kissed Jasper on the forehead before the two sat down together. Marcus looked into Hattie's soft eyes. Her hair was adorned with daisies. Marcus' cheeks turned a rosy red, and his insides oozed with warmth.

'Isn't it swell to be free?!' she said, sounding like an advert from the 1960s. 'Eh, Tiger?'

'Yeah, yeah, yeah!' exclaimed Trevor, who got up and shuffled back to where the crowd had once stood. 'It's boogie time!' he declared, dancing all by himself.

Marcus looked to Hattie, smirked, then glanced back at Trevor, but saw that he'd vanished, and that the music had ceased. The other rave-goers were nowhere to be seen. Only Marcus, Hattie, and Jasper remained on the beach. All was silent, save for the crackling fire and the trickling waves. The full moon cast a beam across the gentle ocean waters.

"I really miss you guys," said Marcus, heart throbbing with a chemical empathy.

'We really miss you too...' said Hattie, her voice tinged with longing. 'I just wish you'd come back...'

'He can't,' said Jasper, 'he's taken the wrong turns...'

Marcus shook his head. "I know, mate. I know." He stared into the spitting firepit, which spewed embers up in the air. "But I'm not the only one, am I?"

Jasper's face turned comically pale.

"What the frig did you even do?" Marcus asked with a chuckle.

'He, erm,' said Hattie, feeling the need to speak for her quiet friend, 'he made some people upset.'

Marcus erupted into laughter. Jasper grew pale, mortified, while Hattie glared at Marcus with a scolding look.

'Stop it, dick – you're not that funny.'

Jasper burst into sudden tears. Marcus felt a surge of guilt and wrapped his arm around the distraught lad. "It's alright." He hugged Jasper a little closer. "You're gonna be okay."

'You don't know that!' Jasper sobbed. 'You don't know what they'll do to me!'

Marcus glanced at Hattie. She bit her lip, then turned her attention to Jasper. 'I'm sure it'll be fine. Just work hard and keep your head down.'

Jasper shook his head and pulled away from Marcus. 'I could've been a dreamer in a past life,' he mused, which to Marcus sounded like the most insightful thing anyone had ever said. Jasper carried on:

'But I was born at the time I was born. And I faced the consequences of my nature in the current environment. What else is there to say?'

Marcus nodded to himself. "So true!"

Jasper looked at Marcus, wiping the remnants of tears from his eyes. 'And you'll be nothing either.'

Marcus smiled with incredulity. "Eh?"

'None of us will.' Jasper turned to face Hattie, who regarded him with concern. 'We're all destined to be nobodies. Apart from the Smiths.'

"The Smiths," Marcus echoed, bobbing his head to an imagined tune.

'Look, Jas,' said Hattie, reaching to pat him on the knee, 'we can all be a someone in our own right. We just have to make an effort. And we've got to play the cards we're dealt.'

'I'll never make do,' said Jasper. 'Don't never lose that flicker of hope. Play the world's game on your own terms.'

"Inspired," said Marcus. "But how?"

Jasper rubbed his hands together. 'Dream big, start small.'

"M'kay..." Marcus scratched his chin. "Dream big, start small..."

'Wow, guys... so profound.' Hattie laughed and rolled her eyes. She looked at Marcus with a wry smile. 'But really, I think a bit of spice is all we need, isn't it? A splash of technicolour...'

'Jesus...' Jasper feigned a shudder. 'You do make me cringe sometimes.' He clasped his stomach and retched out a performative gag.

Marcus stood up and called the other two into a circle. They each held one another by the waist and gazed into the sparkling campfire. "Guys," he began, "I wanna go back to how we used to be."

Hattie peered up at his face. Her mesmerising eyes were full of colour. Marcus felt the urge to lean in for a kiss, but Jasper was there, and he would doubtless have something to say about it. Marcus pulled his friends even closer together, as though his arms were a force of attraction.

"You're coming back with me, Jas. I'll get you out. I've got partners, you know."

'Partners...' said Jasper, his voice a ghostly whisper.

"Partners. Mhm." Marcus peered over at Hattie, whose dreamy eyes beamed at him with admiration. "And we'll come and pick you up too – when the time is right."

Hattie smiled warmly, though her eyes appeared lazy. 'Thanks, hun.' She squeezed his hand and strolled off across the beach, her white summer dress billowing in the breeze. She turned back to give her ex a reluctant, sidelong stare.

"I like your wreath," called Marcus, admiring the daisies in her hair. "Looks good on you."

Hattie's eyes dimmed. She peered down at her feet, hesitating, thinking of whether to respond, before smiling sadly and stumbling away. Marcus and Jasper were left alone in the sands, listening to waves as they crashed against the shore.

In a flash of lucidity, Marcus was overcome by the urge to run after his ex, confess all that he felt for her, lament those poor decisions he'd made in his time, but in the end, decided against it, as a nagging voice told him it was all too late. Finally, he took a deep breath, gave his friend Jasper one last hug, and said:

"*MaxSimi*, Exit."

* *

Marcus was jolted awake. The tight hood covered his eyes. After a long, vacant moment, he sighed and spoke some more instructions to *MaxSimi*. The tall machine whirred and knocked him out, taking his mind to a dreamless sleep.

12
Songs of Praise

08/10/17

Hattie was seated in the front row of the Sports Hall, waiting for the officials to arrive. The loudspeakers blared with upbeat jazz, which contrasted oddly with the sombre mood of the occasion. The faces of the Bunker displayed the collective anxiety that had built over the last few days.

At last, a procession of officials arrived. Davey, Ted, 'Freddy Krueger' and Eddie all sat down at the back of the stage. Commander Tommy took his place at the podium, clutching the stand with shaky hands. Hattie could see feigned gravitas in his eyes.

Tommy adjusted the mic to his mouth. Through the speakers, his breath whistled like a harsh wind.

"My friends," he began, "the rumours you've heard are all too true." He licked his lips and turned to Eddie. Eddie stood up, handed a little golden pellet to Tommy, and swiftly returned to his seat.

"Have a look at this – have a look at it..."

The audience all leaned in together, staring up at the golden bullet that Tommy held between his fingers.

"The self-same make," he began, "as the ones used in o'twelve, and o'nine, and o'seven, and those three dreadful incidents in o'four, and all the rest – used to pick off our men from afar!"

The crowd began to mutter with collective disdain.

"Those cowards, those 'Retreaters', too afraid to take us on face to face, launched a sniper attack, and now, three of our lads, slaughtered like lambs, for no other purpose than to make a statement!"

The crowd growled with hatred.

"We will not have this! I will not have this!" Commander Tommy cried, waving his hands in the air like an impassioned preacher. "I will not stand by, I will not sit there and take it, while my only son lies in a hospital bed!"

On cue, Little Ted pulled the projector screen down and displayed a large image of the gravely wounded Chief. His face was bloodied and bruised, and his entire torso was wrapped in a straitjacket of bandages. The crowd began to wail, as if they'd witnessed the death of a brother-in-arms.

Tommy raised his arms to induce silence. "My friends: I feel I must tell you that our little dark age has returned. Our peace has been shattered. And what's more, those people are becoming bolder. They always know where we are, whereas we, we have no clue where these vermin could be. Far as I know, they could be based overseas. But regardless – it's time to wise up, it's time we exterminate these animals, these freaks of nature, the ones who were inoculated from the disease, and the ones who refused us its antidote!"

A rage that masked grief stirred within the Bunker. Hattie squirmed in her seat, uncomfortable, for she knew that Tommy had repeated a lie.

"We shall mourn the deceased in a proper fashion. We shall give them the honour they deserve. Killed for nothing – no, I want them to rest with dignity." Tommy shook his head. "But I plead for you now to pray for my Noah. He's a fighter – he's a fighter, he's seen a lot worse, but still, he's struggling, he might not make it..."

A crocodile tear rolled down his cheek, which the Bunker lapped up dearly. Somewhere behind her, Hattie could hear Tiger start to wail, which made her throat swell a little.

"It's alright," said Tommy, softly breathing into the mic. "It's alright." The Bunker's cries subsided. "Be grateful, for our excellent medical team. My son's in good hands. I won't let him go gently into that good night. He's still fighting, he's still going."

Tommy peered down towards the front row, where the medics were seated. "Look at them – these fantastic people. Please, come up; I'd like to show you my thanks."

One by one, the medical staff stood and walked onto the stage to shake Commander Tommy's hand. Dr Jones, in particular, was met with booming applause. "Sorry for your loss," Tommy grumbled, before waving the doctor off the stage. At last, it was Hattie's turn to receive praise. Hattie approached Commander Tommy and accepted his hand. Its cold, tight grip startled her. She peered up at the man, whose shoulders were broad and overbearing. His dull eyes flickered with passion.

"You'll do well for my Noah, I'm sure."

Hattie smiled in return and stepped off the stage, failing to grasp what Tommy had meant.

* *

Tommy finished his speech, and a small concert was held, unifying the crowds as Olivia, supported by the rest of the Bunker's band, sang the lyrics of the Bunker's 'Stately Anthem', before moving on to some other warlike chants.

Once this long charade was over, Hattie returned to the medical wing. Noah lay asleep in the emergency room. Eva Novak, a senior nurse in her early thirties, was watching over him. Hattie knocked on the door. Eva stood, exchanging a polite half-smile with Hattie before stepping out of the room, her blonde hair wafting behind her as she left.

Hattie sighed and, clutching her little book on psychiatric conditions, sat down in the corner chair and began to read. She kept an eye on Noah as he lay still, his monitor beeping gently.

8.2.4 – Narcissistic Personality Disorder

Her eyes shifted to a passage that rang a bell.

Origins of NPD can be multifaceted, rooted in both genetic and environmental factors. There is evidence suggesting a hereditary component, but environmental influences, particularly those in early childhood, play a substantial role. For instance, children raised by parents who alternate between over-praising and devaluing them may develop narcissistic traits as a defence mechanism. Such inconsistent parenting might make them feel they must be perfect and without flaws in order to be loved. These children, in an effort to gain their parents' approval, might begin to see themselves as special, entitled, and superior to others. Over time, these thought patterns often solidify to establish a narcissistic personality.

Hattie glanced over at Noah, whose head had started to move. At last, the young man stirred from his sleep, and rubbed his face with his hand. Hattie cleared her throat and gave him a gentle smile.

"Afternoon."

Noah creased his brow and glanced at Hattie, head still resting on the pillow. "How long was I out for?"

Hattie shrugged. "I'm not sure. Ten or eleven hours, I think." Looking down at her lap, she snapped her book shut and slid it beneath her chair. "Rest is good, though. You obviously needed it."

Noah stared at his limp wrist, where the IV needle was still in place. His tired eyes were tainted with frustration.

"Don't think I even need this thing, y'know." Noah scratched his neck. "I'm feeling much better today."

Hattie let out a soft giggle. "That'll be the painkillers. Dr Hans prepared a batch yesterday."

"Painkillers?!" hissed Noah, as if uttering a swear. His IV bag swelled and dripped like a lava lamp. "I don't need *those*." Noah tried to form an angry scowl, but his sedated face was a little paralysed.

"Don't worry. Eva only gave you exactly what you need. Just a little dose of tramadol."

"Still," he scoffed, "I just think that sort of thing's a bit shameful, really..."

Hattie gulped and, deciding to change the subject, said:

"Noah, if you want to talk about things – about what happened on the road, I mean – I'd be happy to listen. But only if you're comfortable." Hattie nodded to herself. "It isn't good to keep things bottled up."

Noah rolled his eyes. "Yeah, yeah." He gazed up at the ceiling, where a surgical light beamed down on his face. "You sound just like *muh-mah*," he muttered, sighing with weary regret.

Hattie looked down at her feet.

"Everyone thinks you're really brave," she said, pushing her hair back into a bob. "We're all rooting for you."

Noah let out a dry chuckle. "Let me guess," he began, "Tommy made it seem like I was dying, didn't he? All those bandages he had me wear 'round my chest..."

Hattie bit her lip.

"Still," he said, "I suppose it's necessary – for the cause. Always for the cause. The ends justify the means, always."

Hattie clenched her teeth. "I mean... it wasn't just for show; you really were in a terrible state. It was a nasty ordeal, what you had to go through. What you *all* had to witness."

Noah grimaced. "I can't believe it. Three men killed, under my watch."

Hattie allowed her hair to drop. She was struck by a resurgent wave of anguish, reflecting on the loss of yet another friend.

"We got sloppy," continued Noah. "We got sloppy – and now we've paid the price for it. And Tommy, y'know – he's just trying to protect me. He knows full well it's all my fault."

Hattie shook her head. "Oh, come on – that's so not true..."

"Yes, it is." Noah's heart monitor kept bleeping at its slow pace. "He's just playing the sympathy card for me, making out like I'm some kind of brave soldier when I'm the one who's fucked it all up..."

Sensing the despair in his eyes, Hattie leaned forward and reached to hold his hand.

"I've got no business being the Chief." Noah's shoulders appeared to untense. "I just got lucky. Got it all handed to me on a silver platter."

"Nonsense." Hattie gave him a warm smile. "You've completely earned the title. You've done so much for us as Chief. What about 0012, eh?"

"That wasn't because of what I did. Alby was the one who saw them on that hill."

"But you're the one who organised the charge... you're the one who whittled them down to two – and now," said Hattie, placing her hand on his arm, "now, those men, they're still out there, sure, still a threat... but they'd never be able to destroy us, what, just Dalton and Mirza..."

Noah kept quiet. Hattie squeezed his arm and finished her pep talk:

"Had it not been for what you did in o'twelve – we might *all* be dead by now."

She watched with delight as Noah revelled in her songs of praise. His eyes appeared to brighten with a newfound confidence. "Thank you, Hattie." He held her hand up and regarded it as though he might kiss it. "Yeah. If it hadn't been for me, we'd have *all* been fucked."

"Exactly. You're a legend."

"I *am* a legend," he repeated, stupefied by the nurse's nurturing aura. Hattie smiled sheepishly. Wriggling her hand free, she leaned back in her chair. Noah gave her a flirtatious look before reaching for the remote on his bedside table. He switched to the *Landview* channel, which displayed a lush scene of the English countryside, wildflowers and forestry covering the endless fields. Meanwhile, Hattie returned to her psychology book. Every so often, she'd glance up at Noah and find his eyes fixed on her face. Each time this occurred, Noah would give her a smile or a wink before averting his gaze. Hattie wasn't sure whether to be charmed or unsettled by this curious routine. Nonetheless, she carried on with her book, checking her plastic pink watch every other minute, waiting for her time in this place to come to an end.

13
Forbidden Fruits

Friday morning on the Estate

Jasper lay awake on his rock-hard mattress, trapped inside a pitch-black container. His tired musings were rudely interrupted as Pete swung the steel doors open. The bright white light of the cloudy morning sky swept into his cell, making him recoil.

"Get up."

Obligingly, Jasper stood to his feet and, already dressed in his tattered orange jumpsuit, allowed Pete to lead him out into the yard. At its centre, the Estate's wind turbine danced in the breeze, its pronged blades cutting through the air. Surrounding it, the rest of the field-slaves stood in a huddled group, flanked by four Scouts clad in hazmat suits.

Pete grabbed Jasper by the collar and heaved him over to the others before standing in front of the slaves with a clipboard. A cool breeze swept through the air. Jasper blinked and took it all in – the expanses of the fields, the vast atmosphere, the Georgian-style mansion that towered to the side. And the sky! Jasper peered up to watch the outlines of a distant white sun, which glowed behind dense fluffy clouds. A rush of euphoria passed through his tired mind, while the other field-slaves remained sullen and depressed.

"Sharp." Behind his gas mask, Pete glared at a grubby-looking slave called Crispin, who had been sentenced to the farm in o'twelve for 'disrespecting officials'. "Warehouse duty."

The young man nodded his head with a strange, jerky movement, as if to say, 'not bad, not bad'.

"Marshall." Jonathan, a silver-haired ex-judge, looked expectantly at Pete. "Also warehouse." The old man sighed and looked at his feet.

"Farthing." Here, Pete addressed a young woman who had attacked her partner with a knife in o'eight. "Fields." Alice rolled her eyes.

"Parker." Sue wrung her clammy hands together. "Orchards." The woman sighed with relief. The others stared at her with palpable jealousy.

"Singh." To his delight, Mo was told he'd be picking fruit with his girlfriend, Sue, this morning.

"Forsythe." Pete turned towards a sullen young man named Gareth. Upon hearing the word 'fields', Gareth gnashed his teeth and whispered a curse under his breath.

"Watch it, freak," warned Pete, who moved on to Baxter Harding. Baxter, too, would be working the fields, as would his old associates, Tom Bateman and Harry Dickinson. This came as no surprise, for they had been a part of Mickey Ratford's attempted coup and were usually assigned the most miserable of tasks.

"Wycliffe." Sarah, Mickey's old girlfriend, was to be sent out to the fields as well, guilty by association with the widely hated man.

"MacNair." Pete gazed towards Maya; his wild eyes lecherous behind the bug-like goggles. "Picking for you today, darling." Maya responded with a shudder. Pete sighed, then turned back to his clipboard.

"Creak." Brandon stood frozen, arms dangling by his sides. "Fields."

"Carr." Donald tilted his head, his arms folded. "Warehouse."

"Huxley." Jasper peered into the soulless eyes of the masked official. "Picking for you today," said Pete, voice tailing off as he tucked his clipboard under his arm.

"Right then," he continued, "you've all heard the news."

Jasper stared off into the distance. At the edge of a massive green field, he could see the Estate's perimeter fence. Outside it, a group of three youths was stumbling around, searching for something on the grass.

"... but in any case, we're still business as usual. And we've got some busy months ahead. You'd better keep your heads screwed on. If not" – here, Pete left a deliberate pause – "well, you'll be headed the same way as lazy boy Derek..."

The slaves grew uncomfortable. Pete let out a cruel chuckle before opening the back doors of the new van and waving them all inside. Each of the field slaves took their places on the benches.

They sat in pitch-black as the van started up, rumbling down a track. Behind them, the Scouts tailed the van in an old Land Rover.

"This nightmare never ends," said Jonathan, as the wheels hit a bump on the road.

"S'alrigh', Jonno," said Crispin, in his guttural cockney voice. "Just go'a see it through."

Pete slammed on the brakes, causing the slaves to jolt in their seats. Pete came around and opened the doors of the van. Behind him stretched abundant orchards.

Sue, Mo, Maya, and Jasper got up and went to exit the vehicle. Crispin patted Jasper on the arm in a show of solidarity. "S'alrigh', my son."

Jasper nodded before stepping down onto the ground. Pete looked him up and down, then slammed the back doors and climbed back into the van, skidding it off towards the warehouses, followed by the Land Rover.

'Kazza', a young Scout in his late twenties, would be the fruit-pickers' supervisor today. The man, clad in orange, held a crumpled sheet of paper in his hands and had a Glock pistol strapped to his side. He'd already taken his mask off and wore the hazmat gear as though it were a tracksuit.

He led the four slaves towards a stack of plastic bins and handed them one each. "When they're full, bring 'em back," 'Kazza' said, laconic as ever, before slumping into a deckchair and whipping out his phone. Sue and Mo stumbled off together. As Jasper strolled away with a plastic bucket, he found himself being followed by Maya.

A gust of wind swept over the land. The ripe apple trees rustled, and Jasper's eyes became wet with tears. His greasy hair blew about in tufts. Meanwhile, Maya pinned her hair back in a ponytail. Jasper glanced at her. He'd never seen her like this before – her sharp eyes saddled with bags, and her orange jumpsuit all in tatters. Once, the old teacher had taken pride in her appearance, but her time on the Estate had robbed her of that pleasure.

The two strolled further up the orchard row in silence, until Maya stopped and turned to a tree, reaching into its foliage and plucking at its fruits. Jasper stood nearby and began to do the same, placing Granny Smiths into his bucket. He turned around sharply upon hearing a crunch and saw that Maya was eating one of the apples. Her face was filled with a fervent look. Instinctively, Jasper checked over both of his shoulders and, seeing that the coast was clear, began to nibble on his own apple, avoiding the mouldy patch that had formed on its skin. Maya glanced over at the young lad and gave him an approving smile, before she finished hers off and started another. Jasper stared at her with admiration and, once they'd both finished eating, Maya took his apple core and buried it with hers, covering it in the soil beneath one of the trees.

"They won't know, will they?" Jasper asked, nervously wringing his hands. "They won't be able to tell?"

"Of course not," said Maya, wiping her hands clean. "They don't count all the apples on the trees, mate. And Charlie doesn't give a toss – I'll tell you that much."

Jasper turned to check if 'Kazza' was looking. 'Kazza', still slouching in his fold-up chair, appeared occupied by his own distractions. Maya, meanwhile, touched Jasper on the arm and gestured for him to walk with her along the edge of the orchard. A vast wheat field stretched to the side. In the distance, Jasper noticed a group of field-slaves uprooting it under the watchful eye of an orange-clad Scout, who clutched an SA80 rifle.

"Only five years, then?" Maya asked.

Jasper swallowed hard. "Y-yep. Only, only five years."

"Don't worry," Maya chuckled, "I'm not, like, jealous or anything. It's just – how come *you* got away with a temporary sentence? Whereas Donnie and Brandon are stuck here for life?"

Jasper hesitated. "I mean... I'm not entirely sure. Perhaps it's—"

"Must be your age," Maya blurted. "Mustn't it."

"I suppose," said Jasper. Abruptly, he turned and reached into a nearby apple tree, rootling in its foliage and plucking at its fruits. Maya crossed her arms and stared at him. Jasper avoided her gaze as he frantically dropped apples into his bucket, in the forced, mechanical manner of an angsty robot. As an apple fell from his grasp, he gasped.

"Bloody hell. You're not half awkward, are you?"

Jasper spun around and twisted his face into a scowl, trying to rebuke his ex-teacher. Maya burst into laughter. "Aww... I'm sorry...

I'm sorry. I'm only teasing, pet." She slapped Jasper on the arm and got to work on the apple tree next to his.

"So," she continued, filling up her plastic bucket, "what d'you reckon you'll do when you get back to the Bunker?"

"Well," Jasper began, "I suppose I'll just try and keep my head down. I'll, I'll try and work my way into Tommy's good books, and then of course I'll see, see if I can—"

"Weren't you and Hattie Osborne a thing back in the day? Or have I got that totally wrong?"

Jasper frowned.

"Only curious," she added.

Jasper took a moment, then gazed beyond the trees towards a distant wind farm, which stood atop a hill, towering above the swathes of Sparrowman fields. Although they no longer generated power, the blades of those relics kept on spinning in the wind nonetheless.

"We could've been," Jasper replied, trying to sound enigmatic. "But the circumstances were never right. And I was never given a proper chance."

Maya gave him an intense stare. "Uh-huh." She reached to hold his hand. "You're a nice boy, Jas. I think you just need a bit more confidence. And you've got to stop trying to be something you're not. You're alright as you are, I think."

Jasper glanced suspiciously at his ex-teacher, his guard up, wondering if she was trying to play a nasty trick on him. But Maya's face displayed her sincerity. She gave him a faint smile and turned back towards her tree.

Jasper let out a sigh. He looked back towards Maya and, scanning the woman's face, he could see that her wrinkled cheeks glowed with a long-lost passion. Jasper's heart wrenched with a poignant affection. He shook his head, finished with his current tree, then stumbled off and moved on to another.

* *

Friday evening in the Bunker
Hattie was sitting alone at dinner when one of her colleagues approached.

"Hi, Hattie," said Mateo Dacosta, his eyes shining with delight. "Can I sit here?"

"Sure." Hattie gave the man a faint smile as he scrambled onto the bench opposite. She continued to pick at her food, then looked up at his face. Mateo quickly averted his gaze and began to eat his dinner, shoving a lump of mash into his mouth.

"It's terrible, isn't it," he said, releasing a loud gulp, "that we might have to go back to rationing..."

"Yup." Hattie stared idly at the ceiling. She was too tired to engage with this bland topic of discussion. Everyone in the Bunker had already exhausted it over the last couple of days.

"Are you alright, by the way?" he asked, letting out a grating snicker. "You seem... upset."

Hattie rolled her eyes. "I'm fine."

"Of course. Of course." Mateo took a sip from his glass. "You've been through a lot recently. I apologise, I apologise."

Normally, Hattie found male awkwardness charming, but Mateo's was just annoying and tiresome. An intrusive thought called for her to chuck her drink in his face.

"Are the other girls being mean?" he asked.

Hattie peered over at the table behind, where the Bunker's young women were chattering away. She returned to her food, ignoring Mateo's question.

"Hattie?"

"What?!" she snapped. Stunned, Mateo's wry smile turned into a frown. The two stared at each other. Mateo blurted out a repugnant "SooOOOorrrrRRRRrYYYY!", before taking his tray and moving to another table, sitting down all by himself.

'No wonder the Scouts turned him down,' she thought to herself, furiously chewing on a lump of steak.

After she'd finished eating, Hattie, grabbing her tray, couldn't help but eavesdrop on the girls' table. Melissa, dominating the conversation, wittered on about that "freak" Ursula Wolf from the class of o'eighteen, and how she'd allegedly tried to "attack" Melissa's new beau, Bobby, with a "blunt instrument". Hattie had no desire to listen to Melissa's bullshit, and quickly walked away, dumping her tray at the canteen's serving station. She felt Mateo's piercing gaze trail behind her as she trudged towards the door, like a pesky fly that wouldn't leave her alone.

Dropping onto her rock-hard bed, Hattie stared up at the buzzing ceiling light. She reflected on the events of the morning. Noah, now almost fully recovered, had been discharged from the emergency room and, before heading up to Level 2, came into Hattie's office with a proposition.

"I'd like you to come to dinner with me," he'd told her.

And how Hattie had smiled at him, said she appreciated the invitation, but that she couldn't make it – how she'd lied about needing to "run errands" in the evening.

Hattie wiped her tired eyes with her fingers. Reaching over to her bedside, she opened up her laptop and continued watching the film she'd been trying to finish for the last two days.

Look at that subtle off-white colouring. The tasteful thickness of it...

But Hattie couldn't focus on Patrick Bateman's monologue. Her scattered brain was bogged down in a trance. She slammed the laptop shut and dumped it on the duvet as she propped herself up, staring at the pyramids she'd painted all those years ago, the ones that flanked Commander Tommy's portrait. Once oblivious to her inner drives, Hattie could see it all too clearly now: how her naïve young mind had been trying to make a statement against Tommy's tyranny. But now, in her maturity, Hattie could see how wrong she'd always been. How, despite Tommy's flaws and deceit, the real world truly was a dangerous place. And now, three Scouts were dead. Her old friend Walter, slaughtered senselessly by those pack animals. And Dr Jones, hollowed by the loss of his only child – an empty husk of the man he'd once been.

Hattie wiped her eyes, reached into her bedside drawer, and took out a lump of tobacco. She stuffed the dry leaves in her mouth and chewed away, hoping that this might provide her with a trickle of pleasure, but if anything, the nicotine made her feel even more numb and inhuman. As she lay there, Noah's voice came back to her, trying to extend an olive branch.

'Come and see me.'

Hattie spat her tobacco out with disdain, sending the brown mush into her bedside bin. Driven by some overpowering urge – at last, allowing herself to be led by natural instincts – she found herself in front of the mirror on her wardrobe. Although her eyes were saddled with bags, she still looked good enough. Glancing over at the childhood photos on her plain concrete wall, Hattie shook her head and moved towards the door. She turned back and rushed to apply a light layer of makeup and some lipstick, before finally stepping out into the hallway, passing through its exit. She began to ascend the helix-shaped steps, which spiralled through the stairwell like an oversized gene.

Eddie Lee, the official on night-watch, allowed Hattie to strut past without saying a word. Approaching Level 2, she found that the entrance was sealed, and called down to Eddie. Eddie came pacing up, and the dutiful guard unsealed the door with his master key.

Moving through its modest lobby, Hattie entered the corridor marked 'A', which felt vastly more spacious than the ordinary floors. Its tunnel stretched so far that she could scarcely see its end. Dinner was over, but Noah would no doubt be happy to see her in his chambers.

Marching through the hall, Hattie could hear aggressive music blaring from within a few of the rooms, causing the steel doors to vibrate on their hinges. Inside one of them, number '26', she could clearly make out a young man's groans, followed by an older woman's gasps. Hattie quickly shuffled past, and, glancing back at the door marked '31' – Marcus' desolate suite – she reached the far end of 2-A. After a moment's hesitation, she knocked on the door to number '54'. The wounded Chief opened up, smiled, and waved for her to step inside.

14
War Footing

Hattie sank down into Noah's recliner chair. Her body nestled into the soft leather as she pulled a small lever at the side, sending her legs swinging up. Noah chuckled, offering her a drink which she accepted with pleasure. From his mini-fridge, Noah took out a flask of fresh lemonade, a product of the greenhouse in the Garden Space, and added a touch of vodka to it. Hattie accepted the cup and sipped the concoction, which tasted strangely of sweet antiseptic. Noah prepared a similar glass for himself, then sat on his bed, casting a curious gaze at the young lady who had come to visit.

"Done with your 'errands', then?" he teased with a chuckle.

Hattie blushed, returning his tease with a shy smile. "I'm sorry, I just – I felt a bit apprehensive about coming here, is all."

"No worries. But I can only spare ten minutes," said Noah, taking a generous gulp of his drink. He glanced at the clock, adding, "Tommy's called a meeting for 9 o'clock."

"Really? Why so late?"

Noah swirled his drink around. "He's been making the decisions in my absence. Wants to send a dispatch to the farm tonight." He raised his glass and drained the remaining contents in one go, wiping his lips with the back of his hand.

"Shouldn't be mixing alcohol and tramadol," Hattie said, half-teasingly. "Naughty chap, you are."

Noah grinned and shook his head. "Don't worry: I've stopped taking those painkillers. No need for them anymore." He stretched his arms and grimaced, holding a hand against his healing ribs. "Almost done with the antibiotics too."

"Really?" Hattie raised her brow. "I thought you had, like, nine days left on your course..."

With a dismissive shrug, Noah brushed her comment aside. He leaned back on his bed, watching Hattie with an amused expression. As he stared intensely at her, Hattie returned his smile, though a lingering fear overcame her, causing her to wonder if he was playing some sort of mind game.

Eventually, Noah averted his gaze, rubbing his face. The fatigue showed on his features. Hattie glanced towards his bedside table, where a framed photo rested upright. Anastasia, the late wife of the Commander – Noah's biological mother – looked radiant in the picture. Her expressive blue eyes were full of joy, and her long blonde hair came down in golden locks.

Seeing where Hattie was looking, Noah allowed a sigh to escape from his lips.

"Miss her every day," he said, eyes marked by a vacant expression. Hattie felt a lump in her throat, admiring his vulnerability. Both of their mothers had passed away in the Bunker, despite surviving the initial outbreak. Hattie's mother had lost her life in o'six following a botched cancer surgery, while Noah's mother had succumbed in o'four, owing to a prolonged battle with bipolar disorder. Noah, Hattie realised, had never truly come to terms with his loss. Tommy had taught him well to keep emotions at bay. Hattie glanced over at the poor chap – this Chief of Scouts, this rugged young man, who, to her mind, still seemed a lost child.

Moved by a natural instinct, Hattie stood up from the chair and embraced him tightly. They sat together on the edge of his bed. Noah froze into a statue as Hattie pressed her head against his stone-hard chest, although he did pat her back in a comforting gesture, as if to say 'there, there'.

In the protective warmth of Noah's muscular frame – his broad shoulders, and those trunk-like arms – Hattie allowed herself to release all the tears she'd been trying to keep down. Noah, silent and unsure of himself, remained an awkward plank until he finally pulled himself away.

"I should be heading out," he said, pointing to his watch, "it's nearly nine already."

He stood, reaching for his jacket. Hattie looked down at her feet, sniffling and wiping at her face, ridding herself of all those self-indulgent tears.

"I'm so sorry, Noah, I didn't mean to—"

"No, no, don't worry, you're fine," Noah assured, adjusting his collar. Not quite sure of what to do with this emotionally unstable young woman, he cleared his throat and asked if she would like to accompany him to the meeting.

Hattie's eyebrows knit together. "But isn't that—"

"Yeah, yeah, yeah, it's fine. It's fine. Tommy won't mind." Noah reassured her with a smile. "I think he trusts you."

He extended his hand, offering it to Hattie to help her up. Together, they left the room and made their way through the corridors. As they crossed the threshold into the Scout Theatre, the young couple proceeded down the narrow aisle and took their seats. Half the Scouts were already in attendance, though Commander Tommy was yet to arrive.

* *

That same evening, the Retreaters were making their way up to the Peak District. The journey was lit by a sliver of moon, and the full beams of their armoured truck.

Ashley Mirza had spent the last two days exploring old police compounds and had stumbled upon a 'Gurkha', once used by SWAT teams. Marcus had told him there were either twelve or thirteen people at the Estate needing rescue, and this was certainly a vehicle fit for the task. Currently, Ashley was skilfully manoeuvring the enormous car through bends in the road, while Dani Dalton, sitting in the passenger's seat, was busy manning her drone. Her face was caked in powdery makeup, her thin lips embellished with a glossy purple lipstick.

Seated in one of the back seats, Marcus stared out through a porthole, watching the eerie night scene as they made their way up the empty A6.

"These bastards have it all coming to them," said Ashley, repeating a sentiment he'd expressed many times already. "Forcing people into slavery – even for Tommy, that's totally beyond the pale..."

Dani Dalton turned to look at Marcus, then scoffed and returned to her tablet screen.

"Marcus," began Ashley, "no one's going to die because of this." He swerved past the wreck of a toppled oil tanker. "We've checked the comms. Like I said, the Estate still seems like it ain't so well-guarded. So it'll just be a quick operation: in, and out. Free the slaves, build up our numbers, and pile more pressure on Tommy." Ashley licked his lips. "It's exciting, my friend. You've made this all possible. Might finally get that scumbag out of power. Real change, at last – all thanks to you."

Dani raised her brow, then whispered something in Ashley's ear. Marcus was able to read the movements of her lips:

We'll see about that...

Marcus grunted, irritated by Dani Dalton's lack of respect. "Still don't believe in me, huh?"

"Of course we do," said Ashley.

"No, no." Marcus jabbed his finger at the old Prime Minister. "I want *her* to answer." Dani's attention remained fixed on her tablet, ignoring the hostage's complaints. Marcus snapped his fingers near Dani's ear, causing the lady's head to turn. She narrowed her eyes at him. Marcus looked away to diffuse the tension.

"I don't trust him," Dani told Ashley, still staring at Marcus. "We shouldn't be giving him a gun."

Marcus returned Dani's gaze, with an incredulous smirk on his lips. "I mean, d'you want me to help you with this little 'project' of yours, or don't you?"

The two stared each other down for twelve seconds straight, until Dani swivelled around. Marcus smiled proudly to himself.

The Gurkha's wheels slammed against a violent pothole as it sped across a desolate stretch of road. Marcus asked Ashley how long it would be until they arrived.

"A little while, still."

Marcus nodded, peering out of his tinted window in quiet anticipation. Shadowy hills loomed on the horizon, their outlines visible against the night sky.

* *

Meanwhile, Hattie and Noah were seated in the front row of the Scout Theatre on Level 2-B. The rest of the Scouts stared at the young couple in awe. Dennis, sitting in the row behind, patted Noah on the shoulder to congratulate him. All the while, Hattie stared ahead at the concrete wall. Unnerved, she could sense Trevor's jealous gaze boring into the back of her head.

The air fell still as footsteps began to plod down the aisle. Hattie turned around. There he was: Commander Tommy himself, dressed in formal military attire. He stepped into the spotlight and cleared his throat. His voice boomed without the need for a microphone, as he proceeded to rant about those "bastard" Retreaters, and how they were going to "sniff out" those "dastardly dogs" "soon", in order that they could finally be "put down". However, the current policy was to keep everything "on lock" in case Dalton and Mirza launched another attack. Half of the Scouts would be sent into the hills to guard outposts on a rotation basis, ensuring that the Bunker's entrance and its hydroelectric dam were secured at all times.

"All the same," said Tommy, his voice laced with paranoia, "the Estate's still at risk. We've only got five men out there. Seven-hundred-and-thirty-seven acres of land. That simply won't do. It just won't. Not in these times." Tommy looked down at Noah. "Son, I know it's your decision – but I strongly suggest we get some more guys out there, ASAP."

Noah nodded in agreement. Tommy turned to the others, and continued:

"Dani knows she could do real damage if she disrupted our food supply. It would be a total fucking disaster. Existential." He left a long pause, scanning the room for any dissent.

"Respectfully, sir," said Dominic, a weaselly Scout in his late twenties, "I feel it's best that we don't spread ourselves too thin. If something did happen to the Estate, it's less than half an hour away; they'll radio us and then we can—"

"Time is always of the essence in these matters, my child," said Tommy, wagging his finger to and fro. Dominic bowed his head, then started to twiddle with his thumbs.

"Anyone else got something to add?" asked Tommy. "No?"

"Good. Now," he said, waving his hand at one half of the crowd, "You lot will head to the Estate. Tonight." Tommy nodded resolutely. "Yes: the roads should be safe to drive on. Just keep your headlights off. And of course, you'll need to take an alternative route. And Noah," he said, folding his arms, "I'd like you to stay here while you recover. Albert, you'll be leading the team to the farm."

"Yes, sir." Albert rubbed his hands eagerly. The chosen Scouts stood and left, heading down to Level 4, where their rifles were waiting in storage. "As for the rest of you – I'd like you to head up to the hills. Make sure we've got protection on the outside." Tommy waved with a purposeful gesture, instructing the remaining men to leave the room. Meanwhile, Hattie and Noah were kept in their seats as Tommy towered above them, hands propped on his hips. His wrinkled lips turned into a smile; his eyes gleaming with a thinly-veiled lust.

"So, this is Gina's replacement," Tommy mused, admiring his son's new woman. "Good for you then, eh lad." With a pat on Noah's injured shoulder, he strolled down the aisle, leaving them alone in the theatre.

"Are you okay?" Hattie asked, noticing Noah's grimace as his bullet wound ached.

"Mhm." Noah gritted his teeth. He took a sharp breath to compose himself. "He wouldn't do that on purpose, by the way. It's just," he gulped, "sometimes Tommy can be forgetful..."

"Right." Hattie bit her lip. "Look, I erm—"

"Yeah, yeah," said Noah, "you'd best be heading off. But listen," he paused for a moment, "if you'd like to come to dinner another day – then I could certainly have that arranged. Just the two of us, I mean. And," he went on, "I think my dad's got a pool party coming up soon, if you wanted to tag along..."

"Dinner sounds great. I can do whenever." Hattie smiled. They stood and embraced for a while. Noah kissed her on the cheek before she made her way back to her stuffy room on Level 12-A.

15
Breakout

The dispatch of Scouts drove through wild backroads. Their journey was guided by moonlight, for it was too risky to turn their lights on.

In the leading Jeep, Albert had taken the wheel, with Dennis in the shotgun seat. In the back sat Trevor, and Bobby, who had recently been reinstated as a Scout.

"Everything alright, Tiger?" Bobby asked, watching Trevor with a sidelong stare. The young lad appeared to be in a sulk. He turned around and gave a dispassionate nod, though his eyes were drooping with despair.

"Hey, kid," Dennis said, his voice softer as Albert navigated the car through the forest. "This'll all get easier, I promise you. All of us – we've all got our own demons. We all feel your pain. You ain't alone in this."

The rest of the men mumbled words of agreement. Trevor continued to lean with his head in his hand, staring vacantly through the window.

A voice crackled through the static of the car's radio.

"Eh?"

Albert turned the volume up.

Jesus Christ! screamed the radio. *Get here now! Get over here right now!*

As the men listened in horror, Albert pressed a button and spoke into the mic.

"What the hell's going on, Pete?"

More static.

We're under attack...

The radio cut off.

Albert panicked and floored the accelerator, switching on the car's full beams. The four Jeeps followed suit. Eventually, they skidded onto the A616, and were seven minutes away from their final destination.

**

The air of the Estate cried with piercing sirens. Outside, the chain-link gates had been busted open. The body of a Scout, clad in blood-splattered orange, lay dead near the checkpoint.

At present, Marcus and Ashley stood outside the slave-yard, Ashley fumbling desperately to unlock the fence's door. He slid a thin sheath into the padlock and, at last, managed to break it open. Both entered the yard, and, one by one, they started breaking the locks on each shipping container, Marcus using the technique that Ashley had taught him earlier that day.

Marcus, under Ashley's cover, rushed to free Mrs MacNair, Gareth, Crispin, and finally, Jasper Huxley.

"Jesus Christ." Marcus's heavy breaths faltered. He stared at Jasper for a moment, the feral boy lying half-naked in his cell, his grubby face filled with confusion.

Marcus threw himself to the ground, covering his head as hellfire rained down over the yard. Three of the Scouts, aiming at the Retreaters, were shooting from the mansion's windows. Marcus scrambled behind a shipping container and, alongside Ashley, returned fire with his pistol, hands shaking. Dani emerged with an AK, abandoning her drone for a moment, and began spraying bullets at the mansion. She managed to fell two of the guards, their bodies dangling from the windowsills like orange ragdolls. The four freed slaves started running from the containers while Ashley and Marcus provided cover. Sprinting through the exit of the slave yard, each of them jumped into the armoured truck outside.

Dani climbed back into the truck, while Ashley and Marcus continued to free the remaining captives, Ashley watching the windows, anticipating the last guard's appearance.

Marcus managed to open the lock for old man Jonathan and was working on another when Dani's urgent voice rang out from the truck:

"Get back!"

"What's going on?" called Ashley.

"I – I see them! On the drone! They're coming!"

Marcus's racing heart sank. The growls of engines grew in the distance, coming ever closer.

Ashley sprinted towards the Gurkha, but Marcus remained in the yard, attempting to bust open another container. At last, he broke the lock, but before Brandon could step outside, Marcus was forced to take cover as the last guard, Pete, began firing down at him. Ashley fired back, shattering several windows in the process. Pete let out a cry and vanished from sight. The gunfire ceased.

"Get out!" yelled Ashley. The Scouts could be heard driving down the track, rapidly approaching the Estate.

"Go and fetch Donald!" hissed Brandon from within his metal box. "He's in the one – to my left!"

Marcus bit his lip and, compelled by a sense of obligation, moved towards Mr Carr's container, desperate to free the old teacher, despite Ashley's frantic protests. In the distance, the glare of the Jeeps' headlights could be seen. Marcus finally managed to force open Donald's cell. "Come on!" he urged, motioning to both Brandon and Donald to follow him out of the yard. All three of them darted towards the Gurkha, leaving behind the six slaves who had yet to be freed.

As they neared the vehicle, Brandon fell to the ground, and the sound of a sniper shot pierced the air.

Marcus, heedless, refused to look behind as he jumped into the safety of the truck. Panting, he slammed the door shut and stared out the window, watching as Donald struggled to lift a lifeless Brandon.

"Let him go!" cried Ashley. But Donald chose to ignore his pleas, and, in a heartbeat, fell to the floor, his head erupting in a cloud of blood. Another shot echoed through the atmosphere.

The approaching Jeeps crossed into the Estate, entering its car park. Ashley pulled the handbrake and the Gurkha skidded off. The silver Jeeps were unable to stop the behemoth in its tracks. They swirled like sharks before giving chase. After speeding through the battered gates, the Gurkha veered off the track and raced through a field. The Jeeps tailed behind; their speed hampered by the bumpy terrain. One of the Scouts began firing at the Gurkha with an SA80. The freed slaves shrieked in unison, fearing that death was imminent.

"Marcus!" cried Ashley as the rear was peppered with bullets. "Marcus, return fire!"

"But—"

"They're going to take our tyres out! Do it!"

Fear clamped Marcus's throat. He swallowed hard and, grabbing Dani's AK-47, opened the small hatch on the vehicle's roof. As though emerging from a sewer, Marcus poked his head into the air of the night before opening fire on the Jeeps. Their bulletproof windscreens cracked and splintered with each round. He focused on the lead vehicle, and eventually, its front windscreen clouded with a powdery white, blinding the driver. A Scout leaned out of a window, guiding the way. Marcus could see that the face belonged to Tiger. A sniper shot ricocheted off the roof of the Gurkha, forcing Marcus to duck.

Jasper, face pallid and aghast, turned to look at his friend. Marcus, for his part, felt as though he were in a dream, observing himself from afar, marvelling at the absurdity of it all. Ahead in the field, Ashley accelerated towards a solitary figure clad in orange, clutching a sniper rifle. The man fired a useless shot and began to run, but it was too late: the Gurkha ploughed straight into him, and its wheels crushed the body of the killer.

The car reached a narrow road and sped down its crumbling path, flanked by a network of wooden telephone masts on either side. At Ashley's instruction, Marcus resumed firing at the pursuing Jeeps, being careful not to shoot Tiger in the face. At last, a bullet pierced the windscreen of the foremost vehicle, instantly killing the driver. The Jeep swerved violently and smashed into a mast. Marcus watched the wreck, where Trevor's crushed head dangled limply from the side window.

The remaining Jeeps continued the chase. Marcus reached down and, grabbing a fresh magazine, reloaded the AK. Rising, he picked off one of the Scouts, who had been firing an SA80. Marcus kept firing. He feigned running out of ammunition. Another Scout leaned out, aiming his rifle from a window. Marcus shot one dead, then another. The macabre game continued until the Jeeps screeched to a halt and abandoned the chase, seeing the futility of their pursuit against a better-prepared enemy.

"Marcus," said Jasper, as Marcus clambered back down into the vehicle, slamming the top hatch shut. "Wh—"

Jasper stopped himself, unnerved by the wild look in Marcus's eyes. The rest of the slaves seemed petrified too, save for Crispin Sharp, whose face was full of awe at what the young lad had accomplished.

* *

With the massive AK on his lap, Marcus resembled a child soldier. He turned to look at Ashley.

"What now?" he said, his expression weary, though his body trembled with adrenaline.

"Well," Ashley began, "I suppose we get our new recruits back home." The Gurkha looped around a roundabout and pulled onto an empty motorway. Dani sat in sombre silence, her eyes fixed on the tablet screen as she manipulated her drone to follow the vehicle.

"'ome?" asked Crispin, rubbing his greasy mitts together.

"That's right: back to the Project." Ashley peered over his shoulder. "What d'you call it, Marcus?"

"The Retreat..."

Ashley let out a dry chuckle. "That's how you refer to us, innit? Retreaters? Fuckin' hell," said Ashley with a snicker, a sound echoed by Crispin. The rest of the field-slaves, however, remained eerily silent.

"Oh, c'mon, lads," said Crispin, trying to engage the others. "Cheer up. We're ou' of it now. Free at las', free at las'..."

Jonathan solemnly shook his head, while Gareth groaned and muttered a curse under his breath, lamenting the terrorists who'd rescued them. Meanwhile, Maya sobbed with confused, cathartic tears. She leaned on Jasper's shoulder. The young lad, nauseous and uncomfortable, began to freeze up, too scared to do or say anything.

Still fiddling with her remote, Dani looked up from her tablet and gazed at young Jasper.

"Blimey." Dani fiddled with one of her earrings. "Look how you've grown..."

Jasper gulped; Dani kept watching him. There was a strange affection in those sullen green eyes. Ms Dalton and her husband,

Vernon, had helped look after Jasper as a baby, before they were exiled in o'zero along with the rest of the 'Retreaters'. Dani smiled faintly at Jasper, then turned back to her tablet screen.

Marcus slapped Jasper's unoccupied shoulder, offering him an odd, crooked smile. "Bet you're pleased to be out, aren't you," he said, with a touch of regret in his monotone voice.

After driving through the night for three hours, winding through old motorways and passing desolate Surrey villages, the Gurkha finally reached a gate. Ashley swung it open, drove them up a slope, and parked between the Range Rover and the Bunker's old delivery van. He called the slaves out and led them up to the ruins of a medieval abbey, while Dani and Marcus trailed behind. Jasper stared at the distant London skyline before Ashley called for him to enter the hatch and head down the ladder. Jasper complied, moving towards the bright light that lay at the bottom of the tunnel.

16
Life's Work

Descending into the Earth's depths, Jasper let go of the ladder and stepped onto the cold, hard ground. He found himself standing in a strange, underground shelter, which felt like a scene from 3000AD.

"Fuckin' 'ell," said Crispin. "It's li'e Back to the Future in 'ere…"

Jasper watched as the young chap paced down the hall in his clunky, restless manner. Inspecting the long rows of cubicles, Crispin turned to face the others, who lingered near the ladder, gazing around the brightly lit chamber.

Meanwhile, Ashley Mirza and Dani Dalton called for Crispin to come back, and gathered everyone in a circle.

"We'll all be staying here, for now," said Ashley. "We've got water, electricity, and enough stored food to last us… what, about a year?" Ashley looked to Dani, who shrugged her shoulders.

"Yeah," continued Ashley. "I reckon about a year, what with the nine of us." He chuckled to himself. "I must warn you: the stuff we've got here isn't the nicest, but it's edible – it'll do the job." Ashley rubbed his hands together as he stared at the grubby slaves. Their dry mouths appeared to water at the thought of food. "You know what? I'll fetch you something up now. God knows you lot need a bite to eat!" The man strolled off towards the far end of the complex and disappeared through a door, with Dani following behind. Marcus, who had stayed behind with the freed slaves, exchanged a lingering look with Jasper before finally embracing him. Jasper returned the hug with forceful enthusiasm, his stomach pulsing in and out as he burst into tears.

"It's alright, mate," said Marcus, patting Jasper on the back. Meanwhile, the rest of the slaves loitered off in a group, inspecting their new home, before Maya MacNair asked Marcus where they might get some water.

"Kitchen's over there." Marcus pointed to the little room where Dani and Ashley had gone to. "Take it from the tap." Immediately, the slaves went off. Jasper remained with Marcus.

"The things they made us do..." he sobbed. "We had to, we had to, toil in the fields all day, and they made us sleep in little boxes, and—"

Jasper's wails intensified. Marcus, uncomfortable, suggested that they go and get a drink with the others. Jasper seemed to come to his senses. Sniffling, he allowed Marcus to lead him off to the cramped kitchen room, where Dani and Ashley were preparing hot food. Once Sue was done, Jasper stuck his head under the gushing tap and took long, deep gulps of water.

Ten minutes later, dinner was served. The field-slaves and the Retreaters all sat down at a long table together, one which Ashley had set up in one of the Retreat's empty storage rooms. Ashley and Dani had set up nineteen chairs in there, having anticipated a greater number of arrivals.

In hungry silence, the group tucked into some cooked beef jerky and canned sweetcorn. Old Jonathan growled and groaned as he ate, wrinkly chops covered in yellow juice, which prompted Crispin to chortle like a maniac. Marcus felt sick upon hearing this. The young man's laugh sounded like Trevor's.

"So," started Crispin, wiping his mouth, "wha's with all 'em fuckin'... *beds*?"

Ashley swallowed a mouthful. "It's *MaxSimi*. It's a virtual reality setup. That's what we've been doing since we got here – sixteen years back, now."

"Oh. Well tha's a bit sad, innit." Crispin let out a nonchalant laugh, while the others continued to devour their food.

"Just a way to pass the time, I suppose," said Ashley. "And besides – they'll never find us in this place."

"W-what do you mean?" said Jasper, clenching his teeth. "Are – are they out looking for us?"

Ashley turned to the young lad and saw that his face was ghastly pale. "No, no, no, that's not what I meant. Relax, relax."

On this cue, Marcus turned to pat Jasper on the arm. "You're alright now: we're safe," he assured, trying to calm his friend's nerves.

"That's right," Dani's voice started, causing the others to jump. She turned to the rest of the table, who by now had finished their meals. The former Prime Minister had an air of majesty as she spoke, which enticed the others into silence.

"This place," she said, "is a total secret. It was built during the War. We wanted to see how people would react to living underground, in the event that nuclear weapons were deployed against the United Kingdom. The Survival Project. It was all classified – no one knew about it. The engineers thought they were commissioned to build some kind of seed vault. That's what their contracts specified." Dani smiled to herself. "But *MaxSimi* – I'm sure they knew what we were up to. We shipped in their most up-to-date models and had a team of engineers set them up. Three-hundred devices, all in all, designed to keep people happy and docile for long-term living. But of course," she said, sipping on a glass of water, "the *release* took place before things could get going. So the experiments never took place." She rubbed her palms together. "But when I suggested to the others that we come and stay here – after Tommy kicked us out – we found that the Project was empty. No one had thought to occupy the place. It was perfect. Utterly perfect, I tell you." Dani nodded to herself.

"And Tommy doesn't know where this is?" asked Sue. Dani didn't answer, compelling Ashley to respond:

"Nope. No one knew about the Project. Apart from Dani and the old Defence Sec." He looked up at the ceiling and performed a prayer gesture, paying tribute to a deceased friend.

Meanwhile, Jonathan, the ex-judge, lifted his chin at Dani. "May I ask – why didn't the government use this place to house members of the public?"

Dani turned to stare at the man. Jonathan, flustered by Dani's piercing gaze, scrambled to elaborate. "All I mean is, one might have saved many lives in the initial stages of the pandemic, had one pursued that..."

"No, no, no. It's not that simple. You see," Dani cracked her knuckles, "it's not fair to pick who gets to live and who dies." Jonathan knitted his brow, as though to call the old Prime Minister a hypocrite. Dani appeared to spot this, but continued nonetheless:

"Our policy wasn't to save: it was to contain. We did everything we could to keep people calm. Make them think that help was on the way. But it wasn't," she said, with a note of regret in her voice, "it simply wasn't. There was nothing anyone could do. It was far too late by that point." Dani paused for a second. "I tried to keep things together, but the disease – it just wasn't going to stop. It was awful. Awful."

The group sat in solemn silence for a while, reflecting on the horrors of the pandemic's early days.

"All those broadcasts..." said Maya, her eyes brimming with pain, "you told us it'd all be okay..."

"That's right," said Dani. "We were trying to keep the peace. The daily updates, the readings, the national hymns: white lies and empty words while the world tore itself apart. And I must say, it worked. It really worked. There was very little violence or looting on UK streets – much less so than in other countries. Our people passed away with minimal suffering. That deliberate disease – some might think it a curse, but I don't think it's that simple." She inspected the slaves at the table. "And look at us now, blessed survivors, positively thriving in the rubble..."

Dani let out a hoarse, sarcastic chuckle. The others looked sullen and depressed. At last, Crispin raised his chin in an attempt to lighten the mood:

"Least we go' our lives, dun' we? Still got 'ope for a be'er future..."

"Yeah. I used to tell myself that too." She held the table with both hands, and released a forceful sigh. "But in the end, it's all rubbish. Nothing but a cope. Our friends are gone. Our families, too. And our lives were all for nothing. What more is there to say?" She licked her glossy lips. "I aspired for so much more. I wanted to rescue the whole lot of you from the Estate. But we failed. Could barely manage half. And look at you – look at us. We're no soldiers, we're just ordinary people. Nothing but *civilians*," she said, with a disgusted emphasis on the last word, treating it as though it were a swear.

"But we can always return for the other slaves." Ashley gave him a forced smile. "It ain't over yet..."

"Yes, well." Dani raised her eyebrows. "Life has a way of disappointing you, doesn't it."

Gareth muttered something under his breath, then vigorously shook his head.

"No, no, believe me. I've been around long enough to know." Dani nodded with an air of wisdom. "Twenty years ago – I had it all. I thought the world was my oyster. I really did. I remember it all so clearly." She closed her eyes and breathed in through her nose, before spiralling down the rabbit hole of her regrets.

"December 14th – election night. How Big Ben struck, and the exit polls told of my victory. 44%. 44%! Seven points higher than projected! Oh, and how I would change it all: revive the stagnant economy, modernise our institutions, invest in our children's future – make our country great again. But two months into my tenure, it all got scuppered after a dispute in some poxy backwater. All my aims had to be put on the backburner." Dani bit her lip, eyes welling with tears. "And those sadists. Those monsters. I remember being told of that dreadful weapon, a modified flu virus, released by our near-defeated enemy, already sweeping over the world undetected. We thought we'd seen light at the end of the tunnel, but no! Those bastards had to drag us down to the depths of hell *with* them!"

Ashley stood up and tried to console Dani. But the Prime Minister jerked away from the embrace, refusing to be patronised. "You know, we thought the War might go hot. And it did, of course: just not the way we expected. So yeah, we were lucky. Me, my Vernon and our two boys, and my officials already stationed in our state-of-the-art bunker, in the arse-end of nowhere, I thought, we'd be okay, at least, wouldn't we? We'd all be secure; we'd be safe from what was happening? But no! Tommy! Fucking Tommy! Why on Earth did we let that bastard in?! Oh, why didn't I trust my instincts?!" she spat, face turning bright red. "And the way he manipulated everyone, how he turned them all against us, got all the soldiers to shove us out into hell! Left us for dead on the surface, and for what? For what?! And now," Dani cried, flailing her arms in the air, "here I am, left with nothing. *Nothing.* Tommy took it all away – don't you see? They butchered us, the Scouts picked us off one by one! All my friends and family – all of them are gone!" Dani's voice began to tremble. "Don't you get it?! Don't you get it?!" she cried, before bursting into frenzied tears. Ashley went to comfort her, while the others sat there, stunned. Jasper stared down at the table, his chest rising up and down with each heavy breath. Meanwhile, Marcus sat there in grave silence. At last, he rose from the table and offered to introduce the new recruits to their *MaxSimi* machines.

* *

Midnight in the Bunker

The medical staff were roused awake by Big Davey, who flickered their bedroom lights on with the outside switches. Up on Level 7-A, they were forced to tend to Dennis and Bobby, who had been severely injured in a car crash. Pete was taken in with a shard of broken glass in his eye. Meanwhile, nine body bags were delivered to the morgue on Level 1.

Having been informed of the news, Tommy sat alone in his chambers on Level 5, staring at his sleek marble bust that sat on a corner table. In his hand, he held a glass of whiskey, although he felt too sick to drink. His aquarium glowed, and his little orange fish swam and bobbed about, oblivious to the horrors that had befallen the Bunker.

Tommy stood up, set his drink down, and began to drum on the tank. He grumbled with laughter as the fish stirred with fear, their benevolent God watching over them with his massive eyeballs. Tommy quickly grew bored of tapping the glass. He returned to his chair and downed his whiskey all in one. Looking down at his glass pipe, he reached for it and took another hit, careful not to inhale too much chemical smoke, and finally stepped out of his room. Dressed in a dark-red gown and a pair of slippers, Tommy made his way up the Bunker's stairs and passed into Level 3.

He held a small gas lantern as he stumbled through the pitch-black passageway. At last, he arrived outside an unmarked door, and slammed on the steel to rouse the inmate awake. Inside the cell, a man's deep groans could be heard.

Tommy licked his lips and cracked a smile. Putting on a mock-lady voice, he called out, "My darling... my darling... it's me, Prim... let's get the hell out of here..."

Otto remained silent. Tommy scoffed and rattled the door open. Inside, Otto lay sprawled on the floor in his sweaty orange jumpsuit.

Tommy set the lantern down and began to lean against the wall with his arms folded. Leering with disdain at the man beneath his feet, Tommy watched as Otto tried to avoid his gaze.

"What do you want?" asked Otto, breaking the uneasy silence. Tommy's eyes lingered on him for a moment before he breathed sharply and started to talk.

"I've got some more updates, friend-o." His lips curled into a cruel smirk as he set himself down on the floor and crossed his legs. "Your stepson was killed in an accident."

Otto's eyes seemed to widen.

"Well, I say accident – it was more a deliberate act. Would you like to know who did it?"

Otto's eyes shimmered in the flickering light.

"Marcus X." Tommy left a deliberate pause. "That's right. He's still kicking about. Got taken in by Dani and Ashley. Came driving to the Estate in a large, armoured vehicle. And the lads – well, they didn't stand a chance. It seems the boy did a lot of damage."

Otto said nothing, his head turned away. Tommy reached down and clicked his fingers near Otto's ear. Reluctantly, Otto turned to look him in the eye.

"Yeah. I've been arrogant, you know, these past few years. Sloppy. Really sloppy. Letting my son drive a fancy car with no armour – thinking the coast was clear. But I admit – I was wrong. Dreadfully wrong. And now, nine more men are dead. Brings the toll up to *sixty-eight*. And your son," said Tommy, closely inspecting Otto's face, "just another stat to the tally; just another young soul lost to old men's pride." Tommy let out an ironic chuckle. "And those bastards managed to take some of our workers, too. But only some. A lot of them they left behind. Your old chums Brandon and Donnie were killed in the onslaught. We'll have them buried out in a ditch somewhere. As for you – well, we're gonna have you stationed on the Estate, once the coast is clear. Do what we can to replace the manpower we lost."

Otto closed his eyes and took a deep breath.

"So, tell me," said Tommy, "how do you feel about all that?"

Otto refused to speak.

"You and your reserve, eh?" Tommy thumped Otto on the shoulder. "Come on, tell me! I promise I won't get cross."

Otto glared at Tommy. Both of his eyes were jaundiced and bloodshot. "Sounds like Dani's got something in the works. You'd better watch yourself."

Abruptly, Tommy's cruel smile turned into an inhuman scowl. "Dani can't get me. No one can! I'm blessed – I'm blessed!"

He stood up and paced around the room. Otto recoiled, vigilantly watching the crazed Commander. "And Dani knows that. She can't stand the fact! She thinks she can scare me to submit, but failure follows her about like a big dog on a leash! No, no! This is just a wake-up call! Dani *wants* me to come and sniff her out! And I will! I'm going to stock up, bolster up, re-arm ourselves and build ourselves stronger, move away from the peace that's finally passed. But I know. I know I'm the prized star of this show. The people love me, the Almighty has placed His faith in me – and I'll carry my weight until I reach the very end!" concluded Tommy, froth flying from his mouth as his voice tailed off. He grabbed his oil lamp and slammed Otto's door shut, before making his way down the gloomy corridor.

Tommy reached his chambers and slumped down into his armchair. His body shook with a restless paranoia, but nonetheless, he managed to resist taking another hit from his pipe, as he had merely been microdosing to enhance his connection with God, and was far from being hooked on the stuff.

17
MaxSimi Dreams

08:30

Hattie ate breakfast at the girls' table. Having stayed up all night attending to four wounded Scouts, her eyes were dry with exhaustion. The air of the canteen felt heavy and oppressive, and the paranoia in the Bunker was palpable. Word of what had happened had already spread. The Commander had arranged an emergency assembly for 11 o'clock, in order to address the situation.

Meanwhile, the girls bombarded Hattie with relentless questions.

"Pete's lost an *eye*?" asked Grace, her voice full of disgust.

"Was *Noah* involved?" Melissa enquired, her face ghastly pale.

Hattie sat there, frozen, too scattered to respond properly.

"Ladies, ladies," said Charlotte, waving her hands in the air. "One at a time." She nodded at Hattie, who wiped her eyes as she started to speak.

"It all feels like a dream. I don't know what to tell you." She reached down to take a disheartened bite from her piece of unbuttered toast, while the girls, agitated, began to murmur.

"But why would he do it?" asked Olivia, referring to Marcus. "I don't understand..." Her blue eyes were drooping, and her parted lips quivered, which made Hattie feel a little sick.

"Me neither..." Hattie was on the brink of tears. Charlotte reached to wrap her arm around her shoulder, and the girl burst out crying. The two went off together while the rest of the canteen turned to watch, staring in cold silence as they left through the door.

* *

Down in the Retreat, Jasper was preparing to make an escape of his own.

He lay down on his small surgery bed as Marcus, standing above him, guided Jasper to roll the *MaxSimi* hood onto his head.

"Just say 'Go', right?" said Jasper, his voice muffled underneath the hood's fabric.

"Yeah," said Marcus. "And what's the word for when you want to leave?"

"Exit."

"Good." Rubbing his hands together, Marcus said, "Have fun, mate. I hope you enjoy it as much as I do." Finally, he left Jasper alone, strolling off down the corridor. Allowing himself to sigh with relief, Jasper spoke the commands as he'd been taught.

"*MaxSimi*, Go."

A posh woman's voice appeared in his mind's eye. *Are you sure?* Jasper gulped. "*MaxSimi*, I'm Sure."

In the blink of an eye, he found himself standing in an endless white space. He'd been taken to a virtual purgatory.

A little book appeared in his hands, titled USER GUIDE. Jasper flicked through its cold, laminated pages and turned to the contents section. He tried to read through the leaflet but stopped after five minutes, becoming bored and restless.

"*MaxSimi*... Take Me Somewhere Nice."

Where would you like to go? was the voice's response. Jasper paused for a moment, then started to pace about the empty white chamber, lost in his thoughts.

"*MaxSimi*... How About London?"

Certainly.

In a flash, Jasper was standing in Oxford Circus, surrounded by massive rows of grand buildings. The road was packed with black cabs and red double-deckers. Tourists were flooding the pavements, holding cameras and taking flash pictures. Overwhelmed by the teeming human life, the hustle and bustle of civilisation, the deafening sounds, and the lingering smell of fumes and coffee, Jasper took a deep, trembling breath through his nostrils.

Stepping into a small café to the side, Jasper's insides panged with a strange unease. Despite never having been here before, his mind had done a good job of constructing this place. Nonetheless, something seemed a little off about it. Jasper pushed past the queue of customers and grabbed a little brownie from the till, then, acting on impulse, screamed and ordered the baristas to make him something. And so they did, preparing an instant coffee. Jasper smiled. Smacking the poor barista in the face, he strolled back out into the street, stuffing the delicious brownie into his mouth and washing it down with his piping-hot drink. He tossed the empty cup into the air, hitting a passer-by in the face. This turned out to be none other than good old Dennis, who rubbed his forehead and groaned with pain. He threw Jasper a pitying look that said, 'What'd you do that for, kid?'

"Piss off!" hissed Jasper, shooing Dennis away with his hand. Compliantly, Dennis began to walk away. Jasper smirked, and began to stalk him through the street. Dennis's walk turned into a run, and Jasper chased behind, shoving through crowds of mindless NPCs until a foot tripped him over. Jasper fell to the pavement. His head smacked against the concrete, although this brought no physical pain. Looking up, he saw Hattie standing there, staring down her nose at the wild, manic boy.

"The hell's gotten into you?"

"Hah!" Jasper stood and got up close in her face. "I don't give a shit about you anymore," he insisted, trying to gauge her reaction. But his wry smile vanished after the girl began to weep. Jasper, overcome by a wave of horrible guilt, started to fidget with his hands. "I'm sorry... it's just—"

"I know," said Hattie, wiping her tears away. "You're not the thing you used to be."

Jasper looked down at his feet.

"No... You're better. You're back to being you."

Jasper looked up. Hattie caught his gaze with her soft blue eyes. Her face was radiant, her wet cheeks glowing bright red. Jasper felt an intense pang of warmth, as if he'd been seen for the first time in his life.

The two shared a close embrace in the busy street together, forming a small island as the crowds streamed past, attending to affairs that didn't matter all that much. Finally, the two broke away from each other, though Jasper's hands lingered on Hattie's hips.

"I *am* better," he insisted. "And I hope I'm enough for you now..."

Hattie smiled warmly. "Don't be silly. You've always been enough." The two hugged each other once more, Jasper kissing her forehead while his heart fluttered with joy. The sounds of traffic filled the air.

"Let's get out of this concrete nightmare," she said, taking his hand and leading him away. "I'm sick of this grey city." Jasper followed behind, smirking every now and then as Hattie glanced back at him with a giddy look in her eyes.

"Where d'you want to go, then?" Jasper called. "I can take us anywhere you want..."

Hattie stopped in her tracks. Jasper stood with his hands in his pockets as she considered her options.

"What about the beach?"

"Sounds like a plan." Jasper smiled and instructed the machine to whisk them off to the Seychelles.

* *

Back in the Bunker, Hattie was sitting in a dimly lit theatre. The Sports Hall was packed with all the citizens. The crowd sat in silence. The air felt charged with a current of dread, as they awaited the Commander's arrival.

* *

The intense sun seared Jasper's eyes. Seeing his discomfort, Hattie took a pair of aviators and carefully placed them on his face.

"Better?"

"Better."

Jasper took in his surroundings. Beneath their feet was soft, pristine sand. Beyond that, a vast, peaceful expanse of turquoise water. The cloudless sky was an ocean blue.

"I've been gone for a while," said Jasper, awed by the beauty of it all, as the hot sun warmed his dry, pale skin. Hattie stood by his side, wearing a blue summer dress. Her long hair blew in the gentle breeze.

"You've always been here," said Hattie, adjusting the shade of her sunhat. "You just couldn't see it." She gave him a warm smile and led him over to a pair of sunbeds, where they lay in silence for a while. The resort seemed deserted, yet Jasper had never felt so connected to the world.

A lone parrot shrieked in the undergrowth, startling him, causing him to turn and look behind, where a cluster of palm trees stood, obscuring opulent villas nestled in a tropical field. Jasper's mind flooded with blissful serotonin, imagining that this might have been his in a previous life.

An elderly butler came strolling through the sand, holding a silver platter. He set it down before the pair, unveiling a whiskey bottle and a large packet of crisps.

* *

The back doors of the Sports Hall were shoved open. In came a troupe of twenty-four Scouts, the sound of their boots echoing throughout the room. Noah entered, followed by Commander Tommy and the rest of the Bunker's officials. Pete was absent, still in a drug-induced coma.

Tommy took the podium. His hands shook with a drug-induced fear. His eyes darted about as he inspected the crowd, clearing his throat to deliver his words.

* *

Stuffed with crisps and buoyant with booze, Jasper and Hattie splashed about in the sea, giggling and messing about with each other, before heading back to their luxury villa.

Dani Dalton and Maya MacNair were in attendance. They both sat at the end of the long dining table, while Jasper took his place opposite them, Hattie by his side. The butler came in and laid bowls of French fries in front of them before leaving them to settle their dispute.

"Mr Huxley," said Ms Dalton, munching on a long chip, "I'm afraid I can't give you the control that you desire."

"No way." Jasper shook his head. "That just won't do."

"No, it won't," echoed Hattie, clasping her partner's hand for moral support.

Mrs MacNair cackled with laughter. "What do *you* know, then?"

"I know Jasper's new to the game," said Hattie. "But he's brilliant. He's a lovely, nice boy. He deserves the life that Dani was given."

"Is that so?" Ms Dalton raised an eyebrow. "Well, I'd like something in return, if I'm to give it all up."

Jasper turned to Hattie, who held his hand tighter. "It's okay," she said, giving him a soft peck on the cheek.

Jasper turned to Dani Dalton, eyes filled with resolution. "Take a look at this." He grabbed a small wooden angel from Hattie's cupped hands and slid it across the table. Dalton picked it up and inspected it, before throwing a sinister glance in Hattie's direction. Hattie seemed to freeze in her place.

"Mhm. This'll do." Dalton tucked the figurine into her satchel. She took a handful of chips, stuffed them in her mouth, then stood up and left. Maya trailed after the old Prime Minister. She paused to stare down her nose at Hattie before smiling at Jasper. Jasper ignored her. Maya frowned and pulled the door shut on her way out.

Jasper gave Hattie a warm hug as she started to cry. "It's okay," he said. "You and I both know it had to be done."

"I know," she assured, burying her face into Jasper's chest. "But a part of me's gone missing..."

"Yeah. I know how you feel." Jasper began to stare at the wall, where a grand portrait of him had appeared, depicting him as the lord of the manor.

Their butler returned, informing the young couple that their coronation was scheduled for that afternoon.

* *

First, Commander Tommy called Dr Hans up to the stage. The ex-chemist told them all the expected news – his annual findings proved that Disease X still persisted in the air. He read a few obscure, jargon-filled excerpts from his papers, explaining the methods of his research. Tommy slapped him on the back, thanked him, and allowed the scientist to return to his seat.

Finally, it was Tommy's turn to take the spotlight. It was time to release those simmering words. He took a deep breath, and finally, allowed his lips to run loose.

"The rats are back. The rats are back. They've done it now. Those bastards. Those bastards." Tommy grabbed a cup of water with his shaky hand and took a massive gulp. A rattling sigh escaped from his nostrils, amplified by the microphone.

"You know these people. You know what they've done. We're the last bastions, and you all understand that, don't you?" He scanned the audience's faces, but their reaction was ambiguous. "Don't you?!" he screamed, leading to a stunned silence. He raised his hands with righteous anger. "Those bastards – don't you know what they did?! They butchered our boys! They took all our labour away, and now they'll force us to starve!"

The crowd became stirred. Tommy bared his teeth and went on:

"We must ration from now – it's an unfortunate fact! But don't forget who forced my hand! The ones who hate you! The globalist rats!"

The projector screen flashed with an image of Dani Dalton, sitting in a circle with other former world leaders. She grinned at the camera with a sinister, doctored look.

"They orchestrated it all! They took our lives away! They took everything we had, and now she, she wants to take what little remains!"

Tommy jabbed his finger at the image of Dani Dalton's pixelated face. A long pause ensued as the crowd seethed and breathed, processing the weight of it all.

"All of it," said Tommy, soothing himself with a deep inhale, "all of this could've been avoided, but for the dark hearts of the Élite..."

The audience shuffled in their seats. A collective sense of despair washed over them.

"This deliberate outbreak – make no mistake, they'd been planning it for a very long time. *Agenda 35*. And the *Cabal* certainly got what they wanted. But I ask you now – after everything, after all the attempts they've made, will you sit back and surrender your lives to these vermin?"

The slideshow switched to a gruesome image of Tiger's mutilated body, sprawled halfway out the window of a wrecked car. "Will you sit there and take it while Ms Dalton does this to our children?!"

The young children in the audience, already sobbing, escalated into shrieks of horror at the sight of this ghastly image.

"Our children," said Tommy, "our dear, dear children. Yes – she's coming for them too. She hates what we have, our joy, our innocence – in their minds, the *Retreaters* tell themselves, if they can't have these things then we can't either! But we will! We will! I shan't let them deprive us of our future!"

The crowd clapped and cheered with thunderous applause. Some of the adults had begun to wail, including Hattie. All that pain – the loss of her friends, their betrayals, and the life she'd been denied by that terrible pandemic – that excruciating pain pulsed through her veins and made its way out her lungs, screaming, screaming and screaming, hysterically, as she ceded control to that wonderful orator. Commander Tommy's words were like a song, the way he composed them. Tommy carried on with his passionate cries:

"And we have hope! We have leads! That vile boy, X, he's our way in. I know it, we can sniff him out..." Tommy nodded to himself. "Yes. Our efforts won't be fruitless. The whole country must be searched. No stone in these lands shall remain unturned. And we will not stop," said Tommy, wagging his finger, "not this time. Make no mistake: these people are past it now – pure evil. This, I tell you, shall be the final push. Oh, what a relief it shall be to be rid of all this – this, our heavy, heavy burden!"

The crowd clapped in unison. The Scouts stood to their feet to give an ovation and were joined by the rest of the Bunker. Tommy smiled into the crowd. "Thank you. Thank you." He revelled in the praise for a while, then gestured for them to hush and be seated. "Today, I want you to remember the dead. I want you to think on the lives that those scumbags took from us. But in spite of it all, don't let those bastards bring you down. That's what they want, isn't it? They want you to wallow in fear and dread; they want you to lose your love for this world. Do not let them take this from you. Don't ever give in!"

The crowd murmured in agreement.

"My friends – go back to your lives, rejuvenated. Live all your days as if they're the last. This, I say, shall be our rebellion. Our hearts burn with an endless summer, while theirs, theirs remain cold, rotten, riddled with parasites. Be grateful for this place, for it's ours and ours alone: this, the last stand of humanity; the only chance we have against the powers that be!"

Another round of applause, and the Commander was done. His officials followed him as he left the Sports Hall. The Scouts walked down the aisle, as did the regular citizens, who headed off back to their ordinary affairs.

* *

The World King sat in his opulent court. The air was thick with tension and the scent of ancient stone. He listened as his new personal adviser, Mr Carr, informed him of ongoing events in the 'Thousand-Day War'.

"Tommy's forces are soon to arrive at the shores. Wha' on Earth shall we do, sir?"

Jasper reflected for a moment. "What would Dani have done?"

"Well," said Donald, "a' imagine she would've launched a recruitment drive. She would've enacted the Draft."

"No, no," said Jasper, dismissively waving his hand, "I won't have that. Let not the common man partake in the Élite's struggle." Donald's brow raised in awe at the King's profound words. "Instead," Jasper added, "I believe we must find new innovations. New strategies. Do you think that is wise?"

"Most certainly," said Donald, diligently bowing his head. "And wha' were you thenkin' in terms of specifics?"

"I was thinking," said Jasper, "that we could launch a wave of terror on Tommy's realm. Make them feel isolated. Like they're trapped on a desert island, with no escape."

"Interestin'..." Donald nodded to himself. "Interestin'..."

"Perhaps the use of a tactical weapon. Yes; I think this can be justified." Jasper scratched his chin. "After all they've inflicted on us..."

Donald smiled. "A' completele' agree." He patted his King on the arm. "Ye know, a' always believed en ye, laddie."

Jasper smiled back, though his eyes were filled with a lingering sadness.

"You were one of the few."

Donald bowed his head, then strolled off. Jasper stood up from his throne and went to visit the new Queen Consort in their shared chambers.

Mrs Huxley looked up from her book. She put it down and stood from her corner chair, giving the King a warm hug. Jasper gazed into her soft blue eyes. She stepped away and began to apply a thin layer of makeup, while her King took a steamy shower. They were preparing for the ball that evening. Although Jasper would have much preferred a cosy night in with the love of his life, appearances were there to be kept, and there were people from the past to be proven wrong.

* *

19:24

Hattie finished her shift in the medical wing, exhausted and scatter-brained. It had been a long day of tending to and monitoring the patients. Thankfully, they'd all been discharged, aside from Dennis, who remained in critical condition.

Dr Andersen and Dr Jones were to stay overnight to keep a close eye on the wounded Scout, while Hattie, Mateo and Eva were allowed to head to bed. At present, Hattie was strolling by herself through Level 12-A, locating her room at the far end of the hall.

She threw off her work clothes and searched in her cupboard for her new swimming costume, given to her by the Bunker's stylists. She covered up with a silky red dress before applying makeup and a dash of rose-scented perfume. Grabbing her mobile and using the local Bluetooth network, Hattie sent the following text to Noah:

Up in a min. Can't wait to see you :)

Immediately, Noah tapped out a response.

me too. tonights gonna be sick...

Hattie smiled to herself and left the room. The ceiling lights continued to buzz, illuminating the vivid artwork that covered her walls.

* *

Jasper and Hattie stepped into a familiar scene from their past.

This time, circumstances were rather different. Jasper was attending the summer ball as a VIP. The crowds stared and gawped at the King and Queen as they strolled arm in arm, making their way to the serving station. The people in the queue dispersed to make way for them. Jasper poured Hattie some wine, and for himself, took a glass of whiskey and ice. They clinked glasses and proceeded to sip on their drinks.

Despite his new rank and status, Jasper couldn't help but feel sick with insecurity, feeling the eyes of the attendees fix on his Queen. In her silky blue dress and her hair braided back, the young lady resembled a Disney princess.

"Alright, Jassy?" exclaimed Tiger, slapping Jasper on the shoulder. He jolted and turned around. Tiger grinned at him.

"Lookin' dapper," he said, admiring the frills of Jasper's tux.

"Thank you, Trevor." Jasper looked away. Tiger went to greet Hattie, taking her hand and giving it a kiss. Resentment stabbed at Jasper's heart as Tiger flirted with his Queen, but familiar inhibitions clamped his mouth shut. At last, Jasper downed his drink, and, asking *MaxSimi* to give him some extra courage, rolled up his sleeves and grabbed Tiger by the scruff of the neck.

"STAY IN YOUR LANE!" spat Jasper. The entire hall fell silent as they looked upon the unfolding scene.

Tiger burst out with a nonchalant chuckle. "Ooh, Jassy here thinks he's 'ard cos his mind made him King!"

Jasper slapped Tiger in the face. Stunned, Tiger fell back and clasped his cheek, which had swollen red with pain. He looked up at Jasper.

"What the fuck?!"

Tiger proceeded to lunge at Jasper, tackling him to the ground.

"HELP! HELP!"

Two security staff came and dragged a kicking and screaming Tiger away. Jasper stood up, adjusted his hair and shrugged his shoulders as if nothing had happened.

"Are you alright?" asked Marcus, who was hovering nearby.

"Yeah, yeah," said Jasper. "I'm fine." Raising his arms to appeal to the others, he proceeded to tell a joke about how he "could do with another drink". The crowd roared with laughter. Jasper smiled proudly to himself. He caught Hattie's eye, and the two shared an intense stare. Hattie beamed at him with palpable admiration. Jasper felt a surge of longing in that moment and, as the ball returned to its ambient chatter, he approached her and leaned in for a sloppy kiss. The two stood together, making a lewd display of their affection. Jasper looked up to check if Marcus was watching. And there he was. The poor chap stood with his hands in his pockets, with the angsty look of one who'd been replaced. Jasper smirked and returned to Hattie's lips, pressing against them, until at last, he pulled away and, speaking over his shaky breath, asked Hattie if she would like to go somewhere private. The girl nodded with enthusiasm, and the two strolled out of the Hall, making their way down to Level 5.

The two entered Jasper's grand, stately room, and dropped down together at the end of the king-sized bed. They smooched for a while, enveloped in each other's arms, before they engaged in two minutes of passion, which culminated in Jasper finishing early.

* *

When Hattie knocked on Noah's door and entered his chambers, she was greeted by the scent of rosy candles. Noah was sitting on his bed, dressed in a frilled dinner suit which covered his swimming trunks.

The two opened a couple of Sparrowman Brews, and clinked bottles, before sipping away on the aromatic beer. Hattie checked her little pink watch.

"When's our food coming?" she said, letting out a playful sigh and twirling a strand of her hair. Noah glanced at her, the corners of his lips curling into a smile.

"We've got a while still."

He set his beer down and took a deep breath. At last, he leaned in to give Hattie a snog. As they lost themselves in the warmth of each other's embrace, Tommy's painting watched sternly from the door. The room was filled with the sound of soft moans and loud grunts.

Fifteen minutes later, Hattie and Noah lay smiling in each other's arms, but their intimate moment was shattered by a knock. Both scrambled to put their clothes back on. A member of the dining team came in through the door, wheeling in a cart topped with two silver domes. The dinner lady told them both to "enjoy", and the couple were left to eat their steak platters in peace.

18
No Legacy

Jasper woke up from his day-long *MaxSimi* dream, and removed the tight hood from his head. He stretched his arms, stood up, and with a spring in his step, made his way over to the bright kitchen. Dani and Ashley were inside, sitting at the counter, munching on stale rolls of chemical bread.

"Alright, lad?" Ashley asked. "What're you after?"

"Just water."

"Alright." Ashley cleared his throat. "How're you finding it so far?"

Jasper bent his head beneath the tap. He took a big swig, released a satisfied breath, then wiped his mouth dry. "I just had the best dream of my life."

"Glad to hear it," said Ashley with a smile.

Jasper glanced at Dani, whose gaze lingered on the floor. The lady finally straightened her back and wiped her weary eyes. "I apologise for my outburst earlier. I'm not sure where it came from."

"Don't worry," Jasper said, shaking his head. "I know you've lost a lot..."

Dani nodded solemnly.

"But," chirped Ashley, "there's always a way to get it back."

"Doubtful," said Dani. Jasper took a deep breath and, grabbing a stool, sat down with the two Retreaters.

"Tommy's shafted us all."

"And that'll be his undoing," Ashley declared.

"Perhaps in a few more decades," said Dani, taking an idle sip of coffee, "the natural order of things will return."

"Decades?"

"That's right."

Jasper furrowed his brow. "But – what about in the meantime? Why did you even break us out? It can't have been for nothing..."

"Breaking all of you out was the one chance we had to turn the tides. Cripple their farm and build ourselves a proper army. But we failed. And when I look at you all, I don't see capable soldiers. I'm sorry. Besides, there's just not enough of us to make a difference."

Jasper crossed his arms, bewildered by Ms Dalton's pessimism. "But you don't need numbers in this fight. This war's about strategy, not attrition. That's what I understand."

"And you'd be correct," said Dani, "but they're doubtless going to re-arm. We got lucky with our armoured truck; caught them off guard. But next time we go back, it won't be Jeeps that'll chase us, it'll be bloody tanks."

"Perhaps they won't wise up to what we're doing," said Ashley, though his eyes betrayed his doubt.

"Don't be ridiculous." Dani sighed. "I guarantee you: we will be outclassed next time. There's no need to deny it. I already know this war's all but over. Seizing the boy – seizing Marcus – when we encountered him alone in that yard, it gave us a little spark of hope, but in the end, this war has but two outcomes. One, we stay in hiding. We get to live in peace. Perhaps Tommy's regime will fall apart by itself. Two, we go out guns-a-blazing. Try and do the job ourselves. But we would get ourselves killed in the process," Dani said, scratching her scaly neck. "I know which one I'd prefer."

"Yeah..." said Jasper, "it's certainly *easier* to sit and do nothing, isn't it." Dani looked at him with suspicion. Jasper continued:

"I've been taking the path of least resistance all my life. Still got nothing to show for it."

Dani scoffed. "I'm not being a coward. I'm being a realist. One has to know when to give up."

Jasper peered over at Ashley, who remained silent, anticipating what the young lad had to say.

"Believe me, I myself have been a 'realist' too." Jasper nodded to himself. "I've denied myself things that should have been mine. I tell myself all these elaborate stories for why I can't get what I want. It's too risky; maybe another day; perhaps I don't deserve it..."

His face was etched with a lingering pain.

"Spent eighteen years like that – a rational coward. I could've been so much more... I could've become who I've always been, deep down. But by circumstance, and by choice – I felt like the world was

plotting against me. But it wasn't. I just never took enough chances."
His mind returned to all those late-night events and the times when
he and Hattie had been close. Jasper, too scared to ruffle feathers,
had always been stifled and inhibited in her presence. "There's so
much more to this miserable life – if only we took a stand..."

Dani reflected for a moment. Her stomach rose with each breath
she took through her nose. At last, in a hoarse, muted tone, she gave
a response:

"What exactly are you suggesting...?"

Jasper shrugged, unsure of the specifics. "I don't know," he said,
placing his hands on the table. "But it seems to me like we've got to
play this smart. Hit Tommy where it really hurts."

"Like the dam," said Ashley.

"No." Dani crossed her arms over her chest. "I've already told you,
that's never going to work."

"Why not?" asked Jasper.

"Because," said Dani, "there are too many things that could go
wrong. There's no guarantee it would play out how we think. It
might well solidify Tommy's power. But even if it didn't... we'd be
returning to a Bunker with no water or electricity."

"So what?"

"I could never rule over such a place."

"But what about the Retreat?" Jasper gestured towards the open
door. Outside, long rows of hospital beds stood, the vast majority of
which remained unoccupied. "Why not bring them back here?"

"Five hundred mouths to feed..." said Ashley. "We'd run out of
supplies pretty damn quick..."

"But we could seize the Estate too – produce whatever food we
needed." Jasper smiled at them both. "Come on... you know this
could work. Why are you acting like it won't? I thought this was
what you wanted!"

Dani pressed her eyes shut. "I just can't... it's just—"

Jasper laughed incredulously. "But what?! Come on, why won't
you believe me?"

Ashley looked at Jasper with concern. Dani opened her bloodshot
eyes, which were welling with tears.

"Last time we tried something like this – five years ago – my two
boys, and the last of my colleagues – my lifelong friends... all of them

were slaughtered. And I was the one who organised the charge. But I messed up. And I got them all killed. These things, you play them out in your head... you imagine the joy that comes when they're done... but in the end, it'll never turn out how you want it to."

There was a moment of silence. Dani stood up to leave. Jasper implored:

"Let me try. Just let me take a stab at this."

Dani stopped in her tracks.

"Yeah." Jasper's voice was full of resolve. "I'll take full responsibility."

"Kid," said Ashley through clenched teeth, "you have no idea what you're getting into..."

"No, no, I do." Jasper stared at the ceiling. "I just can't let this life pass me by. You might be happy to spend your days reliving the past. But for me – I've got nothing. Nothing. And that's got to change. It has to. I won't let my future be wasted away." Jasper looked over to Dani. Dani reflected for a moment. At last, she looked into Jasper's eyes and smiled with faint admiration.

"Ashley," she began, "go and wake the others up, would you?"

Ashley nodded, glancing at Jasper. He passed through the door and headed down the aisle, rousing the sleepers from their *MaxSimi* dreams.

* *

21:24

In the makeshift dining room, Jasper sat at one end of the long table. Dani sat opposite, while the others took the chairs on the sides.

"Now," said Ashley, turning to the freed slaves, "Jasper's got a plan he'd like to share with you all."

Jasper took a deep breath, clasping his hands together. "Well," he started, "I just think – we can't sit about here for the rest of our lives, not doing anything about our situation..."

"Why not?" hissed Sue, folding her sturdy arms. "What's wrong with this place?"

"Let him talk," said Maya. She gave Jasper an admiring look, which caused him to freeze up in his seat.

"You alrigh'?" asked Crispin.

Jasper, petrified, broke away from Maya's gaze. "Yeah, yeah, fine..." He cleared his throat. "What I'm saying is, there's erm, there's nine of us here. I think that's enough for us to really do something – something against the Bunker..."

Marcus's eyes seemed curious, as he watched Jasper intently. Jasper continued:

"Ashley, Ashley said we could blow up the dam – that would really make a statement..."

Gareth grimaced with disgust, as if to say, 'such a vile proposal'. Ashley noticed this, and asked, "Got something you wanna add?

Furious, Gareth gnashed his teeth and declared:

"You know what you are, Ashley Mirza? You're an evil scumbag!"

Dani looked up, and, with a slow, sharp movement, leaned over the table to thwack Gareth in the face.

"Se'le down!" said Crispin, after Gareth started growling like an angry shih tzu. "They've done a lo' for us, these Retrea'ers." He then turned to his pal, Jonathan, and, imagining that the old judge had something to say, asked for his opinion on the matter.

"Well," said the judge, twirling his silky grey hair, "history shows that revolutions must be planned carefully. Toppling an oppressor – you must understand, this isn't a mere intellectual exercise. It's something that must be done pragmatically, with great forethought and precision."

"Damn straigh'!" said Crispin, violently ruffling Jonathan's hair. Jonathan shut his eyes with discomfort, but his crusty old lips cracked a smile nonetheless.

"But how could we do it?" asked Marcus.

Jasper scratched his chin. "I don't know. I'm hoping to work out an exact plan with you guys."

Jonathan chimed in once more. "I'm sympathetic to your ideas, young lad. I really am. The things that they did to me – to all of us – so arbitrary, so unjustified..." He shook his head. "But nonetheless, I'm not sure I agree with your proposition. Destroying the dam could have all kinds of repercussions."

"Like what?" said Sue. The portly woman had a certain disdain in her voice, hearing this posh, privileged man speak with such self-assuredness.

"A man like Tommy Smith," he answered, "is not a man you want to have trapped in a corner. A man like that becomes dangerous under pressure."

"I don't understand."

"Well, no surprise there." Jonathan smirked as Crispin hyped him up, grabbing him by the shoulders and shaking him about in his seat.

Sue crossed her arms, before saying that Crispin and Jonathan were both "wankers". Ashley hushed Crispin before he could offer a comeback.

"Enough, enough. Let's keep this sensible." Ashley turned to Jasper. "I think it's a brilliant plan, mate. If we managed to do it, we could have them all out in a flash. There's no way Tommy's regime would survive such a disaster."

"How so?" asked Maya, propping her head in her hand.

Ashley glanced over to Marcus, then fixed his gaze on Maya. His eyes flickered with excitement. "Marcus tells me that it's the Scouts who hold all the power in the Bunker. Tommy's foot-soldiers. If they were to stage a revolt, the officials would be powerless to stop it. But Tommy keeps the men in line with all those privileges, what, just for being young and having a willy?"

Sue groaned with resentment. "Bunch of wankers, the lot of them."

"Right," said Ashley, "and it seems to me, based on what the kid's told me" – here, he nodded at Marcus, who was busy examining his fingers – "based on what I've heard, the Commander controls the people with two things. The stick – well, you already know all about that, I'm sure."

"Yup," said Crispin with a sigh.

"But on the other hand, you've got the carrot. Rewards for toeing the line."

"It's all about the lifestyle," said Marcus. "That's what Tommy offered us. We do his bidding, we be his soldiers, and he'll give us anything we want."

"Yeah." Crispin rubbed his palms. "Li'e a deal wiv' the devil, innit." He turned to Gareth. "Isn' that righ'? Bloody ridiculous, 'ow unfair it is, eh Gazza?"

Crispin's stony face became tinged with a furious flush. Crispin continued to prod the bitter lad:

"The way they fuckin' turned ya down, even when ya finished top on all of Jackson's tests... Christ, I remember ya, gettin' the 'ighest scores in shootin' I've ever seen..."

Gareth clenched his fists, his chest rising with each indignant breath.

"Come on, ma'e, they dun' give a damn abou' ya... Tommy certainly don't. And y'had every righ' to act the way you done, when he said you was a reject."

Gareth pressed his eyes shut. His nostrils flared in, and out, as he inhaled, and exhaled. At last, his dry lips peeled open, and the others were left at the edge of their seats while he psyched himself up to declare:

"I suppose Tommy's just a bit of an arsehole, really."

Crispin smirked, having achieved his intended result.

"But I *still* don't agree with you bunch of half-wits."

"Right then." Ashley cleared his throat. "Where were we?"

"The dam," said Dani. "The importance of lifestyle."

"Ah, that's right. Yes." Ashley drummed the table with his hands. "We get rid of electricity, we get rid of the water supply – no one will want to stay in there any longer. Sooner or later, they'll come up for air. Especially since we've taken one of their fuel shipments – they can't rely on their backup generator to keep things going."

"Erm, excuse me?" Gareth crossed his arms. "Aren't you forgetting something? You know, the killer disease X that's lurking in the air?"

The other slaves bellowed out with laughter. Maya caught Jasper's eye and shrugged her shoulders to mock Gareth's naivety. Jasper responded with a nervous chuckle.

"Yeah. In case it wasn't obvious – it's gone. It's cleared. There ain't no fuckin' lurgy in the air – not these days, in any case." Ashley crossed his arms. "You've all been fed a bunch of lies..."

"It's an absolute disgrace," said Jonathan, "all that rubbish Tommy spews out to keep people trapped in there." He released a heavy sigh. "It sickens me to say it – but one can't help but admire what he's achieved. All the systems he's put into place."

"So le's tear 'em apart!" exclaimed Crispin. "Build a big bomb – ma'e the dam go *boom* – then wai' for the Scou's to turn on all 'em pricks. Fuck Tommy, fuck Noah, fuck the rest of 'em, too. Me, I'd pay good money to see 'em die in a slow sor' of way." He let out an odd, repetitive chuckle, which sounded like the howls of an agitated fox.

"But you could never predict how this thing would turn out," said Dani. "Tommy might cling to power. Or we might end up with someone even worse in his place."

"Exactly," said Sue. "You lot are a bit bloody sure of yourselves, aren't you, thinking you can pull this off without nothing going wrong."

"Oh, enough wiv' it now, you miserable bint!" Crispin snapped, "all you do is mope abou' an' complain! Why dun' you come up wiv' a fresh fuckin' idea, then?!"

Infuriated, Sue shot up from her chair, ready to exchange blows with Crispin. Ashley had to intervene, standing up to pacify her while Crispin bellowed with mocking laughter. As chaos ensued, Jasper rubbed his weary eyes and, in a moment of impulse, whistled sharply with his fingers. The room fell silent. All eyes turned towards him.

"Can I speak?! This is *my* meeting." A deliberate pause ensued. The whirs of distant machines filled the silence. "None of us wanted to end up here. But that's where we're at. And we've got two choices – we can live out our lives, miserable, always longing for more, or we can actually *do* something about it!"

Marcus and Crispin mumbled their agreement. Undeterred, Jasper continued:

"And yes, things can go wrong. And yes, things don't always pan out as expected. But who are *you* to judge?" He shot a glance at Sue. "You used to peddle drugs to kids. For extra sandwiches. Fucking sandwiches! But you want to challenge *me* for saying we should take a risk?"

Sue's gaze fell to the floor. There was a passing of shame in her eyes. After a moment's pause, Jasper posed a question to Ashley and Dani. "Do you really enjoy living like this? Trapped underground, living in a fantasy, hoping that things will magically improve themselves? Because I sure as hell don't." His gaze swept across the room. "This life – it's a stale one. There's no zest to it. Just comfort, just pleasure. One that, in the end, will never really last. We can't go on like this, plagued by quiet resentment, with nothing to look forward to apart from *MaxSimi* dreams."

"And what's wrong with those machines?" asked Sue. "I think they're bloody brilliant."

"I know they are," said Jasper, "but they're dangerous, too. They'll mess with our heads if we use them too long." He stared at Dani and assessed her face. Once a bold and alluring Prime Minister: now a sour old lady who resembled a crackhead. "Every now and then, you wake up, realising – you need to make a change. And today was that day for me." He swallowed hard. "I've got little to show for my time here on Earth. I don't want to die like that. All of us: we have the potential to make things better, to have our names written down in the history books! This plan – to take down Tommy, to blow up the dam – this could be our 'Great War'. Be rid of a tyrant, and restore Dani as ruler of the U.K., and set an example for the rest of the world. Show everyone that, despite everything that we've lost, humanity lives to see another day..."

As Jasper fell silent, everyone stared down at their feet, save for Dani, whose eyes were kindling with a long-lost passion. She played with one of her tear-shaped earrings.

"Well, Jasp," she said with a wide, toothy grin, "you certainly make a hell of an argument."

"He certainly does," agreed Ashley. "Got a way about him, this one." His brown cheeks flushed red. The air was charged with a current of optimism. Marcus patted Jasper on the arm.

"Blimey," he chuckled. "Where did that come from, then?"

Jasper shrugged. "I just... can't stand to see injustice, I suppose." Marcus nodded, but his gaze lingered on Jasper with a hint of scepticism.

"Right then," said Jasper, drumming his fingers on the table. "Let's get to work on this thing."

"Right-o," said Ashley.

The group began brainstorming ways to execute their plan. The discussion was led by Jasper, Dani, and Ashley. Crispin contributed with the occasional witticism while Jonathan offered words of wisdom. Maya regarded the others with a smile as they tried to show off their knowledge of military strategy, while Sue sulked with her sturdy arms folded. Gareth remained quiet, and Marcus, despite his occasional contributions, felt deeply unnerved by it all. The way Jasper spoke of killing Scouts as though it were a dispassionate chore. The way Mrs MacNair fawned over Jasper, despite being twenty years his senior. And, most disturbing of all, the way Jasper spoke with such self-assurance. His confident gestures, his hearty laughter, and his commanding aura sickened Marcus to the core. And Marcus grew even more bitter still, observing his meek friend over the course of that meeting, as he finally came into his element.

19
Forget the Past

Strolling through Level 2-B, Hattie and Noah made their way towards the pool. Both wore swimming gear under their dinner clothes.

"I'm still not sure about this," said Hattie, clutching her man's arm. "You sure he'll mind if we don't show our faces?"

"Gotta be done," Noah insisted. "Besides, you'll be fine. Just a chill one tonight, I promise."

At last, they reached the entrance to the pool, where the party was soon to take place. Noah swung the door open.

The massive room was dimly lit. The pristine pool glowed with a turquoise hue. Along its edge, several tables had been set up, where Pete was already sitting, alone.

Hattie and Noah made their way over, their clogs echoing against the wet, tiled floor. They both took their seats at one of the ornate tables, which resembled furniture from an antique garden.

"Alright?" said Pete, who was smoking a fat cigar. His left eye was covered with a pirate's patch. "Good dinner with the missus?"

"Yeah." Noah patted Pete on the arm. "You're looking good, my friend."

"Cheers." Pete flicked his head towards Hattie. "This one's a fuckin' hero, in't she."

Hattie responded with a reluctant smile. Pete gave her a lustful look, then turned as Dr Hans and Eva entered the room. Dr Hans gave everyone a naïve, childish wave. He scurried over excitedly, almost slipping on the floor in the process. His wife struggled to keep up.

Dr Hans took the seat next to Hattie and greeted her cordially. Before Eva sat down next to her husband, Hattie gave her an awkward nod. The attendees began to exchange small talk. Next to arrive was Mr Jackson, whose appearance Hattie always found rather amusing. She smirked to herself. With his bristly moustache and wide brown eyes, the man looked like an angry drill sergeant, though he was generally alright when you spoke to him one-on-one. Hattie's smile, however, was quickly wiped away as Bobby and Melissa entered through the door.

Dragging Bobby by the arm, Melissa paced her way over, her ginger hair wafting with each elegant step. She leered down at Hattie and gave her a frosty greeting, before leaning to give Noah a hug and a kiss on the cheek. As she did this, Hattie felt a pang of nausea. She looked over at Bobby, who lingered like a lost child. He fiddled with his bandaged wrist until Melissa led them both to sit down.

The party poured themselves drinks and, after a few minutes, the atmosphere lightened. Everyone became a little livelier. Nonetheless, Hattie kept her guard up, for she knew who was soon to arrive.

The party fell silent as the door swung open once more. The rest of the officials streamed into the room.

Tommy, Ted, Davey and Eddie entered one-by-one. Each man was dressed in a frilly tuxedo. Freddy hadn't shown up, as he was currently stationed on watch at the Estate. The checkpoint on Level 5 had been left unmanned. Ted turned around and gestured for another person to step inside. Hattie's heart sank upon seeing that it was Tiger's mum, Prim.

The procession of officials made their way towards the tables. The others stood up and exchanged hearty greetings. Tommy went around shaking everyone's hand. When he got to Hattie, he paused, sized her up for a moment, then took her dainty hand and kissed it softly.

Tommy instructed everyone to be seated. Prim continued to stand. She was dressed in a tattered garment, her red-dyed hair dishevelled and faded. Her eyes bore a hollow expression.

Tommy stood in front of everyone and, ceremoniously, cracked open a fresh bottle of whiskey. He poured a glassful, raising his drink for a toast.

"I'd like to thank you all for your service. These last few weeks haven't been easy. But each of you, in spite of it all, you've shown excellent spirit. You've all done excellent work. And for that, I thank you." Tommy gave a pleasant smile. "To the Bunker!"

"To the Bunker." Everyone took a sip of their drinks. Tommy sat down and propped his feet up. He ordered Prim to kneel and massage his feet. She obliged him. Hattie tried to catch Melissa's eye, whose gaze trailed off in the distance. Meanwhile, Bobby was sitting with his shoulders hunched and his neck bent over. Hattie observed him closely; the discomfort in his eyes was palpable. She felt a pang of sympathy for the man, who, evidently, was a touch out of his depth.

The air reeked with the stench of cannabis. Tommy had lit a joint and was passing it around with his officials.

"You sure you want to do that?" warned Eddie, as Little Ted took it into his hands. "What about last time?"

"Leave him be," said Tommy, with a certain nonchalance in his tired voice. Prim was busy rubbing his ankles. "Can a man not make his own choices?" He nodded at Ted, who, in turn, took a drag from the blunt. He exhaled a thick cloud and let out a hearty cough. His eyes, already watering, turned bloodshot.

Hattie, meanwhile, began to feel tense with unease. She shot an anxious glance at Noah.

"What?" He took a sip of his beer.

Hattie leaned into his ear. "You said this was going to be a 'chill one'..."

"It is," said Noah.

"What's the matter?" asked Pete, his gaze becoming fixed on Hattie once more.

Noah shrugged his shoulders. "I dunno. She seems a bit strung-up, doesn't she." Hattie gave Noah a look of bewilderment. While taking a drag of the joint, he met her gaze and returned it with a vacant stare.

"Nothing to worry about, my dear," insisted Pete. "You're among friends now." He licked his lips at the girl and returned to his chatter with Big Davey. Noah took another hit and offered Hattie the blunt. She declined.

"Oh, come on," he said, cracking a smile. "Don't be such a wuss-puss."

The other men chuckled. Hattie's heart fluttered, her skin becoming clammy with sweat under the expectant eyes of the attendees. Finally, she gave into their demands and took a tiny puff of weed. Everyone laughed and broke into sarcastic applause.

"Wasn't so hard, was it?" teased Noah. As if paralysed, Hattie's face froze into a nervous, twitchy smile.

"Are you alright?" Melissa asked, leading everyone to stare at the timid young woman. Melissa gave Hattie a scornful look and added, "I think there's something wrong with her..."

In search of support, Hattie turned to Noah. But her man, nonchalant, was engrossed in his phone. "So, Hans," he said, "what's, like, your favourite ever drug?"

Dr Hans gulped. "What, to make?"

Noah put his phone away. "To take!"

The men erupted in boisterous laughter. Eva appeared to tense, anticipating her husband's response.

"Well," said Dr Hans, "when I was a student, I must confess, I did try a little tab of... how you say it on the street – is it Mary? Or Molly? MDMA, anyway... hmph, this experience was very... *interesting*, yes?"

The others cried out with a sarcastic "Oooooooh!", acting all impressed.

"You're a nutter!" Jackson laughed.

"Off the rails," Pete added.

Dr Hans smiled sheepishly. "Or perhaps it was ketamine. That horse tranquiliser really make me 'gallop', eh-heh!"

"Oooh, yaaas!" said Noah, mocking Hans' German accent. Hattie gave her boyfriend a disapproving look, scolding him for his thinly-veiled cruelty.

Dr Hans began to fidget with his hands. "But yes, erm... what I can say is that this batch of LSD I have produced, I hope you all agree that it's—"

"So, anyway," Tommy interjected, belching a little, "I was thinking, you deserve more appreciation, my friend. If you don't mind me saying – and Eva, I hope you won't mind either – I think you deserve a little more *excitement* in your life. What'd you say to that?"

Dr Hans didn't respond.

"Prim," continued Tommy, "go and do him a dance, would you please?"

Hans shook his head. "No, really, I... I would rather not—"

Thumping electro sounds blared from a speaker. On cue, Primrose got up and stumbled over to Dr Hans. Eva folded her arms as the other men roared with laughter. Hattie, mortified, edged her seat away as Primrose leaned over the scrawny scientist. Little Ted, his face flushed, yelled out with vicarious arousal:

"Go on! Give it to him! Give it to him!"

Meanwhile, Hattie was staring at the dimmed ceiling, which rippled with light reflecting from the pool. Dr Hans squirmed in his seat as Primrose gave him the time of his life. A sharp pang welled up in Hattie's throat. She felt an overwhelming urge to dive into the tranquil waters and escape this horrid scene.

Eventually, Tommy called Primrose away. Dr Hans gasped with relief, as if he'd narrowly avoided a drowning.

* *

Twenty minutes later, Hattie found herself caught in a monotonous conversation with Mr Jackson. Noah was in the pool, splashing about with Big Davey, and Melissa. Bobby observed from the side, his casted wrist dangling limply over his lap.

"Recruitment," Mr Jackson barked, "that's how we win this fight. Yeah?" Hattie wiped away a speck of spit from her cheek. Jackson carried on spluttering:

"The lads from '18 and '19 are near ready to go. I've fast-tracked their training. And of course, we're reassessing all the rejects, too. That Mateo Dacosta bloke seems a good bet. But we'll have to see how he fares in the re-takes, of course."

Before Hattie could respond, Mr Jackson had already pressed ahead. "And women. Yep – even the women. Might take a few to training; see which ones have what it takes to be Scouts. Would you be interested in that?"

"No, no!" Tommy cried from his lounger, "that most certainly won't be happening!" He laughed and returned to his magazine.

"Of course, sir!" barked Jackson, who turned back to Hattie. "Boss always gets what he wants. But me, I believe in equality. Level the playing field, yep, no qualms with that. However," he raised his voice, "I won't have any of that Femi-Nazi tosh those woke celebs used to spew, yeah? Not for me, thank you very much, yeah?!"

"Too bloody right!" said Teddy, flicking his butane lighter. "To hell with that kind of thing!"

"Precisely!" said Jackson. He gave Hattie a wink, then stood up and dove into the pool. Hattie was left alone, clutching a lukewarm cup of wine.

As Pete began to approach her, Hattie held her breath. But she let out a relieved sigh as Eva pulled up a chair next to her and shot Pete a fierce look. Pete span on his heel and re-entered the pool, climbing down the metal ladder.

"What a fucking creep," Eva muttered. She took a prolonged swig from her cup of whiskey. Her eyes were glazy and unfocused. "Whole lot of them are. 'Inner circle', I don't care, they can fuck right off."

Hattie sat with her arms folded, observing Noah as he swam with Melissa tailing behind, who cackled while splashing him with water.

"But," Eva continued, "I think you've lucked out with that Noah. He's a good lad, really."

Hattie couldn't help but crack a smile as Noah carried on swimming in circles around the pool, ignoring Melissa's splashes. At last, she turned her gaze to Eva. "You think so?"

"Most definitely." Eva gestured towards Tommy, careful not to catch his eye. "Especially considering who his daddy is."

"True." Hattie let out a quiet chuckle. "Yeah. Noah and I have got a lot in common. All his nasty behaviour – I know it's all an act. I hope so, anyways."

"All an act," Eva echoed. Before the two women could say anything further, they were forced to seal their lips as Little Ted and Eddie Lee took seats at a nearby table.

A few moments later, Dr Hans re-entered the room, holding a small green briefcase.

"A-ha!" exclaimed Tommy, rising from his lounger. "What have we here?"

The partygoers all stood and swarmed around a table, where Dr Hans had opened his case. Inside was a large batch of drugs – LSD tablets, powdered meth, and tramadol pills, each placed in little sealed baggies. Hattie felt nauseous, watching as Tommy stared down at the stash and licked his lips.

"Right," he said, "let's get this thing started, shall we?" He ruffled Dr Hans' bald head and pushed him out of the way before taking everyone's requests. Noah asked for a tablet of LSD, and before Melissa could chime in, Hattie blurted out that she'd like the same. She threw angry daggers at the redheaded fiend, before gazing up at her handsome boyfriend.

"I'm impressed, Hat." Noah smiled with approval. "I didn't think you had it in you." After each received a tablet, they both sat down on a lounger together. Hattie watched Noah as he placed the tablet under his tongue. With her trembling finger, Hattie followed suit.

"How long do we need to wait for?" she asked with a slight lisp.

"'Bout an hour."

The two sat in silence for a while, watching as the others took their pick for the night. Tommy went last, grabbing a bag of crystalline powder. He poured it onto
the table, shaping it into a line.

"He'll be alright," assured Noah. "He's only microdosing."

Hattie raised an eyebrow, disconcerted, as Tommy snorted the ice in one go. Then he laughed, grabbed Little Ted, and tossed him into the pool, before himself went tumbling down into the choppy waters.

* *

Thirty minutes later, Hattie, Noah, Melissa, and Bobby had retreated into the sauna, while the others let loose outside. Melissa was scolding a glassy-eyed Bobby for having allegedly flirted with Eva earlier, while Noah's eyes darted about the place. Hattie was hyperventilating, and her pale skin was riddled with goosebumps.

"It's finally kicking in," said Noah. "I can feel it!"

Melissa turned away from Bobby. The corners of her thin lips curled into a smile.

"What's it like?" she asked, propping her head in her hand.

"It's unbelievable. Wow." Noah cracked a smile. "What about you, Hat? How are you doing?"

Hattie opened her mouth to speak, but found that her words were struggling to come out.

"It's... erm... I'm, it's—"

"Bloody hell," said Melissa, appealing to Noah. "Properly *schlepped*, isn't she?"

Noah observed the petrified girl, and asked if she was alright.

"Y-yes," Hattie managed to stammer, remaining frozen in her seat. Her hair was drenched with sweat from the sauna's heat.

"Err. D'you want to head out, maybe?"

Hattie shook her head.

"I had the same thing on my first trip," said Bobby. "You've just got to think happy thoughts and—"

Melissa shot a hostile glance at her man, who immediately silenced himself.

Hattie, meanwhile, was plagued with terrible visions. The world around her seemed to be melting, and the others' faces were distorting into spirals. A woman's voice cried in her ears, imploring her to be "cautious", for she was in "great danger".

"Mum! Mum!"

The deep bellow of a foghorn sounded from outside. She was overcome by a rush of unease, powerless to stop the bottled-up feelings as they started to rise to the surface.

"She needs to get out of here," said Noah.

Melissa stared at him with beady eyes. "Are you sure?"

"I'm sure." Wrapped in a towel, Noah stood and grabbed Hattie's hand. She recoiled, curling into a corner like a startled animal. In Noah's grey-tainted eyes, she felt she could sense something predatory.

"Hattie... Hattie..."

But she refused to budge. Another horn blew. A vision of her assault flashed before her eyes. She watched herself from a third-person perspective as those vile boys tried to drag her out of the hall, on that fateful night in August 0015.

"Fucking creeps..." she whispered, pointing an accusatory finger at Noah. "You're a fucking creep, just like the rest..."

Noah reached for her hand again, but she slapped it away.

"I'm not," he insisted, "I'm not. I'm just trying to help..."

As if in a dream, Hattie found herself rewatching the trial of her tormentors. Derek Platt and Reece Jenkins. Tommy had sentenced them both to the Estate for their crime. While working up there, Jenkins died of Disease X in November 0016. A wave of grim satisfaction crossed her face as she recalled that Platt too had met his end, contracting the disease in late August of this year.

"It's going to be okay," said Noah. Hattie's mind returned to the room. Her boyfriend's face appeared to soften, and his eyes became a little more colourful. Hattie finally accepted his hand. Noah led her out of the sauna. The two sat down on a bench and dried off, before heading towards the changing room. Meanwhile, Tommy was splashing around the pool in manic laps. Little Ted watched on from the side. A sudden guffaw made Hattie jump. She glanced over at the tables where the men laughed, engaged in mindless banter. Davey, with his arm wrapped affectionately over Hans' back, was spurting out all sorts of nonsense at the scientist, who, for his part, appeared to ignore the fact that Pete was busy licking his lips at Eva, who slumped in her chair, woozy under the spell of alcohol and Hans' tramadol. Eddie was busy sleeping by the poolside, while Primrose sat in a corner, curled in a ball like a traumatised child.

At last, Hattie and Noah reached the door to the locker room, but before he could swing it open, Tommy jumped out of the pool and cried:

"Leaving so soon?"

The room fell silent as the others turned to look. Noah scratched his neck.

"Yeah... it's just... Hattie's not feeling so well."

Tommy dried his hairy body with a towel, and wiped his face.

"First timer, eh?" Tommy gave Hattie a sickly smile. "You'll be fine, my love." He blew her a charming kiss and made his way over to the couple.

"Do you recognise me?" he asked, "do you know who I am?"

Hattie gulped. "You're the Commander..."

Tommy raised his hand. "And how many fingers do you see?"

"Five..."

"There you go," said Tommy, addressing his son, "your lady-friend seems fine to me."

Noah turned to Hattie. The palpable terror in her eyes was evident. Then he turned back to his father.

"It's just – I think she's getting flashbacks. She's had some really nasty things happen in the past."

"Flashbacks, flashbacks." Tommy waved his hand in dismissal. "Listen – we've all got our own shit to deal with. She's really no different to the rest of us."

"But it won't be any fun keeping her here. It'll bring the mood down." Noah fiddled with his wrists. "Please. She needs some time alone, to try and come to her senses."

Tommy folded his arms. At last, he rolled his eyes and allowed the two to go and get changed. Noah grabbed Hattie's arm and led her through the door of the locker room, before gently closing it shut.

The two dressed into proper clothes and headed out. As they strolled through the gloomy corridor, Hattie felt her muscles loosen up. Noah took a deep breath, and clasped Hattie's hand tightly. "He'll want us both to come back at some point – the night's not over yet."

"No," Hattie said, stopping in her tracks and pulling her hand free. "I can't go back in there. I can't."

"But Hattie—"

"ENOUGH!" she boomed, her voice sharp and unfaltering. "Just spare me the constant bullshit, for once!"

Taken aback, Noah stared at Hattie. Hattie returned his gaze, scowling with determination, though the muscles in her face were twitching with adrenaline. On her urging, they retired to his bedroom. The two sat there for the rest of the night while painful memories surged within Hattie's mind. Noah put on a children's cartoon on his plasma TV to try and comfort her. But Hattie paid no attention to the talking animals on the screen. Instead, she chose to stare into her past as it flashed before her eyes, refusing to retreat into mind-numbing distractions.

20
Chinook

One morning in October

The Retreaters were crammed in the back of the Gurkha. Ashley was driving them to their training grounds for the day.

"I still think this is a profoundly stupid idea," hissed Gareth, who was sitting in the back. "But a certain Thatcher wannabe won't listen to reason. Look at her: absorbed in her *gizmos*, as ever."

Dani, sitting in the front, turned around and told Gareth to be quiet, then carried on fiddling with her pronged remote control.

"Such an oddball, you are," muttered Maya, who threw a scathing look in Gareth's direction.

"Yeah, shu'up, twat," laughed Crispin, who thumped Gareth on the chest. "You wan' this jus' as much as the rest of us do. Jus' be honest abou' it, ma'e."

In response, Gareth shot Crispin a furious glare.

"Ooooh, sorry," said Crispin, with mock fear in his voice. He swivelled to look at Marcus and Jasper, who were both sitting together on a separate aisle. "Gazza's in a foul mood today, inn'e!"

"That's odd," quipped Jasper, with a wry smile, "normally a ray of sunshine, that one…"

"Ha! You're no' wrong there, my son." Crispin let out a chortle and turned around once more. "We nearly a' the dam ye'?"

"No," said Ashley. "We've a while to go, still."

Reaching a junction, the black car spun its way around a roundabout before speeding down onto the motorway.

* *

Meanwhile, Hattie was only starting to wake. She'd been fast asleep in Noah's bed, recovering from the acid trip that had kept her up for twelve hours straight.

Hattie rubbed her eyes and opened them to see Noah emerging from the bathroom, steam trailing behind him. He had a towel wrapped around his waist.

"How long was I out for?" Hattie asked, reaching for the glass of water on the bedside table.

"Seventeen hours," Noah replied, rummaging in his cupboard.

"Jesus." Hattie propped herself up and took a sip of water. "Weird night, huh?" she remarked in a nonchalant tone.

Noah turned to Hattie, narrowing his eyes at her.

"Yeah. You were freaking out. It was hard getting through to you; you were so stuck in your own head." As he was getting a pair of boxer shorts from the cupboard, his towel slipped, exposing his rear end. "Do you remember anything?"

Hattie nodded slowly. "It's coming back to me." Under the spell of Dr Hans' LSD, she'd been haunted by the ghosts of her past: the men who'd tried to use her, the cruelty of the Bunker, and the losses she'd accumulated over the years. And no one to guide her through any of it! Noah had been useless throughout the trip, engrossed in blasting his headphones and spouting meaningless drivel every now and then. So the whole experience had been a nightmare. But now – perhaps because her adrenal glands had worn themselves out – Hattie couldn't feel any fear. The memories were still there, sure, but their grip over her had weakened. Her long-standing fog had finally cleared.

"We need to head out soon," said Noah, stepping into some camouflaged trousers. "There's a whole-Bunker assembly after breakfast."

Hattie drank more water. "Why? What's happening?"

Noah, having put on a white T-shirt, leaned against the wall, arms folded. "I have to give a speech," he said, glancing at the floor.

He offered to help Hattie out of bed, but she waved him away. After a quick shower in his ensuite, she put on one of his oversized t-shirts and some tracksuit bottoms. Together, they made their way to the Scouts' dining hall on Level 2-B.

Inside, about two dozen men sat around tables. The remaining Scouts were on the hills, manning vantage points. The mood was sombre. Joining Bobby and Melissa at a table, Melissa gave Noah a smutty smile. She proceeded to witter on about the "wild time" they'd had at the party, and how he and Hattie should've stuck around to see the "happy ending". Bobby, for his part, kept to himself, his head hunched in shame. Hattie turned to Melissa and, taking a deep breath, proceeded to chastise her for the way she rejoiced in making others feel uncomfortable, not least her miserable and long-suffering so-called 'boyfriend'. Melissa's jaw dropped mid-bite, revealing a mouthful of mushy food. She'd never seen Hattie be so honest before.

After eating their scrambled eggs and toast, the group moved to the Sports Hall on 6-B where the Bunker's citizens were gathered. Hattie and Noah took their place on the stage with other officials. Although the entire room's eyes lingered on her face, Hattie felt strangely at ease in the spotlight.

Tommy summoned Noah to the podium. The Chief's voice echoed through the hall, projected by the speakers, as he read from the script that Tommy had written. He proclaimed that today was the "beginning of the end". The Scouts were to undertake a mission to an old military base to source weaponry and equipment, so that they could grow into a "veritable army". Once they'd located everything on their checklist – new ammunition, tanks, explosives, even a helicopter – they'd then proceed to scour the entirety of Britain to "weed out" the Retreaters and get rid of them forever. To power their fight, they would use their emergency fuel reserves, of which they had "plenty", in spite of the "cowardly" attack that had occurred earlier in the month. Then he mumbled something about being a "survivor", how the Retreaters had nearly taken his life but he still remained standing, in spite of their "barbaric" efforts, and in spite of their "tireless persistence". And how the Bunker, too, would end up surviving this threat, thanks to their "brave young soldiers". The Bunker duly applauded and cheered the Chief of Scouts, who returned to his seat next to Hattie. Hattie looked at him through the corner of her eye. She could see that Noah's neck was twitching with adrenaline, and that his palms were layered in sweat.

* *

Down South, the Retreaters were getting busy with their drills at an old Kent reservoir, named Buck's Haven. They had spent the entire morning practising their assault on the Bunker's dam, running up to the wall while Ashley shot at them with rubber pellets. Their task was to set down the 'device' – which currently took the form of a wooden log, as a stand-in for the missile they planned to obtain – against the base of the wall, light it on fire, and avoid getting themselves killed in the process. However, the Retreaters' new recruits, still unaccustomed to combat, had failed each and every round of practice, with Ashley picking them off one by one with relative ease.

Ashley, who had returned from his position on the watchtower, gathered them all into a circle near the slanted wall of the reservoir. Dani was sitting in the Gurkha, zipping her prized drone around the cloudy sky.

"For fuck's sake," said Ashley, "this ain't gonna work if you lot don't up your game..."

"I dunno what you want from us," Sue retorted, crossing her arms as she pulled a chippy face. "We're doing our utmost best..."

"Nah." Crispin, who had his hands in his pockets, started to kick at the grass under his feet. "You're le'in' us down, is wha' *you're* doin'."

"Now, now," said Jasper, "there's no need for that. Let's just stay calm, yeah? We'll get it right eventually..."

"Except, I don't know if you will," said Ashley. "Everyone, aside from Marcus, has fallen totally short. Not sure if you lot are cut out for this."

"'Course we are," said Crispin. "Bu' this whole tactic ain't gonna work. Why're we sendin' these two chicas to help us ta'e the guards ou'? They've go' no fightin' experience, and it shows, dun' it."

Maya shrugged. "Thought *I* did a pretty good job..."

"An' Johnno," said Crispin, slapping the old man on the back. "This one ain't exactly the fi'est bloke in the world, is he? Why're we le'in' him be a par' of the attack?"

There was a long moment of silence. A harsh breeze blew across their faces. Drizzle started to fall over the waters of the reservoir, and, a few seconds later, reached the field where the Retreaters stood. They stepped back into the shelter of the Gurkha, slamming the car doors shut.

"Fuckin' hell," said Ashley, wiping his face with frustration. The car's roof pattered with droplets. "This thing ain't gonna work." Dani glanced over at him as he continued to rant. "Took ages to train the old ministers. Years. And even then, we still couldn't beat the Scouts."

"But we can't give up," said Jasper. "We've got to see this thing through. Or else, what the hell are we going to do for the rest of our lives? Mope about and complain about how unfair it all is? No bloody way – I'm never going back to that frame of mind."

"'Ear, 'ear." Crispin leaned forward to Ashley, and slapped the man on the shoulder. "We've jus' go'a switch gears a bi', dun' we?"

"I dunno." Ashley shook his head. "It's pretty worrying... twenty rounds of practice, not once did you manage to get the device set up..."

Jasper stared into space for a moment, before his eyes sparked up with an idea.

"There's another way to get this done."

Ashley turned around. The others followed suit, anticipating what the lad had to say.

"The problem is that the hill's so well-guarded. I doubt we'd ever win against them, charging up there – especially on foot. But," he said, wagging his finger like an admonishing preacher, "who says that this has to be a direct confrontation?"

"Okay..." said Ashley, "what exactly are you suggesting?"

"Maybe, like, if we do an attack somewhere else?" Maya added. "Get them distracted?"

"Exactly." Jasper pointed his thumb at Maya. "Like a false flag type of thing: that's what I was thinking."

Outside the car, the drizzle began to pass. A ray of sunshine slithered through a gap in the clouds.

While Ashley remained silent, deep in thought, Jonathan spoke up. "I'm not sure what you mean by that, Jasper. A *false flag*?"

Jasper's cheeks turned red. "No, not a false flag – I didn't mean to say that. *Diversion*, that's what I meant."

"I understand, lad." Jonathan gave a patronising smile. "It's important to be precise with our words."

"Great." Jasper rolled his eyes. "Now – I reckon we should try and attack the farm again. Storm through the gates, set fire to the mansion – that sort of thing. Enough to cause a panic. Enough to draw the Scouts away from the Bunker."

"There's no way they'd let the hill go unprotected," said Dani. "There'll always be a few men to deal with."

"Maybe so. But they'll be manageable," Jasper said with a nod. "Ashley could take them out with his sniper."

Ashley shrugged. "I suppose..."

"And then," Jasper continued, "we head up to the dam – try to drive up the valley, if possible – and detonate the missile. Watch as all the water comes gushing out." His eyes lit up with colourful visions. "It'll be incredible. And it won't be that difficult."

"I dunno, mate," said Marcus. "I doubt it'll be as simple as you're trying to make out..."

Defensive, Jasper folded his arms. "Why not?"

"It's just – how's the attack on the Estate gonna work? And what happens if that goes wrong?" Marcus gritted his teeth. "Look. I know you wanna get Tommy really badly – believe me, I do too – but it seems like there are too many things that are completely out of our hands, here."

"Nah." Jasper scoffed. "We'll find a way. Just have to grow a pair. Believe in ourselves for once..."

"Hear, hear," said Jonathan.

"I have to say," said Dani, "I do rather like the sound of Huxley's plan." She turned to Ashley, and asked him what his thoughts were.

"I'm not sure." Ashley crossed his arms. "It might work. But we'll need to think it through, before we jump into anything."

Switching the Gurkha's ignition on, Ashley steered them away from the reservoir, driving through a boggy field. Eventually, they reached the main road, whose broken surface crumbled under the wheels of the car.

* *

Tommy was standing outside the Bunker's gates, clad in a hazmat suit. He watched in awe as a Chinook whirred overhead. The convoy of Scout Jeeps made its way through the heather field, followed by a large, rumbling tank. The helicopter landed on a flat patch of grass. Its blades came to a halt. Two Scouts emerged from the cockpit.

Meanwhile, the procession of Jeeps parked in a line. Noah stepped out to shake his father's hand.

Tommy slapped Noah hard on the back. "Good job, son," he said, his voice seeping through the holes of his mask. "Everything's shaping up nicely..."

The other Scouts stood outside their Jeeps. Tommy strolled over to greet them one-by-one, before running his hand along the surface of the camouflaged tank. The air was heavy with the smell of combustion.

"We'll start the search tomorrow," called Noah, rubbing his gloved hands together. "Beginning with Surrey. There might be clues we didn't see in September."

"No, no. I want this done ASAP," said Tommy. "You'll start tonight. Yes?"

Noah nodded obediently. Tommy smiled once again, and wrapped his son in an embrace. "The Retreaters – listen to me, lad. They're finished. The future's within our reach, you know." Tommy chuckled. "You and what's-her-hame – you're going to churn out some little ones for me now, aren't you?"

Noah swallowed down a gulp. "It's exciting. And, err, yeah. Hattie's a nice girl."

"She certainly is," said Tommy. A touch of regret showed in his eyes. "Oh, son... I wish you two had stuck about for all of Saturday evening... t'was a *wild* time we had, in the closing hours..."

Noah wriggled out of his father's arms. "I'd better get these lot in. We need to start preparing." He returned to his car and led the Scouts into the Bunker. The five Jeeps and the tank parked inside the ground floor, near the entrance. Tommy stepped inside and, after pressing a panel on the wall, the concrete gates began to drag themselves shut.

* *

Having postponed their drills for the time being, the Retreaters spent the afternoon at RAF Redhill to procure equipment. A missile had been stripped from the wing of a Typhoon fighter jet, and was currently locked away inside the Gurkha, waiting to be deployed in their 'dambusters' scheme.

After dining with the others, Marcus and Jasper stepped out to the surface of Surrey. Beyond their hill lay endless fields, woodlands, and the shadows of distant towers. Though the sun had set, the moon and a myriad of stars illuminated the sky.

Jasper pushed the trapdoor shut, camouflaging it with the surrounding grass. Marcus handed him a cigarette and lit its end for him. The pair stood in silence, gazing at the night landscape as they exhaled plumes of smoke.

"It's exciting," said Jasper. "Feels like the whole world is in our hands."

Marcus remained silent. He took a drag from his cigarette and, already sick of the taste, stamped it out with his foot on the dewy grass.

"Don't really like these things, to be honest," said Marcus. "Prefer a bit of chew, myself."

"I don't know," Jasper said in a low voice, "cigarettes just feel a bit more more – liberating, I guess you'd say..." With an almost theatrical flair, he took in a deep breath of smoke and, parting his lips, expelled it out into the wind. Marcus' teeth chattered slightly in the cold.

"God, it's so good to be out of that concrete dumpster..." Jasper added, taking in a deep, invigorating breath. The sound of rustling trees filled the atmosphere.

"Yeah," said Marcus, folding his arms around his chest, "it's just – I miss everyone." He tilted his head. "I want my old life back."

Jasper bit his lip. "I miss them all too." He finished his cigarette and flicked it down the side of the hill. The butt smouldered for a moment before extinguishing itself in the grass. "What happened to Tiger and Ace – it wasn't anyone's fault, Marcus. You do know that, don't you?" Jasper glanced at Marcus, whose face appeared ashen. He continued:

"And they'll be with us forever. All those memories..." Jasper's voice wavered. "All those memories – the good *and* the bad – *MaxSimi* will keep them alive. But Hattie," he began, his voice shaking, "Hattie's still trapped. We can't let her go to waste in there."

Marcus sighed. "You're right."

Jasper pressed his eyes shut, feeling his chest tighten. He took a deep breath and allowed himself to spill all those pent-up thoughts.

"That's what it's all about for me, to be honest. I want to see her again. Marcus, I don't know how to say this... but I really like her. Really. And that's always been the case..."

Marcus didn't feign surprise. He looked deep into Jasper's eyes, and told him that it had always been clear, despite Jasper's attempts to conceal the obvious truth.

"Don't worry though," said Marcus, "it's fine. She's always really liked you, too – as a friend, I mean."

"No." Jasper shook his head vigorously. "That's just not enough..."

"Mate," said Marcus, patting Jasper on the shoulder, "Hattie's just – she's probably moved on to other things, y'know. Noah, he erm," Marcus cleared his throat, "he told me he was after her, or something. And, you know, you can never be sure: but you know how it usually goes, when a guy like that goes for a girl like her..."

"Nah, nah," said Jasper, waving his hand, "Hattie's different... she doesn't care about people's rank and title – unlike the other girls..."

"I guess... but still, you've got to remember that she and Noah have a surprising amount of things in—"

"Stop it!" snapped Jasper, flailing his arms up with passion, "you're completely off the mark about her!"

"No, I'm not."

"Yes, you are," continued Jasper, "and really, I think you're just trying to mess with my head, to be honest!"

Marcus scowled. "What the hell do you mean by that?"

Jasper let out a derisive laugh. "It's your insecurity, isn't it? You know she'd never take you back. You screwed up, cheating with Liv. I mean, Liv, for Christ's sakes! What the fuck were you thinking?!"

Tears began to show in Marcus' eyes. "Why are you bringing this up? I don't know why you've become so—"

"And not only that," interrupted Jasper, "but you couldn't even protect her, could you? When Derek and Reece came down to the ball? The way they knocked you to the floor, and you lay there, frozen, like a stupid fucking lemon. Who was it that went and fetched Davey? Me! Me! *I* was the one who saved her! *I* stopped those dirty cunts from stealing her away!"

Marcus shoved Jasper, nearly knocking him to the ground. Regaining his balance, he turned around and swung at Marcus' face, and missed. Marcus kicked Jasper in the shin. Jasper collapsed onto the grass, wincing in pain.

"She'll never love you," Marcus hissed, "so just stay in your fucking lane!"

Jasper's eyes flashed with rage. He screamed and grabbed Marcus' leg. Marcus tried to shake him off but lost his balance and fell to the ground. Their childish scuffle came to a sudden halt at the sound of a distant whirring in the sky.

Their eyes widened in terror. There it was: an aerial object, gliding across the horizon. A floodlight beamed down from its base, scanning the barren landscape below. Jasper and Marcus scrambled back down the ladder, nearly slipping on the rungs in their haste to get back through the tunnel.

21
Dambusters

"Ashley!" cried Marcus. "Ashley!"

But the man gave no response. Jasper and Marcus ran through the long corridor where the Retreaters were asleep in their cubicles.

At last, they located Ashley's bed and shook him awake. The man rolled off his *MaxSimi* hood and wiped his eyes.

"What is it?" he grumbled.

"It's – there's – in the sky... it's—"

Ashley hushed Marcus and told him to slow down. Marcus took a deep breath and said:

"A helicopter."

Ashley winced with confusion. "A helicopter..."

Marcus nodded to confirm. Ashley furrowed his brow with disbelief.

"I saw it too," said Jasper. "It was flying over London. Coming towards where we are, it looked like."

Ashley stood up and, without saying a word, scurried down the hall. Jasper and Marcus followed behind as he entered a side room. Inside, the man started to fiddle with a large radio system. Twisting its dials around, the thing buzzed with white noise until at last, he located a frequency that happened to click. They waited, and waited, until – as Ashley had expected – sharp male voices began to speak over the static.

Crossed into Surrey.

Acknowledged, said a crackling voice that belonged to Noah Smith. *We're still on the M1. Should be on the M25 in twenty minutes or so.*

Copy that. Whirring blades could be heard in the background. *Surrey now in sight. Taking a look around the Hills.*

Marcus gritted his teeth. Ashley looked towards Jasper and told him to fetch Dani. Jasper nodded and scrambled off. Marcus, for his part, was instructed to head back up to the surface to keep a close eye on the chopper's trajectory. He clambered back up the ladder, fuelled by adrenaline, and emerged into the ruins of the abbey.

High in the sky, the blades of the Chinook were beating through the air. It was busy scanning through a distant forest, using a floodlight to see through the dark canopies.

"Jesus..." Marcus wiped his eyes in disbelief. The helicopter moved closer and closer to their location, until at last, it buzzed around half a mile above his head. The floodlight swivelled around, catching sight of a clearing in the trees.

The Chinook stopped, pivoted in the air and, ever so slowly, began to lower itself, before becoming stationary once again.

Peering through the depths of the woods, he could see that its spotlight was fixed on the Retreat's car park.

Clenching his jaw, Marcus turned around, muttered a curse, and slipped back down into the depths. Holding himself up on the ladder, he peeped through a crack in the hatch as the helicopter shifted upwards and, after flying a few miles south, began to lower itself down into the woods.

* *

Marcus raced back to the radio room. Inside, Ashley hunched over the station, his eyes flicking in their sockets as static voices came over the speakers. Dani sat tense and alert, clutching a notepad, while Jasper nervously drummed his fingers on the edge of the table.

"We've been made," Ashley said, the colour draining from his cheeks.

Marcus stood with his lips parted. On the radio, Noah's voice was discussing what the pilot had seen: in a little clearing in the Surrey woods, atop a large hill, a bullet-riddled Gurkha and the Bunker's old delivery van, parked there discreetly. The Scout convoy was currently on the M25, headed down towards Surrey. Once they'd regrouped in the hills somewhere, Noah said, they'd start to search the area to try and find the exact location of the Retreaters' base.

Ashley stepped out to wake the others up. All of them came into the room, sick and unnerved by how roused Ashley had become. Dani, who remained silent, could provide no reassurance.

"They won't know exactly where we are, though," said Marcus, trying to quell the panic that was building in the air. "They'll never find the entrance – right, Ashley?"

Ashley shrugged, staring gravely at the floor.

"Maybe not," he said. "But they'll cut all our lights out should they find our solar panels."

"What about the generator?" asked Marcus, forcing cheer into his voice. "Yeah. We'll be alright. We've got a ton of fuel. And besides, there's enough water supply and tinned food to last us like a year!"

Ashley solemnly shook his head. "Less than that, I imagine. Much less. And as for electricity," he said, looking over at Dani, "that'll run out within a couple of months, even with the diesel we stole from the Bunker..."

"But we'll survive," said Marcus, "will we not?"

Jonathan chirped in, "It'd be no way to live, son."

"Li'e bein' trapped in a cave," said Crispin, with a strange touch of gravitas in his voice.

Jasper took a deep breath. "We can't let them do this to us. We can't just sit here and take it." He peered up at the low ceiling. "We've got to fight back!"

Crispin nodded in agreement.

"You go ahead, son," said Sue with a note of dismissal. "I think I'll be staying right where I'm at, thank you very much."

"Suit yourself," said Jasper. He sized her up and down. "You've done nothing but try and drag us down this whole time. I'm hardly surprised you're backing out of it now."

"Oi," she said, stepping up to his face. "Don't you try starting on me, you fucking wrong'un. Think you're the man now, do you? Well I think you're getting too big for your boots, me personally!"

Marcus glanced at Jasper with a sidelong look, flashing the whites of his eyes. Meanwhile, Maya tried to get Sue to back down, telling her to "keep calm". "Us bickering won't achieve anything, will it?"

"No, it won't." Dani moved over to an unoccupied bed. She dropped down onto its end and, clutching her knees in her hands, looked up at the others. "Ashley," she said, "how long do you think we have?"

Ashley shrugged. "No clue."

"The helicopter landed quite far away," said Marcus. "Four or five miles, I reckon."

"So we've still got time to make a run for it," said Jasper. "Get the hell out of this place."

Gareth laughed. "Quit playing the fool, Phaethon."

Jasper sized Gareth up and, on impulse, shoved the slender lad in the chest. Gareth let out a surprised yelp and, before he could retaliate, found his arms pinned back by Crispin.

"Come on Gazza... it ain't worth it..."

"But this *scumbag* thinks he's better than us!" screamed Gareth. "Someone's got to stop him!"

"ENOUGH!" yelled Dani. The others fell silent. Dani wiped her clammy palms. "Jasper's right. We've got to leave while we still can."

"No way," said Sue, folding her arms in her typically stubborn fashion. "I ain't sticking my head up there. And I don't care what you try to tell me. Had enough of you and your silver tongues."

"Very well," said Dani. "But as for the rest of you – those who choose to stay... you should know that we'll starve to death down here, if we don't act. Even if they can't find the entrance, they'll make sure we can't escape. But we've got a window of opportunity, right now. The missile's in the car. There's still time to carry out Jasper's plan." She nodded to herself. "And the Scouts are on their way down here. The Bunker's not so guarded. It should be relatively easy to get to the dam."

Jasper's eyes lit up with excitement. He turned to Marcus. "What do you think?"

Marcus shrugged his shoulders. Jasper turned to the others, awaiting their responses.

"Fuck it – I'm in," barked Crispin. He went to gather some things and enthusiastically returned with a rucksack. Meanwhile, the rest of the freed slaves were still plagued with doubt. Ashley, for his part, was mulling over whether to support Dani and Jasper in the plan. At last, he opened his mouth to speak:

"It's gotta be quick – and we've got to assess the situation on the ground first. See how many Scouts have been kept on watch."

"Of course," said Dani. She instructed Ashley to go and fetch some weapons before leading Jasper up the ladder. Marcus and Ashley tailed them, followed by Crispin and Maya. The others remained behind, too frightened to venture up to the surface.

"Good luck!" cried Jonathan. His voice echoed up through the hollow exit tunnel, before dissipating in the air.

After a minute's climbing, the Retreaters emerged on the hilltop. The night was eerily still, and the full moon was dampened by cloud cover.

* *

The gang hurried down towards the car park and entered the Gurkha. Dani set her spy drone up and climbed into the shotgun seat before Ashley revved the engine and sped them down towards the road. Not bothering to open it, Ashley crashed through the locked wooden gate. The armoured truck's tyres screeched on the narrow country lane as Ashley spun the wheel, veering the car to the right. Back in the boot, the Retreaters' rifles and a carton of diesel clunked about. The massive aircraft missile they'd brought back during the day jutted awkwardly over the top of the seats. Jasper glanced towards the strange, greyish object, which resembled an alien worm.

Ashley sped them through country villages, while Dani hovered her drone high above the M25.

"Jesus Christ..." said Dani.

"What's the matter?" asked Ashley, whose attention was fixed on the bumpy road ahead.

"Look."

Jasper leaned forward to observe Dani's tablet screen. It displayed nine silver Jeeps, speeding in a line across the motorway.

"Is that a..."

Jasper cut himself off, for he already knew what it was: a colossal tank, trailing shortly behind the cars.

Ashley puffed with an anxious sigh. "No worries, no worries." His eyes darted about, as if calculating something. "We need to take a different route." The Gurkha swivelled past a roundabout and launched itself onto another country lane. A black-striped sign marked the start of a national speed limit. The massive car's wheels thudded against potholes and cracks in the tarmac. Maya let out a yelp and reached for Jasper's hand, which he clasped tightly.

"It'll be alright," he said, and the two gazed at each other. Marcus, meanwhile, stared out the window with a look of dissociation.

The Gurkha continued to speed through an endless maze of narrow lanes, while Dani tracked the procession with her drone. She kept an eye on the Jeeps as they made their way through a village before pulling onto the same stretch of road on which the Retreat's entrance was situated. Before she could see them locate the gate, Dani was forced to pull the drone back, keeping it within the Gurkha's range.

"The others'll be okay, wun' they?" Crispin asked, but received no answer.

As Dani shifted the drone over Surrey woods, its camera picked up on a set of canopies that appeared to be whirring about. Out from the trees, the Chinook rose by its spinning rotor blades. The helicopter made its way northwards, destined for the Retreat.

* *

After a two-hour journey, the Retreaters entered the Peak District, and stopped on a road near the Bunker's broad, flat-topped hill. Pulsing with adrenaline, Ashley stepped out of the Gurkha and signalled Marcus to take the driver's seat. Marcus, visibly shaking, complied with the instruction. Assembling his sniper, Ashley disappeared into a dense, coniferous forest. Taking this as his cue, Marcus accelerated up towards the dam.

Nestled in a high valley, the concrete wall stood imposingly. A torrent of water gushed from its base in a cascading waterfall. The watchtower, barely discernible from the bottom of the slope, became a hive of activity as its little orange men began firing down at the Gurkha. The car's sturdy cage pinged with the impact of bullets. Marcus, taking an unprecedented risk, began to manoeuvre the vehicle up a steep and bumpy incline, tracing a zig-zag path towards the dam wall. Dani's seatbelt clattered about, unfastened, her attention fixed solely on her tablet and remote.

Meanwhile, Ashley, concealed within the distant woods, started to eliminate the Scouts on the watchtower. One by one, their heads exploded in a splash of blood, their lifeless bodies toppling into the valley below.

Pulling up near the base of the dam, Marcus, Crispin, Jasper and Maya disembarked, leaving Dani inside the vehicle. As they grappled with gravity, they hauled the missile from the boot and struggled to secure it on the precarious slope.

"It's gonna roll down!" Crispin exclaimed. "There's nowhere to pu' it!"

Forced to drop the missile as a Scout fired down from the watchtower, they scrambled beneath the car and watched helplessly as it rolled down the slope. They braced for an explosion, but the missile remained intact, wedging itself into a crevice halfway down the valley. A sniper shot echoed through the wilderness air, and a bloody mist sprayed from the watchtower.

All clear, Ashley confirmed through the walkie-talkie. *Go and fetch the missile.*

Scrambling back into the Gurkha, Marcus buckled up and, joined by the others, sped down the steep slope. His hands trembled as adrenaline surged through him.

"Slow down!" Dani hissed. "We can afford to take our time."

Marcus glanced over at her. The lady still hadn't deigned to put on a seatbelt. Petrified, Marcus returned his gaze to look straight ahead but, before he could hit the brakes, the wheels met a sudden bump in the terrain. The Gurkha lifted from the ground, and the vehicle was suspended in the air for a second, before it landed, but the tyres bounced upon impact, and the occupants shrieked as their car rose again, then began to fall down the valley, spinning uncontrollably, its strong cage thudding and slamming against the rocks, Dani's body flinging about like in a human tumble-dryer, crashing into Maya, before, in a flash, the abrupt flight ended, the Gurkha left in a smoky heap at the bottom of the hill.

Are you alright? hissed a voice on someone's walkie-talkie. *Guys – are you okay?! Talk to me, please!*

Jasper, aching all over, scurried out of the toppled car, followed by a disoriented Crispin. Together, they helped Maya, who screamed with excruciation, and then extracted a lifeless Dani. Her head flopped about as they dragged her from the wreck. Her neck seemed unnaturally twisted. Checking Dani's pulse, Marcus, who was physically unharmed, fumbled with his walkie-talkie.

"Dani, she's – she's not..."

After a pause filled with dread, Ashley's voice crackled back on the radio, instructing them to carry on with the mission.

While Jasper tried to comfort the severely injured Maya, Marcus and Crispin took a red fuel carton from the ruined Gurkha's boot, and scrambled up the valley by foot. They wriggled the missile free from the crack in which it was stuck and, after a minute or so of clambering, found a suitable spot for it, near the dam's wall. They set the explosive down and doused it with the Bunker's biodiesel, before lighting its outer shell on fire, and sprinting back down the slope, regrouping with the others in the forest at the bottom of the valley some ten minutes later.

"How the hell are we gonna get out of here?!" said Jasper. He gritted his teeth, clutching his shoulder, which had been dislocated in the crash. Maya, meanwhile, was resting on her back in the thick undergrowth. A bone could be seen sticking in her elbow, bulging under the skin as if trying to pierce its way out.

Ashley, level-headed as always, had his sniper trained on the dam. But before he could shoot at the burning missile, his forehead erupted in blood, and he collapsed into the grass. A gunshot echoed from afar.

Instinctively, the group took cover behind trees. Crispin seized Ashley's sniper and ammunition, while Jasper supported Maya. They clung to each other, darting towards cover. Another shot ripped through the air, the bullet pinging off the forest floor.

"We'll find a car there," Marcus said in a calm and strangely matter-of-fact tone, gesturing towards a farmhouse at the forest's edge, standing isolated in an open field. As the Bunker's sniper fired again, Maya let out a yelp.

"Fuck it," hissed Crispin. He peered out with the rifle, aiming through its scope towards the Bunker's hilltop. Upon spotting a gunman near the radio tower, Crispin's shot pierced through the air, the noise assaulting their ears.

"Agh," he spat, hastening to reload. Weaving through the trees, he left cover to fire another shot, then cracked a smile. The Bunker's lone sniper had been taken out. Crispin then turned his attention towards the base of the dam, where they'd propped up the missile, and began to fire, again, and again, and again, until the torched shell finally exploded. The dark sky flashed with a malevolent red. The others plugged their ears at the deafening boom. Looking up, they saw their mission had been a success. A massive hole gaped in the concrete wall, gushing a torrent of water in a white stream. Eventually, the wall cracked and crumbled further, eroding under the weight of the escaping reservoir, its waters pouring down the valley. Before the flood could reach the woods, the Retreaters ran towards the field in which the farmhouse stood.

After ten minutes of jogging, the Retreaters approached the isolated building. Far off in the distance, they could hear the blades of a fast-approaching helicopter.

The four scurried through the barn's doors and found it was stocked with relics from the Bunker: disused rifles, rusty old Jeeps, and a tank once used by the British Army.

"What's all this?" Jasper asked.

"Old gear," said Crispin, panting with exhaustion. "Stuff we though' we didn't need after o'twelve." The ex-Scout propped himself against the decommissioned tank and clutched his knees, wheezing out asthmatic retches. In shock, Marcus stood idle as Maya lowered herself to the floor, groaning with pain.

"Can we get one of these things to work?" said Jasper, nodding towards the old Jeeps. "Can't one of you hotwire it?" he added, addressing Marcus and Crispin.

Almost casually, Crispin shrugged his shoulders and, as the chopper's sounds drew ever closer, he stumbled over to one of the Jeeps and smashed its window out with a rock. He reached inside, swung the door open, and fiddled around near the wheel, sweeping the broken glass aside in order to sit down. After several attempts, he finally started the Jeep. Jasper and Marcus helped Maya up, and the three hurried into the car.

Crispin drove them out of the barn while the Chinook flew overhead. In a flash, the chopper caught sight of their vehicle and began to pursue. Crispin drove through a bumpy field before veering onto the main road. The chopper's searchlight trailed the

Jeep, and bullets rained down like hellfire, some pinging against the car's metal cage.

"It's alrigh'," assured Crispin, seeing Maya panic. A bullet struck the rear window, creating a spider-webbed shatter. "These things're rock-solid."

Crispin followed the road as it cut through a dense, overhanging forest. Obscured beneath the canopies, the Jeep briefly evaded the helicopter's floodlight.

A wail burst from Marcus, and he began to cry. "It's pointless," he said, tears streaming down his cheeks. "It's all so fucking pointless..."

"Shu'up." Crispin continued to speed along. A large slope rose to the right, covered in trees. Marcus continued his weeping. Crispin brought the car to a skidding halt, reached over, and slapped Marcus in the face. "Snap ou' of it." He took a deep breath, and grabbing Ashley's sniper rifle, told the three to escape while he created a distraction.

"But you can't—"

"Just fuckin' do it!" snapped Crispin, as he stepped out of the car and disappeared up the forest slope, without saying another word.

Muttering a prayer, Marcus composed himself, took the wheel, and pressed his foot on the accelerator. The Chinook caught sight of them once again, fixing its light on the rusty old Jeep as it drove along the road. Marcus continued as machine-gun fire rained down on the car. Suddenly, the storm of bullets ceased, and the chopper appeared to pause in mid-air. The Jeep continued to speed away. Jasper kept an eye on the helicopter. Its spotlight turned to focus on the hillside, where Crispin was firing Ashley's sniper rifle. Someone on board returned fire. A brief flash on the hill was followed by a reverberating shot. A silhouette collapsed from the chopper, but another man soon took his place.

I'm gonna polish off all these bastards, me, said Crispin, speaking via Marcus' walkie-talkie.

Marcus reached a junction and turned the car right. A few minutes later, the road passed through a valley. The Chinook disappeared from sight, although the atmosphere flashed with distant gunfire.

"We should turn back," murmured Marcus. "We can't leave him behind..."

"Forget it," said Jasper, "he'll be alright. He knows what he's doing. And besides, we need to get a move on..."

Marcus tried to reach Crispin via his walkie-talkie, but there was no response.

Before the chopper could return, Jasper instructed Marcus to hit the brakes. The car came to a stop. Looking into the dense forest surrounding the road, the three climbed out and disappeared into the undergrowth.

As expected, the Chinook, having dealt with its brief distraction, rose up into the sky and began to skim the terrain with its bright light. The three survivors continued to run through the trees until Marcus slowed down and waited for the others to catch up. Jasper supported an injured Maya, helping her to keep moving. They caught up with Marcus, whose eyes were frozen over with a hollow expression.

"You alright?" asked Jasper.

Marcus shook his head vigorously, as if to snap himself out of a trance. He turned back to the others and waved them along.

The three stumbled through the undergrowth. Spotting a white river ahead, they jumped into the gushing stream and allowed themselves to be carried by its currents.

The Bunker's Chinook began to fly above the forest, casting its floodlight through the dim trees as it scoured the floor for signs of life.

PART III

22
Graveyard

Five hours later, the black sky was tinged with a twilight blue. Dawn was about to break.

The convoy of Jeeps returned to the Bunker, parking in front of the wide-open gates. The tank followed shortly behind, coughing and spluttering with exhaust fumes as it crawled along the field. Noah stepped out from the lead Jeep, and the rest of the Scouts streamed out of their cars, following his cues. They began to approach Tommy, who loitered alone by the gates. The man was clad in a fluorescent orange suit, and wore a gas mask over his face.

The Bunker's helicopter landed with an overwhelming sound. Its rotors whipped tufts of grass about violently as it touched down on the ground. Five crew members emerged from the cockpit. "We lost 'em," said one of the Scouts.

Tommy clenched his jaw and pressed his eyelids shut. Flaring them open, he shot a pointed look at the man who had spoken and, struggling to contain his anger, asked in a low, growling voice where the survivors had last been seen.

The man audibly gulped. "Their car was pulled up by the roadside. Think they went into the woods. But saw no signs of them there."

Tommy scowled. "Look again."

Noah interjected, suggesting that the Scouts should get some rest, and, in any case, the helicopter's fuel was running out.

"It's been a long night – we can't keep going without—"

With a wave of the hand, Tommy compelled his son to stop talking. "We've got to act tonight. They might be headed to the coast... they'll disappear out of our reach." He took in a shaky breath, a rare display of real emotion. "No, no – this can't have been for nothing..."

Noah nodded solemnly. Tommy raised his arms and, addressing the others, said he'd fetch Hans and obtain some "go-powder" for their mission, as they needed to remain awake for the time being. Tommy retreated into the gates of the Bunker, while Noah and the others, on his father's request, went to collect the bodies of Ms Dalton and Mr Mirza from the bottom of the valley. Pete's corpse had already been retrieved from the top of the Bunker's hill, where he'd been stationed on watch with a sniper.

* * *

Meanwhile, in a local village about an hour down the road, the three survivors had passed out. They'd taken shelter inside an old church and were currently sleeping in its clock tower. A giant rusty bell dominated the space of the room.

Jasper awoke from a nightmare to darkness. He clenched his teeth and cradled his arm, which felt twisted and torn, as if the muscle had been wrenched from the bone.

The young man lay with his eyes open for several hours, until the translucent clock face was finally illuminated by morning light. Marcus awoke shortly after this happened, while Maya remained in a deep sleep. Jasper crawled over and, taking her delicate hand, checked her pulse. He sighed with immense relief.

"What the hell are we gonna do with her?" said Marcus.

Jasper looked into Maya's comatose face. With her black hair fanning out over the floor, the woman appeared to be at peace. Dropping her wrist, Jasper hoisted himself up and, limping, began to make his way down the bell tower's metal ladder, with Marcus following closely.

"Where are you going?" Marcus called, as their footsteps clanged on the metal rungs.

"We need supplies," replied Jasper, his voice low and grave.

They stepped out of the desolate church, its stained-glass windows depicting faded scenes of good and evil. They made their way down a cobbled road. Jasper spotted an old corner shop. The boys went inside and scanned the shelves, only to find them empty. A skeleton lay near the counter, clad in tattered rags.

Holding their shirts over their noses, the two fled the shop, gasping for fresh air outside.

"For Christ's sakes," said Marcus, fidgeting like a frightened child, "we're gonna die out here..."

"Man up," Jasper grumbled. "We'll find a way," he added, gazing at the cloud-heavy sky. A bitter wind brushed their faces, and they shivered in the breeze. Aimlessly, they continued through the village. Jasper felt a pang of sadness looking at the yellow-brick buildings, many of which had shattered windows. The streets outside were littered with miscellaneous debris: glass shards scattered on the road, and plastic wrappers whirling about in the wind.

Through chattering teeth, Marcus asked, "What do you reckon? Should we give up?"

Jasper shook his head and walked up to a small cottage, pulling open the front door, which someone had left ajar. Inside, the furniture remained intact, albeit covered in heavy dust. Marcus followed him in and, opening the kitchen cupboards, found a stash of tinned food. He grabbed an old shopping bag and filled it with tinned cans, matches, and firelighters, plus a silver pot and a frying pan. Meanwhile, Jasper located the master bedroom. Two skeletons lay tucked in the double bed. Searching in the closet, Jasper found fresh clothes. He dressed himself into a pair of trousers, dry socks, a white t-shirt, and a woolly Christmas jumper covered in snowflakes. He also chose an outfit for Maya, and told Marcus about his findings. Marcus quickly changed into some dry clothes as well. Jasper then went to the bathroom and gathered some medicine. They both grabbed winter coats and left the old home, clutching their filled shopping bags. Five minutes later, the two returned to the church, its high spire towering over the sea of slate roofs.

* * *

Inside the clock tower, Maya had shed herself of her ruined clothes and sat completely bare. She directed the two boys to avert their gaze as she slipped into the new outfit Jasper had picked out for her. Grimacing, she attempted to stand but was unable; hindered by broken bones. Attentively, Jasper went over to her and, at her asking, poured some paracetamol pills into her hand. Maya downed the painkillers in one go. Jasper kept a pill for himself and swallowed the expired medication dry.

Marcus was engrossed in lighting a fire and boiling tinned beans in a small pot. As the contents bubbled and splattered, Jasper found himself salivating. At last, the baked beans were ready. Jasper wolfed down his portion before passing some over to Maya. Maya thanked him and brought the bowl to her lips before tipping the contents down her throat.

"What are we thinking, then?" asked Jasper, who stared up at the towering ceiling. "I think we should make a move..."

"No," said Marcus. In his hands, he held his small Glock pistol and was trying to wipe it dry. All his belongings had been saturated in the river last night.

"I think he's right," said Maya. "We need to lay low – gather some strength."

"But what if they search for us here?" Jasper asked.

Marcus shook his head dismissively. "If they're out looking for us still, the chopper will see us if we try and move about. Staying here's our safest bet."

"I'm not saying we should hit the road," said Jasper. "Just that we could try to make our way out of the Peak District. On foot, that is. Be subtle about it, yeah?"

"But the chopper," said Marcus, his voice terse.

"What'd you mean?" asked Jasper.

"It'll see us if we stay out for too long."

"Not necessarily..."

"It's just too risky." Marcus folded his arms. "And we can't afford to be reckless anymore," he said, letting out a sigh as he looked down at his broken walkie-talkie.

Meanwhile, Jasper had begun to inspect his Glock pistol. Absentmindedly, he tried to pull the trigger, causing all three of them to startle as the gun went off, the bullet ricocheting off the metal bell and cobblestone wall before coming to rest on the wooden floor.

"Sorry, I – I just wanted to see if it worked..."

Marcus chuckled and, trying to lighten the sombre mood, joked: "Seems like it does."

Jasper and Maya gave obliging laughter. Nonetheless, their faces were marked by pain and exhaustion, their eyes wide with fear of what was to come.

* * *

Bolstered by Dr Hans' powdered crystal meth, the Scouts patrolled the woods where the survivors had vanished. Noah remained stationed in his Jeep, huddled by the radio to maintain communication with his team. The Chinook had shifted its focus to a nearby river, where it was presumed that the Retreaters had escaped. The chopper made its way downstream, using its powerful camera to zoom in on the streets of a distant village.

Inspecting Baslow – over.

Noah activated the radio's dashboard button, "Acknowledged. Over." The Chief of Scouts sighed heavily to himself. Noah had refused the go-powder, and his mind was carried down by the weight of fatigue.

* * *

The echo of distant rotor blades filled the air outside the bell tower. The trio inside fell silent. Marcus went to retract the metal ladder, and they each took up positions in the corner, anticipating the arrival of the Scouts in the village.

* * *

While the men in orange continued their search in the woods, Noah sat in his car, awaiting a report from the Chinook.

Can't see anything in Baslow, the radio buzzed, *no signs of anyone on the ground – over.*

"What about in the buildings? Can you see anything inside?"

Negative, said the chopper. Noah wiped his weary eyes and, reaching for his walkie-talkie, enquired if the men in the woods had uncovered any clues.

Nothing here, Dominic replied.

Hold on... said another crackling voice, which belonged to Bobby Stephens. *I think I've found something...*

Animatedly, Noah swung the car door open and hurried towards Bobby's location. A cluster of Scouts were gathered around the young man.

"What is it?" Noah demanded, pushing his way through the throng of orange-clad men. He looked down and saw a trail of fresh footprints in the mud. The surrounding grass was trampled, and the prints led about fifty metres to a gushing river, where they abruptly disappeared. An idea sparked in Noah's eyes and, instructing his men to return to their vehicles, he dashed back to his car. Firing up the engine, he pressed the radio button and urged the Chinook to keep eyes on Baslow. He released the handbrake and revved the Jeep forward, leading his Scouts towards a tranquil country village.

* * *

The chopper continued to fly near the church. Jasper, Maya and Marcus stayed huddled in separate corners of the bell tower, bracing for an imminent assault.

After a nerve-wracking wait, the growls of engines filled the air of the village outside. Shadows flitted across the translucent clock-face. A car pulled up nearby.

Jasper took a deep inhale. Marcus's eyes glazed over with a dissociative terror, while Maya had begun to hyperventilate.

"Quiet," hissed Jasper. "It's going to be okay."

The church doors swung open with a resonating creak. Footsteps echoed ominously within the dim chamber. Ever so carefully, Jasper peeked over the edge and scanned the scene below.

Three men in orange were scouring through the pews, each clutching an assault rifle. Jasper pulled back quickly as one of the Scouts turned around.

"What's up there?"

Jasper recognised the voice as Bobby's.

Footsteps drummed against the wooden floor below, reverberating through the church. "Think that's a belfry," said Noah.

"A 'belfry'?"

"Yeah." Noah seemed to hesitate for a second. The trio of survivors clenched their eyes shut. Maya continued to pant with frantic breaths. Marcus glared at her and pressed his finger on his lips, imploring her to be silent. Another set of footsteps was followed by hushed murmurings, which echoed from below, until, without warning, a barrage of gunfire pierced the floor of the belfry. Jasper cowered in the corner as Maya was cut down by the assault. The bell chimed in the onslaught of bullets. Marcus rose, shattered through the clock face, and plunged into the abyss below. Jasper quickly followed, landing on a cushion of grass. Instinctively rolling to absorb the impact, Jasper was on his feet in seconds, sprinting through the graveyard to the main road, where a Scout Jeep was parked. The Chinook passed overhead, but by the time it had registered the escapees, they had already entered the vehicle, with Marcus at the wheel, speeding them away. Three hazmat-clad Scouts emerged from an old cottage and opened fire at the fleeing Jeep. Marcus swerved, trying to evade the bullets, but a few struck the reinforced windscreen, spider-webbing it with cracks. Eventually, the Jeep veered onto the lawn, aiming for the orange-clad men. Two dodged just in time, but the third was too slow, and saw himself crushed under the heavy vehicle. Marcus jerked the steering wheel right at a T-junction, following a sign that pointed to the M1.

23

Ashes to Ashes

Seven hours later, up on Level 1, Commander Tommy and Big Davey were inspecting the dead. Pete's remains had been placed into a silver urn, the cremation having already taken place. Meanwhile, the corpses of Ms Dalton and Mr Mirza sprawled on the morgue's cold, metal beds. Above them, the ceiling light immersed the room in a slightly bluish hue.

Still dressed in hazmat gear, Noah sprinted into the room and, before he could utter a word, Tommy questioned whether he'd taken a skin-prick test.

"But Dad—"

"Procedure, son. Follow it."

Noah hesitated, before retracing his steps as he paced out of the room, leaving the door ajar as he moved back to the stairs.

"We can't afford to drop our standards. Not even in a crisis," Tommy said to Big Davey.

"Right you are, sir..." said Davey with a forceful nod. Tommy turned to the big man, who appeared to shake in his boots, unnerved by his master's piercing gaze. Tommy turned away and, taking his smartphone out, began to take pictures of Dalton and Mirza's lifeless faces. He then instructed David to prepare the bodies into their boxes.

By the time Noah returned, the cremation chamber had been put into operation. The pungent scent of burning flesh caused Noah to cover his nose. The flames of the chamber danced in Tommy's glassy eyes, his focus squarely fixed on his dead adversaries.

Noah, wringing his hands together nervously, broke Tommy's trance as he swivelled to look at his son. A genuine tear was rolling down his cheek. Noah cleared his throat and began, "Got some news to share..."

Tommy remained silent. His eyes displayed an empty, broken look, one of a man on the brink of collapse.

"The survivors," Noah continued, swallowing hard, "we found them in a village. Took Maya out, but the others... they got away... and they killed Dom in their escape..."

Noah tensed up, bracing for an outburst, but his father stood motionless, his expression blank and his breath trembling. He lowered his gaze, and shamefully bowed his head. "What now, son? Where do we go from here..." he said, his voice a ghostly whisper.

"We go an' get those bastards, of course!" Big Davey bellowed, voice filled with a hateful enthusiasm.

"That's what I'm thinking," said Noah, who kept a vigilant eye on his father's face, watching for changes in the microexpressions. "Once the chopper's refuelled, we'll head back to Surrey. Check if they've gone back to their base camp."

With a distracted nod and a sigh, Tommy instructed Noah to "get a move on". As Noah exited, he glanced back at his father, asking if he was alright. But Tommy refused to answer, and shooed the boy away with his hand.

* * *

In the meantime, Jasper and Marcus, each clutching an SA80 rifle, were staggering through Surrey woods. They had abandoned their stolen Jeep several miles back, having successfully outpaced the Scouts. The Chinook, likely low on fuel, had given up its chase on the M1. Moreover, they'd managed to keep a safe distance between their vehicle and the pursuing convoy of Scout Jeeps.

Upon reaching the crest of a low-level hill, they saw that, in a clearing in the trees, the Retreat's solar panels were riddled with bullets. Hardly surprised, they moved past and made their way towards the old abbey ruins, destroyed by the Scouts' explosives. The rubble had been flattened and scorched by an explosion, so that hardly a trace remained. The Scouts had clearly tried to locate the Retreat's entrance with a bombing campaign. Fortunately, as he patted his hand on the ground, Jasper found the secret hatch still intact beneath a patch of unscathed grass. Unlocking the seal with the code that Ashley had taught him, Jasper peeled the trapdoor open.

Descending the long ladder, their heavy rifles clattering on their backs, Jasper and Marcus found the lights in the Retreat still humming.

Jonathan, who had been waiting for the entire time, went to greet the two exhausted young men, who were jarred by his initial enthusiasm. The old judge's eyes fell heavy with concern.

"Where's everyone else?" he enquired, his Adam's apple bristling as he swallowed down a gulp.

Marcus simply said that the others "hadn't made it", before stumbling off to his *MaxSimi* cubicle. Jasper, however, continued to linger there, feeling obliged to elaborate.

"A lot went wrong," he said, running his fingers through his hair. "But the plan... in spite of it all – it worked." Jasper's body shook, muscles torn from an hour of running through hills. He let his rifle drop to the floor, his legs trembling from fatigue. Jonathan's gaze fell on the SA80.

"Stole it from the Scouts," Jasper explained. "Found a stash in their Jeep." Wiping his face, Jasper went to sit down on a vacant bed, while Jonathan stood with his arms folded. Jasper hunched and allowed his arms to dangle down at his sides. "The others... they didn't make it," he said, his voice quivering, as a vivid image of Maya's convulsions flashed before him, her flesh rippling with the impact of bullets, and the life disappearing from her pretty brown eyes.

Jonathan took in a deep breath and spoke a quiet prayer.

"John," said Jasper, "We've won. Our nightmare's over – it's time to let the healing begin..."

Jonathan knitted his brow. "What about the Scouts? What if they come back for us?"

Jasper stared at the ceiling. "We'll just have to wait them out."

"But those *knuckleheads* tried to bomb us!" cried Gareth, who was pacing over to the two. His feet scuttled along the sterile corridor. "We could feel the explosions down here!"

"Don't worry," said Jasper, his voice distant. "Dani said this place could withstand an attack like this. And besides," he added, pointing at the hefty rifle, "we'll be able to fend them off if they ever breached the entrance." Seeing that Gareth was eyeing it up, Jasper reached down to grab the SA80 and held it closely to his lap.

While Jonathan went off to prepare a meal for Jasper, Marcus stayed silent in his cubicle. Jonathan asked him if he wanted anything from the kitchen, to which the young lad gave no answer.

After devouring his corn and gulping his water down, Jasper thanked Jonathan for the meal, retired to his curtained cubicle, then, resting his rifle by the bedside, laid down and asked *MaxSimi* to put him to sleep.

24
Bubbling Up

The Commander sat alone in his chambers, slumped in his leather armchair. In his trembling hand, he held a glass of untouched water. The men would arrive at any minute.

With sullen eyes and a haggard expression on his face, Tommy stared into his little aquarium, where the goldfish looped about mindlessly. Beneath them, a plastic treasure chest at the bottom of the tank opened and shut with a whirring electric mechanism, releasing streams of oxygen bubbles.

A knock on the door, and the remaining officials streamed in: Davey, Ted, Eddie, and their associates, Dr Hans and Mr Jackson. Noah was absent, having set off to return to Surrey, while 'Freddy Krueger' remained stationed on the Estate.

Taking their places on the sofas, each of the men shook the Commander's hand. Tommy's grip was strangely limp. His back was hunched, and the skin on his face looked more wrinkled than usual. His normally well-kept beard was unruly, its grey strands prominent in the harsh light of the room.

Since Tommy failed to break the silence, as was customary, Eddie cleared his throat and initiated proceedings.

"Sir," he said, glancing at the others, "I think I speak for all of us when I say how grateful we are – for all that you've done for us."

No response. Eddie continued:

"We owe you our lives, sir. Without your courage, or your leadership, none of us would be here today…"

The others murmured in agreement. A sigh escaped from Tommy's lungs. "I've only tried to do the right thing, boys. That's all I've ever wanted for us all."

"Of course," said Eddie, "of course. And we'll get the last of those bastards soon, I'm sure…"

Tommy took a sip of water and, with great care, placed the glass down onto its coaster. He gripped the armrests of his chair and, releasing the tension in his shoulders, said:

"I'm grateful for all that you've done for me, too. All the loyalty you've shown me over the years." He nodded at Eddie and decided to change the subject. "Tell me, how long do we have on the generator?"

Eddie stared at the floor. "Four or five days until we run out of fuel. Our emergency reserves – they've been used up by the Scouts in their efforts. We'll need to save some for cooking and for our emergency lighting system."

Tommy pressed his lips together. "And what about the reconstruction? What's the news on the dam?"

The air grew tense with silence. With anxious, darting eyes, Tommy examined each of his men's faces, which seemed mask-like and rigid, as though they were trying to conceal an uncomfortable truth.

"Sir," said Eddie, beginning his reluctant response, "Barry tells me that it, erm, might take a while..."

"And why's that?"

"Well – he said, to plug up a hole of that size – it won't be an easy job. And with the structural damage to the wall, it's going to be very tricky..."

Tommy crossed his arms. "I see."

"And," Eddie added, "it's erm... he said it's going to take a long time to fill it all back up, even once we've managed to sort out the breach."

Tommy leaned forward. "Can't we divert more streams into the reservoir?"

"I'm not sure." Eddie scratched the back of his neck. "Sir, you must understand – I'm just trying to tell you the situation for how it is..."

"And I can appreciate that." Tommy turned over to the others and asked, "What do you think we should do?"

The men stared at the floor. Little Ted stayed mute, refusing to stick up for Tommy's ideas. Tommy glared at Ted with palpable hatred, which could be seen in the whites of his eyes. At last, he turned back to Eddie, who began to speak once more:

"Given the circumstances, sir – I think there are two options. First, we remain as we are. We'll have to do without electricity for a while. Rely on our bottled water stash to meet people's needs." Eddie paused, wary of the Commander's reaction. Upon being prompted, he continued. "Secondly, we stay at the Estate for the time being. Have everyone live there – temporarily. The farm's large enough to accommodate us all, considering the outhouses as well as the mansion. It's all fenced off, it's safe – and we can patrol the perimeters."

"No way!" Big Davey blurted, his forehead creasing as he scowled with disapproval. "Tha'ss a rubbish idea!"

"I'm not so sure, my friend," Dr Hans said to Davey. Tommy shifted his gaze to the scientist, who began to fiddle with the golden ring on his finger. "I think perhaps this is the best option..."

"Why?" Tommy enquired.

"Well," said Hans, "considering the safety issues in the Bunker – no sprinkler system now, and the lack of emergency exits... perhaps this is the best way to move forward. We do not really want to live in unsafe, unhygienic conditions."

"I have to say, sir," said Jackson, who had been unusually quiet today, "I think he might be right..."

A long pause followed. The aquarium bubbled and the ceiling lights buzzed. Tommy's carved statue watched proceedings from its resting table.

"What about my fishies..." said Tommy, with a flicker of despair in his voice. "I can't just leave them here..."

"You can bag them up and take them with you." Dr Hans' lips were tight with a naïve smile. "The Sparrowmans have a koi pond, yes? Perhaps they shall make some new friends in there..."

Tommy gave the man a look of faint disgust. "That's not going to happen." Hans' face fell.

"We're not going to mix with those people," Tommy continued, clasping his bony knees together. He scoffed to himself, noting the confusion in Hans' eyes – the doctor gasped with a sudden realisation.

"Sir, if this is about the annual reports... I can assure you, we can keep up the pretences, as we all have done for the last fifteen years—"

Hans stopped himself after Davey nudged him on the shoulder and gestured towards Tommy, who leered at the scientist with a palpable disgust. Hans peered down at his feet, his hands fidgeting nervously.

"I apologise, sir. I shouldn't have brought that up."

Tommy's gaze lingered on Hans for a moment, before he gave a gentle nod, as if to forgive him for this impropriety. At last, he sighed and, rising from his chair, waved the men out of his chambers. As they made their way to the door, Tommy called for Hans and Little Ted to stay behind.

After the others had left, Tommy approached Hans and instructed him to get to work on a big batch of fentanyl.

"To keep people happy, in these troublesome times," he said, repeating a familiar slogan.

Dr Hans hesitated, before giving a reluctant nod and leaving in silence. Little Ted remained in the Commander's quarters, staring over at his imposing bust.

"You seem awfully quiet today. Are you on medication still?" Tommy asked, easing the door shut. He pressed his ear against it, listening to Hans' footsteps as they echoed through the corridor.

"Yes, sir," said Ted, wringing his hands. "They're a lifesaver – the new pills that Hans made for me... I feel I'm finally in control of my life and—"

"God. Look what's happened to you, mate. Lost your edge!"

Little Ted looked down at his watch. "Listen, sir, I'd better get—"

Tommy hushed Ted with a flap of the hand and made a tsk sound with his teeth before ambling over to his bedside drawer. From it, he took out a glass pipe and a bag of crystals. "Here – take a look."

Little Ted peered down at his master's contraband. "But isn't that—"

"Listen," Tommy interrupted, "I don't see how it's any different to you guzzling those pills, mate. Plus, Big Pharma and the government – you know what they used to do? They used to force them on free spirits like yourself! Make you docile, make you obey their sick agenda!"

Ted, whose face was now covered in flecks of Tommy's spit, stared back at him blankly.

"Well, colour me shocked," Tommy added, waving his pipe in Little Ted's face. "Aren't you going to take me up on my extremely generous offer?!"

At last, Little Ted gave a begrudging nod. "Okay." Tommy then loaded some crank into the end of the pipe, took a small toke himself, and passed it to Teddy, heating it up with his butane lighter.

"Just a little bit for your first time, my child," he said, watching Teddy intently as he torched the bowl with a blue flame. "We're only microdosing..."

After taking a small inhale, Teddy erupted into a violent, hacking cough. As he opened his eyes, Tommy noted, with a smile, that they appeared more bloodshot and wild than he'd ever seen them before.

25
Into the Depths

Five days later

Back in the Retreat, Jasper and Marcus were busy setting up the radio. Jonathan supervised the two as they tried to get the system working again.

Another explosion, some fifty metres above their heads, caused the ceiling light to sway. Jasper felt an instinctive jolt of surprise, though by now, they'd all become accustomed to the periodic bombings. The Scouts had returned to Surrey, destined to root out the last of the Retreaters.

Jasper settled into the chair in the room and began to turn the dials at random. More and more white noise, until they chanced upon a foreign broadcast, produced by an unknown entity.

"The hell is this?" said Marcus.

Jonathan leaned in closer. "I think it's an old public service announcement. Seems to be on a loop..."

The synthetic voice droned on with unintelligible messages, its signal intermittently distorted by static. Disturbed by the haunting frequency, Jasper decided to change the channel until, finally, he paused, sensing he'd stumbled upon something significant.

"Listen..."

A brief crackle, and the signal settled into a steady hum, reminiscent of the sounds of an ocean floor.

"Is this the one?"

All three strained to hear, remaining silent. There was a sharp crack, and then another. Eventually, the static gave way to a discernible male voice:

Nothing in the blast range – over.

Jasper and Marcus exchanged uneasy glances. They recognised the voice as Noah's.

Let's go again. Drop northwards this time.

Copy that, said another transmission, accompanied by a chopping noise in the background. Noah's voice returned, and after a sigh, instructed the helicopter to conduct another bombing. The helicopter complied, and again a small tremor reverberated through the walls of the Retreat, although this one felt a little more distant.

"They'll never find us," said Jasper, his lips marked by a smug smile. Meanwhile, Marcus stared down at the concrete floor, his expression sombre. Jonathan gazed at the ceiling, arms folded, eager for this nightmare to end.

"Are you *sure* the dam was fully emptied?" he asked in earnest.

"I'm sure," said Jasper. "The size of the hole – there's no way they could repair that thing."

"And we saw a tonne of water pour out," added Marcus, his eyes staring off into the distance.

"Right," said Jonathan, "right... one just needs to be patient, I suppose..."

"Exactly." Jasper clapped Jonathan on the shoulder. "Give it a few more weeks, and I guarantee you – they'll be plunged into darkness. Only a matter of time."

"Of course," Jonathan murmured, doubt edging his voice, "of course..."

Boys!

The three jumped as Tommy's voice crackled over the Scout's frequency. *Come home. Come home. Something weird's going on over here...*

Commander, this is the Chief speaking, said Noah, his voice calm and formal. *What's the matter?*

Stop what you're doing. Come back – please. The Bunker... it's—

An abrupt pause.

Just do as I ask, son.

Okay, said Noah. *You heard him, lads. Time to head back...*

The signal dissolved into white noise. The three Retreaters remained in the radio room, exchanging glances as they processed what they'd heard. Eventually, Jasper rose from the swivel chair, headed back to his *MaxSimi* bed, grabbed his SA80 rifle, and slung it over his shoulder. He beckoned the others over, glancing at Gareth and Sue as they slept in their artificial dreams, the curtains of their cubicles drawn open. Jasper declared that they needed to prepare for "one last push". Following Jasper's instruction, Jonathan went over to Dani's old cubicle to grab one of the former Prime Minister's spare drones from a cardboard box. Marcus, meanwhile, retrieved his SA80 from his bed, cradling the weapon in his trembling arms.

* * *

Back in the Bunker, the lights had completely cut out, after the emergency generator ran out of diesel on Monday. Since then, life underground had become a struggle. Claustrophobia pervaded the air of the complex. Never before had it become so apparent, the fact that, for nearly two decades, the people had been cut off from the colourful world above their heads – one that most had experienced and enjoyed first-hand. Although only two days had passed since the power cut, several incidents had already occurred, including petty thefts, an old man's suicide, and a little girl's attempt to sneak up to Level 0. Davey, who was on watch, apprehended the child on Level 3, and she was due to receive questioning once the Commander had a moment to spare.

In an attempt to soothe his people's frayed nerves, the Commander convened an assembly in the Sports Hall. The aisle was lined with a set-up of oil lamps, taken from emergency storage, which provided the hall with a dim source of light. The audience were concealed by shade, their faces hardly visible.

On the stage, the Commander gestured frantically with his arms as he spouted drivel about the "Cabal", "Agenda 35", and how Dani Dalton had played a central part in it all. Little Ted stood beside him, displaying printed photos of Ms Dalton and Mr Mirza's lifeless faces. The Commander's agitation grew as he tried to rile the Bunker's inhabitants against their shared enemy, the Retreaters, now all but confined to history. However, the atmosphere remained suspended with fear. The flames of the oil lamps flickered and hissed, casting shadows over the hall's four walls.

The Commander paused for a hasty gulp of water. Out of the blue, a man from the crowd cried out:

"Don't let us starve down here, Tommy!"

Stunned, Tommy wiped his mouth and leaned into the microphone before saying the following:

"No, no, no. We'll be alright for food, everyone. I can promise you that." He shielded his eyes as he scanned the faces in the crowd to identify who it was that had dared to speak.

"Barry Townsend…" he said, with a menacing softness in his voice, "there's no need to get yourself worked up like this. Please, have some composure. The Estate will provide everything we need. If not, we have emergency reserves. We have plenty. Enough to get us through winter, and beyond, in order that we may enjoy the quality lives that you've all been given."

Barry crossed his arms and muttered something under his breath. Tommy stood quietly, waiting for applause from the audience, but the Bunker refused to indulge him. His face twisted into a scowl at the lack of response.

"Sometimes," he went on, "the Almighty puts rocks in the road. But I promise you now – this will be but a temporary misery. Mark my words. Those bastards will never bring us down, not from the grave, not ever."

The Bunker offered him half-hearted applause, but a sense of unease still lingered in the air. Tommy felt a knot in his stomach. The dark eyes of the crowd loomed over him, as though their unspoken pact was approaching its natural conclusion. Having exhausted his supply of rhetoric, he dismissed the assembly and instructed them all to return to their rooms, and await further instructions. As the people began to file out, Tommy observed the elders, the groups of women, and the mass of children. Most disturbing of all were the twenty-ish Scouts, who'd returned to the Bunker from the hills on his command. The faces of these men were taut with an unspoken resentment, and they walked down the aisle with tense, rigid movements. Licking his lips, Tommy understood that it was time to confront all the enemies that lurked inside his Bunker, in the absence of an external threat.

Still on the podium, he turned to address the officials seated behind him. He ordered Big Davey to man the checkpoint on Level 5; Davey complied. Tommy emphasised to the others that the Bunker was to become a "fortress" in these "uncertain times". He dismissed all his men, but kept Ted behind, who was still clutching the pictures of the two dead Retreaters. With a glint in his eye, Tommy addressed the little man and instructed him to follow along. The two walked down the aisle, extinguished the flames of the emergency lights, ascended to Level 5, and entered Tommy's chambers. There, a large stash of crank awaited them both. They consumed the whole lot as Tommy drivelled on about their "colleague" Eddie Lee, and his alleged desire to launch a "coup d'état", with the aide of a "clandestine network" of "two-faced conspirators" who were "aligned with the goals of the Free Thinkers and, by extension, the Retreaters themselves". Little Ted absorbed every desperate word as Tommy, high on his own supply, masterfully pulled the strings of his paranoiac puppet.

* * *

Three hours later, Noah and his crew reached the Bunker, exhausted from their shelling campaign in Surrey. Leaving the gates open to allow light to filter through, the Scouts drove into Level 0 and took chemical showers before removing their gear and, somewhat begrudgingly, took the sham skin-prick tests. Impatient, Noah refused to follow procedure: once the tests began, as they always did, to display negative results, he allowed his men to descend into the depths without the usual thirty-minute wait.

The twenty men made their way down to a pitch-black Level 2, guided by small gas lanterns that had been placed in the halls. The other Scouts had already returned to the Bunker from their stations on the hills, and could be heard in their rooms, blaring music and movies on their gadgets, all of which were soon to die, once the batteries expired. Meanwhile, Noah checked his chambers to see if Hattie was around. No sign of her. Noah furrowed his brow and turned around. While he still had time, he headed back to the spiral staircase, making his way down to Level 12, to see if Hattie was present in her old room. Using his master key, he unlocked the bedroom door and saw that she wasn't there either. Turning to leave, Noah spun his torch around. He gasped, springing backwards. His father's portrait sneered at him, dangling from the door which teetered on its hinges. Hattie had painted a desert scene on the walls surrounding Tommy's face. While running his eyes along the pyramids, rising high and mighty over barren sands, Noah felt a weird flutter in his gut. Frowning, he creeped past the door and crossed into the shadows of the hallway.

Inside the other bedrooms of 12-A, Noah could hear the sounds of hushed conversations. Pressing his ear against one of the doors, number '28', two men – a gay couple who pretended only to be friends in public – could be heard inside:

"I don't know how much more of this I can bear to stand..."

"I know, I know. It's ridiculous. I don't understand why he won't let us out. What exactly is wrong with that fucking lunatic?"

Noah, uncomfortable, backed away after Colin Carrington began to violate confidentiality, saying something about Disease X and how Tommy was using it as a "pretext" to keep people "trapped and powerless" inside his "purgatory of delusion".

Eventually, when Noah reached Level 7, he entered Corridor A and searched the medical wing. No sign of Ms Osborne – or anyone, aside from a comatose Dennis, who lay lifeless in a hospital bed. Noah then stepped into Corridor B, and began to check the common areas, to see if Hattie was hiding away there. Holding a flashlight, he opened the library door and, peering inside, saw only a group of teenage boys. They fell silent and turned to Noah with nervous, guilty expressions, like meerkats caught in the open desert. Noah closed the door and continued checking the common rooms, until, at last, he ventured into the dark Garden Space, its hexagon lights now completely cut out. For the time being, the willow trees and lush grass would remain intact. The air was charged with the agitated buzz of bees, troubled by the change in their environment. A few children continued to play on the grass, guided by the lights from their mobile phones. Noah made his way along the path and, stopping in his tracks, saw that Hattie was sitting on a bench with her older friend Charlotte.

As he approached, Noah heard Hattie saying the f-word. The way she said it was so gratingly obvious, even though the girls were trying to keep their voices down. Seeing them sitting face-to-face, leaning right into each other, Noah felt they were discussing something important. He hid behind the curtain of a willow tree to eavesdrop on their muted conversation.

* * *

"... so God knows how long we've got left in this place," Charlotte remarked.

Hattie's eyes, illuminated by the gas lantern near the bench, flashed with fury. "It's ridiculous," she said, almost hissing, "how they're trying to tear our lives apart... fucking Retreaters. Marcus and Jasper – I'm still trying to figure out what's going on with them..."

"I tried to warn you about those two," Charlotte replied, pressing her lips into a patronising pout.

Hattie turned away, slumping on the bench. "It's just – they were always so good to me, you know?"

"Were they really? Or were they just leeching off you?"

"What do you mean?" Hattie asked.

"Taking advantage of your good nature. Like, look at Marcus. All the shit that went down after the ball..."

Hattie grimaced.

"And I know you guys ended things," continued Charlotte, "but you seemed so quick to forgive what he did... I never understood that, to be honest."

"I don't know, Char. I think it's just... I could tell how sorry he was. Seeing what Derek and Reece did to me – it really messed him up." She began to examine her fingers. "But I know he'd never set out to hurt me. Not on purpose, at least."

Charlotte scoffed.

"What?"

"Always quick to see the good in people, eh?"

"I guess..." Hattie turned to face Charlotte. "What, is that meant to be a dig?"

"Nah. It's not just that. I think your main issue, Hats, is that you're a massive pushover. Like, good for you, putting up with people's shittiness, but I don't think you've ever realised, you are allowed to be angry sometimes... you don't have to let everyone walk all over you..."

"No, no. You're right." A sigh escaped Hattie's lips. "Always blowing in the breeze, aren't I."

"Like a plastic bag..." Charlotte began. Hattie scowled, refusing to sing along. "Floating through the wind..."

"Yep," Hattie rolled her eyes, "that's actually so funny, isn't it. Good old Hattie, always sleepwalking, never far from the next disaster... hah, hah."

Charlotte's face fell. Hattie's eyes shimmered with tears in the flickering light.

"I always thought," Hattie continued, her voice trembling, "that it was a good way to be, you know? Not stressing about the things I can't control... But it hasn't made me happy. And I've let myself be fucked over far too many times. Never looked after myself like I should."

There was a long silence.

"Where do you think this is coming from?"

"I mean, drugs did help. Has to be said." Hattie let out a dry chuckle, though her head remained bowed. "But really, I've always known these things. Even before the acid. I think it started with mum. Her diagnosis – it made me grow up so, so fast. All those sleepless nights by her bedside... clinging to the hope that it'd all be okay..." She shook her head. "So, there we are. Aged five – forced to see all these things that a kid shouldn't see. Moulded into a caregiver. And don't get me wrong, I do like looking after people – it's just... it's a little much sometimes... a little unhealthy..."

"Go on," said Charlotte.

"After mum went... I found other people to try and heal; little pet projects – thinking I could fix them if I *just* tried hard enough..." Hattie rubbed her eyes. "And so, my first target was Ursula. That's why I used to play with her all the time. Make her feel included. Poor girl: the other kids really had it out for her. And," she took in a deep breath, "after that, I moved on to Jasper. When he became more reclusive... when he started to *change*... I felt obliged to take him under my wing. Marcus helped out a bit, too." She gritted her teeth. "Like adoptive parents, I suppose."

"Yep. No, I totally get it." After a pause, Charlotte scratched her chin and asked, "And why d'you think Jasper's... y'know... why'd he turn out like that?"

Behind the willow tree, Noah almost gave his cover away, swatting a bee off his neck.

"Jasper's just... I read something the other day about 'HSPs'. Highly Sensitive People. I reckon he's one of those, for sure." Hattie nodded to herself. "Life's not been too kind to any of us, really... but Jasper's never coped. No confidence, no parents, nothing to set him straight. When he was younger, he seemed happier, more at peace... but things, I think, mounted over time. Especially after puberty. Especially with Tommy always getting on his case twenty-four seven."

"Bit up his own arse, isn't he?" Charlotte remarked.

"Tommy?"

Charlotte shook her head. "Jasper."

"I don't think so." Hattie reflected for a moment. "In some ways, perhaps."

"I reckon that's what he's getting from the Retreaters: a means of enacting revenge. Like he wants to make us suffer, because he himself's such a miserable twerp."

"No way." Hattie folded her arms. "He'd never..." Her voice tailed off. "Look," she began, "the Retreaters are the scum of the Earth. Dani got screwed over, yeah – but that doesn't make it right what those lot have done to us. That's pretty damn obvious. Marcus, I feel, got dragged into it. Jasper, probably the same. But Tommy – you have to admit," Hattie lowered her voice, "you have to admit, he's erm... he's a bit of a—"

Charlotte cut her off, glancing around. Noah ducked behind the tree trunk. After a pause, Hattie continued:

"You know what he's doing to Tiger's mum, don't you? Up on Level 3?"

"No..." said Charlotte, her intonation rising. "What's going on with her?"

Hattie whispered her response. Noah peeped his head out from behind the trunk, trying to hear. As he shuffled beneath the willow tree, getting within earshot of the bench, another bee buzzed onto his neck. Startled, he flapped it away. But the bee came back with a vengeance. Panicking, Noah's legs propelled him forward, and he stumbled through a curtain of leaves. The girls turned and, seeing Noah there, immediately fell silent.

* * *

Exposed, Noah stepped away from the willow tree and approached the girls on the gravel path. Hattie and Charlotte sat frozen. Noah stopped by the fountain for a moment, shone his torch on the dried relic, and then aimed it at the bench. "It's alright. I couldn't hear much."

Charlotte kept her eyes fixed on Noah. He assured her, "I was just curious. I'm not gonna get you into trouble." However, her look of concern remained. Noah added:

"Believe me – my dad's got bigger things to worry about. He won't care to hear about this."

Charlotte nodded gratefully. On his cue, she left Hattie and Noah alone, heading along a gravel path lit by yellow lanterns.

Reunited, Noah hugged Hattie. "Rather naughty of you," he said as they separated, "violating confidentiality like that. Those are 'sacrosanct' rules, I'll have you know."

Hattie blushed. "Sorry."

Noah laughed. "Only teasing." He sat on the bench and Hattie joined him.

"In truth, he's a bit of a *wanker*," Noah remarked, applying an awkward degree of emphasis.

"Huh?" Hattie regarded her boyfriend with suspicion.

"I said, he's a bit of a *wanker*."

Hattie's brow creased. "Who?"

"Tommy," Noah replied. "Isn't that what you were gonna say just then? Before you cut yourself off?"

Hattie didn't respond.

"How Tommy's a *wanker*?"

At last, Hattie broke into laughter. But Noah's expression was grave. She let out a half-chuckle, closely inspecting his face. "Why, what's he done now?"

"It's just... everything about him, really." Noah puffed out a sigh. "The hypocrisy... the ego... and the way he treats people like we're" – he paused, racking his brains for an apt metaphor – "worker bees in a – a big beehive..."

Hattie snorted with laughter. "Interesting description, Noah." She gritted her teeth, peering up at the ceiling. Above their heads, the hexagonal lights were off, devoid of any current. "So Tommy's the keeper of the hive then? Or, like, the evil queen who gets off on bossing everyone around?"

Noah's gaze, meanwhile, trailed off in the distance. Through the gloom of the Garden Space, a row of greenhouses could be made out at the far end.

"Does he even *have* a soul?" he asked, in full earnest. Hattie cast him a wary glance. His cheeks had turned pale.

"It's alright," Noah added, "just be honest."

Hattie arched an eyebrow. "You really want me to answer that?"

Noah nodded.

"Alright then..." Hattie took a deep breath to compose herself. "Okay, so, you know that book I've been reading?"

Noah turned to her. "The one about mental problems?"

"Mhm. That's the one." Hattie peered down at her feet. "Well, I read about this condition, which I think describes him to a tee."

"Really?" Noah fiddled with the scruff of his shirt. "Which one?"

Before Hattie could continue, Noah's phone alarm started ringing.

"Ah, shit. Better head off. Got a meeting at 5 o'clock. The 'Commander' wants to have a word with all the Scouts." He rose to his feet and looked down at Hattie, his eyes twinkling in the lantern's light. "We'll discuss this later."

"Alright." Hattie blew her boyfriend a kiss and waved him goodbye. She trailed him with her eyes as he strolled down the gravel track. Letting out a sigh, Hattie gazed over at the park's central fountain, the one that Tommy had commissioned to be built in o'nine. Its basin was dry, no water spewed from the top anymore, but the ornament retained a certain allure all the same, with its intricate patterns and its expert design.

26
Chemical Dust

30/10/0017

22:28

Hattie was sitting in the corner chair of Noah's darkened room, dressed in a red robe. She'd just returned from a long, stressful shift in the medical wing and was currently reading her little textbook on psychiatry. A lingering unease had settled in her stomach. Several of the patients they'd seen that day had complained of ailments without an obvious cause – headaches, chest pains, dizziness, and above all, an intense nausea. Hattie sighed, her lungs rattling. She suspected that a wave of hysteria had swept over the Bunker, the somatic display of a social disease.

As Hattie neared the end of the book, she turned to the final chapter, which listed a number of unclassified conditions. Her eyes gravitated to the section that was titled STOCKHOLM SYNDROME.

> *Though not officially recognised in the diagnostic manuals, Stockholm Syndrome offers an intriguing insight into the psychological interplays within manipulative and controlled environments, notably where the dynamics mimic those of domestic abuse or hostage situations. The phenomenon is characterised by unusual emotional bonds between captives and captors, particularly where both parties hold shared values or goals. A system of reward and manipulation may also be used in order to maintain the captive's loyalty.*

> *The validity of this phenomenon continues to spark debate among mental health professionals, as it underscores the challenge of discerning true allegiance from coercive compliance within such environments.*

But before she could continue reading, the door creaked open. Noah came in, turning off his torch. The candlelight was dim, and it was hard to read his features, although Hattie sensed something was up through his tense, rigid movements, and the unusually high pitch in his voice.

"How're we doing?" he said, almost squeaking his words.

"Fine." Hattie set her book aside. "You?"

"Yeah, yeah," said Noah. "I'm good, I'm good..."

Hattie gave him a closer look. Although his face was half-concealed by shadow, she could see his watery eyes shimmer in the flickering light. Acting on instinct, she stood up and hugged him. Embraced in his trunk-like arms, she felt a rush of comforting warmth.

"It's okay, Noah." Hattie nestled her head against his chest, her fingers caressing his back. "We'll get through this..."

Noah puffed out a sigh and said, "Everything's turned to shit." The depth had returned to his voice.

Pulling back, Hattie looked up at him. "What happened at the meeting?"

Noah stepped away and dropped down onto the bed. "Tommy – he's... I think my dad's losing it... and the other guys think so too..."

"What d'you mean?" Hattie asked, folding her arms.

"He kept saying how 'screwed' we all are," said Noah. "That our days are numbered somehow."

"That's nonsense," said Hattie. "Sounds like paranoia to me..."

"Yeah. I'm not sure..." Noah reached into his mini-fridge, still nice and cold, although the blue light had ceased to function. He took out a half-empty flask of vodka and swigged it straight. He passed it to Hattie, and she did the same, sitting next to him at the end of his bed.

"What about the Retreaters?" she asked, wiping the booze from her lips. "You're gonna take them out, right?"

"Yep. That's what Tommy has in mind." Noah grimaced. "But we're almost out of fuel. There's barely enough for a trip to the Estate, even. So we'll have to march down to Surrey at this rate. On foot. That'll be fun..." Reaching for his phone, he began to play some cheery music to lighten the mood, but stopped, seeing that his battery was about to die.

"Maybe he has a point. Maybe we are kind of fucked."

"Don't talk like that," said Hattie, injecting cheer into her voice. "There's plenty of food and water stockpiled, isn't there? We'll survive. And besides, the Bunker's seen worse." She offered him a forced smile.

"But the truth's out, Hats. Everyone knows about X. What the real situation is, up there." Noah turned to look at the dim concrete ceiling. "But Tommy won't budge. He'll never let us leave this place..."

Hattie cast Noah an uneasy glance. At last, she cleared her throat, and said:

"I know your dad's not perfect. And I don't always agree with his methods. But he's done a lot for us, hasn't he?" A faint smile crossed her lips. "And, once the Retreaters are out of the picture, we can finally start healing..."

"Err," said Noah, "I guess?"

"Yeah..." Hattie nodded to herself, eyes wandering off into the distance. "Build ourselves back up, after all the shit they've put us through. And Tommy – it's affected him too, hasn't it? It's made him cold, made him ruthless, so that he can ward them off; keep us safe from those killers outside..."

"You think he wasn't like that before?"

Hattie shrugged. "I mean, you know him better than I do..."

Noah clasped his hands together. After hesitating, he admitted:

"He's certainly got worse over the years. I can tell you that much."

"The crank's a new thing for him, isn't it?" Hattie enquired.

"It was coke before that," Noah replied, "but the stashes we used to find during missions – it all kept getting weaker over time. So he wanted something fresh. Hence, Hans' lab on Level 0. Plus, the tobacco and cannabis farms that he had us set up on the Estate."

"And the whole forced labour thing?" Hattie peered down at her feet. "I get that it's supposed to be a punishment... but what he's done to Prim in particular, is just—"

Hattie stopped as Noah shot her a stern glance. There was a flicker of shame in his eyes. "Prim's being kept on 3 for the other guys, Hattie. Not him. She's an 'outlet for the lads': Ted's words, not mine."

Hattie shook her head. "But that doesn't make sense. Why not just send her out to the Estate? At least then, she could help work the fields and do something productive..." Hattie shuddered. "Christ, listen to me, justifying this shit. I mean, why's she even being held captive in the first place? Prisoner for life, what, because of something her husband did? For getting on Tommy's bad side? Jesus!"

Impassioned, Hattie rose from the bed and grabbed her psychiatry manual from the corner chair. She flicked it open to a dog-eared section, and displayed it to Noah.

"Have a look," she said, sitting down next to him. "Tell me this doesn't ring a bell..."

Noah had to squint in order to read the book's tiny letters. After finishing, he hesitated, before slapping it shut and handing it back to Hattie.

"Yeah, I dunno about that," said Noah. An irritating smirk came over his lips. "Besides – they're all mad themselves, aren't they? Psychologists?"

"For fuck's sakes, Noah!" Hattie exclaimed, thumping him on the shoulder. "I'm serious!"

Noah winced, irritated by the shrillness of her voice. "What, so, you reckon he's a bit doo-lally, then? Great... like I wasn't already aware."

"He needs help," Hattie said, clenching her teeth. "It makes me nervous, the fact he's getting so high all the time... especially with all the stress he's been under lately..."

Noah let out a sharp cackle, although his eyes glistened softly in the light. "And how exactly are you gonna help my father? Huh? What, because you read a little book about so-called 'disorders', you think you're Sigmund Freud all of a sudden?"

Hattie smacked Noah in the face and rose from the bed. "Why don't *you* come up with something, then?! Maybe try and stand up to him for once in your life!"

Recoiling from the pain, Noah peered up at her. Seeing the tears in his eyes, Hattie felt an instant pang of regret. She sat down and draped her arm over his shoulder. "I'm sorry – I shouldn't have lashed out like that. I'm sorry. But I hope you realise – someone needs to do something about that man!"

Noah, wiping his tears, took a deep breath to regain composure. Then he turned his gaze to Hattie. "So what are you suggesting?"

Hattie moved her arm off his shoulder. "I'm not sure. But I know he needs to come off the drugs, for one. Maybe we could stage an intervention. Or get the guys to have a word."

"He won't listen to them."

Biting her lip, Hattie asked, "What about you?"

Noah wiped his eyes once more. He turned to look at the framed photo on his bedside, admiring his deceased mother's face. "Fine," he sighed, "I can give it a shot. If it'll get you off my case..."

"You promise?"

"Yeah, yeah." Hattie smiled and reached for his hand. Noah returned her tight clasp with a loose squeeze. "Now," he said, a prolonged yawn escaping his lips, "will you please let me get some bloody rest?"

Hattie smiled and kissed him on the cheek, leaving a smudge of lipstick. She took her robe off and hung it on the door, smothering the Commander's portrait. Noah, meanwhile, had started to undress from his sweaty day clothes.

After Hattie blew the candles out, the young couple climbed into the duvet together. Despite the air circulation system being out of order, Noah's chambers remained comfortably warm. The two stayed close together in the bed as they tried to drift off, although they shuffled about, tossing and turning, their tired minds unsettled by a stream of racing thoughts.

* * *

Three levels below, Tommy sat alert in his leather chair. His meeting with the Scouts had only fuelled his paranoid suspicions, adding to his belief that dark forces were at play, conspiring to wreck what he'd built over the years.

He stared at his personal bust, carved from marble that glistened coldly in the light of his oil lamp. In that moment, he felt an immense pang of self-hatred, repulsed by the contours of his face, all the wrinkles and marks that had accumulated over the years, captured boldly by the sculptor's expert hand. No longer the Adonis he'd been as a young, virile man in his prime, Tommy, in his maturity, now looked more like a gargoyle.

Hunched over his desk, he reached for his little notebook and started reading through its contents. The self-hatred was compounded, Tommy cringing at himself as his words laid it bare: the insatiable ego he'd been trying to satiate, all the power he'd been amassing, the little empire he'd established to try and prove a point, propelled by some unknown force, but it was useless, for none of it had ever really mattered, and in any case, all of these things were destined to fall apart.

As he flicked through the pages, he stopped on a diary entry with a bold header that read, **STORY OF MY LIFE – 1st January, 0001.**

Below, he'd scrawled down a poem with leaky ink during one of his coke episodes:

A bright Star rose, above the ground,
And tried to steer the course of the Earth,
But the Danis and Joes and naysayers of this world,
Felt threatened by my Star's magic twirl!

But the bright Star moved with a skilful grace,
And was held by most in high regard.
The masses could see how It shone so bright
And put a stop to the ministers' fight.

Yes, we booted them out: free at long last!
But my Star is a merciful thing.
No deaths at my hands, even let them run free,
Orange suits did those ministers receive.

Not a peep from them yet,
Perhaps they failed to survive.
Or worse, what if they are still alive?
What will happen if those scumbags start to thrive?

Ms Dalton, you see, she's a wicked old thing,
Though alluring her eyes do deceive.
And though others may whisper with rumours and lies
About the man I could very well be,

The world's been placed, inside of my hands
And my Star steers its course every day.
I just happened to be the right man at the hour,
And was cast in this role by God's Epic Power.

But there's always a price
That a Star comes to pay
If It flies too high,
If It burns too bright...

Tommy wiped his sore forehead. These words, once profound, now seemed devoid of any charm they'd ever held. Instead, they read to him as the manic ramblings of a man with a chip on his shoulder.

With a long and indulgent sigh, Tommy turned to re-read his scripts for all the plays that he'd written: GOOD AND EVIL for Spring 0010, LONG ROAD AHEAD for Winter 0011, VICTORY SCREAMS! for Summer 0012, among many other titles. All of them followed the same old pattern: tired tropes, repetitive plot-lines, and familiar 2-D characters. Enjoyable, perhaps, and always good fun for the kids, but all in all, he knew he had been trying his hand at a task that simply wasn't his.

Tommy snapped the notebook shut. Grabbing his pipe, inspecting it with trembling fingers, an intense thirst began to pulse in his mouth. Tommy leaned forward and, with heavy limbs, heaved himself up from the massive armchair. As he made his way out of his room, wearing his dark-red gown, he looked over at the neglected aquarium where a school of putrefying goldfish floated at the surface.

* * *

Tommy stepped into Corridor A of Level 8. Sitting near the entrance was a burning oil lamp, which marked where the communal bathroom was situated. Its hissing flame flicked shadows across the walls. Treading along the red carpet, Tommy passed silent rooms, where the people were asleep. At last, upon locating number '27', he stopped and rapped on the door. A few moments later, Dr Hans appeared, with eyes that looked dry and tired.

Tommy requested another "refill" of his "special ice", fidgeting with his hands.

Hans bowed his head. He stepped back into the room and reached into a drawer, while Tommy leaned against the doorframe, staring longingly at the golden locks of Eva's head, who, turned away from the door, was tucked fast asleep beneath the duvet.

Dr Hans returned with his small green box, and took out a bag of crystalline substance. He handed it to Tommy and, before he could return to bed with his wife, Tommy clicked his fingers and performed a sharp whistle. A flicker of irritation crossed Hans' face as he turned around.

"Doctor, doctor," said Tommy, in a sickly sing-song voice, "there's something else I need you to do."

"Oh?" Hans crossed his arms. "What's that?"

Tommy grinned and told the man to get dressed. There was a "special chemical" that had to be produced before sunrise.

"What do you mean?" asked Hans, as he pulled on a red polo shirt and a pair of tight trousers.

"You'll see." Tommy gave him a cheeky wink and, patting him on the back, led Hans through into the dark hall outside. Near the exit, the lantern's fire flickered and spat.

27
Lab Leak

23:11

The same night, after making their way up to the Peak District in a hotwired Audi, careful to take alternate routes, Marcus, Jasper and Jonathan were sitting in the car, tucked away in the shadows of a forest. All their windows were rolled open, and the sounds of bristling leaves filled the air. Marcus was busy operating one of Dani's spare drones. The tiny craft hovered high above the Estate, zooming in on the grounds with its powerful camera.

On the iPad screen, the farm seemed eerily silent, devoid of signs of life, save for the outhouse near the barbed-wire entrance. Its window glowed with yellow light, and a black silhouette was lurking inside.

Marcus, clicking buttons on the remote, began to raise the drone and drift it to the west. It passed over the terrain of the Peak District, barely visible, as the moon's light was dimmed beneath heavy clouds.

Soon, the drone was hovering above the Bunker's hill at a high altitude. Marcus manipulated its camera to zoom in on the punctured dam. A pile of concrete rubble lay at the bottom of the valley. The flood of water had dissipated, seeping away into the soil. Marcus zoomed out. No little orange men could be seen in the area: all the Scouts' watch-posts were unmanned.

Marcus furrowed his brow. On the other side of the hill, the Bunker's concrete gates had been left wide open. He lowered the drone and tried to zoom in, but the three Retreaters were unable to see anything through the shadows of Level 0.

* * *

Meanwhile, Tommy led Hans up the gloomy, winding staircase. They greeted Big Davey on the landing outside Level 5, who was slumped in his chair, with an oil lamp by his side. To justify the late-night excursion, Tommy mentioned something about a safety issue in the lab, one that Hans needed to address. Davey bowed his head and muttered "Yes boss", although his beady eyes trailed the two as they climbed the stairs towards the ground floor.

Tommy took out his phone and, using its flashlight, tried to find his way in the artificial cavern towards the corner laboratory. He spotted a shiny metal vat that towered above his head. Shining the light towards the far wall, he saw a stack of chemical barrels. His eyes appeared to spark with an idea. He passed his phone to Hans and told him to hold it while he reached into his pocket, taking out a glass pipe which he filled with crystals, then heated with his lighter. Tommy took a deep drag of the intense smoke and, expunging it into Hans' face, asked the chemist whether he'd like a little toke.

"No," said Hans, firmly raising his hand, "I'm quite alright, thank you."

"Suit yourself," said Tommy. "Might need you awake for a while, is all."

Hans began to fidget with his hands. "Sir... if this is about your request for fentanyl – I'm sorry, but we still don't have the specific precursor for that one... and in any case, in the absence of electricity, it's going to be very difficult... impossible, even..."

Tommy's eyes were blank, but his face seemed to twitch with a manic energy. Feeling uncomfortable with the silence, Dr Hans added:

"Thus, I don't know what you want me to do, sir. It's just not possible. But I can always—"

"So you won't do cyanide either, I take it?"

Hans looked into Tommy's eyes, and saw that his boss wasn't joking.

"No, sir," he said, "I really don't think so..."

Hans suppressed a gulp. Tommy's empty eyes seemed to see through him, as though the man wasn't there. The chemist stood frozen, like a deer stuck in headlights, before he broke away and, turning on his heel, began to wander through the shadows of the laboratory. With Tommy's flashlight, he began to scan all his old equipment: the beakers, the tubes, and the piles of papers – all the ingredients he had used to produce the Bunker's drugs, now defunct and obsolete.

"What is this for?" Dr Hans asked, with feigned confidence in his voice, though he couldn't suppress the tremble in his throat.

Somewhere in the dark, Tommy's voice responded, telling him that it was for no one in particular and that, in any case, it was none of Hans' business.

"I've given you a task," he continued, "and that's all you need to know. The rest is up to you."

"Fine." Moving towards his old desk, Dr Hans sat down and, using the phone's little light, began to flick through old drafts of the annual fabrications. At the bottom of the stack, he found the first report he had ever written, drafted in o'two at Tommy's request.

> *The H5N1-X strain ("Disease X"), a unique biochemical anomaly, has demonstrated unprecedented survivability in the hostile exospheric conditions above ground level. This report elucidates the mechanisms through which this tenacious pathogen defies conventional biological limitations to persist in the tropospheric environment. The research utilises advanced cross-analytical spectral chromatography, alongside multivariable hyperbolic regression models, to validate the existence of these pathogenic aerosols. Furthermore, I introduce a novel bio-analytical framework that hypothesises a self-replicative air-to-air transmission mechanism unique to Disease X. These results offer a theoretical substrate for the continued necessity of subterranean habitation to safeguard our people against the airborne threat.*

Dr Hans closed his eyes tightly, ashamed of the lies he'd helped Tommy spin. He jumped in his seat, startled, as Tommy stood behind him, placing his hand on his shoulder. Hans scrambled to hide the papers, and pretended to look over instructions for the synthesis of MDMA.

"This needs to be done," said Tommy. "And it has to be something you can't taste in water."

Hans turned around and took a deep breath, trying not to hyperventilate. "I don't know what you intend," he said, lying through gritted teeth.

Tommy scoffed. "Of course you do." He pulled out one of the papers that Hans had tried to hide. "Don't forget," he added, "you're in just as much shit as I am, pal. Just think about what they'll do to you if they ever find out what I've done – what *we've* done. And what they'll do to your Eva, no less."

Dr Hans shook his head in vehement denial. "No," he said, "no... this eventuality will not happen... the people, we can continue to control, it's going to be okay – they understand what you have done, and they respect you, for how you have saved us all from the terrible world outside those gates..."

"Yeah. I'm not sure." Tommy raised his brow and peered towards the end of Level 0, where the massive concrete doors had been left wide open. Little could be seen in the darkness outside. "And besides. It's the others I'm concerned about the most."

"The others?"

"Yes." Tommy propped himself on the desk and held his hands on his hips, leering down at Dr Hans, who sat hunched in his chair. Hans folded his arms as Tommy spiralled off on a pack of lies. It all came so easily to him, like a form of art, although Hans had learned all of Tommy's tells. In the dim light of the room, he watched as Tommy raised his hands passionately, and his eyes darted around in their sockets as he spun the words in his head before speaking them aloud.

"... so he's going to use your Eva as a prize, to try and get Pete on board. You know how much that desperate freak wants a piece of your action. You're very lucky, y'know – a man like you, with a woman like that. Hey, I'm kidding, I'm kidding!" he said, slapping Hans on the chest. "Lighten up. But yes. Seriously. There really are no lengths that Eddie won't go to. Ted told me everything. Listening into their conversation, a little clandestine meeting in the Gardens – disgraceful. Disgraceful. After everything I've done for those bastards." Tommy wrinkled his nose, watching Hans' face intently. The man avoided eye contact as he feigned agreement, the nods of his head automatic and dispassionate. Tommy sighed and, failing to hide the disappointment in his voice, told Hans to stand up, for the work needed to be done as soon as possible.

"Before the others wake up," explained Tommy. Hans looked deep into his eyes and saw a wild, bloodshot look. His dry, scaly lips seemed to cry out with a thirst that water alone could never quench.

"How much do you want," probed Hans. "How much poison would you need?"

Tommy scratched his chin. "A gallon's worth."

Hans raised his brow. "A gallon?"

"Yes." Tommy started to ramble on with a vague explanation, eyes shifting about as he formulated it:

"... in case we need more for the future – in case other threats arise. Can't hurt to be prepared, you know." Tommy turned towards Hans and, in a somewhat defeated tone, simply added:

"Just do as I ask."

Hans rose from his chair, and reached to hold Tommy by the shoulder with unprecedented strength. "This, I cannot do, my friend. It's really just not possible." He passed the smartphone back. "Besides, I really must be going. I'm too exhausted, to stay awake up here and talk with you." As he made his way back to the door, Hans paused, then turned back to Tommy, whose face could not be seen, although the phone's light continued to glow from his hand. His chest heaved with a series of shallow, rapid breaths.

"I will not speak a word of this," Hans assured. "I respect the confidentiality between me and you. As I always have." He gave Tommy a courteous nod and wished him a good night. Tommy didn't respond. His silhouette remained frozen in place. Hans, uneasy, turned away and began walking to the door. His walk quickened as he heard footsteps clattering behind, until at last, he swivelled around and saw that Tommy was hurtling towards him in the darkness.

* * *

Hans screeched as he was tackled to the ground, his skull thudding against the tarmac. Tommy climbed on top and began to bash Hans' head into the floor, again and again, caving in the skull until it started to bleed, and at last, the life disappeared from the scientist's eyes. Tommy stood up letting out a vile bellow. For good measure, he stomped on the man's face, splattering the nose with his boot. At last, he began to scramble away, leaving the body behind as he made his way down towards Level 5. Outside, an oblivious Davey continued to sit, reading a magazine by the light of his oil lamp. He propped his head up and, seeing the troubling look on his boss's face, asked Tommy what was wrong.

"Nothing," breathed Tommy. "Nothing," he repeated as he fumbled with the lock of Level 5, trying to get it open. His shaky fingers dropped the metal key, which chimed on the grated metal floor. Davey put his magazine down and stood up, towering over his boss like a naïve giant. "Boss – wha'ss that you've got there?" he said, pointing to a streak of blood that had splattered on his night gown. Davey peered down at his feet and, agitated, began to hyperventilate.

"Where's Hans?"

Tommy pressed his lips together. "Don't worry. Like I told you: he's just fixing a leak."

Davey shook his head, a tear rolling down his cheek. "But sir – I dun' understand! Why won't you ever tell me wha'ss *really* goin' on?!"

Tommy looked up and, in a flash of rage, punched the imbecile in the face. Davey tumbled back and, under heavy momentum, his massive legs crashed against the safety rail. Tommy licked his lips and, without hesitation, shoved the man downwards. He watched with a perverse joy and laughed like a maniac as the simpleton fell with his arms flailing, as if this could somehow slow the descent, until at last, his body thudded against the lowermost floor, cracking and contorting, blood spilling out from underneath. Tommy released an inhuman cry, as if to claim triumph over a mortal enemy, but panted with exhaustion, as his eyes slowly returned to their baseline empty state.

28
Burned Out

01:07

Tommy lay awake in his chambers, his mind racing with a restless energy. His nails were torn and bloodied from where he'd been chewing them. His teeth throbbed with pain. A gas lantern hissed on his bedside table.

Tommy sat up and began to look through old photos on his phone. He swiped from the beginning – right from '0000' – and smiled faintly as he remembered the life he'd once lived with his then-wife Anastasia, and her little Noah, the blue-eyed boy whom he'd taken as his own. One depicted the three sitting in the Bunker's common canteen, smiling broadly at the camera. A rare moment of warmth and peace in an otherwise tumultuous time. A peace he'd spent his life trying to recreate, but one which, he realised, had been lost in time forever. The woman had killed herself some four years later, an event he'd once blamed on her mental fragility, but which, he realised, was the product of his own moral failings.

At last, the smartphone's battery died.

Groaning with a sound like the growls of a roused bear, Tommy dragged himself from the bed and took another hit of crystal meth. Its chemical flavour seeped into his lungs, and at once, the weariness gave way to a powerful, rhythmic energy, like the warm, steady beats of a human heart. A divine voice began to whisper songs of praise. It told him that he'd done well in his time, but that he would have to give up now, for he'd finally reached the end of the line.

Standing up and feeling several kilograms lighter, Tommy strolled over to his aquarium, whose light had been extinguished. The orange fish lay lifeless, having sunk down to the pebbly floor. Tommy grunted to himself and gave the glass one last tap. The pebbles jostled, and the dead fish shuffled in place. The treasure chest stayed sealed, its oxygen bubbles building up beneath the lid.

Tommy picked up his blazing lantern. Approaching the door, he turned around for a final glance at his chambers before heading out into the dark and silent corridor of Level 5.

Tommy stopped at room number '2', knocking on the door. Little Ted creaked it open.

"It's over for us," said Tommy. "Eddie's planning a coup in the morning. Davey told me everything."

Ted's eyes kindled with a wild fury. "I can't believe it," he hissed. "So ungrateful!"

"I know. I know." Tommy let out a heavy sigh and added, "You can't trust a soul in this terrible life."

Ted shook his head, disgusted. "Such a shame, sir."

"It certainly is." Tommy leaned against the doorframe, looking down at Little Ted. "But I have faith in you still."

"Of course! Of course!" said Ted, knees wobbly with excitement.

"You and I – we're built from the same kind of stuff. Forget about the others. They'll never accept us for who and what we are."

"I agree, I agree," chirped the little fanatic. Tommy felt a slight twinge of regret, which he duly suppressed with a hit from his glass pipe. He passed it to Ted. Ted took a deep drag and, following his boss's lead, the two walked together to the stairs, guided by Tommy's flickering light.

* * *

01:26

Noah and Hattie lay fast asleep. The door was rattled open, and the two were stirred awake, straining to see who was entering the room.

"Son," hissed Tommy, "son, get up. Stop lazing about."

Noah wiped his brow. "What's going on?"

Tommy crossed the threshold. He shone his lamp on the couple and licked his lips before muttering something about a "grave, imminent threat". Noah rose from the bed and, following Tommy's instructions, got dressed and packed a bag. Hattie did the same. As she pulled on a white T-shirt, she noticed Little Ted propped against the doorframe, smoking from a glass pipe. He appeared to shake with a full-body tremor, hands jerking with abrupt twitches.

"Come on," said Tommy, beckoning the two with his finger. "We've got to hurry." Tommy stepped out of the room, followed by Noah. Hattie noticed the butt of a Glock tucked into her boyfriend's trousers. Noah turned to give Hattie a wary glance, reached for her hand, and noted the look of nausea in her face.

All four of them stepped out of Level 2, leaving the pitch-black lobby behind. Inside the staircase, the air was unusually warm, like a slow-baking oven.

"Go on, go on," urged Tommy, gesturing for Hattie and Noah to head up the stairs. "We'll meet you on Level 0. Teddy and I have some business to attend to first."

Hattie and Noah climbed the metal steps, which were coated in a thick layer of fuel. It clung to their shoes as they made their way up towards the Bunker's exit. Glancing down the spiral staircase, Hattie could see flickering shadows and the outlines of flames through the portholes of the doors.

Emerging from Level 2, Tommy and Ted locked the entrance shut. Inside, flames had already begun to roar.

As they ascended the steps, Ted trailed behind Tommy, his face etched by a degree of reluctance. "Come on," called Tommy, "step up. The sooner we leave this place, the sooner we'll be rid of all this burden..."

Hattie turned to Noah, her eyes wide with dread. Noah inhaled sharply and, clasping her hand, asked Tommy if he could visit their loved ones' memorials one last time before they left.

Tommy sighed, begrudgingly permitting Noah and Hattie to head down to Level 1. Noah thanked his father and rattled the entrance door open with his master key. Tommy and Teddy stepped into the shadows of Level 0.

After entering the long, institutional hall of Level 1, Noah eased the door shut, then burst out with sharp, panicking breaths. Hattie clung to the folds his shirt and exclaimed, "What the fuck has he done?!"

"I don't know," breathed Noah, trying to conceal the tremble in his throat, "I don't know – I think... I think he's trying to—"

The two jumped and sprung backwards as Tommy swung the door open. His hands dangled by his sides, like a man in the midst of a shootout. Noah grabbed Hattie and held her tightly against his shoulder, staring at the monster before them. Like a ghostly apparition, Tommy drifted down the hall, forcing them to split as he made his way through. Stopping in his tracks, he turned and entered the space of the columbarium.

In a spur-of-the-moment decision, Noah whipped out his pistol and gave it to Hattie. Holding her by the waist, he told the young girl to make a run for the stairs, and to use force against Ted if necessary.

"The gates," he explained, "they should be open still. Just head out, run as fast as you can. If I don't see you..." He scrambled in his pockets and produced a set of keys. "Here. Take one of the Jeeps. Mine's the furthest to the left."

"But what are you planning to—"

"Just go, just go," snapped Noah, who gave her a peck on the lips to see her off, shoving her on the back to force her out.

Hattie, sobbing to herself, spiralled up the diesel-coated stairs, the metal steps clattering beneath her feet. At last, she reached Level 0. Little Ted lingered in the dark, smoking Tommy's pipe. He glanced at Hattie, his lustful eyes glistening in the darkness.

"What the hell are you doing up here?" Ted hissed. Hattie caught a glimpse of his pistol, tucked into his belt. He extinguished his lighter and disappeared into the shadows. "Where's Tommy?"

Hattie gulped. "Please, just – I don't want to—"

"Silent!" his voice snapped. "Tell me what you've done with him, woman!"

Hattie recoiled as Ted's footsteps echoed through the chamber, advancing towards her. She swung her gun up, flicked off the safety and, with shaky aim, shot into the dark, illuminating the chamber with each round. But she screamed as she was tackled to the ground, the gun flinging out of her hands. Hattie tried to wriggle free as the slender official pinned her down, his bony frame pressing onto her. As he attempted to seize her by the wrists, she grabbed his crotch and pulled it with a sharp twist. Ted screeched, flailing his fist at her face, but lost his composure, so Hattie snatched his pistol, levelled it up, and dispatched a bullet into his forehead. Blood sprayed across her face before his body collapsed on top of her. Rolling him off, she rose to her feet and turned towards the row of Jeeps near the exit.

Sprinting towards them, her focus shifted to the scene outside the gates. The outlines of hills stood prominent against the night sky, and a torrent of rain poured down from the clouds.

Hattie approached a Jeep and paused, panting, leaning against its door. But before she could unlock it with Noah's key, she was startled by the sound of a slam.

"Where the fuck do you think you're going?!" Tommy hissed. Level 0 became immersed in an orange, flickering hue.

Even with Ted's pistol, Hattie felt paralysed by primal fear. She saw Tommy's reflection in the Jeep's wing mirror as he locked the door that led to the Bunker's depths. Flames were dancing behind its glass. Tommy, gun in hand, prowled towards her.

On command, she lowered her weapon and let it drop, keeping her hands up high. Tommy frisked her in a full-body search and took Noah's keys before staring deep into her eyes.

"Fuck me," he said, taking in her appearance. There was a strange allure in his eyes. His beard was splattered with blood. "Look at the state of you." Hattie felt the urge to be sick. Ted's blood and brain matter still clung to her face. Bits had been spewed into her hair.

Tommy looked over at Little Ted's body, and Hans', which lay strung out by the lab. His gaze returned to Hattie. "Managed to ward off his advances, then?" His pupils dilated as he sized her up.

Hattie, petrified, stared back at Tommy. His crusty lips peeled open. Snarling, he ran his tongue over his teeth, before he used Noah's keys to open the car. He waved Hattie into the shotgun seat and, taking his place behind the wheel, strapped himself in with a seatbelt.

"In truth, he was never up to standard."

Hattie recoiled as Tommy locked eyes with her. He carried on:

"I know you didn't want to see it; you were blinded by love."

He'd confused her for his late wife.

"And you know what our child tried to do? Tried to shut me in!"

Tommy twisted the ignition and fired up the engine. Through the open gates, Hattie thought she saw an object flit across the sky.

"Those people," Tommy continued, spewing flecks of saliva into Hattie's face, "they were gonna torture us, they were going to – but little Noah and his new *woman*, huh?! Trying to keep me *in* with the fire! Not a chance, my dear, not a chance!"

Tommy's hand hovered over the handbrake, twitching with a manic energy, but he hesitated.

"No, no, wait a second..." His eyes darted around as if trying to recall a lost memory. "No, it's – I'm sorry. I can't just leave it all *behind* like this... I'm sorry!"

Removing his seatbelt, Tommy declared that he was going to take "one last look", before he and "Annie" could "enter the real world" to "start afresh". Outside, the full moon was cloaked beneath the clouds. Tommy stepped out and turned to the opposite end of Level 0. The fire behind the door raged in his eyes. Shadows flitted across the cavern's walls.

Hattie kept a close eye on Tommy as he lingered around, inspecting his life's work as it erased itself to the ground. But before he could return to the wheel and drive her away, a storm of lights flashed from the field outside, and Tommy's body convulsed, a stream of bullets raining over him. Hattie plugged her ears and turned her head away. Tommy collapsed into a pool of his own blood.

After a long, stunned moment, Hattie opened her eyes and climbed into the driver's seat of the Jeep, trying to get it to start. She had no idea how to operate it, but felt compelled to get away, before the killers out there could come and get her too. As she crawled the car along the tarmac, rolling out of Level 0, she slammed her foot on the brakes as two silhouettes approached, clutching Bunker-issue rifles. Her jaw dropped in disbelief, as she saw that it was Jasper and Marcus.

29
Shells

Hattie watched the two from the window as they approached Tommy's corpse. From their expressions, she could see that their boyish charm was no more. Jasper's eyes, normally timid and bright, were bloodshot and saddled with rage and exhaustion. Marcus, meanwhile, stared vacantly at the Jeep, his eyes hollow, the look of a broken man. Jasper spat gob onto Tommy's lifeless face, while Marcus moved to swing Hattie's door open.

"Hattie," he said, "Hattie – it's alright..."

On his instruction, she returned to the shotgun seat. Marcus lingered outside the car for a moment, staring towards the end of Level 0. The flames behind the sealed door's window flickered in his watery eyes.

"Don't," said Hattie, her voice wavering, sensing that Marcus was about to run towards the fire. He turned around and, ever so slowly, lowered himself into the driver's seat. His neck tensed with a gulp.

Marcus called for Jasper to step inside. Jasper stopped kicking Tommy's body, and scrambled into one of the back seats. Marcus got the Jeep going, and they drove into the storm outside. Far above their heads, a small drone tracked the car's movements.

The three sat in tense silence. Marcus kept his eyes on the gravel track, which crumbled beneath the tyres, while Jasper turned to look through the rear window, staring at the Bunker's open gates with a mixture of dread and elation. Scores of rain streamed over the windows. Marcus switched on the Jeep's wipers and turned to Hattie, seeing that her lips were quivering and her face was deathly pale. She was leaning against the door, as if preparing to make an escape.

"Hattie," he began, "what exactly happened back there?"

He swallowed, and asked, "That fire... that was Tommy, right?"

No response. The girl was too traumatised to speak. Eventually, she gave a reluctant nod, her eyes staring far into the distance.

"That bastard," said Jasper in the back. "Good riddance to that dirty fucking bastard..."

Marcus shot Jasper a wary glance through the whites of his eyes. The Jeep wound its way through a low mountain pass and entered a forest. Pulling off the track and driving through the trees, they located where the Audi was parked. Old Jonathan was sitting in the front, manning the drone. Marcus stepped out and called him over. Jonathan sat in the back of the Jeep alongside Jasper. Marcus fired the engine back up, which caused Hattie to jump, before they finally glided off down the lonely A-road. Pyramid-like hills loomed on either side. In the near distance, they could see a lake, its navy-coloured waters choppy in the breeze.

Breaking the silence, Marcus cleared his throat.

"Hattie – do you know if there's anything left?"

The others remained silent, anticipating the girl's response. At last, she opened her mouth and told them that nothing would remain of their old home. The Bunker's levels had been purposefully set on fire.

"What, even the..." Jasper's question tailed off as Jonathan cast him a stern look. He began to stare out the window, cradling his SA80 in his lap, as he quickly realised what the answer would be: that the residential floors had been targeted by Tommy's rage. Suddenly, Hattie broke out with a desolate wail.

"Hey, hey," said Marcus, reaching to pat her on the arm, "you're safe. What happened down there, I can't even begin to imagine, but all I can say is—"

Abruptly, Hattie shoved his hand away and punched him hard on the shoulder. She punched him again. And again. Jonathan intervened to stop Marcus from losing control of the car, shouting at her and restraining her arm. Marcus, shocked, watched the despair in Hattie's face as she carried on wailing, mourning the loss of their childhood home. Stirred, Marcus took a deep breath. He shifted his attention back to the road, suppressing the lump in his throat. All the while, Jasper's gaze was fixed on the back of Hattie's head, seething away with a lifetime of hatred.

* * *

The three-hour journey passed in a slog.

Marcus parked the Jeep in the Retreat's car park. The other vehicles had been blown to smithereens by the Scouts' bombing campaign. The Range Rover was a torched shell of its former self, while the delivery truck had been obliterated, its metal parts strewn about the mud like the results of an air disaster.

All four of them stumbled through the woods in silence. Swathes of trees had been erased to the ground, the ground full of craters where the shells had been dropped. At last, they reached the top of the hill and located the Retreat's secret entrance, still undiscovered, although one of the blasts had almost exposed the hatch. Marcus reached down to punch numbers into its keypad, and gestured for the others to step inside. Hattie lingered on the hill, her long hair drenched with rain as she stood near the edge, her gaze fixed idly on the horizon, where the shadows of towers could be seen in the far distance.

"Come on," he said. But Hattie didn't listen. Her cheeks were wet with rainwater. Marcus puffed out a forceful sigh.

"It's over. We won. We're rid of them all. Tommy's gone. The officials are gone. And Noah—" he said, abruptly cutting himself off, as Hattie turned to stare at him with a fiery look. Marcus bowed his head, peering down at his feet. With his rifle dangling at his side, he passed through the trapdoor and climbed down the rusty ladder, heading towards the distant light of their underground retreat. Upon reaching the floor, he peered up the long, narrow tunnel, and saw that Hattie hadn't bothered to follow.

A shadow flickered near the top of the ladder as she slammed the hatch down on them all.

30
Abyss

Awake from their dreams, Sue and Gareth stumbled up and approached the others. "What's happened?" asked Sue.

Jonathan looked down at the floor. He told them that the plan had worked, and Tommy was no more, but that things had gone "awry".

"What do you mean, 'awry'?" hissed Gareth, watching Jasper pace around with his fists clenched.

"Everything alright, Huxley?"

Jasper stopped and stared at Gareth with a flash of rage.

"Don't you look at me like that," said Gareth, gnashing his teeth. Before Jasper could square up to him, Marcus intervened, urging both of them to calm down.

"Easy now," said Jonathan, addressing the two squabbling boys. But Jasper ignored the old man's plea. He wriggled away from Marcus, and continued his agitated pacing.

"What the fuck have we done..." he whispered to himself, though the others could easily hear.

"Keep your head," said Marcus, but to no effect. After muttering a curse under his breath, Jasper turned and, in a loud, booming voice, cried:

"This was all for fucking NOTHING!"

The others grew pale. Jasper's voice echoed through the chamber's sterile walls. After a long, mournful silence, Marcus tried to grab Jasper by the arm again, only to be shoved away.

"It's Noah," said Jasper, "isn't it? That's why she hates us. Like you said – we're no good for her, are we?" Jasper's voice quivered. "So what're we even doing? Why even bother trying if it'll never be enough?!"

"Jasper, for God's sake, just stay here and—"

Marcus cut himself off as Jasper stormed down the corridor.

Retreating to his little cubicle, the enraged lad drew the curtain and lay down on the bed. He fumbled to fit the hood back over his head and, barking instructions to *MaxSimi*, brought himself into an electric nightmare.

* * *

Commanding the voice to do as he asked, Jasper was transported to the Bunker. He currently stood at the front of a crowd, gazing down from the stage in the Sports Hall. By his side, Tommy and Noah had been made to kneel at the edge, dressed in orange jumpsuits. Big Davey had been apprehended as well, as had Little Ted.

"My friends," said Jasper, raising his arms like Jesus on the cross, "I hope you can see where the *true* evil lies." Jasper turned and, nodding to Donald, who was sitting at the back of the stage, instructed the man to stand up and dish out the punishments. Grabbing a cricket bat, Donald stood up and, with a single swing, thwacked Davey and Teddy on the back of the head. Their bodies collapsed to the bottom of the stage. In the front row, Dani and Ashley rose to their feet and began to applaud. Donald prepared to strike Tommy but, before he could build momentum, was halted by Jasper, who called Dani up and told her that the honour was hers. Dani obligingly stepped up to the stage and, taking the blunt instrument from Donald's hands, proceeded to strike Tommy in the skull, cracking it, causing the man to tumble to the floor. Dani gave the bat to Jasper. Jasper stretched his arms out and, huffing and puffing to psyche himself up, prepared to strike Noah. His gaze scanned the crowd, seeking out Hattie. There she was, at the back of the hall, standing with her hands behind her back. Her eyes were filled with sorrow, and she shook her head, pleading with Jasper not to do the necessary deed. Jasper responded with a menacing smile and, after letting out a primitive growl, smacked Noah to the ground. Jasper jumped off the stage and, like a predator locked on its prey, swung some more, and some more, beating Noah's head into a mushy oblivion. The Bunker's crowd watched in amazement, stunned, before one by one, they rose to their feet like a sea of meerkats, and began to clap and cheer with mindless applause, egging on the brave boy, this Free Thinker, the one who'd known better than any of their leaders but the one whom they had forever turned away from all his life. Jasper threw the bat to the floor and, in a fit of rage, channelling some violent, wicked energy, summoned a rifle from *MaxSimi* and fired away into the crowd. The people shrieked and ran. Jasper let out a horrendous laugh and continued the slaughter – his oppressors, his personal tyrants, all the wicked men and boys who had conspired to kick him down, keep him buried underground, stripping all the light and the colour from his life and shattering his dreams of an escape. A fat man fell. Jasper cackled as his 'friend' went to pick him up. He mowed this one down with a vile glee too. There was something so pathetic in the way they all reacted, something so generic, as if their lives had meant something in the short time they'd been allotted.

Panting heavily, Jasper stopped firing as the rest of the crowd streamed out towards the stairs. The nozzle of the SA80 smoked with lingering fumes. Jasper blew them away and, tossing the gun to the floor, turned back to the stage. Dani looked at him in mild surprise, while Ashley stared, positively stunned. Donald, meanwhile, folded his arms with disdain, shook his flabby head, and said:

'A' though' you were better than this, Jaspur...'

Ignoring these patronising words, Jasper climbed onto the stage and, looking down, admired the gruesome scene he'd created.

But what to do next?

What else was there to see in this tiresome place?

Dani patted Jasper on the shoulder, wished him good luck, and began to stroll towards the exit. Ashley followed the old Prime Minister. Jasper turned and, seeing that Donald had disappeared, realised he was the only one left in the room.

Jasper scoffed, stepping over pools of blood as he made to the doors and out. In the staircase, he could hear the masses of feet as the Bunker's survivors shuffled up in a stampede, escaping from the depths into the vast world beyond, the one that lay outside the gates.

"Hope you enjoy what you've been GIVEN!" Jasper screamed, his voice bristling with self-righteous anger. The final citizen left the stairs, leaving him all to himself. He began to lean over the rail and, mesmerised, peered into the endless, spiralling steps that wound into darkness. The metallic structure of the stairs chimed faintly under his feet, like the ringing of a distant bell.

At last, Jasper smiled. With a sudden resolve, he hoisted himself up, and let himself tumble into the abyss. A sharp breeze brushed against his face. He closed his eyes, relishing a brief rush of adrenaline, until his body smacked against the floor which jolted him awake into a sterile bed.

31
Satellite

Panting, Jasper pulled off the *MaxSimi* hood, feeling queasy and exhausted by his own self-indulgence.

All those lives that Tommy had ruined. All those people, brought to ashes. Jasper closed his eyes, filled with a strange serenity, as a sudden intuition told him that – while awfully sad – the story of the Bunker never mattered all that much. For even whilst alive they'd just been mere matter still: the contortions and spirals of clusters of cells, forever repeating themselves, living on and on and on until at last, they'd been put out in a fire. Their dreams now resided in a chemical dust.

Jasper opened his eyes and stared at the ceiling, lying wide awake inside the silent Retreat. To him, the Bunker now seemed a distant dance. Animate, sure, alight with sparks of joy and brief flickers of passion, but on the whole, theirs had been a dull and forgettable display. Most people had never appealed to Jasper; a few names already flushed out of memory.

His throat began to swell, for he realised that, by now, even Hattie Osborne seemed a phantom. Attraction, intimacy, even the act of love itself – nothing but tools for DNA's spread. And Hattie's phenotype had been naturally appealing: her agreeable nature, her pretty face and her humble intelligence all fuelled the exhausting pursuit, like a hyena trying to chase down a gazelle. But Hattie would remain forever out of reach: his worthless personhood had been determined non-select.

Jasper's vision was blinded as he stared into the light. His head felt uncomfortable on the pillow, as if someone had twisted his neck. The eyes were bloodshot with exhaustion, and the synapses fired with painful messages until, after a minute, all of Jasper's ideations had completely fizzled out.

The *MaxSimi* CPU buzzed with a static sound, like a TV without any signal.

* * *

Up on the surface, Hattie lay on the hillside, watching the sky with a pained look in her eyes. Behind her head, the Retreat's hatch was swung open.

"Hattie!" exclaimed Marcus, clambering up from the tunnel. "Hattie – I'm so sorry..."

No response. A gust of wind broke the silence. The grass on the hill was dewy; the soil was waterlogged from the torrent of rain that had recently passed. Marcus approached Hattie and lowered himself down next to her. He gazed into the sky, where the stars were still obscured beneath a fog of heavy clouds.

"Why," said Hattie. Marcus looked over at the distraught young girl. She continued to lie there, staring into nothingness.

Marcus shook his head. A crow cawed in the woods. The canopies rustled in the breeze. "I just – I thought this could have all been avoided... I thought it would've worked in a different way..."

Hattie pressed her eyes shut, and took a deep breath through her nose.

"Noah and I—"

She stopped herself and glanced at Marcus, noticing the anguish in his face. His gaze was fixed on the skyline, where London towers stood. Gritting his teeth, the boy spoke:

"I never meant to hurt anyone. I just wanted my old life back – I wanted things back to how they were. And, in all truth – I seriously missed you..."

His eyes brimmed with tears, and he shuffled away from her, ashamed, trying to hide his grief-stricken face. She gazed over at him, and after a long silence, propped herself up by her elbows.

"I know," she said, biting her lip. "I know. It's just," she continued, her voice tailing off as she let out a sigh, "you could've just told me how you felt..."

Marcus froze up as he processed these words. A sore lump swelled in his throat, and he raised his head, as if trying to plead with a force that wasn't there. With regret flushing over him, he turned to Hattie, who immediately saw his unspoken agony. She reached out to hold his hand and, taking her lead, the two stood up.

Hattie stared into her ex-boyfriend's eyes, and, with a mixture of pity and the remnants of love, led him off for a stroll through the last parts of the woods that the shelling had left untouched.

* * *

Jasper sat at the end of his bed, staring blankly at the wall. His stomach rumbled, but he had no desire to eat anything.

Reaching into his bedside counter, Jasper took out a Glock pistol and, after ensuring that it was loaded, bowed his head with resolution. Possessed by some strange, unknowable force, he rose from the bed and walked out of the segregated cubicle, acting on instinct, thirsting for the release that was about to come. He saw that, in the Retreat, all the others were fast asleep, their curtains drawn shut. Hattie and Marcus had seemingly left, and were nowhere to be seen. Jasper's heart pounded with an all-too-familiar feeling.

Making his way to the ladder, he began to climb its rungs. His body was sore, his muscles all torn, but the pain made no difference to his resolve. Straining himself, he ascended towards the sealed lid at the top of the tunnel. Finally, he heaved it open and, with a smile, rolled onto the wet grass of the hill. Staring up into the night, he relished an icy breeze as it brushed his face.

His hand moved towards the gun that he'd tucked into his pocket, and he sat up to admire the City of London. Turning his head, he began to look into the forest that lay behind him, but was unable to see through the darkness.

He stood up and, making his way towards the edge of the hill, started to admire the landscape, taking in the beauty that remained of this world. But before he could raise the gun, Jasper paused, and winced, seeing that something was dancing in the sky.

A lone star, drifting through the atmosphere.

Tears brimmed in his eyes, and his lungs rattled out a sigh. His stomach panged with the shame of a lifetime wasted, watching the satellite as it drifted, aimlessly, towards the ground, before passing from sight beneath the distant horizon.

A loud shot cut through the air. The atmosphere returned to its breezy silence.

32
Spotlight

Marcus drove alone through the Peak District. All around him lay a vast, surreal, natural beauty, yet his eyes remained fixed on the vacant road ahead. The cloud cover was thick, but the dome of the sun could be seen underneath. All those terrible thoughts that he'd been trying to suppress with *MaxSimi* dreams, started to resurface once again.

That dreadful memory of the distant gunshot, while he and Hattie were taking a walk, reminiscing about better days. How they'd sprinted out of the woods, petrified, thinking that the Scouts had returned, only to find the lifeless body of their beloved, lifelong friend.

Marcus, closing his eyes, turned the volume of the music up, the booming, repetitive dance track which he'd loved in his time. His racing thoughts were pushed to the background of his mind, but carried on trying to take centre stage.

Leaving behind a flat valley, the road spiralled out into an expanse of heather plains. To the left stood a lone cottage. A ridge of hills curtained the horizon to his right, blurry in the light of that hazy afternoon. The Estate was somewhere nearby. Marcus pressed on, with full knowledge of what had happened to the officials stationed there: 'Freddy Krueger' and the five Scouts, catching wind of the Bunker's destruction, had abandoned their posts and gone astray. The other day, Gareth had managed to get in touch with the Sparrowmans via radio, who shared all the news and, last week, had arranged for the last field-slaves to be taken to the Retreat. Mo Singh, Alice Farthing and Mr Ratford's four associates were all released, as was Otto Walker, having been stationed on the farm in the wake of the Retreaters' assault.

Marcus, hoping to receive more goodwill from the Estate, was making his way over, in an attempt to barter for some food and extra fuel. The lights were about to go out, as the Retreat's generator was almost out of the Bunker's biodiesel. Moreover, none of the residents were particularly impressed by the cans of mushy beans, the expired protein bars, and the stale chemical bread that was kept in stock. It had been nearly eighteen years since it was stored there, and although still edible, nothing about their meals satisfied or produced any pleasure.

Following the arrow-sign that pointed to the Sparrowman Estate, Marcus turned onto a track. A trio of youths was loitering up ahead. Marcus carried on, expecting the three to scurry away, but the boys remained in place, forcing the Jeep to come to a stop. Its tyres scraped against the dirt as Marcus slammed the brakes.

Rolling the window down, Marcus snapped at the children, yelling for them to move out of the way.

"Or what!" cried the eldest, whose face was plump and round like the moon.

"Just do as I ask," warned Marcus. But the big lad scoffed, smiling with glee. With his tall, stocky figure, the boy resembled a hippopotamus standing on its hind legs.

"We ain't doing any more graft for you daft cunts," said the hippo.

"Damn fucking straight, motherfucker!" squeaked the littlest lad, who looked about thirteen. He folded his arms in an attempt to look tough. Meanwhile, the middle child, a boy of fourteen or fifteen, continued to puff on a poorly-rolled cigarette. His thick-rimmed glasses were fogged up with ashy smoke.

"You shouldn't be doing that," said Marcus, "not at your age..."

"Shut yer ruddy gob!" snapped the four-eyed child. He finished the last of his cigarette and, trying to intimidate Marcus, tossed the stub down and stamped the end out with his shoe.

"You'd best be scooting off," said hippo-boy, "else our dad and the gang'll come n' do a dani-handla on ya."

"Is that right?" Marcus chuckled. "Well – I'm actually here to see your folk, believe it or not. I want to make a deal."

"Thought they already made it clear what they thought 'bout your attempts to scrounge from our lands." Hippo-boy raised his chin. "Yep. Heard all about you and your begging on the radio."

"Yeah! Stick it up yer pie-hole, daft motherfucker!" squeaked the pipsqueak, desperate to impress the older lads. The four-eyed kid strolled over to the Jeep and, calling the others ahead, began to stand right outside Marcus' window.

"Come on, guys," said Marcus, "I just wanna talk to your parents. What's your issue with me, huh?"

"You lot..." Hippo-boy jabbed his finger at Marcus. "You think you can just come in 'ere and take whatever you please. Well, sorry to break it to ya – them times have passed now."

Marcus shook his head. "But our power's nearly run out. We need some extra fuel, or we're gonna go *crazy* down there. You understand what I'm saying?"

The hippo bellowed with laughter. "And is that meant to scare me, aye tommy-dazzla?"

"No, no, I mean it. You don't understand..." – Marcus began to gaze at the swathes of Sparrowman fields – "you've got all this land to keep you busy. Whereas us, we've got absolute fuck-all to do in our lives. Nothing but sleep and electric dreams to look forward to now."

"Go and cry me a river then, will ya," said the one with glasses. The others laughed with cruelty. Frustrated, Marcus rolled the window up. With a sardonic wave, he began to speed the car down the track once more.

"Oi!" cried the big one, who hurled a rock at the Jeep, which pinged straight off the protected window. Marcus chuckled to himself, watching the lads chase after him as he approached the gates. His amusement was quickly deflated, however, as a strange man emerged from the little out-house and brandished an assault rifle at the windshield. Marcus came to a skidding halt and, fearing retribution from the Sparrowman clan, swerved the car around, before speeding back the way he came. The three youths cried with victory shrieks as the Scout Jeep retreated to the main road, never to be seen again.

* * *

Marcus pounded the steering wheel with his hand, crying out with frustration. In two days' time, the Retreat was set to run out of the Bunker's biodiesel. In the absence of solar panels, their lives would be plunged into darkness, and they'd be forced to start over yet again. It was all too much, he thought, swerving the car along meandering bends, all this looping about, these exhausting, aimless attempts to find life in a world that had already passed them by.

As he made his way through the barren countryside, surrounded by plains on either side, Marcus turned on the Jeep's inbuilt radio, and clicked a button, hoping to speak with someone at the Retreat.

"Anyone there?"

The radio responded with static.

"Just wanted to let you know – I'm doing okay."

No answer. Marcus kept going nonetheless.

"Nearly got in trouble with the Sparrowmans. Things could've gone really bad, actually." He nodded to himself. "Yep. They're still pretty pissed at us. They really don't wanna help us out anymore. But I gave it my best shot, still." Marcus licked his lips, adding, "And, y'know, perhaps they'll come around. We'll just have to wait them out for a while."

Marcus glanced at the rusty remains of a hatchback, which lay on the side of the road. His eyes lit up as he heard a faint breath over the radio.

"Hattie?"

A pause. The radio crackled, and a male voice replied:

It's Gareth.

Marcus rolled his eyes, feigning cheerfulness as he said:

"Alright, mate. Did you catch all that?"

Yep, was the laconic response.

"So?" said Marcus. "What d'you think we should do?"

Another crackle. *I knew you were running a fool's errand.*

Marcus puffed his cheeks out. "Yeah, well. Someone's got to try something 'round here, haven't they."

I mean, said Gareth, *what the hell were you thinking? Do you imagine yourself as some sort of silver-tongued salesman? Or a diplomat, perhaps?*

"Piss off, wanker. At least I made the effort."

They already told us they weren't going to help. Give us the field-slaves back, and that's it. No more contact. But you wouldn't listen, would you? Always thrusting yourself into action, never stopping to think about the consequences! Didn't you ever hear the tale of how Icarus—

"Fuck off!" Marcus snapped.

Gareth chuckled on the other side of the signal. Marcus blurted out another insult, then declared that he was "heading home" to the Bunker.

Well, have fun with that, said Gareth, with a snide cruelty in his voice. Enraged, Marcus switched the radio off and slammed his foot on the accelerator. Exiting the low valley, he began to snake his way through Woodhead Pass. Bloodstains could still be seen on the surface of the bridge, where those unfortunate boys had been butchered by Ashley Mirza.

* * *

In the radio room, Gareth sat in the chair with his hands behind his head, stretching out languidly. Hattie, meanwhile, had been standing behind him, anticipating updates on Marcus' unplanned trip. A sickening dread filled the girl, worried that her friend would get himself killed.

"What an idiot," said Gareth, appealing to Hattie. "Thinks he knows better than the rest of us mere mortals. No?"

Hattie's face was taut with anguish. Abruptly, she turned around and left the room. As she hastened through the corridor, Sue, who was snuggling up with her boyfriend Mo in his cubicle, called out to ask Hattie if she was "alright". Ignoring her question, Hattie entered the Retreat's kitchen, where Otto and Jonathan were seated at the counter, their wrinkled hands cradling mugs of steaming coffee.

"Marcus," she said, with panic in her voice, "Marcus – he's—"

Otto stood up and, quickly spotting the disturbance in her face, began to comfort Hattie with a hug.

"It's alright. It's alright." He looked down at her. "What's happened?"

Hattie shook her head, tears building in her eyes. "Marcus said, he said, he's going back to the Bunker, I don't know what he's going to do, and—"

Otto held the distraught girl gently by the arms, hushing her softly. He turned to Jonathan, who remained at the counter, sitting with a grave expression. At last, the old judge stood to his feet, and said that they'd better get going, before Marcus had the chance to do "anything silly".

* * *

Meanwhile, Marcus' Jeep was winding through a steep valley, soon to arrive at his final destination. All the while, his entire body stirred with pain, as he reflected on the untimely death of his lifelong friend – one of few he'd ever truly connected with.

Tears stung in his eyes, but he kept the rush of emotions inside, distracting himself with the electro music that thumped through the loudspeakers. Those soft, melancholic sounds brought him to a trance, although the underlying message failed to resonate. Instead, he found himself returned to a distant night, one where he'd seen Jasper's pain on full display.

* * *

August 4th, 0015
The Sports Hall had been lit with disco lights. A DJ played tunes catered to the under-18s, as the boys and girls danced awkwardly on two sides of the room. Ever so slowly and all at once, the rhythms of that gentle song, now playing in the car, seemed to bring the children together. Taking their cues from Bobby and the older boys, Marcus and his friends began to gravitate towards the girls. He remembered how his ironic robot moves had caused all the girls to giggle. And how Hattie had cast him a starry-eyed look of admiration. Seeing this, Marcus approached her and took her by the waist. Hattie, his girlfriend at the time, peered up at him with rosy cheeks and a flirty smile on her lips.

After twenty minutes of frenetic dancing, the two strolled off to the drinks table, where the dinner lady, Barbara, poured them a glass of shandy each.

'Thanks, Barb.'

The woman nodded pleasantly. Marcus and Hattie took their cups and refreshed themselves.

'God, I'm shattered!' Hattie exclaimed, wiping the booze from her lips.

'Really?' Marcus polished off the rest of his drink. 'I'm just getting started...'

He began to stare over at the dance floor. Ursula Wolf, in the year below, was standing by herself.

'Jasper's wifey over there.'

Hattie gave Marcus a pretend nasty look, playfully bumping him on the arm.

'Don't be mean,' she laughed. But her bright smile fell as she spotted Jasper, who was lingering alone in a corner of the room, holding a cup and sipping it occasionally. Marcus too caught sight of Jasper's location, and rolled his eyes with disdain.

'He's got to put himself out there,' he said. 'He can't stay this way forever.'

Hattie grimaced a little. 'It's not his fault... You know how nervous he gets with these sorts of things...'

Marcus creased his brow. At Hattie's urging, the young couple cut across the floor, moving past crowds of lively pre-teens and sweaty adolescents, before finally approaching their shy and awkward friend.

'Jasper!' Marcus said, thumping him playfully on the arm. Jasper's cup jostled and he nearly spilled it on the floor.

'How're you doing tonight?' said Hattie, giving him a bright smile. Jasper exchanged a fake one and took a big gulp from his drink.

'Err... good. Yeah, good...'

Marcus scratched his neck. He turned back to the dance floor, where Ursula Wolf remained by herself. She looked quite pretty in that bright yellow dress. 'Listen, mate,' he began, 'I think you should go make a move.'

'What?' said Jasper, leaning in to hear Marcus a little better. A loudspeaker blared overhead.

'I said, you should go make a move,' Marcus repeated, flicking his head towards the lonely young lady.

Jasper blushed and vehemently shook his head. 'Nah, nah. I'm alright.'

'She really does like you,' said Hattie in a patronising tone. 'It's rather sweet, actually.' In response, Jasper gazed into her eyes and, in that moment, Marcus recalled the sheer longing that he'd seen there: all the quiet desperation, and the bitter resentment, how it *showed so clearly on Jasper's face, after trying to keep it locked down for so long. Marcus sighed and, grabbing Jasper by the shoulder, began to give his friend a pep talk.*

'I know Wolfy's not the belle of the ball or anything, but you've got to admit – and don't take this the wrong way – but a guy like you... I think you ought to be adjusting your standards, is all.'

'Well, cheers for the advice,' snapped Jasper, awkwardly trying to stand up for himself, though his hands were visibly shaking from Marcus' confrontation.

'Just trying to help.' Marcus shrugged and, slapping Hattie on the back, began to lead his girlfriend away. Hattie turned to look at Jasper one last time. Marcus grabbed her by the waist, and the two began a slow dance as the DJ started playing a soft R&B track.

Marcus whispered into her ear, 'You may have been right about him...'

Hattie gritted her teeth together.

'I mean', she began, 'why'd it take you so long to realise?'

Marcus pulled her into a forceful embrace; the two clung together for a while. Marcus peered up, watching the door as it was shoved open.

In came the predators: Derek Platt and Reece Jenkins. Marcus held Hattie's head closer to his chest, seeing the look of frustration and lust on the two men's faces. Unfortunately, they caught wind of Hattie's location and, moving through the dispersing crowd, began to approach the young couple in a successful bid to tear them apart.

* * *

Marcus shook his head violently, trying to get rid of his painful recollections. But despite his efforts, he couldn't suppress those haunting flashes of how the two Scouts had knocked him down to the ground, and their attempted assault on Hattie. He remembered the way they'd seized her arms and tried to drag her away, until Big Davey, alerted by Jasper, intervened to stop the two men in their tracks.

The Jeep continued down the bumpy gravel road, heading towards a flat-topped hill where the Bunker's transmission tower stood alone. Wild fields sprawled beneath, blanketed in heather and budding cotton flowers. A chinook and a tank lay abandoned near the wide-open gates.

As he neared the Bunker, Marcus pulled up and, stepping out, crossed the threshold of Level 0. Tommy's decaying corpse lay strewn on the tarmac. Holding his nose, Marcus rummaged through the trouser pockets and grabbed a set of keys. He walked across the dim cave, stepping past the remains of Hans and Ted, until he found a large plastic bin near the curtained-off lab. From it, he retrieved a mask and a crumpled hazmat suit. Dressed up in the old uniform, Marcus unlocked the door that led into the Bunker's depths.

Using his phone as a makeshift torch, he descended the winding steps of the pitch-black stairwell, filled with the stench of fumes. The door to Level 1 had been left unlocked, the entire floor ominously intact. Marcus ventured inside. One of the doors gaped open, which led to the columbarium. He stepped through and peered into the gloomy chamber, whose shelves were lined with rows of urns: engraved boxes and china vases, holding cremated ashes. Noah's body, decaying, was sprawled on the floor. His skull had been bludgeoned under the force of Tommy's foot.

Looking down at the body with a flicker of pity, Marcus left Level 1, returning to the stairway. He entered Level 2 and crossed the lobby. Trapped heat wafted over his hazmat suit as he unlocked another door, which led to Corridor A. With his flashlight, Marcus scanned the ashy residue of what had once been a red carpet. Near his feet lay the charred remains of a broken oil lamp, with shards of glass scattered around it. The steel doors remained intact, but nothing could be heard from inside the bedrooms.

Marcus turned back and descended the stairs, paying no attention to Levels 3 and 4, until he reached 5. There, the checkpoint chair had been molten into a contorted pile. Through the porthole in the door, Marcus saw the aftermath of Tommy's arson in the desolate Executive Suite.

Level 6, however, presented a different scene. The Schoolroom floors had been left untouched.

Marcus peered into one of the classrooms. The teacher's desk was piled with textbooks and a stack of unmarked homework. The pupil's seats were all empty. On one of them, a silly message had been carved into the surface of the table: an oval-shaped willy, accompanied by a smiley face. Marcus peered up at the concrete walls: black-and-white posters of historical figures, faded quotes and unfunny teacher's jokes, dangled sadly downwards. A wave of dysphoria swept over him as he took in this bleak snapshot of the past. Too upset to explore the rest of the rooms, Marcus left Level 6, bogged down in a tired trance.

Upon reaching Level 7-A, the medical wing he had seldom ever visited, and 7-B, which housed the common spaces including a small library, games rooms, a barber's shop, a chapel, and the now decayed Garden Space, Marcus, overwhelmed, stepped out feeling dizzy. He leaned over the safety rail to catch his breath, stomach churning with malaise, longing to be done with this venture, but gathered himself nonetheless, and continued his descent down the spiralling staircase. The air was still warm from the fire that Tommy had started.

At last, Marcus arrived at Level 12. Entering the scorched, sooty corridor that was marked with an 'A', he managed to locate the door to Hattie's room. Using Tommy's key, he opened it up to find that the interior had been left untouched, save for a cloud of smoke that had seeped in through the cracks. Marcus wiped the soot from his goggles and, shining his light on the walls, marvelled at Hattie's murals. Her green and flowery fields, her concrete high-rise hell, and her drab and dreary desert – Marcus finally understood what she'd channelled into the making of these things. On the last wall, unpainted, lay a collage of printed pictures, which displayed shared memories. Unable to bear the sight, Marcus swiftly left the room. Taking a deep breath, he resolved to make his way to 13-B.

Marcus unlocked the door to Jasper's little cell with Tommy's key. After a moment's hesitation, he stepped inside and closed the door behind him. The room was bleak and stale, with barren concrete walls. The single bed was unkempt. Marcus turned his attention to the desk and, with his gloved hand, lifted Hattie's carved wooden angel, the one she had made for Jasper as a Christmas present, back in o'nine, a time in which the two had truly been close. How thoughtful she'd always been! Marcus set the figure back down, next to an empty tin of chewing tobacco.

Sinking into the rock-hard mattress, Marcus removed his mask. As he stared at the ceiling with an empty expression, he found his thoughts returning to a rare moment, one in which Jasper Huxley had taken the spotlight.

* * *

5th August, 0015

It was the early hours of the morning. Jasper was hosting the afters for that dreadful summer ball. Marcus remembered how self-conscious he had initially looked, with all his friends lurking in his room. Someone was playing dampened music on a speaker. Normally, these kinds of events would take place at Marcus' or Trevor's, or occasionally Walter's, but that night, Jasper had agreed to let everyone in.

The lights were off, as it was technically curfew, although Jasper had set up a blue lava lamp on his desk, which he'd acquired from some girl a couple of years below them, in exchange for helping her with science homework. Chemistry, Marcus remembered – something about particle bonds.

Trevor had brought a bottle of whiskey to try to help them all forget the horrors of the night. Meanwhile, Hattie was sitting on the edge of the bed, her head hunched over. Marcus had no idea how to comfort her. Earlier, she'd been taken in for an interview on Level 3 to give testimony about Derek and Reece's assault, and had arrived at Jasper's room later on, to everyone's surprise. Jasper stood in the corner, sipping on a flimsy cup of whiskey.

'Otto will be so pissed,' Trevor joked, nudging Walter on the shoulder. 'Am I right, Acey?'

'Yup,' said Walter, slurring his words. 'You're gonna be in such shit.' He took out his vape and began to inhale, savouring its nicotine contents. Breathing out a cloud, he let out an 'aaaahhh' and passed the pen to Trevor. Trevor took a hit and, trying to get Jasper more involved, offered it out to him.

'I dunno, Tiger... is it really any good?' Jasper was uninitiated to the stuff.

'It's bloody brilliant,' Trevor replied. 'Sense of freedom you don't get with that baccy-chew rubbish. Liberating, is the word for it.'

Jasper nodded and, in amateurish fashion, slobbered his lips around the mouthpiece, taking a sharp inhale. He coughed and spluttered. *The others giggled. Jasper, determined to prove some kind of point, took another hit and spluttered some more, but this time, managed to retain most of the vapour in his lungs. As Marcus initiated a countdown, the others joined in and clapped in unison, including Hattie, whose face appeared to brighten while Jasper performed this self-imposed challenge, trying to keep all the steam in. At last, Jasper's throat gave way, and he let it all out in a spluttering cough. The others went 'wheeeyy' and burst into applause, but quickly subdued themselves, worried they might wake the neighbours. Marcus remembered how an emboldened Jasper sat down on the bed, right between him and Hattie. How Hattie had complimented Jasper for his 'willpower', which Jasper lapped up with a gratified smile.*

The rest of the night went by in a blur. With Jasper's surge of confidence – one which, in the end, didn't last beyond those few drunken hours – he dominated the conversation in a way that Marcus had never seen. It was like he'd become a real person for the night – showcasing his emotions, coming up with clever jokes, being a part of the banter, laughing whole-heartedly and proving, deep down, that he relished the company of others. Marcus remembered how close Jasper and Hattie had been in those moments, the closest they'd been since Jasper hit puberty, before he'd buried himself away and become a self-contained shell of a human being.

Marcus also remembered the respect Trevor and Walter showed to Jasper. When the night was over, at the ripe hour of 03:18, each of them gave Jasper a tight, hearty squeeze, something they'd never done before in their lives.

'This was...' began Walter, utterly schlepped on Otto's whiskey, 'the best... friggin' night of my friggin' life...'

Jasper's eyes seemed to well up with emotion as Walter continued to wrap his arms around him. At last, the two broke away. Jasper saw him and Trevor out as they stumbled down the hall, returning to their rooms on upper floors. Marcus went in for a hug and wished Jasper good night. Marcus lingered in the doorway as Jasper helped a tipsy Hattie to her feet. Marcus watched, overcome by a wave of jealousy, as his girlfriend gazed into Jasper's face with that bright, mesmerising smile she reserved for those she truly admired. Jasper held her closely, resting his chin on the top of her head as she clung to him. Jasper's cheeks went red. And Marcus remembered the searing yellow pain that had throbbed inside his own chest, one that had been building for a long time, sparked up by the events of that horrible night.

After Hattie wished Jasper goodbye, she and Marcus stumbled down the hall and up the stairs together. She reached to grab Marcus' hand. Her tight clasp was met with his limp grip. Marcus, ashamed, felt too exhausted to respond to her enthusiasm. After they reached her room, Hattie struggled to open the door. Fully sober, Marcus helped her, turning the metal lock with her key. Hattie thanked him and, with rosy cheeks, gave him a soft, inviting look, as if asking him to sleep in with her tonight. Ashamed – for his inability to keep her safe, for the fact that Jasper connected so seamlessly with her, so unthinkingly, those life-ruining inhibitions having let him be just for the night – Marcus turned down Hattie's unspoken request. After giving her a defeated peck on the forehead, he trudged down the hall with his hands in his pockets. Hattie watched him go, before easing the door shut.

In his room on Level 13-A, Marcus lay awake in bed, staring at the ceiling. His heart throbbed with a painful, restless flutter, as he dreamed of a life that had yet to be accomplished.

* * *

The phone battery died out. Marcus' light was extinguished. Darkness engulfed him in the quiet, lonely room.

He continued to lie there, unresponsive, staring at the ceiling with his arms at his sides, breathing in the monoxide fumes, ready to join his friend and just be done with the agony of it all.

* * *

A lone car approached the Bunker's gates. After crossing the threshold of Level 0, it came to a sharp stop. Otto, Jonathan, and Hattie stepped out. Hattie peered down at Tommy's rotten corpse. His eyes, sunken and clouded, stared emptily into the abyss. Swarms of flies buzzed all around.

Making their way over to Dr Hans' old lab, the three found a large plastic bin filled with abandoned masks and used hazmat suits. They pulled the gear over themselves and, after Otto dished out some instructions, the three stepped down into the Bunker with their flashlights. Otto searched the upper levels, while Jonathan took the middle ones. Hattie, meanwhile, had opted to head down to the lower floors. Immediately, she searched Marcus' room on Level 13-A, before stepping out and, following a sad intuition, made her way into Corridor B.

* * *

Marcus heard a set of urgent footsteps in the corridor outside. He raised his brow, completely indifferent, expecting it to be 'Freddy Krueger' and the last Scouts, back to enact revenge on the boy who'd plunged their lives into darkness.

The steel door shook with a knock.

"Marcus?"

His face fell. Marcus sprung up from the bed. He took a rattling breath and pulled the bedroom door open, revealing an orange-clad figure on the other side. The girl removed her mask and, looking into Marcus' face, Hattie jumped in to give him a hug. Marcus pressed his eyes shut. Hattie moved past and, spotting the angel figure that she'd given Jasper for Christmas in o'nine, stumbled over to the desk by the bed and began to hyperventilate, breathing in the Bunker's fumes. Trying to keep that dizzying heat out from the hall, Marcus closed the door and watched as Hattie set her flashlight on the desk and, both knees cracking, allowed herself to drop onto Jasper's single bed, overwhelmed with emotions that had long gone suppressed. In the dim light, Marcus could see that Hattie's lips quivered. Her blue eyes flickered as they brimmed with tears, until the wooden angel fell from her hands, and she began to wail. Marcus took a deep breath and stumbled over to the bed. He felt those buried feelings stirring up inside himself and, allowing himself to feel the lump in his throat, finally gave up on holding it down. He felt the pain surge as it made its way out, impossible to stop even if he tried and, falling onto bed, allowed himself to cry for the very first time, weeping for it all; the horrors he'd witnessed, the damage he'd inflicted: all the countless lives he'd helped to destroy! And the countless chances missed, all those rejections of the life that lay before him: how little he'd appreciated it in his time! Instead, always being dragged into worlds that didn't exist, pursuing ideals that had never been his, trailing hell and ashes on that poorly-chosen road.

As his spirits passed through him in an exorcising fit, Marcus found his hand clamped against his lips, muffling the screams that continued all the same. His gaze turned up to the low-hanging ceiling, until at last, he looked around and could see, in Hattie's face – beneath all the sobs, and beneath the ugly tears – that a spark of life remained. Her cheeks glowed with the passion of their sorrowful life. In that moment, she had never looked so radiant and endearing.

Allowing himself to follow his instincts, Marcus leaned in to give her a hug. Hattie returned the favour, and the two embraced each other, wailing away with their shared agony.

*
**

Late afternoon
Stepping outside the Bunker's open gates, Hattie and Marcus stood together, having rid themselves of the Bunker's hazmat suits. A cool breeze swept over their faces, as they stared into the wilderness that stretched before them. Green hills rolled across the horizon. The sky was immersed in fiery streaks and a vast expanse of purple. The red winter sun had started to set.

Holding a box of effects that she'd salvaged from the Bunker, Hattie turned away and treaded off towards the car. Otto and Jonathan were waiting inside. Marcus stood alone for a while, breathing in the fresh, icy air, before heading over to the car and sitting in the back, with Hattie close to his side.

Otto got the engine going. The car inched along the track. Gravel bits jostled underneath the tyres. Sharp, gusty winds blew across the windshield, but inside, the passengers were comfortable enough.

The three-hour journey went by in a breeze, all four of them accepting the silence. Night had returned by the time they reached

Surrey, although the sky was free of clouds, and the atmosphere teemed with constellations of stars.

Acknowledgements

'Songs of Praise'

For most of my life I haven't been very open with my emotions – and I don't want to disturb anyone with a sudden outburst – but I'd like to take a moment to highlight the amazing people who helped me throughout this mad project of mine. THE RETREAT would have never seen the light of day without them.

First, I'd like to thank my mum for cheering me on whilst THE RETREAT was in the works. My mum is genuinely one of the nicest people you'll ever meet and she certainly looked out for me during my writing binges. Especially as I started to ignore chores and other responsibilities. Although her weekly nagging to take the bins out was a step too far (in my opinion).

Next, I'd like to thank my dad for his words of encouragement, his guidance and his help in making this book the best it could possibly be. My dad is not only a creatively gifted guy but also knows his stuff when it comes to marketing and making things like this work. I really appreciated his constructive feedback on my manuscript, which helped me give more life to the opening scenes and polish certain aspects of the story later on. For example, Dani Dalton would never have existed without my dad's advice.

I'd also like to thank my friends for not calling me stupid for trying to write a book. And for listening to me ramble on about it. I promise to stop doing that.

Also, a shoutout to my family at large for supporting my dreams. Although I'm not sure this book is quite up your street. Granny, you might want to read something that's a bit more cheerful...

Simona's professional reading and detailed report on my manuscript was extraordinarily helpful in helping me see its strengths and weaknesses, and allowed me to bolster Hattie's character arc. Onur's cover art also turned out brilliantly. I feel it captures the essence and overall heart of the story, and I really appreciate his patience during the design process as we mulled over different options.

Author's Note

Although this book obviously isn't an autobiography, I imagine people will want to psychoanalyse it. And yes, there are certain elements of myself I recognise in the three protagonists of this story. I grew up with a very emotionally sensitive personality, certain long-lasting traumas and undiagnosed inattentive ADHD, which led to me developing severe anxiety, to add to the fun (and which ruined even basic social interactions, a lot of the time). So that's where the 'mental health' elements of THE RETREAT came from. However, after a few years of effort and quite a lot of pain, I'm now at a place where I'm content with where I'm at and confident in myself.

I really wish I could've been more mentally and emotionally present in the past, rather than letting my teenage years be dominated by fear, scatter-brainedness (pretty sure that's a word?) and awkward oscillations between extreme inhibition and bouts of impulsivity. But you can't live with regrets.

And if anyone reading this is struggling, please know that your life can get unimaginably better in a short space of time, if you tackle your issues head-on. Also - I hope you realise that there are many, many people out there who care deeply about you and your well-being, whether that be family, friends or others in your community. Please don't let your struggles go ignored, don't be ashamed to seek professional help (it's become a lot more normalised in recent times, especially with the impact of COVID), and please don't feel that you have to walk this path alone. No one is an island.

Here's to happier stories in the future.

Printed in Great Britain
by Amazon

31973526R00164